THE NEW AMPLIFIED
PILGRIM'S
PROGRESS

*From this world to
that which is to come*

Adapted from
John Bunyan's Original Text
by James Pappas Jr.

Published by

DESTINY IMAGE® PUBLISHERS, INC.
SHIPPENSBURG, PENNSYLVANIA
www.destinyimage.com

Previously Published under ISBN 0-7684-2051-2

Art direction and design: Matthew McVane
Cover illustration: Nathan Greene
Body illustrations: Frederick Barnard and others
ISBN 13 digit: 978-0-7684-4147-5
ISBN 10 digit: 0-7684-4147-1
ISBN Ebook: 978-0-7684-8813-5
Adapted By James Pappas Jr.

Destiny Image Fiction
An imprint of
Destiny Image® Publishers, Inc.
P.O. Box 310
Shippensburg, PA 17257-0310

For Worldwide Distribution
Printed in the U.S.A.

This book and all other Destiny Image, Revival Press, MercyPlace, Fresh Bread, Destiny Image Fiction, and Treasure House books are available at Christian bookstores and distributors worldwide.

For a U.S. bookstore nearest you, call **1-800-722-6774**.
For more information on foreign distributors, call **717-532-3040**.
Reach us on the Internet: **www.destinyimage.com**.

CONTENTS

SPECIAL THANKS TO

*Mr. and Mrs. Jim Pappas Sr. and Mr. Darryl Manning
and a very special family that prefers to remain unnamed.
By their faith and support this book was made possible.*

*Thanks also to Marilyn Morgan and Sue Gibson
for their generous gift of time. Their efforts have made this
book better than it would otherwise have been.*

PREFACE

ALTHOUGH FOR the most part the language in this edition is quite modern, there are some patterns of speech borrowed from Bunyan that, hopefully, will lend a bit of an old English flavor to the story. All biblical quotations are from the King James Version, which was newly published in Bunyan's time. At times I have quoted from the writings of others who have expressed ideas more fluently than I could have done. In those instances I have enclosed these lines in quotation marks. Also, you will note that some of the characters along the way say, "thee, thine, thou," etc., but I trust the reader will quickly catch on to these simple usages from an earlier era.

This work is totally unabridged with nothing left out or shortened. However, where I felt that an amplification might aid in spiritual understanding or add a bit of adventure, I have taken that liberty.

I have undertaken this work with loving reverence and have tried to deal faithfully with the intent and content of the original. Should there be any mistakes in interpretation, I trust that in the resurrection Mr. Bunyan will forgive me.

Jim Pappas Jr.

John Bunyan

Dedicated to Linda, the beloved wife of my youth.
She whose patience and self-sacrifice are
more appreciated than I can express.

INTRODUCTION

HE IMMORTAL allegory that Bunyan crafted in his prison house was set in the framework of a dream. Although it is not the basis of this work, I too have a dream, which is as follows.

In my dream I see myself newly arrived in the New Jerusalem. With my friends and family I am walking the streets of the Celestial city and pausing frequently to admire some new wonder of creation. As we round a corner and come into a spacious park I seem to hear someone laughing. Not just a chuckle or two here or there but large bellyfuls of genuine amusement. Coming near to its source, I see a large bear of a man reading to his children. Then, as he reads on, he comes to a tender moment and, soft-hearted gentleman that he is a tear etches a salty trail down his cheek.

Curiously I draw near and looking over his shoulder, I perceive that the man is reading *The New Amplified Pilgrim's Progress*. Then the man turns and I see that the reader is none other than John Bunyan himself! There is a pause, a mutual acquaintance introduces us, and for the first time John Bunyan, the genius tinker from Bedford, looks upon his admiring adaptor. He stands, I extend my hand, which he grasps firmly only to pull me into a crushing Bunyan bear hug. Next in my dream he stands me back a pace, looks me squarely in the eye, and says, "Well done, James, old chap. Thank you. What do you say we have a grand reunion of all the people who have been helped to this place by our little books?"

And so it is that on the appointed day they gather on a grassy knoll overlooking the Tree of Life—thousands by multiplied thousands coming to pay tribute to God's faithful servant, John Bunyan, the tinker. And from those thousands I hope that a few, here and there, from these modern times might stroll across to me and say, "Thank you, sir, for taking Mr. Bunyan's masterpiece and putting it into a tongue I could comprehend."

Should you, dear reader, wisely decide to join us on pilgrimage because of this version of John's little book, I shall be most pleased to meet you. I may not know you by sight but you may meet Mr. Bunyan and myself on the little knoll that sits on the west side of the Tree of Life. We will meet there at sunrise on the first Sabbath following the first new moon after the coronation of the Lord of The Hill. Until then, faithful friend, I shall bid thee a fond adieu and dearly hope to meet thee in the Kingdom.

Affectionately yours,

Jim Pappas Jr.
ADAPTOR

As I slept I dreamed a dream.

. . . and, as he read, he began to weep and tremble.

CHAPTER ONE

*A*N MY JOURNEY through the wilderness of this world there came a time when I found myself caged up in a very dreary dungeon. Now how I came to be in that place, and what befell me there, is not for me to relate in this little book. What is for me to tell is the story of my dream. For, you see, while I was shut up in that most loathsome place surrounded by profligates and felons, I seemed to breathe the very atmosphere of heaven. Yea, 'twas there that I laid me down to sleep; and as I slept, I dreamed a most wonderful dream.

In this amazing dream I saw before me the most miserable man I have ever seen. He stood before the front door of a very tumble-down and miserable excuse of a house. He was dressed in garments that would scarcely merit the title of clothing in the genteel place where you dwell. Rags is what they really were! More frayed and tattered than the clothing on any bag-man beggar you are ever like to see. His face was very sad and was, for the better part of the time, turned away from his house. In his right hand he held a little black book, and upon his back he bore a huge burden—a great big black bundle of a burden that looked as if it must shortly press him down to the ground. 'Twas a very mysterious burden that he carried, for, as large and heavy as it looked to me, I soon perceived that it was invisible to those about him. But you can be sure that it was quite real to him; aye, just as real to him as the burdens of your soul are real to you.

Now, as I beheld in my dream, I saw him open the book and read; and as he read, he began to weep and tremble. He bowed lower and lower, as if his weighty burden was somehow growing even heavier. Finally, unable to endure any longer, he cried out with the most mournful voice I have ever heard, saying, "Oh, alas! Woe is me. Woe, woe, woe! Is there no one to help me?"

But to his despairing cry there came neither answer nor reply. He looked left, down the winding, twisting lanes of his tumble-down town and saw nothing but other people clothed in rags just as patched and worn as his own. He looked right, up the twisting, winding streets of his tumble-down town, and again saw nothing but more people in the same miserable state. In this dejected frame of mind he turned to enter his little tottering shack of a house. Once within that dreary little one-candle cottage, he tried his very best to act as normal as possible, lest he should alarm his wife and young children. But try as he might, he could not contain the moans and groans that forced themselves from unwilling lips. Finally, noticing that his wife and children kept stealing quick, sideways glances at him, and seeing that keeping his silence only seemed to add to his sorrows, he decided to open his heart to his loved ones. And this is what he said:

"Oh, my dear wife, and you, my tender children! I, your poor father, am all lost and undone. And why all lost and undone, do you ask? 'Tis because of this huge burden strapped tightly to my back."

Then said his dubious wife, Christiana, "Uh, burden? What burden, my dear?"

"I don't see any burden, Papa," piped up Matthew, his eldest son.

To this the man replied, "Can you truly not see it?"

"No," they chorused, all as one voice.

"Oh dear! What can I say?" he groaned. "For whether you can see it or no, this weight is about to crush out my life!"

"Dear, dear," said his wife, her brow deeply furrowed with grave concern, "an invisible burden so heavy as to crush out your life? What can it be?"

"Hear me! Hear me well, my dear ones. I have been reading words from this my little book."

At this his family exchanged one of those knowing glances that shouted silently, "Oh no! We were afraid something like this was going to happen."

At last Samuel, with strained politeness, ventured to ask, "And uh . . . ahem, what do the words in your little book say, dear father?"

"They tell me that this, our city, will soon be burned with fire from heaven!"

"What!" cried his ashen-faced wife, with a shocked expression. "Burned down!"

"Yes! Burned to ashes!"

"No!"

. . . he opened his heart to his loved ones.

"Yes!" he insisted, even more earnestly. "And in that fearful over-throw, we shall all miserably come to our ruin!"

"Oh, my dear husband!" she exclaimed, dropping her head into her hands with a moan.

"And as for a way of escape," he added despairingly, "I can see none."

"None!" she exploded.

"None?" cried Joseph, fearfully.

"Nun?" burbled baby James.

"No, none! None at all," he answered sorrowfully. "We are doomed to perish with this miserable town of Destruction!"

Now at these words his family was put into a state of shock. Not that they believed that what he had told them was true, mind you. Oh no! Certainly not! But rather because they conceived that he had gone stark raving mad! Therefore, since it was getting on toward evening, they served him a spot of hot tea with a touch of lemon and honey, wrapped his neck with a heavy, grey woolen rag, and bundled him off to bed. "There," said his wife as she latched the door quietly behind her, "a good night's sleep ought to settle his brains a bit."

But the night was just as troublesome to him as the day. Therefore, instead of sleeping peacefully, he tossed to his left and cried out: "Ah, woe is me! Lost and undone am I! All lost and undone!" Then there would be sighs and tears as he rolled onto his right moaning, "Ah, what shall become of me, wicked man that I am?" And so he spent the long lingering hours of darkness.

Now when morning was finally come, Matthew, his eldest, donned his sunniest smile and cheerfully addressed him saying, "Are you feeling happier now, dear father?"

"Yes, how goes it with you, dear husband?" sighed Christiana, trying her best to squeeze a touch of optimism into her fatigued voice.

"Worse!" he moaned.

"Worse!"

"Yes! Worse and yet more worse!" he continued.

"Oh, dear!" she cried with more impatience than concern. "What more can we do for you, poor man?"

To this he answered, desperately, "We must set ourselves to study and pray that we may know how to escape this city of Destruction."

"Escape!" she exploded. "My dear husband! There is nothing to escape from! Now come to your senses before the magistrates declare you to be a lunatic and cage you up forever!"

"No! No!" he cried. "I am in my right mind. There is danger—and we must escape forthwith. But how? Only how?"

"Husband!" snapped Christiana, her pot of anger beginning to boil over, "come to yourself this instant!"

Now, thoroughly convinced that their husband and father was indeed going quite mad, they sought to drive his affliction away by treating him with the utmost hardness and disrespect. Sometimes they would scold him, sometimes mock and mimic him. At other times they would totally ignore him. But as you well know, this is no way to treat a soul in distress. Not only did it fail to help him, it actually added to his burden because now he began to fear all the more for his family's salvation.

This added burden of worry drove him more often than ever to his chamber where he would pray for their souls as well as his own. At other times he would walk all alone in the fields, sometimes reading from his book, and sometimes praying. And thus for many a day did he spend his time.

Now, as my dream unfolded, I saw him once again walking in the fields. He was, as before, reading in his little book, and still groaning under his heavy burden, which, by now, was even larger than before. At last he burst out as he had done earlier, crying: "Oh wretched man that I am! What shall I do to be saved?" And as before, so now again, there was no reply.

I saw also that he cast hungry eyes this way to the left, and that way to the right, seeking some place to flee for his escape. Yet he continued to stand, trembling, out in the midst of the field, because, as I perceived, he could not tell which way to go. Then, from the right, I saw a man named Evangelist approaching, who addressed him thus, "Good day, Christian."

"Good day," moaned the man woefully. "But pray tell, sir, why did you address me as Christian?"

"Because if you continue to read from that little book in your hand, a Christian is what you must surely become," said Evangelist with joyful assurance.

"Hmm. Even though my name is now 'Graceless'?" asked the man doubtfully.

"Aye," said Evangelist earnestly. "Though your name should be called death itself, yet would the reading of that Word give you life!"

At this, a look of great puzzlement came over Christian's face, and he asked sincerely, "How can these things be?"

Then answered Evangelist with much gravity, "'Tis because that within that book of yours abide the words of He who spoke the universe into existence."

"Ah, I think I see. And who are you?"

"My Employer has named me Evangelist."

"Ah, 'tis a wonderful name you have, sir. But as for me, there is only woe. Woe, woe, and yet more woe!"

"Good sir, why are you all the time crying out so sadly this way?"

"Because, sir, I perceive by this book in my hand that if I remain in this city of Destruction, I am doomed to die."

"Ahh . . ."

"And, I find that I am not willing to die, neither am I able to come to judgment."

Do you see yonder wicket gate?

"And why not willing to die, since your life here is obviously filled with such sorrow?"

"Because," answered Christian dolefully, "I fear that this burden upon my back will sink me into the grave; yea, and lower than the grave. In fact, I fear that I shall perish eternally."

"I see," nodded Evangelist sympathetically.

"And good sir, I am not even fit to appear at the bar of judgment, much less attend my own execution."

"Ahhh. Now I understand," said Evangelist with a tear or two welling up in his eyes.

"So, you see, good sir, 'tis the fear of these things that makes me cry out."

"Ah. And your fears are well founded. Here, look into this roll."

I saw then that he gave him a parchment roll, and as the man unrolled it he saw written therein these words: **"Flee from the wrath to come!"**

"Oh no! Oh, more woe to me than ever!" groaned Christian. "'Tis true what I believed! I must indeed escape this place!"

"Aye," agreed Evangelist. "You should even now be fleeing as if for your very life!"

"Yes, I know."

"So why are you standing here, lingering at the edge of Destruction?"

"Sir, my little book informs me that I must flee; this parchment roll affirms that I must flee; you earnestly instruct me to flee. I can clearly see that a storm of destruction is about to sweep down upon our city as an overwhelming surprise. So, I know full well that I should be running, and I truly want to be running, but good sir, I . . . ," and at this the man began to weep and stammered, "I honestly don't know which way to go! Can you help me?"

"Look!" urged Evangelist, pointing across the plain, "Look over there across that wide, wide, field. Do you see yonder wicket gate?"

Christian strained his eyes to see through his tears, but was finally constrained to confess, "I . . . uh . . . no."

"Hmmm. Then, tell me, do you see yonder shining light?"

Wiping away his tears and stretching his eyes even more, he was finally able to say "I . . . I think I do."

"What color is it?" asked Evangelist, hoping with all his heart that the man told no lie.

"Uh, to be perfectly frank, sir, I can barely see it. But it seems to be white . . . I think."

"Good! Good, good, good! That's it! All you need to do is to keep your eye on that light!"

"But I can scarcely see it."

"No matter about that. As you follow what little light you have, you will find it grows ever more brilliant in your eyes. Soon the things of earth will grow strangely dim. Only remember! Always move toward the light. If you do, you will surely be led to the wicket gate."

"Indeed? Well, that's easy enough. And where will said gate take me?"

"That gate is the trail head into the path that leads to the Celestial City," answered Evangelist joyfully. "Go directly thereto and you shall learn how to inherit eternal life."

"I shall, good sir," he said, hitching up his britches and tightening up the frayed cord that served as his belt. "I shall!"

"See that you take not your eyes off of the light," warned Evangelist solemnly.

"Oh, I shan't," he answered joyfully. "Oh, I didn't dream that finding the way could be so easy! Simply follow the light! Thank you, sir! Thank you very, very much!"

"'Tis my greatest pleasure," answered Evangelist, whose eyes were now swimming in pools of tearful joy. "My greatest pleasure in all the world."

So I saw in my dream that the man began to run. Now, he had not run very far from his own door when his wife and children, seeing him, grew alarmed and began to cry after him.

"Mama! Look!" cried Joseph. "Papa's running away from home!"

"T'um home, Daddy!" burbled baby James.

Christiana called out sternly, "Husband! Where are you going?"

"To life! Life! Eternal life!"

"Oh no! He's gone and fallen clean off his wagon," blurted out Matthew. "Papa! Where are you going?"

"Never mind where he's going!" urged Samuel. "Just get him back into bed before he hurts himself! Father, come back!"

Christian flees Destruction.

Christiana, seeing not the slightest slackening of his pace, screamed out after him, "Graceless! You get back here this minute! Do you hear me? Come back this instant!"

"Life! Life! Eternal life!" shouted Christian as he galloped on with his clumsy burden swaying heavily from side to side.

"Graceless! You best obey me!" threatened his wife sternly.

"Mama!" shouted Matthew. "He's put his fingers in his ears! Now he can't even hear us!"

"Oh, the fool man!" cried his wife. "That book of his has so rattled his brains that he can't even listen to reason! Graceless!"

"Papa, you crazy fellow!" called Matthew. "Come back before you hurt yourself!"

To this, teary-faced little James pulled his thumb from his mouth and cried piteously, "T'um home, Daddy!"

Now by this time all the commotion had aroused the entire neighborhood and begun to draw quite the crowd. Said one, "Come look! It's Graceless! Look at'm stumbling across yonder meadow."

"Aye," observed a second. "Ee's finally flipped 'is wig, 'e 'az." Another called after the fugitive, saying, "Hey! Fool man! Come back before you lose your way!" To which yet another answered, "Ah, let the fool go! Better off we are without the likes of him around here."

Then there came running up all huffing and puffing a stout, mulish looking man named Obstinate, who asked, "What's all the excitement, lads?"

"Oh," answered the first, nonchalantly chewing on a straw, "the fool has finally lost his mind and runs amuck!"

"Aye," cried the second, "straight into trouble 'e goes."

"Yup! Sure 'nuff. The egg has finally cracked, it 'as," declared the third.

Then said Obstinate, "So! He's finally made a break for it, eh?"

Now at this moment there came up a whimpy wisp of a man named Pliable, who gazed after the fleeing man with a worried look and whined, "Oh dear, oh me! Oh, neighbor Obstinate, I just knew this would happen, what with him reading that Book all the time!"

"Yes, brother Pliable," Obstinate answered gruffly. "We should have taken it away from him as soon as we saw the distemper begin to settle upon his soul."

"Oh dear! Oh me! Now what can we say to save the dear soul?"

"Say! Nay!" blurted out Obstinate. "'Tis not what we say that will do—but what we do that will do."

"Uh . . . your meaning flies clean over my head, dear Obstinate," said Pliable, his scrawny face mirroring his inner confusion. "Uh, please, do clarify."

"Foolish Pliable!" exploded Obstinate. "Can't you see, bumpkin? He has his ears all stopped up! He will understand no language but that of animal power!"

To this Pliable looked even more lost in the mist and said meekly, "Uh . . . clarify more, dear sir. A bit more, do clarify."

"Grrr," growled Obstinate impatiently. "Can't you see, silly head! We must needs go fetch him back by force!"

"Oh! Of course, by force. Heh, heh, heh. By force of course. A splendid idea!" exclaimed the enlightened Pliable with a smile and a bony clap of his skinny hands. "Simply splendid! Shall we be off?"

"Yes. Off with us!" ordered Obstinate bowing low to Christiana with an expansive sweep of his fine feathered hat. "Don't worry your pretty little head, Madam. We'll unscramble his brain yet. Graceless!" he bellowed after the fleeing figure of Christian. "Hold up a bit!" Then he set off at a piggish waddle of a trot with Pliable loping easily behind shouting, "Sirrah! Wait up! Wait up!"

Now, even with his fingers in his ears, Christian could faintly hear their shoutings. But he dared not look back, no, nor even slow his pace because he had read in his Book that, "No man having put his hand to the plow and looking back is fit for the kingdom of heaven."

But because of the burden upon his back, it was not long before his pursuers drew alongside. Then the gasping Obstinate shouted between puffs, "Hey! (puff puff) Graceless! (puff puff) Hold up!" Christian, thinking they might have come to join him on pilgrimage, slowed his pace to a brisk walk and said, "Why, good neighbors! Have you come to join me on my journey?"

"Join you!" snorted the portly Obstinate. "No! (puff puff) We are here (puff) to persuade you (puff) to go back with us!"

"Oh, that can by no means be," declared Christian, "for you dwell in the city of Destruction; and sooner or later, you, with that city, will sink down into a place that burns with fire and brimstone! Therefore, good neighbors, come along with me and deliver your souls."

"What!" snapped Obstinate gruffly. (Puff puff) "And leave our friends and comforts behind us?"

"Yes, because all that you leave behind is not worth one-millionth part of that which I am seeking to enjoy."

"And what do you seek (puff) that is worth leaving all the world for?"

"I seek an inheritance that is incorruptible, undefiled, and that will never fade away."

"Where?" wheezed Obstinate, struggling to keep pace.

"It is laid up for me in heaven," answered Christian, "and kept safe for me there."

Then Obstinate cast a knowing glance at Pliable before saying, "And when shall you receive this uh . . . 'inheritance'?"

"I shall receive it at the time appointed, as shall all of them that diligently seek it," said Christian, extending his little Book toward Obstinate. "Here, you may read about it in my Book if you will."

"Tush!" snapped Obstinate, brushing the book aside. "Away with your silly Book! Will you go back with us, or no?"

"No! I can't, because I have put my hand to the plow."

"Plow! I don't see no plow," sneered Obstinate, looking about to see if he had missed something.

"'Tis not a plow as you understand plows, neighbor Obstinate. What I mean is . . ."

"What!" interjected Obstinate. "Invisible plows now? Oh, come on, neighbor Pliable. Let us turn again and go home without him. His rooster brain is obviously so stuffed with his own ideas that he cannot bear sound reason."

"Now, now, don't revile the dear man, friend Obstinate. Actually, my heart inclines to go with him."

"What! Another fool born? Who knows where such a brain sick fellow will lead you! Best you come away with me and be wise," said Obstinate, snatching Pliable by the arm.

"Nay, but come along with me, neighbor Pliable," answered Christian, grasping his other arm. "You can have all the wonders that I spoke of and many more glories besides."

"More glories besides?" exclaimed Pliable, his eyes growing wide with wonder.

"Aye. And if you don't believe me, read of it here in my Book."

"Grrr! Books begone!" groused Obstinate defiantly as he rattled Pliable's bones with a snapping jerk toward Destruction. "Who knows but what the whole business is a pack of lies!"

"No!" cried Christian earnestly as he tugged Pliable a step closer to the Celestial City. "What is written here is all true! Behold, it is confirmed by the blood of the One who made it."

"Well, neighbor Obstinate," said Pliable, planting his feet firmly, and retracting both arms with all the dignity of a queen upon her throne. "I find myself coming to a point of decision."

"Being what?" scowled Obstinate suspiciously as he crossed his arms and leaned back on one leg.

"I think I intend to go along with this good fellow and to cast in my lot with him," said Pliable decisively.

"What!" snorted Obstinate incredulously. "And leave common sense and good reason bleeding all dead on the ground?"

Then Pliable raised his chest, crossed his arms and said in a firm and princely manner, "M'thinks that friend Graceless here knows just as much of these things as you do."

"What!" squealed Obstinate, the convulsing of his portly frame sending a cascade of salty sweatlets down his face.

"Yes," said Pliable with calm assurance. "So am I persuaded."

"Tush! Lunatics! The both of you. Why, why . . . he doesn't even know the way."

"Eh?" queried Pliable, turning to the pilgrim. "Uh . . . tell me, my good companion, do you know the way to this desired place?"

"Oh, yes," exclaimed Christian confidently. "A man named Evangelist showed me the way to a little wicket gate that lies just before us."

"Where?"

"Over yonder meadow," said Christian, pointing straight ahead.

Pliable squinted his eyes tightly, stared fixedly in the indicated direction for a few moments, and then finally confessed, "I uh . . . I see no gate."

"There is no gate!" bellowed Obstinate triumphantly.

"Then, do you see yonder bright light?" urged Christian, eagerly pointing again. At this, Pliable peered intently through scrunched up, shaggy eyebrows and, at last, managed to answer, "Well, I . . . uh . . . Yes . . . I guess I sort of think maybe I might."

At this Obstinate roared with wide-eyed astonishment, "Sort of think! Good heavens, lad! Will you risk life and limb on the basis of a 'sort of think?'"

"Good! We need only keep our eyes fixed upon that light until we come to yonder wicket gate. Once we get there, we shall receive further instruction about the way."

Back to reason and common sense with me.

"Well! That certainly seems easy enough," said Pliable eagerly. "Let us be going! Would you care to join us, Obstinate?"

"Absolutely not! I will be no companion of such misled fanatical blockheads as you two! Back to reason and common sense with me!" And with that, Obstinate spun on his heel and strutted back toward Destruction.

Then said Christian, as they began their journey toward the light, "Ah, dear neighbor, Pliable. You cannot know how happy I am to have you join me on this fine celestial journey!"

"As am I," said Pliable with a crooked-toothed grin, "Indeed, as am I."

Then, as Christian cast a longing glance at the retreating figure of Obstinate, he said with a heavy heart, "Oh, if only Obstinate could understand the powers and terrors soon to come upon our doomed city. Then he would not count it such a light thing to turn his back on eternal life."

"Oh well," said Pliable nonchalantly, "Obstinate be his name and Obstinate be his brain. No use crying over spilt milk. Can't fetch back water gone under the bridge, I always say, I do. But come, neighbor Graceless . . ."

"Oh, please, call me no more by that name, sir," interrupted Christian, "for I am now named Christian."

"Indeed? And how did you come to be called by such a wonderful name?"

"'Twas given to me by a great man named Evangelist."

"Evangelist, you say? Hmmm, never heard of the chap. How did you chance to meet him?"

"He came with a message from heaven because he saw me reading in this Book."

"Hmmm," said Pliable, obviously impressed. "Well, 'tis a beautiful sounding name, to be sure. To be sure. But come, neighbor Gr . . . heh, heh, I mean, Christian. Tell me more about our rewards and how we shall get our hands on them."

"No need to take my word for it," said Christian, opening his Book. "Here, I will read to you from my Book."

"And do you truly think that the words of your Book are certainly true?" asked Pliable greedily.

"Oh yes, absolutely! For it was made by Him that cannot lie."

"Cannot lie! My, what a nice person he must be. Uh . . . tell me, what sorts of things are written in your Book?"

"Well," answered Christian joyfully, "it speaks of an endless kingdom to live in . . ."

"Eh? Endless, did you say?"

"Aye, indeed I did!" glowed Christian, warming to his subject. "And there we shall be given everlasting life so that we may dwell in that kingdom forever."

"My, my! Eternal life in an endless kingdom!" said Pliable, rubbing his hands together in eager anticipation. "And what else?"

"Well, there are crowns of glory to be given us, and garments that will make us to shine like the sun."

"Really!"

"Oh yes."

"And . . . and what else?"

Then answered Christian with a faraway look in his eye, "In that place there shall be no more sad farewells nor crying, for He that is owner of the place will wipe away all tears from our eyes."

"Wonderful!" gushed Pliable, rivers of sweet emotion surging through his breast. "Simply wonderful! And who shall we have for our company there?"

"Oh, dear Pliable," said Christian, his voice choked with emotion, "You cannot imagine! There we shall keep company with angels and seraphims and cherubims. Creatures so beautiful that they shall dazzle your eyes to look on them."

"Dazzle my eyes, you say!" exclaimed the enthralled listener. "Oh my! Go on. Do go on!"

"There you shall meet with thousands, and tens of thousands of the resurrected saints that shall travel with us to that place; none of them hurtful, but every one loving and holy and . . ."

"How lovely."

"Every one of them walking in the sight of God and standing in His presence with acceptance forever."

"Oh! Marvelous! Simply marvelous!"

"Yea," said Christian, with growing enthusiasm. "And there we shall see the elders with their golden crowns, the holy virgins with their golden harps, men that by the world were cut in pieces, burnt in flames, eaten of beasts, and drowned in the seas—and all for the love they bear to the Lord of that place. There they shall all be well, and clothed with immortality as with a garment."

"Marvelous!" squealed Pliable, smacking his palm with his fist. "Absolutely marvelous!"

"But best and better than all these will be the company of the Lord of that place Himself. He who became as one of us, to bring us to His kingdom that we might enjoy His friendship forever!"

"This is absolutely breathtaking, dear Gra . . . er, Christian," said Pliable with an hungry gleam in his eye. "Why, just the hearing of it is enough to ravish one's heart! But, tell me, good fellow, how do we become partakers of these things?"

"The Lord, the Governor of that country, has told us how in this book," said Christian, again holding forth his treasure.

"And what does it say?"

"Well, in brief, if we be truly willing to inherit the kingdom, He will bestow it upon us freely. And . . ."

"Well! I certainly qualify for that! Come! Let us pick up the pace a bit."

"Oh, I cannot," said Christian a bit sadly, "because of this weighty burden lashed to my back."

"Hmmm," said Pliable, puzzling his head to understand what Christian could possibly be speaking of (for, you see, as he looked at Christian's back, he saw there nothing at all).

"Uh . . . strange," said he.

"What is?"

"That there is no burden upon my back."

"Hmmm?" said a somewhat puzzled Christian. "Yes?"

"Tell me," said Pliable curiously, "How did this . . . uh . . . weighty burden come upon you?"

"Well," said Christian, pausing to reflect, "as I recall, it seemed to come upon me gradually whilst I read here, in this, my Book."

"Aha! Then it seems to me that this little Book of yours is not a blessing unmixed with sorrows."

"Aye," confessed Christian ruefully. "It has indeed caused me much grief and has certainly laid a heavy burden upon me."

"Ummm, hmmm," replied Pliable, thanking his lucky stars to be walking in the path of life without such a cumbersome load.

"But I trust that the same light which has shown me my need shall also point me to my deliverance."

"Well, I should hope so!"

Then Christian turned to Pliable and, holding forth his little Book, said, "Would you like to read it?"

"Oh, dear me, no!" exclaimed Pliable, drawing back as if being offered a serpent's egg. "I, uh . . . I rather prefer to pursue my journey without such a burden as this book imposes, thank you." Then, under his breath he added, "Although, to be frank, I don't see what this burden business is all about, for on his back there is nothing at all. Nothing at all."

I saw next in my dream that, without realizing it, Christian had taken his eyes off the light. Therefore, they strolled past the stepping stones set there for the use of watchful pilgrims and came instead to the edge of a miry, mucky slough; a very miry, mucky slough that had been laid in that place by the enemy of souls. Now, as they proceeded, they heard the slurshy squishing of the marsh muck gurgling beneath their feet. They felt the ooze of the bog beginning to creep over the tops of their shoes. Alarmed, they sought firmer terra by taking a few steps to the left, only to have the muck deepen and go climbing up past their knees. They next turned hopeful steps off to the right only to feel the bog rising inexorably, all cold and clammy up their thighs and into their pockets. Then, deciding that going off to either side had been a serious error in judgment, they determined to forge straight on—assuming that surely things could only get better. But it took only a few more steps to discern the depth of their mistake by finding themselves fallen chest-deep into the mushy, miry muck of the slough. Now the name of that slough was Despond. And here they wallowed for a time, until both were covered from head to toe with the black, smelly ooze of the place.

Here, for a time, they struggled on in grunting silence expecting soon to find solid ground for their searching feet. But alas, this was not to be. Now, of the two, I saw that poor Christian, because of his burden, had much the worse time of it. Therefore he began to sink lower and lower into the mire. Then a frustrated and angry Pliable hissed, "Ah! Neighbor Christian! What muck have you gotten us into now?"

"Truly, I do not know," exclaimed Christian wearily.

"So!" snarled Pliable, all wet and bedraggled. "Is this part of the happiness you have been promising me all this time?"

"Blame me not, gentle neighbor. I know not what has come upon us."

"Well," spouted Pliable as he spat out some sort of slippery slime, "if we fall into such misfortune so close to home, what may we expect between here and our journey's end?"

"Whatever it may be," called out Christian with what little courage he could muster, "we shall find that country to be cheap enough."

"Bah!" shot back Pliable over his shoulder. "'Tis already too cost-ly! Just let me escape this miry muck with my life, and you can keep your shiny dreams all to yourself!" And with that, he gave a desperate struggle or two and managed to slosh his way back out of the mire.

"Ah! Oh me!" he gasped, finally able to reach solid ground, where he lay gasping for breath. "Free at last!" Meanwhile Christian strug-gled on, all the time sinking ever deeper into the mire.

After a time Pliable groaned to his feet, slurshed off the outer layer of malodorous muck, and turned staggering steps towards home. As he wearily ambled off in the direction of Destruction, he cast a parting jab over his shoulder, saying, "Adieu, foolish Graceless! Farewell to you and all your misty dreams of golden glory!"

"Pliable, wait!" wailed Christian sorrowfully. "You've somehow gotten out on the wrong side of the slough!"

"Pah!" shot he over his shoulder. "Better out on the wrong side—like me, than in on the right—like you!"

"But, you have turned your back to the light!"

"Bah!" he snapped again, pausing to point an accusing finger. "To be the more honest with you, I never saw any such light as you speak of. And I frankly doubt that you do either. Fare you well, foolish dreamer!"

And thus did Pliable turn his back on eternity to tread his slurpy-shoed way back to Destruction.

Meanwhile, poor Christian was left to tumble in the Slough of Despond all alone, moaning, "Ah! Oh, dear me!" But weary and half drowned as he was, he still struggled on toward that side of the slough farthest from Destruction and nearest to the wicket gate. Now, because of his weighty burden, he was sunk deep into Despond. Yea, so deep as to scarcely discern the faint glow of distant light. Neither could he tell how much farther it was to the other shore. Whether a few yards or yet many leagues, he had no way to tell. Therefore, being quite exhausted, he clutched a large clump of cattails that only seconds before had been the abode of a large bull-frog, and paused to rest. There between gasps, he paused to reason with himself thusly:

"Oh, dear me! Who can tell who is worse off? Is it Pliable in his return to yonder doomed city? Or is it me in this murky slime of death? Oh, if I can just somehow get out!"

With that, he resumed his desperate struggle toward the light until, at last, he reached what seemed to be the distant shore. But there he found, to his dismay, that he had not enough strength to climb the steep bank. After resting for a time he tried again, saying between clenched teeth, "Out! Oh, I've got to get out or I shall die!" But because of the water-logged burden upon his back and his weakened condition, he lost his grip on the weeds and slowly slid back down, deeper than ever, into the ooze. Then said he, in total despair, "Oh, weary. So weary. 'Tis certain that I shall never get out of this place alone. If only Pliable were here so we could help each other, for certainly help is what I need. And if I cannot find it, I fear that the beginning of my journey shall be its end. I wonder if the Lord of the far country might be able hear me from so far off. Shall I try? Or shall I die?"

Then Christian hung all his hope on the mercy of his King and cried out, "Oh, Lord of the far country! Send help, I pray!"

Now scarce had the echo of his words died away when a power-fully built man appeared on the edge of the bank. He looked upon him with loving concern, and said, "Hello. Who goes there?"

"'Tis I, Christian," sputtered the bedraggled pilgrim, spitting out a piece of duckweed or two.

"Ah, I heard that you were coming," said the man, "but what are you doing over here, wallowing in the Slough of Despond?"

"'Twas certainly not my idea, sir. I was sent this way by a man named Evangelist."

"Uh huh."

"And as I was travelling the path into which he set me I fell in here."

"But why did you not come across on the steps?" asked Help earnestly.

At this, Christian felt a bit sheepish and asked, hesitantly, "Uh . . . steps?"

"Yes, steps! Over there."

"Are there really steps?" queried the embarrassed pilgrim, stretching his neck to see.

Upon hearing this, there came a sympathetic tear into Help's eye as he tenderly sighed, "Tsk, tsk, tsk. Of course there are steps, dear Christian. 'Tis not our Lord's intention that His children should sink into Despond. Why did you not use them?"

"Well," said he, a bit chagrined, "I suppose I must have been so fearful about the destruction behind that I gave no thought to the dangers before."

"Hmmm," answered Help, sympathetically kneeling down with outstretched arm. "Here, give me your hand!" Then, taking Christian's hand in his own, he hoisted the poor bedraggled pilgrim clean out of the bog, saying, "There you are! Out with you!"

"Oh, thank you, good Sir," said the grateful pilgrim as he stood dripping into his own puddle. "Thank you very much! You have sure-ly saved my life!"

"You must thank Him who heard your cry and sent me."

"Yes, I shall," said the shivering Christian. "And, may I inquire after your name, sir?"

"My Master has named me Help."

"Help, do you say? Why, you are the very one I called for."

There you are! Out with you!

"Of course."

"Dear Help, sir?"

"Yes?"

"Do tell, since the only way from the city of Destruction to yonder wicket gate is over this slough, why is not the walkway better mended?"

"Because this miry slough is such a place as cannot be mended," responded Help, shaking his head sadly.

"Oh? And why not?"

"Because whenever there comes a conviction of sin, there will always be a scummy runoff of filth and guilt. This lowland is its natural drain field and therefore is it called the Slough of Despond."

"Aha! And well-named it is."

"Aye, more than you know. For, as the sinner is awakened to his lost condition, there arise in his soul many fears . . ."

"Oh, to be sure. I know all about fears!"

"And doubts?"

"Oh yes. Many doubts."

"And discouraged worries about your salvation?"

"Oh, more than you can know," answered Christian, "more than you can know."

"Well," concluded Help, "'tis all these doubts and fears, worries and guilt, that drain down here and create this place of despondency."

"I think I understand you quite well on these matters," answered Christian, "for certainly all of these things did thickly fill my mind. But tell me, is there no way that the King might fill this place?"

"Ah, He has tried," said Help with a sigh. "He has tried."

"Indeed?"

"Aye. He has poured into this place encouragement and wholesome instruction by the millions of cartloads. But all to no avail."

"Then must every pilgrim suffer in the mire of Despond, as I have done?"

"No. Not if they keep their eyes fixed on yonder light. That light shows the way to some very clear and solid steps."

"Clear and solid, do you say?"

"Aye," nodded Help. "Most assuredly. And placed there by direction of the Lawgiver Himself. I am surprised Evangelist did not instruct you to keep your eye on the light."

"Well, actually he did, sir," confessed Christian. "Three times. I suppose I must have turned my attention upon my circumstances, for truly, I never saw any steps."

"Ah, a very common mistake," said Help sympathetically. "But be assured, the King has indeed placed steps in the very midst of this slough. And they can be found by all who simply keep their eye on the light."

"Ah. A lesson too late learned for this pilgrim," said Christian, with a rueful shake of his head.

"Ah, but take courage. He is faithful and just to forgive you and to cleanse you from all this mire upon you. And the ground is good once you get in at the gate. Godspeed!"

"Thank you, sir. Thank you very much. Farewell."

I saw next in my dream that Pliable had reached the back edge of Destruction and was trying his best to creep back into his house unnoticed. Now although he had made some feeble attempts at wiping himself off, they had been to small avail. Thus it was that when his wife saw this apparition, all miry and mucky, at her back gate, she screamed out in fright. When he was finally able to shush her up long enough to convince her that it was indeed he himself and no mucky vagabond, she handed him a bucket and brush.

"What are these for, my dearest?" he queried through chattering teeth.

Then she sternly informed him that he could by no means come into her home until he had cleaned up. He whined and begged a bit, but she seized her broom, planted her ample body in the only path, and refused to budge. To add to his miseries, one of his bat-eared neighbors had heard the sloshy approach of his footsteps. He dutifully alerted the entire neighborhood which quickly assembled in anticipation of some entertainment.

Said his neighbor to the left, "Uh . . . been for a swim, Pliable?"

Added his neighbor to the right sneeringly, "Hey! Look who's come a sloshing back!"

His neighbor across the street chimed in saying, "So ye've come back now, have ye!"

Then the neighbor across the back fence sniped, "A fool you were to go as far as you did with the likes of that crazy Graceless fellow."

. . . ya been for a swim, Pliable?

"Been for a swim, Pliable?" asked the neighbor to the left again, with a gleeful grin.

To this another added, self-righteously, "Look at yourself—all slimed and bedaubed with dirt!"

At this his wife came to his defense and said, "Well, at least he was wise enough to come to his senses!"

"Bah! Wise nothin'!" quipped one of the local youth. "Seems pretty chicken-hearted to turn back the first time the road gets a little soggy."

Then the neighbor to the left leaned onto the sagging picket fence, smiled a toothless grin, and said again, "Uh . . . ya been for a swim, Pliable? Hee, hee, hee!"

Then they all rollicked and rolled with mirth, and a jolly good time was had by all—all but Pliable, that is. And, in spite of his best attempts at quiet anonymity, he soon became quite the celebrity in

Destruction. Thus it was that for a good long time he went sneaking and ashamed among them. But as time passed, he forgot that he had played the coward and before long, was able to join all the others in mocking poor Christian behind his back. And this was all I saw concerning Pliable.

My view then turned to Christian who, by now, was well on his way toward the wicket gate. Now by and by he espied someone coming down across the field to meet him. This gentleman's name was Mr. Worldly-wiseman. He dwelt in the town of Carnal Policy, which is a very large town just up the road from the city of Destruction. It was his practice to keep a watch on the path that leads to the wicket gate and to intercept those just setting out on their journey. As he came near, he took silent notice of Christian's damp clothing and said with a jolly smile, "Ho there! How goes?"

"Greetings, jolly sir," replied Christian wearily.

"Pray tell, good fellow! Where off to looking so serious and burdened down?"

"To yonder wicket gate, for there I shall be shown a way to be rid of my heavy burden."

"Ahem," said the man, clearing his throat and cocking his ear the better to hear. "Uh . . . excuse me, lad, but did I hear you say, yonder wicket gate?"

"Yes."

At this the distinguished-looking fellow twirled his elegant, waxed moustache betwixt long, tapered fingers, raised one of his bushy eyebrows for effect, and said incredulously, "You're on your way to yonder wicket gate?"

"Yes."

"Tell me you're joking."

"No. I'm quite serious."

"Hmmm. Serious. Very serious. Tsk, tsk, tsk," said the man slowly with extreme gravity. "Uh . . . ahem . . . tell me. Who set you out on this little overgrown path to find relief from your burden?"

Now, by this time, Christian was beginning to suspect that perhaps this pilgrimage business was not all so clear-cut as he had at first imagined. Thus a twinge of doubt quavered in his voice as he answered, "Uh . . . a man who appeared to me to be a very great and honorable person. His name, as I recall, was Evangelist."

"Evangelist, you say!" sputtered the man with a cough, as he stepped back in shock.

"Yes," responded Christian with a puzzled look.

Then Worldly-wiseman raised himself to his full height, smote his palm with his fist, and bawled out, "Bah! Shame on him for his evil counsel!"

"What? Evil counsel, do you say?"

"Oh, evil indeed!" continued the man, reaching out a sympathetic hand to pat Christian on the shoulder. "Why, don't you realize that the way into which he has set you is the most dangerous and troublesome in all the world?"

"Indeed?"

"Yea, verily," he said, leaning back and crossing his arms. "In fact, ahem, it rather appears that you may have met with a few difficulties already. Uh . . . is that, uh . . . perhaps the slime of Despond that I see upon your person?"

"Aye," admitted Christian. "You see, I took my eyes off the light and missed the steps."

"What light? What steps?" sneered the man. "Every man ever seen traversing this dangerous trail has been just as mucked up and slimy as you are!"

"Oh, but . . ."

"And let me tell you something else, lad. That slough is but the beginning of the sorrows you can expect to meet in this way."

"It is?"

"Oh yes!" continued the man confidently. "I have lived here all my life and have seen many a pilgrim come rushing back. From their sworn testimonies I can assure you that you shall meet with wearisomeness . . ."

"I am already weary," interjected Christian.

"Uh huh," nodded Worldly-wiseman knowingly before continuing his list. "And you can also expect painfulness, hunger, perils, nakedness, sword, lions, dragons, darkness, and well, to cut my list short, death and what not all else on the way to it!"

"Oh, my!"

"Aye, oh my indeed!" agreed the man, waxing warm to his subject. "So what do you think about this way now?"

"Well, to tell the truth," put in Christian with a touch of returned boldness, "I don't think I care what I meet in the way."

Mr. Worldly wiseman

"No?" replied his shocked auditor.

"No. Just so long as I can be delivered from this crushing burden."

"Ahh!" said the man, nodding his head wisely. "I see your point. And well taken it is. For certain it is that this guilty burden will crush any man who cannot get it off, as well I know. So then, let us analyze the situation logically. Tell me first, how did you come to carry this great burden?"

"By the reading of this Book in my hand."

"Ah! Just as I feared!" snapped the man with a great show of concern. "You have made the mistake of trying to understand mysteries that are beyond the reach of your feeble mind."

"Actually, I thought it all seemed rather simple."

"Don't interrupt please," returned the man with great show of authority. "And as you read in that little book, you began to feel guilt piling up on your back, didn't you?"

"Yes. You're right about that."

"Uh huh! And as you grew more and more convicted, your mind became unstable. You became distracted and could think of nothing else, right?"

"Yes."

"And then . . . and then, at the very first suggestion of some way of escape, you ran yourself off on this desperate venture to obtain you know not what!"

"But I do know what!"

"What?"

"It is ease from my heavy burden!" Christian declared.

"But of course! But why on earth would you ever seek for ease this way?"

"Well, do you know a better way?"

"Yea, verily! And the true solution is very close at hand."

"It is?"

"Of course it is! And in this way, instead of those great and many perils, you shall meet with much peace and safety."

"Why, sir, certainly I have no desire to play the martyr. Pray tell, what must I do?"

"'Tis simple," said Worldly-wiseman, placing one hand on Christian's shoulder and pointing with the other. "See yonder signpost off to the side there?"

"The one pointing toward Morality?"

"Yes, the same. That village has an old major whose name is Legality—a man of no small wisdom."

"Oh?"

"Oh, yes. A man with a wonderful reputation."

"For what?"

"Why! For being able to help men off with just such burdens as weigh upon your shoulders, of course!"

"Indeed?"

"Yea, and from what I can gather, he has done a great deal of good this way."

"Why," exclaimed Christian, greatly encouraged, "it sounds to be just the thing."

"It is!" affirmed the man boldly. "And since his house is not quite a mile from this very spot, you may go to him and be helped right off!"

"Really?"

"Uh-huh. And if he should uh, perchance not be at home himself, he has a handsome, young son living next door, whose name is Civility. Civility can likely relieve you nearly as well as old Legality himself."

"Indeed! Then I do hope they are at home."

"Most likely they are," encouraged Worldly-wiseman. "Most likely. But, if perchance they should both be off on a hunt or at a party, the old man has a base-born son who, in spite of his doubtful parentage, can do you as much good as his father."

"Well, his base-birth be no fault of his own," said Christian. "If he has a ministry to relieve men of their burdens, why what matter his mother? What be his name?"

"Psychology," said the man. "His name is Psychology."

"Hmmm? What an odd name," mused Christian. "And you say he can remove my burden as well as Legality himself?"

"Aye. Or at the least help you realize that it is not really there. In any case, relief of some sort lies just up this little trail."

"Why, such good fortune!"

"Yes," nodded the man with a gracious smile, "there you may be quickly eased of your heavy burden."

"Sir!" declared Christian, "if these things of which you speak be true, then my wisest course is to take your counsel."

"Yes, but of course!" gushed the man, with a sugary smile.

"Sir, show me the way to this honest man's house."

Then the man came close and, putting his arm round Christian's shoulder, pointed up a steeply ascending, switch-backed trail and whispered, "Do you see yonder high hill?"

"Yes, very well," answered Christian, in awe. "I have been walking in its smoky shadow since I first began my travels."

"'Tis called Mount Sinai," said the man, with a great show of reverence. "Up that hill you must go, and the first house at the top is his."

"Why, thank you, sir. Thank you very much!"

"Think nothing of it, friend. I have saved many a grateful pilgrim from a long and tedious journey. Ta ta."

"Farewell," said Christian as he hiked up his pants and set out with eager step.

"Oh, and uh, when you come back to your right mind, do come visit my shop on your way home," he called after him.

"Thank you. I shall," Christian replied over his shoulder.

So Christian turned away from the light and began the arduous climb toward Mr. Legality's house. But as he came near the base of Mt. Sinai, he found it much higher, much steeper and much more treacherous than he had imagined. Moreover, when he was about halfway up, he found that the main mass of the mountain hung right over the path. Aye, hung over in such a steep fashion that he feared it might break loose and fall on his head. Therefore did Pilgrim come to a halt and begin to wonder what to do.

"Oh, woe is me. My burden has grown heavier than ever, and I can no longer see the light. Worst of all, this dreadful mountain hangs over my head and threatens to crush out my life. Oh me!"

Now from the dark clouds hanging over the summit, lightning flashed down that put him into a fear to go on. To one side yawned a fearful chasm and on the other there arose a sheer and beetling cliff. From out of the hill behind him there shot flashes of fire and belched yellow clouds of sulphurous smoke. These before and those behind made Christian afraid to move lest he should be killed. Then there came a shaking under his feet that put him into a greater terror yet. Here, therefore, he began to sweat and quake for fear. He also began to deeply regret having met one Mr. Worldly-wiseman. Oh, how sorry he was that he had ever taken such evil counsel. Oh, how he wished he could somehow, somewhere, see the light again.

Just when he had begun to fear that he was lost forever, he saw a distant figure toiling up the hill toward him. As the man came closer, he discerned that it was Evangelist. "Evangelist! Oh joy!" shouted Christian. "Evangelist is coming to meet me!" There was hope once again and now his heart was filled with cheer. But then, as he thought of where he was, and how he had come to be where he was, he began to blush for shame. So Evangelist came up to Christian and looked upon him with a severe and dreadful countenance. Then he began to reason with Christian thus:

"What are you doing here, Pilgrim?"

To this Christian had no proper answer and only managed to stammer out, "Uh . . . uh . . ."

Then said Evangelist sternly, "Are you not the man I found crying outside the walls of the City of Destruction?"

"Uh . . . yes, dear sir. I am the man."

"And did I not set you on the path to the little wicket gate?"

"Yes, sir," said Christian, head hung low with shame.

. . . this dreadful mountain hangs over my head . . .

"How is it, then, that you have so quickly turned aside? Surely you must realize that you are now quite out of the way."

Then said Christian sadly, "Uh . . . that is, uh . . . well . . . right after I had gotten over the Slough of Despond, I met with a distinguished-looking gentleman who dwells in these parts. He spoke with me for some long time and persuaded me that I might get out of the shadow of this Mt. Sinai by climbing to its top. There I was supposed to find a village called Morality, whose mayor could relieve me of my burden."

"I see."

"And so I foolishly believed the man and turned me out of your way into his, hoping that I might be eased of my burden by an easier way. But when I got to this place and beheld things as they are, what with this beetling cliff, and the sulphurous fumes, and the thundering ground, I grew afraid and stopped. And I must honestly confess, sir, that I can no longer see the light and that I have no idea what to do."

"Bear with me for a moment that I might show you the words of God," commanded Evangelist.

"Uh . . . Yes, sir," said the trembling pilgrim.

Then Evangelist raised his right hand toward heaven and said in a deep and thunderous tone, "Now 'the just shall live by faith.' But you have begun to reject the counsel of the Most High. You have drawn your foot back from the way of peace and put yourself in danger of losing your soul!"

Then did Christian fall upon his face, crying, "Oh, woe is me, for I am undone!"

"Stand up on your feet," said Evangelist tenderly, stretching forth a kindly hand.

"Yes, sir," said Christian, gratefully, struggling to his feet beneath the increased weight of an already ponderous burden.

"Fear not, poor Christian," said Evangelist gently, "for all manner of sin and blasphemies shall be forgiven unto men. Therefore, be not faithless but believing."

"Ah, is it even so? May I be forgiven?" asked Christian with a touch of hope in his voice.

"Aye, 'if thou canst believe. All things are possible to him that believeth.'"

"'I . . . believe,'" stammered Christian. "'Only help thou mine unbelief.'"

Then Evangelist smiled to hear him quote from his little book and said firmly, "That man that met you in the way was one Worldly-wiseman. His counsel was like to have been the death of you."

"Yes, sir," answered Christian, his head yet hung low.

"The Lord says, 'Strive to enter in at the strait gate' (the gate to which I sent you); 'for strait is the gate which leadeth unto life, and few there be that find it.'"

"Yes, sir."

"He to whom you were sent to find relief, the man called Legality, is the son of the bondwoman which is yet in sin's bondage with all her children. That priestess and her ways are revealed to you in this Mount Sinai."

"Aye, so I see," answered Christian, glancing fearfully upon the many terrors thickly surrounding him. "There are fires and thunderings and this steeply leaning cliff, which I yet fear may fall on my head!"

"It has crushed many others and would likely have done the same to you had you not wisely stopped. But do tell, if Legality and his mother and his brethren are yet in bondage, how did you ever expect them to set you free?"

"I don't know what I thought," confessed Christian.

"This Legality could never set you free from your burden though you should climb this mountain a million times over! You can never be justified by the works of the law, for, 'by the deeds of the law no man living can be freed from his burden.'"

"Yes, I have read that in my book," said Christian, nodding in agreement.

"Then you should have quoted it to the adversary and cut his arguments down to the marrow!" instructed Evangelist.

"I forgot," confessed Christian.

"Which nearly led to your destruction."

"Yes."

"And by which your burden was made none the lighter."

"Nay! But rather more heavy," admitted Christian.

"Therefore, Mr. Worldly-wiseman is an alien," said Evangelist angrily. "Mr. Legality is a cheat, and his son Civility, notwithstanding his cultured style, is nothing but a hypocrite and cannot help you. And as for his base-born son Psychology, I . . . I forbear to comment further."

"Nay but do say more," pleaded Christian earnestly, "for I see that your heart is stirred within you, Dear Evangelist."

"Very well," responded Evangelist. "Had you not asked I would have kept my silence. But since you have asked I shall say more. Morality and Civility are base impostors of the gospel in verity. Yet, even so, their thin veneer of manners and false kindness will never bring peace to a man's soul. Therefore after a time he will once again realize his need and perhaps renew his search for truth. But the teaching of this young upstart knave, Psychology, is worse by far!"

"How so, dear Evangelist?" inquired Christian.

"In that he will tell you flat-out that what you are today you will forever be," answered Evangelist indignantly. "He will teach you that your burden will never be lifted . . ."

"What!" exclaimed Christian, roused to fear by the very thought. "Never lifted, do you say?"

"Aye, verily, never lifted. At best all he can promise is to help you change your behavior and perhaps teach you to deal with your emotions. But as for a real change of heart or freedom from the burden of the past-never!"

"Never?"

"Never," said Evangelist firmly. "All you can hope for is to be able to accept yourself as you are, and to learn to live with reality."

"Verily?" cried Christian. "Oh, how could I live with such a thought? To be free! To be free! That is the very heart-cry of my soul!"

"'Tis a cry that Psychology shall neither hear nor answer."

"Oh woe would be me," moaned Christian. "It would be just as well that I had never read in my little book, or never left Destruction, as to believe that."

"There is more to tell, if you would hear it," added Evangelist.

"Do go on, Dear Evangelist," pleaded Christian.

"Moreover, he would have you blame all of your painful baggage on those who have gone before: an evil mother, a drunken father, an encounter with an evil monster of some sort. And indeed, all of these things may leave their mark on the heart. But through the gospel they may be overcome and put away!"

"Verily? Is it even so?"

"Yea," said Evangelist with divine assurance. "This is the power of the gospel. There is nothing in our lives that we may not overcome through the power of Christ. Yea, it is the chief delight of the Lord of the Hill to take our weakest points and to give us such a smashing victory that they become our strongest!"

"Oh, glorious thought!"

"Indeed. The Great King desires to make of our soul a mighty fortress—a veritable armed castle right here in the heartland of the enemy. He fully intends that no power but his own shall ever reign in our soul."

"Ah!" said Christian, his eyes bright with hope. "Blessed hope. Blessed, blessed hope!"

"So it is, dear Christian," said Evangelist softly. "And if you will but believe His promise of forgiveness, and act as though it were true, all these words of mine will surely come to pass."

"Oh, dear Evangelist," sobbed Christian in hopeful joy. "May it be so with me! May my soul become a stronghold for the king indeed.

May I never give the enemy one small toe-hold from the past whereby he may afflict my soul!"

"Then bring your past to Jesus," commanded Evangelist. "Be forgiven and let the past die. Forgive all wrongs and let the future be pure. Go on from victory to renewed victory—in Him!"

"But how, dear Evangelist," pleaded Christian. "How?"

"Continue on as you have begun, " advised Evangelist. "Keep your eye on the light. Stay on the path and soon your burden shall be taken from you in the appointed way."

"I shall, dear sir," said Christian. "I shall. Now I can see these knaves clearly for what they are. Oh, God forbid that I should ever be thus deceived again."

Then Evangelist raised his hand toward heaven and said in a commanding voice, "I call upon the heavens for confirmation that my words are not my own but those of Him who sent me!"

Suddenly, Mt. Sinai began to smoke and quake with great violence and there thundered forth the resounding voice of Moses saying, "As many as are of the works of the law are under the curse of the law; for it is written, 'Cursed is everyone that continueth not in all things which are written in the book of the law to do them.'"

"Oh, I fear for my life!" cried Christian, dropping to his knees in terror. "Oh, curse the time that I stopped to parley with the enemy. Oh, curse my forgetfulness of the promises. Oh, I have played the part of a thousand fools times ten thousand fools!"

"But," said Evangelist, laying his hand upon Christian's shoulder, "praise be to God that your eyes have been opened."

"And shame to me that they ever should have been closed by arguments that flowed only from the flesh," moaned Christian. "Shame to me that worldly-wise logic should have prevailed against the words of Truth." Then Christian looked up into the eyes of his benefactor and asked pleadingly, "Sir, what think you? Be there any hope for me?"

"Aye," nodded Evangelist, with a tear in his eye. "There is hope."

"May I yet turn and get me up to the wicket gate?"

"You may turn."

"Might I not be abandoned for this sin and be sent back from thence ashamed?"

"You shall not be sent back. For the man at the gate has come to bring 'peace on earth, good will to men.' Come, stand you up."

With these words he gently lifted Christian to his feet and said, "Go in peace."

"I shall, sir. I shall."

Then did Christian turn himself to go back; and Evangelist, after he had kissed him, gave him one smile and bade him Godspeed; so he went on in haste. He did not speak to any man by the way. If any man saluted him or asked a question he would not slacken his pace nor pause to give him an answer. He went on like one that was all the while treading upon forbidden ground and could by no means feel himself safe till he was once again back on the path which he had abandoned. Once upon it he applied himself to his journey with all due diligence until, in process of time, Christian got up to the gate.

CHAPTER TWO

OW, OVER the gate there was written this promise: "Knock, and it shall be opened unto you." Therefore he knocked boldly, and that more than just once or twice, saying:

"May I now enter here? Will he within
Open to sorry me, though I have been
An undeserving rebel? If so, then shall I
Not fail to sing his lasting praise on High."

While he awaited the keeper of the gate, he noticed that the door was curiously marred by many scars. He observed further that there were smoke stains on the stone arch over the door. He saw also the broken shafts and charred feathers from many arrows littering the ground. "Hmmm," said he with furrowed brow. "If I do not miss my guess, I would say that this gate has withstood more than just a simple siege or two."

Soon there came a grave person to the gate named Goodwill, who asked, "Who knocks there?"

"A poor, burdened sinner," replied Christian, "fleeing unto Mount Zion from the City of Destruction."

With that, the gate was thrown open and Christian was so quickly snatched within by two powerful hands that he nearly went sprawling headlong upon the ground. Before Christian could even regain his balance, the door had been speedily shut fast and securely barred behind him. Then Christian, a bit dazed by such hasty behavior, said, "Dear, sir, what was the reason for giving me such a violent jerk?"

Then answered Goodwill, wiping a bead of sweat from his brow, "Did you not notice the scars and burns on our little wicket gate?"

"Yea."

. . . in process of time, Christian got up to the gate.

"And did you chance to hear all the zinging and thumping sounds as I was shutting the door?"

"Yes, I think I did. What were they?"

"Open the door a little and take a peek out to see what they were."

So Christian loosed the bars, cautiously opened the door just a tiny crack and there, stuck fast in the wood about the door, were several burning arrows!

"Oh my! Fiery darts!"

"Aye. Flaming arrows."

"Stabbed into the door!"

"Aye."

"And for whom were these messengers of death sent?"

"For you, dear traveler," said Goodwill gravely. "For you."

"Whence came they?"

Goodwill pointed through the crack at an imposing castle loom-ing large in the shadows of the misty forest, saying, "Look! Across the way!"

So Christian cracked the door just a bit wider and peeked out. "I see a castle hidden in the trees. It has great iron gates, and it flies the black banner. And it seems, sir, that it is not very far off from the wick-et gate you keep. Within a bowshot, I should guess."

While these words were still upon his lips a flaming arrow went zinging (ssffssst!) over his head and buried its smoking shaft in the flower bed behind him. Quickly slamming the door, Christian leaned his burden back against it and swallowing hard said, "I say! This pil-grimage business is dreadfully dangerous stuff, isn't it!"

"Aye," agreed the gatekeeper. "Life and death stuff."

"But who would want to kill a simple pilgrim like me?" he asked incredulously. Then Goodwill answered saying, "Open the door a wee crack and look out again. But, not so wide!"

And so Christian obeyed, and with the utmost caution peeked him out through a tiny sliver of light. Then said Goodwill, "Can you see the dark castle?"

"Aye," answered Christian. "To whom does it belong?"

"'Tis the castle of the enemy, of which Beelzebub himself is the captain."

"It is?"

"Aye. And from its walls he, and they that be with him, shoot arrows at those that come up to this gate, hoping to kill them ere they enter in."

"But I am new upon this journey," said Christian. "Why would he want to destroy me? Surely I am no threat to him!"

"Nay, but you are!" declared Goodwill. "The greatest of God's warriors began just as you have done. And since the evil one has no way of knowing what God's grace may make of you, he tries to nip you in the bud. Besides, it is a principle of the dark kingdom that none shall leave its service without encountering trials, tribulations and death at every step."

"Then I have great cause to rejoice and tremble!" said Christian thankfully.

"Aye, indeed you have," said Goodwill as he bolted the door fast. "But tell me, how is it that you came all alone?"

Then Christian bowed his head in sadness and answered softly, "Because none of my family or neighbors saw their danger, as I saw mine."

"Did any of them know you were coming?"

"Oh yes! Almost the entire town saw me go."

"Then I am surprised that no one followed after to persuade you to go back."

"Oh, some did. Both Obstinate and Pliable came running after me. But when they saw that they could not change my mind, Obstinate went stomping back."

"As the name, so the man. And Pliable?"

"Well," explained Christian with a note of sadness to his voice, "Pliable was happy enough to come along with me, until we carelessly fell into the Slough of Despond."

"Ah. You must have taken your eyes off the light."

"Aye. So we did," admitted Christian.

"What then?"

"Well, for a short time we both tried to press forward. But as soon as the muck got past our waists, he became discouraged and refused to venture farther."

"Ah, alas, poor man! Was not the celestial glory precious enough to brave a few difficulties?"

"Truly, if the truth be known, I am no better that he."

"Why do you say that? Did not he run back? And did not you come straight on?"

"'Tis true," agreed Christian, with his head hung down. "He went on back to Destruction, but I also turned aside back into the way of death."

"Ah. Up to the town of Morality no doubt."

"Yes."

"Uh huh," said Goodwill angrily. "Directed thereto by the carnal arguments of one Mr. Worldly-wiseman, I suppose."

"Yes. But how did you know?"

"Because this wicked fellow attacks nearly everyone with his fleshly reasoning. And frankly, there are few that escape his snare."

"Ah, then I have more reason than ever to be thankful to my Lord," said Christian with a sigh of relief.

"More than you know. And I suppose he was going to have you seek for ease at the hands of Mr. Legality or one of his base-born sons?"

"Aye. Their names were Civility and Psychology."

"Pah! Nothing but cheats the lot of them!" said he with righteous indignation. "But go on. Did you truly take his vile counsel?"

"Yes," admitted Christian. "At least as far as I dared. For I was nearly crushed by the overhang of that fearful mountain."

"That mountain will be the death of all who try to enter in by the works of their own hands," affirmed Goodwill. "Frankly, I am amazed that you escaped being ground to powder!"

"Yea," agreed Christian gratefully. "It is amazing! Thanks be to God! But now, here I am, more deserving of death on the horns of Sinai than to be here talking with you, my lord. Oh, what a blessed privilege! That one so faithless as I should still be allowed within these wondrous walls!"

"No need for surprise on that account, dear Christian. We have no restrictions against any who would enter this place."

"Against none?"

"Against none! No matter what they may have done before coming here, no one is shut out."

"Thank God!"

"Yes," said Goodwill, smiling. "For everything! But come now, good Christian. Walk with me a little way, and I will teach you about the way you must go."

So he took him to the edge of the compound and, pointing to a small, little-trod path said, "Here, look . . . straight before you. Do you see that little path?"

"Aye."

"That is the way you must go."

Christian looked up along the way and then turned to Goodwill saying, "'Tis a bit narrow, don't you think?"

To this Goodwill only smiled and said, "This path through the wilderness of this world was carved out by the patriarchs, the prophets, Christ, and His apostles."

"But it is sooo narrow."

"You're only passing through, dear Christian. And besides, it was wide enough for Christ."

"Truly?"

Goodwill shows the way

"Aye."

"Then, I suppose it must be wide enough for me!" said Christian decidedly.

"It is!" answered Goodwill confidently. "Wide enough for anyone! And with room to spare!"

"Has it a name?"

"Aye. It is called by our Lord the 'Straight Way' and He laid it out using the surveying instruments of heaven itself. This is the way you must go."

"But is it easy to follow?" asked Christian, fearful of getting off the path again. "Are there any turnings or windings wherein a stranger may lose his way?"

"Nay, none. But beware, for there are many ways that come down and intersect with this one."

"Then might I not become confused?"

"Nay, fear not," Goodwill continued calmly. "They are easy to detect, for they are all broad and easy of travel. Only the right way is straight and narrow. You may also detect them because only the right one ascends upwards."

"Ah," said Christian, breathing a sigh of relief. "Then 'the wayfaring man, though a fool, need not err therein!'"

"None need err," smiled Goodwill. "All who are willing to do His will shall know the right way. Now, 'tis time to be off on your journey."

"Uh, one thing more, dear Goodwill."

"Being?"

"Can you cut this burden off my back?" begged Christian. "I cannot do it myself, and back home no one else could even see it. Can you see it?"

"Oh, aye. See it I can. Very well indeed. And a very dark and grievous one it is too!"

"Then, can you help me?"

"No, dear Christian. The place of beginnings is not the place of deliverance. You must be content to bear it until you come to a sacred hill, where it will fall from your back of its own accord."

"When shall this be?" sighed Christian longingly. "When?"

"Sooner than you think and longer than you wish," was the wise reply. "Only be content with your Lord's timing."

At this saying Christian stood tall, tightened his frayed cord belt and said, "Then let me gird up my loins and address myself to my journey. Are there any dangers yet ahead?"

"None but such as have overtaken all men," said he. "But rest assured that with every trial your Lord has made a way of escape."

"That is a comfort. Can you tell me what lies ahead next?"

"Yes. When you have gone some distance from this gate you will come to the House of the Interpreter."

"And what shall I do there?" queried Christian, his eyes now fast on the path to be trod.

"The same as here. Knock and it shall be opened unto you. Seek His wisdom and ye shall find it. Ask for help and it shall be given you."

"I shall," promised Christian as he took the first step of his long journey. "Thank you for your help, dear Goodwill. God be with you."

"Fare you well, good Christian. Godspeed. Godspeed!"

And so he traveled many a mile without further event till he came to the house of the Interpreter. There he knocked over and over until there came from within the voice of the Interpreter saying, "Who knocks, please?"

"Sir, I be a man coming from the City of Destruction and bound for Mount Zion."

"Oh?"

"Uh . . . I was told by the man that stands at the gate . . ."

"Gate?"

"Yes, the wicket gate that stands at the head of this way."

"Ah."

"He said that if I called here, you would show me excellent things that would be helpful to me on my journey."

"Ah, then welcome, welcome. Do come in," said the Interpreter cheerily as he swung open the door. Before Christian stood a dignified gentleman who bowed low before him and said, "Follow me and I will show thee things that will indeed profit thee."

"Most gladly," said Christian eagerly, as squeezed his cumbersome burden through the narrow door.

The wise one led him first into a private room, where he bade his butler come light a candle and open a door into a softly lit and elegantly furnished gallery. Through the open door Christian saw a greater than life-size painting of a very sober and distinguished-looking person hung upon the wall. When Christian first saw it he exclaimed,

"Oh, my! Such a glorious piece of art!"

Now the person portrayed in this amazing portrait had his eyes lifted up to heaven; in his hand he held the Book of Books; written upon his lips was the law of truth; behind his back the world hung in space. He stood as if he were pleading with men for their salvation, and over his head hung a crown of gold.

Then said Christian, "What is the meaning of this fine work of art?"

"The man pictured in this parable is one of a thousand," began the Interpreter. "He can say, in the words of the apostle: 'Though ye have ten thousand instructors in Christ, yet have you not many fathers, for in Christ Jesus have I begotten you through the Gospel.'"

"Then, if this is a parable for the eyes," said Christian thoughtfully, "everything in the painting must have a secret meaning."

"Aye."

"Then do tell, dear Interpreter, what means his upward gaze?"

"It shows that his chief goal is to seek out and to understand the dark mysteries of the kingdom."

"Ah. And what about the book in his hand and the words written on his lips?"

"Ah, 'tis the best of books," he replied proudly, "and out of it come the words of truth written upon his lips."

"And what about his pleading look?"

"This is to show his love for the lost. His mission is to continually plead with the lost, that they might accept the Lord of the way."

"Ah!" noted Christian. "Then the world pictured so far behind him must show his disdain for mere earthly treasures!"

"Ah, good," said the Interpreter with a smile, "well thought out, dear Pilgrim. Well thought out indeed. And the crown?"

"Well," began Christian, as he paused to think a moment, "the crown hangs just over his head, and it be thickly covered with stars. Therefore, might not this crown show us the great glory of his reward?"

"Aye," agreed the Interpreter, with a smile and a slow nod of his head.

"He seems to be a great and noble person," added Christian as he looked admiringly at the painting.

"And so he is," responded the Interpreter proudly. "And he is the only one whom thy Lord has appointed to be your guide."

"Then most gladly will I follow his voice for I can see that he cares for me."

"If you so do, he will guide you safely through all the trying moments of this way, and at last lay thee down in green pastures," said the Interpreter, as he bade his servant close the door.

"Thanks be to God," said Christian gratefully.

"Indeed," replied the Interpreter, beckoning with the hand for Christian to follow. "Come."

Then he took him by the hand, and led him into a very large parlor that was the dustiest, sootiest place you could ever imagine in your worst imaginings! It had dust everywhere! There was dust on the floor, dust on the table, dust on the chairs, dust on the shelves and books and beds. Now, this was not just a thin layer of dust such as you come home to after a long holiday at grandmother's house. Oh, no! This was years of dust piled upon decades of dust. So deep was this dust that it made little puffy clouds about Christian's feet as he walked. Now after giving Christian a few moments to consider, the Interpreter called for one of his servants, named Moses, and said, "Sir, I want you to begin sweeping this room clean." To this the servant answered cheerfully, "Yes sir!"

And begin to sweep he did! And that with a right good will too! And oh, my! You cannot imagine the cloud of dust he stirred up! Oh! Aye, such a cloud of dust that one could scarcely see from one side of the room to the other. Then did Christian begin to cough and spit and sputter as though he were a man about to drown. Said he, between his spasms of coughing (cough cough), "Dear Interpreter, (cough) help!" (cough, cough, cough)

Then the Interpreter called down the hallway for a young maid, named Gospel, to come help them.

"Gospel, (cough) Gospel! Come here, my dear."

There soon appeared a bright young maid in the doorway who curtsied and said with a smile, "Did you call, Master?" (cough, cough)

"Yes, (cough) my child. Come, quickly. (cough, cough) I want you to bring much water, (cough, cough) and sprinkle this room."

And so the maid quickly did as she was bidden. She sprinkled all about the floor and then wet the dust rags and the broom. Soon all the dust began to settle upon the wet floor, and before long all was swept as clean as clean could be.

Said Christian, "What does this mean? (cough) Is there another allegory here?"

"Aye," said the Interpreter with a smile. "Can you guess it?"

The pilgrim thought long, and the pilgrim thought hard, until the pilgrim had run clean out of thoughts to think and had to confess, "No, sir. I can by no means plumb its depths. Please explain."

Then the Interpreter taught him saying, "This parlor is the heart of a man that was never sanctified by the sweet grace of the Gospel. The dust is his desire to evil. It shows the inward corruptions that defile the whole man. Then here comes the law into his life, and, seeing a great need, he begins to sweep things clean! But the girl who brought the water and settled the dust is the Gospel."

"Ah," said Christian, beginning to see a trace of light.

And begin to sweep he did!

"Now," continued the Interpreter, "did you notice that, as soon as the law began to sweep, the dust of evil desire was stirred up?"

"I should say it was!" coughed Christian. "And just as quickly as one corner was swept clean, all the dust seemed to fly through the air and settle even more thickly in another."

"This is to teach thee that the law alone cannot cleanse the heart of sin. Instead it seems to revive it, strengthen it, and increase it in the soul."

"Why is the law so helpless to do more?" asked Christian, a bit puzzled.

"Because the law is only a mirror for thy soul," said the Interpreter. "A mirror may show thee thy need of cleansing ever so clearly. Yet, it hath not power to cleanse thee of one small spot!"

"Ah!" nodded Christian, beginning to understand more clearly.

"So it is with the law. It is very quick to shine thy sins into your face and show thee thy need. But," he said emphatically, "it does not give thee power to subdue one small sin!"

"'Tis true! 'Twas the law that first laid this burden upon my back. And 'twas the law that was near to crush me as I approached the town of Morality!"

"Aye. Aye. The law has more than enough power to point out thy need, but not near enough to relieve it. But! Did you notice the damsel that came to sprinkle the water?"

"Oh yes, verily! I think she has saved us all from a dusty death!"

"Aye," he agreed with one last cough. "In the same way shall sin be vanquished and subdued by the sprinkling of faith."

"Indeed?" marveled Christian.

"Aye. And in the same way shall thy soul be cleansed, and fashioned into a temple fit for habitation by the King of Glory!"

"Verily? Can it be so?"

"If thou canst believe. 'All things are possible to him that believeth.'"

"'Lord, I believe!'" Christian cried out longingly. "'Help thou my unbelief.'"

"Well said!" nodded the Interpreter as he took Christian by the hand and turned to go. "Yea, well said indeed. Come along."

"You mean there is still more?"

"Oh, aye. Much more," he replied, neither turning back nor slackening his pace. "Come along."

I saw then in my dream that the Interpreter led him next into a small room where two young lads were sitting. The name of the eldest was Passion, who, in a very gruff voice was heard to say such things as: "Gimme that toy!" or, "Get outta' my way, you!" The other child was named Patience and from him came words such as: "Thank you," or, "Yes, sir, if you would please."

Then Christian heard Passion bark at a servant, saying, "Hurry up, would'ja!" Not long after that, he heard Patience say, "I would like that very much, thank you."

Then said Christian, somewhat in a puzzlement, "Do tell? Why is the one child so gruffly discontent?"

"Because his governor would have him wait for his inheritance until the beginning of next year. But he thinks he must have it all now. Let us watch," said the Interpreter quietly guiding Christian into a remote corner where they could observe without being seen.

Then Passion snapped, angrily, "Right now, I said! Bring it here, right now!"

In answer was heard a nasal, high-pitched voice from the hallway, saying, "Coming, master Passion."

Passion and Patience

Soon I saw a brow-beaten wisp of a servant come staggering into Passion's presence with fear and trembling. Over his bent back hung a great bag of treasure, as called for by his young master. But I could see that he was quite loathe to pour it out for fear that the lad would squander it all and soon come to want. Then Passion, seeing his hesitation, cried out, "What'cha wait'n for, slave man? Pour it out! Pour it all out! Now!"

And so the servant reluctantly obeyed and poured the glittering contents clinking about Passion's feet. At this the lad chuckled gleefully and ran his fingers through gold doublloons, rubies and diamonds. Then he glanced over his shoulder and said in derisive tones, "Haw de haw, haw, Patience! I gots mine while you gots none. So sit and cry while I have fun. Haw de haw, haw, haw."

Then whispered Christian to the Interpreter, "Such a rude fellow!"

To this the Interpreter only smiled grimly and replied softly, "The story is not yet over, dear Christian. Watch and listen yet a bit more."

Then Passion continued to taunt his brother, saying, "You think the governor's bringing your reward later, don't 'cha? Well, you're dead wrong, pal. Our Lord delays His coming—maybe forever! And if you don't get wise like me, you won't get nothin'!"

"'Tis unfair!" complained Christian.

To this the Interpreter said quietly, "Watch. Watch as the years pass before your eyes."

Then I beheld in amazement as the seasons swept swiftly over the boys and their fascinated observers. Spring, summer, fall, each in their turn, came and went as in a dream. Then I saw, that before winter had well set in, Passion had played away all of his fortune and begun to be in want. Then his scorn succumbed to sorrow and his teasing turned to tears. When he realized his folly and would have repented, there was no one to hear.

Then said Christian triumphantly, "'Tis just and fair! He got just what he asked for."

To this the Interpreter answered, "The story is not yet done, dear Christian. Watch on."

And so Christian watched as more seasons passed over them. Finally, when the appointed time came, the governor of the children came with his book of records to bestow gifts where they were deserved. Then said the Governor, "Greetings from the King, dear

Patience. We are here to bestow upon you all of your Lord's rewards. In addition to your principal, you will receive interest from the King's own bank. Come, gentlemen."

Now at this there came in not one servant, nor two, or even three or four, but many! All of them bent low beneath bags of treasure beyond computation. These they joyfully poured out at Patience's feet to his great surprise and greater delight. But when Passion saw how great was his brother's portion, he was near to be choked with covetous envy.

Then said Christian in astonishment, "My my! So much more!"

"Aye, the King's bank yields the highest interest in the universe. Those who invest in His bank soon find that the interest is many times greater than the principal."

Then Christian saw Patience bow himself courteously and give thanks to the governor for his sound counsel, saying, "I do thank thee for thy wise guidance, dear governor."

Now Passion, finally beginning to comprehend the greatness of the delayed reward, began to rail and curse his misfortune saying, "This is unfair! Completely unfair! All we had was his promise to return, and then He came sneaking in like a thief in the night! Unfair! Unfair! Unfair!"

To this the governor replied calmly but yet sternly, "You were told that your Lord was coming, the same as your brother. And when you were rich, you did not part with even one penny to relieve your brother's poverty. Therefore, although he is desirous and well able to relieve yours, he is forbidden so to do. Go!"

"Go!" snapped Passion. "Go where?"

In answer, the governor sadly lowered his head and pointed out into the darkened courtyard, saying, "I gave you my promise, and you counted me a base liar. Therefore you must take your place in outer darkness with all who refuse to believe. Servants! Bind this knave and cast him out of my presence."

To this Passion had no answer to give but was sent spinning into outer darkness with wailing and gnashing of teeth.

Then said Christian, trembling a bit, "I perceive that I have seen yet another allegory, dear Interpreter."

"Aye. These two lads are figures: Passion, of the men of this world; and Patience, of those of the world to come. The men of

Out, foul flame! Out! Out! Out!

this world prefer to have all their good things now, rather than later."

"Ah! I know their type. Their chief proverb is that 'a bird in the hand is worth two in the bush.'"

"Aye," nodded the Interpreter sadly. "'Tis true. And that saying carries more weight with them than all the divine testimonies of the good world to come."

"But I'll wager that soon they will be like Passion, reduced to rags and sorrow and cast away."

"Aye."

"And no doubt at the very time that good men are just receiving title to their finest treasures."

"Thou hast wisely discerned, sir. Come."

Then I saw in my dream, that the Interpreter again took Christian by the hand and led him to where there was a fire burning brightly against a wall. Now Christian was about to enjoy its warmth when he was gruffly pushed aside by an angry looking man with two pails of water.

"Out of my way, fool!"

The man set one bucket down and then tossed the contents of the other on the fire, shouting angrily, "Out, cursed flame! (Tshhhh) Out, I say! (Psssss) And out again! Take that!" (Tshhhh)

Next he picked up his other bucket and tried again to douse the flames. But no matter how much water he cast upon the fire, he could do no more than make it choke and sputter for a moment. Then the flames would rise again, higher and hotter than before.

"Oh, what's wrong with this miserable worthless water!" grumbled the man. "Out, foul flame! (Tshhhh) Out! Ahh! Out, cursed light! (Pssss) Out! Out! Out! Hah!" (Tsssss)

"What means this?" queried the puzzled pilgrim.

"The fire you see is the work of grace burning in the heart of one who loves God. He who seeks to douse it is the devil."

"But it seems to me that in spite of his best efforts to put it out, the fire burns higher and hotter."

"Ah, yes. Heh, heh, heh," chuckled the Interpreter. "And the reason for that thou shalt soon see. Whilst he goes off to refill his buckets, come, around behind the wall with me."

So he took him behind the wall where he saw a noble-looking gentleman standing with a vessel of oil in his hand. Christian soon perceived that He was often pouring oil into a golden tube that passed through the wall and supplied the fire with fuel.

Then Christian asked, "And what does this mean?"

"This is Christ," whispered the Interpreter reverently. "He, by continually applying the oil of His grace, sustains the flame of love in our hearts!"

"Ah."

"Because of Christ's constant help, it matters not what trials the devil may pour in upon us. The oil of the Spirit floats above them all and the flame of love burns brighter still."

"Aha!" said Christian thankfully. "A good lesson for me!"

"And did you notice how our Lord stood behind the wall to maintain the fire?"

"Aye. I wondered about that. Why so?"

"To teach thee, dear pilgrim, that even when you cannot see Him, Christ is always near. No matter what doubts may come or fears assail, your faith may burn brightly still."

"Then, when I be tempted most," exclaimed Christian, "I can rest assured that He who supplies the oil is still near at hand!"

"Aye. Aye, He is the One that 'sticketh closer than a brother.' And did you notice that His vessel is filled by golden tubes coming from two great olive trees?"

"Aye. I can see how the ever flowing stream renews His stores of oil, but of what are they symbols?"

"These are the Two Witnesses spoken of by John. They are the ones which shall be slain and lie dead in the streets of Sodom and Egypt for 3 days."

"I'm afraid I don't understand," said Christian with a blank look on his face.

Then the Interpreter pointed to Christian's little book and said, "Thou hast a copy of them in thy hand."

"The Testaments, Old and New?"

"Aye. They will provide thee with fuel enough to keep thy light shining through all eternity! And rest assured, dear Christian, that He who pours the oil will never suffer the waters of affliction to overflow thee."

"To God be praises!"

"Aye. Come," he said reaching out to take him by the hand. And so they left the fire burning brightly by the wall. As they were going, they could hear still the old devil shouting, "Out, cursed flame! (Hsssss) Out, out, out!"(Tshhhh)

The pilgrim was then led out to a beautifully landscaped estate surrounding a mighty and stately palace. It was built of precious stones most lovely to behold and atop its walls were turrets and parapets and mighty engines of war. Around it there was a moat with a drawbridge leading to a large, heavily guarded gate of bronze. Walking upon its walls were certain youth all clothed in gold, and it seemed to Christian that they must be the happiest people he had ever seen. Looking in through the great bronze gate, Christian saw broad streets, market places, lovely hanging gardens, and children laughing with their families and pets. At the sight of these marvels he was greatly delighted and asked eagerly, "May we go in here?"

"Aye, someday, if thou art faithful unto death. Come."

Then the Interpreter took him and led him nearer to the gate of the palace; and behold, at the drawbridge, there stood a great company of schoolmen and scholars, all greatly desirous of going in but daring not to take action. Drawing closer, Christian heard two of them conversing as they tried to muster up enough courage to make a move. Said the first, "Well, aren't you going in, dear professor?"

To this the second bowed low, swept his four-cornered cap gracefully toward the guarded gate and answered, "Not just now, lad. After you."

"Not at all. Age before beauty, you know, heh, heh."

"Ah! To the contrary, young man, 'Tis fools rush in!"

Near the side of the moat was a table with a book, a pen, and a writer's inkhorn. Sitting at it was a dignified person whom I assumed to be some sort of scribe or notary. Upon seeing him, Christian asked, "What is the purpose of this gentleman?"

"His work it is to take down the names of all those who have the courage to enter in."

"Ah."

After what seemed to be forever the notary drummed his fingers impatiently on the table and called out, "Come! Come! Come! Is there not one man among you with enough faith to take the kingdom of heaven by violence?"

In response to this challenge there was total silence and downcast eyes. After a few moments, Christian remarked, "No answer."

"Aye, none."

"Do they not desire the kingdom?"

"Aye, with all their hearts. Or at least so they tell us."

"Then why do they wait?"

Then the Interpreter pointed into the city and said, "Look! Look past the drawbridge."

And so Christian looked therein and saw many knights in shining armor guarding the gate. These were armed to the teeth with lances, spears, swords, daggers, maces, clubs, and shields. Moreover, there were catapults, trebuchets, and other great machines of war upon the walls. There were also many battle chariots drawn by matched teams of mighty, black stallions. Christian noticed that the warriors were all on the alert. Yea, so much so that if one of the scholars so much as looked at the gates with longing eyes, the dark knights would bestir themselves and the anxious stallions would paw sparks off the cobblestones with a whinny of eager anticipation. Then was Christian confused and asked, "My! What are all these fierce warriors about?"

Answered the Interpreter, "Their work is to defend the castle from any who would enter in. They are commanded not to yield admittance at any low price."

Then was Christian near to tears, because so far as he could tell, there was no one with enough strength or courage to enter in. Then, he once again chanced to overhear the same two schoolmen conversing as before. The elder of the two, royally attired in his cap and gown, stood, hands on his hips, glaring with furrowed brow at the guarded gate. His younger companion, after waiting in vain for his professor to lead the way, finally turned contemptuously and sneered, "Well! Aren't you going in?"

To this his instructor answered dryly, "Oh no, lad. 'Twas you were here first. Courtesy dictates that I should follow after you."

"Not at all," snapped the youth. "Age before beauty, you know."

"To the contrary," countered the second dryly. "'Tis fools rush in!"

Replied the younger sarcastically, "You said that last time!"

To which the older quipped arrogantly, "So did you."

At last it became obvious that these men, along with multitudes of the same ilk, were hanging back for fear of the armed men at the gate. Just when Christian was beginning to despair, he saw a young man of no apparent distinction marching bravely to the fore. He had a very determined look and, coming directly to the notary's table, said boldly, "I choose to believe the words in my little book, sir. Therefore, set down my name, for I would enter in."

"And what be thy name?" asked the notary.

"Belief be the name, sir. Belief."

"And in what do you believe, good fellow?" challenged the writer.

"In the promises of He who has invited me to enter in."

"Which promises, good sir?"

"The one that saith, 'There shall no man be able to stand before thee,'" the man answered. "Also another which saith that, 'the kingdom of heaven suffereth violence and the violent take it by force.'"

"Ah, weapons well chosen. Your name be writ down, Mr. Belief. Therefore, have on. And God be with thee."

Now, when the armed men at the gate saw that someone was actually putting down his name, they began to bestir themselves and to boast loudly of what they would do to him. And I must inform you that these were not idle threats for they that made them were no ordinary soldiers. Nay, but rather giants conscripted in mass from the town of Gath. The swarthy commander spoke first, saying to one of his heavily bemuscled companions, "Heh, heh, heh. Looky see, mate."

"What?" asked the second, looking up from shining his armor to espy Mr. Belief signing his name with a flourish. "Aha! So! A fool has come to engage us in battle, has he?"

"Good," growled the first, gingerly testing the razor-sharp edge of his sword with his nail. "My blade has been too long thirsting for blood."

"Aye," snarled the second, testing the sharp points on his mace, "and the nails on my club have grown rusty. Come, fool!"

Now Mr. Belief, completely ignoring the swaggering giants and their ferocious threatenings, went straight to the armory to dress for battle. Then Christian, fearing for his safety, asked, "Will he battle them all alone?"

You shall not stop me with your paper swords!

"Only to the eye of appearance," said the Interpreter calmly.

"But look how many there are, and how huge! And see how deadly their weapons and fierce their faces!"

"Heh, heh, heh!" chuckled the Interpreter, merrily. "They are nothing but paper giants, lad. Paper giants who hope never to win a battle."

"What do you mean?"

"Watch. Just watch and see."

So Christian beheld as the man put on his head the helmet of salvation, fashioned about his loins the belt of truth, and strapped over his chest the breastplate of righteousness. On his feet he buckled the swift sandals of the preparation of the gospel of peace which would enable him to dart among his enemies, quick as a ray of light. Then, taking up his faithful shield, which was impervious to fiery darts, and the sharp two-edged sword, which cuts quickly to the very bone and marrow, he stood full abreast at the drawbridge.

"Engarde!" he shouted. Then he was off in a rush against the armed men at the door.

"Stop him!" cried the captain.

"Get him!" shouted his lieutenant grimly.

"Off with his head!" cried one of the giants as he raised a huge headsman's axe.

"Organize, men!" shouted the captain, as they began to scatter in confusion.

"Bring forth reinforcements!" screamed the lieutenant as his weapon went skittering along atop the stone pavement.

"More troops! Stop him!" commanded the captain as he saw his men surrendering ground.

Watching as more warriors rushed to join the melee, Christian grew more fearful than ever and cried out, "He has no chance!"

Amused at his alarm, the Interpreter only smiled calmly and said, "The battle is not over. Watch on."

The men at the gate laid upon Belief with deadly force, but the man, not at all discouraged, fell to cutting and hacking most fiercely, crying out, "You shall not stop me with your paper swords and mache masks. Take that!"

"Auuugh!" groaned one wounded giant.

"Help!" cried another. "Send four legions!"

Then, Belief seized upon his advantage and pushed forward with all boldness saying, "Nor shall I fall back though you call forth a multitude more vicious than you. Back, I say! Hah!"

"Auuugh! Stop!" begged one of the giants.

"Nay! But fall back more yet!" he commanded with a swish/hack of his two-edged sword.

Now by this time, the giants and their reinforcements had begun to retreat in complete disarray. Here and there and everywhere weapons of every sort lay scattered on the ground. One giant tripped over his own feet and became a stumbling block for three more who landed on their heads. Seeing the tide turn in his favor, Mr. Belief gathered up yet more courage and shouted, "Run, feeble cowards! Run for your lives! Take that, hah! And that!"

"No!" blubbered one of the giants piteously. "Have mercy!"

To this, Belief only attacked the more fiercely saying, "There be no mercy for such lying impostors as you. Hah!"

Then the captain himself cried out, saying, "Pity! We will be your slaves! Only have pity!"

At this, Belief staunched the unquenchable fury of his attack and commanded them to throw down their weapons. This they gladly did with a great clatter, all the while trembling with fear. Then he pointed the way to the dungeon to which they eagerly marched with hands raised high above their heads. Entering the gloomy dungeon with obvious relief, they locked the door behind themselves and gladly gave him the key. All the while they kept up a constant whimpering saying, "Mercy, gentle knight. We were only doing our job. Have mercy."

Then, amidst cheering from they that were within, Belief tossed the key into the moat and marched forward into the palace. As he drew near the prize of his high calling, he heard pleasant words from those that walked upon the top of the walls. One said joyfully, "Come in, come in. Eternal glory thou shalt win."

Another said, "Come in. Enter into the glory of thy Lord. Come in!"

Suddenly Christian clapped his hands with joy and exclaimed, "Say! I think I know the meaning of this one!"

"Oh?" said the Interpreter.

"Yes, for look! There are neither dead nor wounded. Nor is there any blood on the ground. But there are masks scattered hither and yon. Those fellows with such fierce faces and shining swords were only actors in a play!"

"Heh, heh, heh! Aye, aye, aye," chuckled the Interpreter merrily. "But they are only seen to be such by the eye of faith. To the faithless, 'tis a different tale. Listen to those two professors over there."

So Christian turned to hear two doctors of theology commenting on recent events. Said the first to his companion with a genteel bow and a gesture toward the drawbridge, "After you, good sir."

"Oh no," demured the second. "I have been teaching here only a few years. Common courtesy demands that I give way to seniority, dear doctor."

"Why do you quake and fear, lad? Yon brave man hacked his way through easily enough!"

"Aye, but did you see his armor? I have none such to protect my innards!"

"Well, does it look like I do?"

"Then do we stand here forever, dear colleague? Ever hoping and desiring to enter in, but never coming to the realization of it?"

"The time is not ripe, that's all," the wise one declared sagaciously. "We must wait for the promise of the latter rain, which will fit us up for the battle."

"Hmmm, yes. I believe so too," said his colleague, with a wistful glance toward the heavens, "but as yet, I see nary a cloud in the sky."

"Hmmm. Nor I," said the elder, scanning skillfully through a periodical. "And, looking here in the church paper, I see not so much as a forecast of clouds, let alone rain!"

"Hmmm," puzzled his colleague, "strange that this illiterate and gullible underling was able to hack his way through before us."

"Aye!" added his indignant companion. "And that without one class in the use of the sharp two-edged sword!"

"Whilst we are veritable experts in its use," grumbled the first.

"Indeed. In fact, I went to an outside university to obtain my degree in swordsmanship."

"Eh! Did you now?" said his companion feigning disinterest. "Well, heh, heh, so did I. In fact, I am licensed by the state to use my sword. How this blustering commoner hacked his way through is a complete mystery to me."

"Oh, beginner's luck, no doubt," surmised the second.

"Or perhaps brute strength," groused the first. "I wonder if we should turn him in for using his sword without a license."

"Say now! That might not be a bad idea. Well, whilst we're waiting for the clouds to form, shall we have a duel?"

"Yes! A splendid idea!" agreed the first eagerly. "'Twill give us something to do and keep our swords sharp besides. Engarde!"

"Engarde!" said the second, drawing his foil.

So they earnestly began their oft-practiced and skillfully choreographed duel. Then Christian turned to the Interpreter and said, "They are afraid!"

"Aye."

"But the defenders are not real!"

"To those who will not take God at His word and move forward," said the Interpreter sadly, "the warriors are more real than you can imagine."

"'Tis a mystery, this faith business," said Christian, shaking his head.

To this the Interpreter nodded in agreement, saying only, "Aye."

"But now," said Christian, looking longingly at the pathway to the Celestial City, "I am ready to be on my way. May I go now?"

"Nay, nay, stay," said the Interpreter with upraised hand. "Stay until I have showed thee a few things more. After that, thou shalt go on thy way."

So he took him by the hand again and led him into a very dark and dismal room, where there sat a man entombed in an iron cage. Looking sympathetically upon him, Christian saw that he seemed very, very sad. He sat with his eyes looking down to the ground, and, as he wrung his hands together, he sighed as if his heart would break.

"What means this?" asked Christian, with an aching heart. "Why is this man locked in this iron cage? And why does his heart break so?"

"Ask him. He will tell thee."

So Christian stepped over to the cage, knelt down and, pulling his face against the bars, asked gently, "Sir, why do you weep and mourn so sadly?"

At this the man sighed deeply and with downcast eyes said, "Because I am utterly changed from what I once was."

"And what were you once?"

"Oh, I was once, in my youth, the same as you. A fair and flour-ishing professor of religion," he answered sadly.

"And what are you now?"

"I am now a man of despair, and am shut up in it, as verily as I am shut up in this iron cage. I cannot get out. Oh, now I cannot!" he cried bitterly.

"But how did you come into this sad condition?" Christian asked gently.

To this question the man shuddered and then moaned, "I stopped praying. I stopped off to watch and be sober. I laid the reins of reason upon the neck of my lusts. I sinned against the light of the Word and the goodness of God. I have grieved the Spirit, and He has gone from me. I dallied with the devil, and he has taken me!"

Christian stood with sympathetic tears in his eyes and, turning to the Interpreter asked, "Dear Interpreter! Is there no hope for such a man as this?"

To this question the Interpreter could only gaze sadly toward the prisoner and say, "Ask him."

Then Christian turned back to the cage and, kneeling before him again, said, "Is there no hope, sir? Must you forever be kept in this iron cage of despair?"

"No!" groaned he. "No hope. No hope at all."

But Christian, unwilling to let him surrender his soul, said, "Why not? The Son of the Blessed is very pitiful. He can yet forgive."

"Not me!" cried the man. "He cannot forgive me!"

Still pressing his case, Christian said again, "But He can!"

"No! He cannot!"

"Why not?"

"Because I cannot repent!" cried he, in deepest anguish. "I have crucified Him to myself afresh. I . . . I have despised His person. I have despised His righteousness. I . . . I have counted His blood an unholy thing. I have done despite to the Spirit of grace. Therefore I have shut myself out of all the promises, and there now remains to me nothing but threatenings, dreadful threatenings, fearful threatenings, of certain judgment and fiery indignation which shall devour me as an adversary."

"Good sir!" exclaimed Christian. "For what price did you sell yourself into this condition?"

"For the same price that buys many a young man," he moaned.

"And what price was that?"

Then the man began to tremble saying, "It was for the lusts, the pleasures, the profits of this world; in the enjoyment of which I promised myself much delight; but now they are gone! And the guilt of every one of those things comes back to haunt me, and to bite me, and to gnaw me, like a burning worm!"

Then was Christian amazed, and turning to the Interpreter, said, "He is the same as the child Passion!"

"Aye," answered the Interpreter, nodding sadly.

Then Christian turned back to the cage and implored the man, saying, "But, sir. Can you not now repent and turn?"

"No!" he groaned. "I told you that I cannot! God will not be trifled with. Time after time I told Him to leave me alone and He has finally obeyed me. He has left me! I have so long refused to listen that now He refuses to speak. I cannot find repentance. Yea, even in His word I find no encouragement to believe. I have shut myself up in this iron cage of disbelief, and now all the men in the world cannot let me out. O, eternity! Eternity! How can I bear the loss of eternity?"

Then the man turned away from his erstwhile helper and continued to moan softly to himself. The Interpreter gently raised trembling Christian to his feet saying soberly, "Let this man's misery be remembered by thee and be an everlasting caution to thee."

"It shall," said Christian, glancing back at the cage. "But pray tell, good sir, why has God shut him up in this iron cage?"

Then the Interpreter shook his head and said, "Nay. 'Tis not God who hath shut him up thus."

"Then who?"

"'Tis Satan who be the builder of cages!" answered the Interpreter, eyes flashing in anger. "God hath revealed Himself as One who came to set the captives free."

"Then why may He not set this man free?"

"Because sin hath blinded his eyes to the mercy of God. He cannot believe that God can forgive him, and what man cannot believe, God cannot achieve."

"Then, if this man were somehow able to believe, could he yet be free?"

"Aye."

"Do tell, are there many that be in such a state as his?"

"Yea, verily. There be multitudes who believe their sins to be so great, that God cannot forgive them. They thus judge their sins to be greater than the power of God."

"Then what I have read is true! 'According to your belief, so shall it be unto you.'"

"Aye," agreed the Interpreter. "Sin hath so badly withered the arm of this man's faith, that it cannot reach forth to grasp God's mercy."

"But did he not know this would happen?"

"Nay!" explained the teacher. "He verily thought that he could lead a life of sinful pleasure and then turn to God at his good convenience. But when the pleasures of sin were past, and he tried to exercise his faith, he found it tightly encoiled by the steel chains of his habits and lusts."

"Then I pray God to help me watch and be sober that I may shun the cause of this man's misery. But, sir, is it not yet time to put me upon my way?"

"Nay," said the Interpreter. "Tarry yet a little longer until I show thee one thing more, and then shalt thou go on thy way."

So he took Christian by the hand again, and led him into a chamber where there was one rising out of bed; and as he put on his raiment, he shuddered and trembled, and cried out, "Aaauugh!"

Then was Christian startled, and turning to his mentor asked, "Dear Teacher, what makes this man tremble and cry out so?"

Then said the Interpreter to the man, "Dreamer, tell this pilgrim why thou didst cry out so."

"All right," agreed the man, who drew up close to Christian's face to tell his tale. "This night, as I was in my sleep, I dreamed a dream; and behold, in my dream the heavens grew exceeding black. There was also thunder and lightning flashing about in a most fearful manner."

"Go on."

"So I looked up in my dream, and I saw the clouds rack by at a terribly great speed."

"Indeed?"

"Aye. And then I heard the great sound of a trumpet, and saw also a Man sitting on a cloud."

"A man on a cloud?"

"Yes!" cried the man, his eyes wide with terror. "His hair was white as snow, His eyes were as a flame of fire, His voice was as the sound of many waters and His . . . His face did shine bright as the sun!"

"Indeed!" marveled Christian.

"Yea, and on His vesture and on His thigh was a name written: 'KING OF KINGS and LORD OF LORDS.'"

Then Christian's eyes lighted up with joy as he shouted, "'Twas our Lord Jesus!"

"Yes," said the man with a shudder. "Yes, I fear so. He was attended with the glittering billions of heaven all wrapped in flaming fire. Also the heavens were in a burning flame."

"'Twas the great day of God!" exclaimed Christian, clapping his hands gleefully.

"Yes!" nodded the man. "Yes. He came near the earth and called with a voice like a trumpet, 'Come forth! Come forth!' With that the rocks rent, the graves were opened, and the dead in Christ came forth prepared to meet their Lord in the air!"

"Glory be!"

"But, there came up as well Annas and Caiaphas and others of that ilk who had pierced Him."

"Yea," answered Christian, "for He promised them that they would 'see the Son of man sitting on the right hand of power, and coming in the clouds of heaven.'"

"Aye. Those vile ones vainly sought to hide themselves, crying for the rocks and the mountains to fall upon them."

"Go on! Go on!" cried Christian, by now thoroughly caught up in the tale.

"And then I heard it proclaimed to those who attended upon the King: 'Gather my wheat into the garner!'"

"Oh! The rapture of the righteous!"

"Yes! And with that, I saw many catched up and carried away into the clouds."

Then Christian smiled and clapped his hands again and said, "Oh! Glorious day!"

"No!" cried the man fearfully. "No! An evil day!"

"What? Why do you say that?"

"Because," sobbed the man. "I was left behind!"

"What?" cried Christian.

"Yes!" he moaned. "Left behind!"

"Oh no!" said Christian sympathetically. "Then what?"

Then the man's eyes grew wide with fear and he shook as he said, "Then I heard it proclaimed by the King: 'Gather together the tares, the chaff and the stubble, and cast them into the lake of fire.' And with that the bottomless pit opened!"

"You saw it?" cried Christian.

"Saw it!" blurted the man, with terror. "I felt it! It opened right beneath my feet! There was this great fiery chasm, and out of its bowels there belched forth sulphurous smoke, coals of fire, and hideous noises."

"So terrible a dream! Then what?"

"Upon this," said the man, calming himself a little, "I awakened from my sleep."

Then Christian, greatly concerned, asked, "But what would cause you to dream such an evil dream. Have you dreamed it before?"

"Oh, aye," answered he. "It comes to haunt me every night."

"Every night! Then can it be God is sending you a warning? Tell me, is there anywhere a brother in the faith who 'hath ought against thee?'"

"Nay," said the man. "None that come to mind."

"Then, by any chance, do you have secret and unforsaken sins?"

"Nay. Nay. None," he said, holding up both hands.

"Sleeper!" warned the Interpreter sternly. "Speak truth."

"Well, all right," he grumbled in protest. "But 'tis only a little sin. A tiny one."

Then was Christian alarmed for the man's soul and earnestly entreated him, saying, "Then you must forsake it, for Moses and the law stand at the gate, and if you have even one stain upon your garments, they will not let you pass through."

"I know. I know," agreed the man, nodding his head. "And that's just what I intend to do."

"When?" demanded Christian.

"Oh, soon," smiled the man assuringly.

"Do it now!" urged Christian.

"Nah!" he declared. "For such a small sin as mine, soon will do well enough."

"But you must!" urged Christian more strongly.

"Soon," nodded the man more agreeably. "Soon. Soon. Very soon."

At this, Christian grew alarmed and said, "But you are in danger of becoming like the man in the cage!"

"Not so!" protested the man vehemently.

"Why not so?" demanded Christian.

"Because," he said a bit proudly, "his sins were gross ones of the flesh, while mine are merely invisible detours of the mind. The tiniest of the tiny."

"But they will grow!" he cried.

"Nay, nay," he said confidently. "It has scarcely grown in years. Nor will I let it."

"But you must . . ." Christian began, until interrupted by the Interpreter who took him by the arm saying, "Come."

"But . . ." protested Christian.

"Come!" commanded the teacher.

"But I must needs convince him!" urged Christian, looking back over his shoulder as the man turned and began making his bed.

"You cannot."

"But he has a sincere intent to change soon," protested Christian again.

"Aye," said he. "And his words are true. But soon never comes. It moves on ahead of us like a receding mirage in the desert. He who thinks to change soon, waits for eternity."

"Oh, dear," sighed Christian sadly.

"Consider well these things," warned the Interpreter.

"I do," he answered soberly. "And they put me in hope, and in fear."

"Good," said he. "Keep all these lessons fresh in your mind. If you do, they will keep thee in the way thou must go."

"I shall, sir," he said thankfully. "The lessons have been good."

"I am glad," smiled the Interpreter. "And now you may be off."

As Christian began to squeeze his burden back through the narrow gate, he turned back and asked, "Sir? Do you think that soon I shall be loosed from my burden?"

"Aye," nodded the Interpreter with a knowing smile.

"When?" he inquired eagerly.

"Sooner than you think, longer than you wish."

His burden fell off his back

"Oh," said Christian with a disappointed sigh.

"And now, dear Pilgrim, Godspeed."

"Ah. I am happy to be on my way, and yet sad to leave you. Farewell, good Interpreter. Thank you for your many good lessons."

As Christian set out on his journey, the Interpreter raised his right hand and called after him saying, "The Comforter be with thee always, good Christian, to keep thee in the way that leads to the City."

CHAPTER THREE

NOW, I SAW in my dream that the highway up which Christian was to go was fenced on either side with a wall called Salvation. Along this way, therefore, he struck out at his best pace, which was not all that impressive by reason of the great burden that hung heavy still, upon his back.

He hiked briskly on in this manner till he came to a place where the path began to ascend a gentle slope. At the top thereof was a skull-shaped hill where stood a cross. A little below the cross in the valley there lay an open sepulchre. So I saw in my dream that Christian, with great effort, struggled to the foot of said cross and gazed with wonder upon One suffering there. And it came to pass that, as soon as he came up even with the cross, the ropes which secured his burden turned to ashes and released the accursed burden from off his shoulders. Striking the ground behind him the hideous mass began to roll, slowly at first but with ever increasing speed. Soon it was tumbling end over end, bouncing and bounding higher and farther at each leap. I watched in amazement until I saw it smash into an outcropping of stone and tumble harmlessly into the mouth of a yawning sepulchre. I am not entirely certain, but I believe that I heard a great splash. Be that as it may, into that bottomless pit his burden fell and I saw it no more.

Then was Christian glad and light of heart and said in a voice choked with joyful emotion, "He has given me rest by His sorrow and life by His death! The Innocent has suffered for the guilty and by His stripes I am healed! Oh, praise Him!"

Then he stood still awhile to look and wonder, for it was very amazing to him that the mere sight of the cross should so effectively release him from his great burden. He looked with love upon His suffering Lord until the springs of his head overflowed and sent rivulets of salty water coursing down his cheeks. Then said he, "Oh, my Lord! Is it truly for love of me that you suffer so? Is it truly my sins that have broken your heart? Oh, then shall I praise you as long as you give me breath."

Now as he stood gazing and weeping at the foot of the cross, behold, three Shining Ones appeared to him, and saluted him. Said the first, "Peace be unto you. Your sins have been forgiven you."

"Is it truly so?" asked Christian hopefully. "Can it truly be?"

"Did not your burden roll down into yon sepulcher?"

"Aye. But it's like . . . well, like when I take off my hat and yet feel it still upon my head. I indeed saw my burden tumble away, but it still seems to be there."

Then answered the Shining One, "'Tis the way of dumb, brute beasts to live life guided by their feelings. But if you wish to understand reality, you must not consult with yours."

"How then?"

"Truth can only be known by believing."

"Believing what?"

"The Words of He who has cast your sins into the depths of the sea!"

"Then, based upon His pledged Word, they are truly gone!" exclaimed Christian joyfully. "Gone! Whether I feel like it or no!"

"Aye, now you understand. And no one can bring them back again, except you."

"How could I ever do that?"

"The same way as the man in the cage did. By ceasing to watch and pray, by turning again to the beggarly elements of this life. By indulging once again in your old ways of evil just as a dog returns to its vomit."

"Oh," cried Christian. "I pray that I might never so do!"

"The choice belongs to none but you."

"Then I will be true!" vowed Christian. "For there are those who trust me."

"Aye. Chiefly, He that suffers in your place. He shall lead you, as a good Shepherd, through all of your travels. When, at last, you come to the far side of your journey, He shall be waiting to greet you. He shall look upon the travail of His soul and be satisfied, for you are precious in His sight. And be encouraged to know that you will look back upon the worst trials of your pilgrimage and shall say, it was cheap enough. Cheap enough!"

Three Shining Ones came to him and saluted him

"Thus I am determined it shall be."

Then spoke the second Shining One, saying, "Christian?"

"Yes?"

"This be for you," he said, holding forth a change of fine garments.

Then was Christian much amazed and said, "Why! A new suit of clothes! Made of fine linen, pure and white!"

"Aye. Put them on."

"Oh, no, I can't. For I have neither gold nor silver to purchase such a fine outfitting as that."

"There is no need for money. These are yours, without money, and without price."

"Then, to whom do I owe my thanks for these goodly garments?" asked Christian as he reverently took the sacred habits from the Shining One.

"To Him whom you behold suffering for you."

"They are His?"

"Aye, His," smiled the Shining One proudly. "He has personally woven them in the loom of heaven. Try them on."

And so Christian exchanged his old tattered, slime-stained garments for new ones, all clean and shining white as snow. Then he looked at himself in astonishment and said, "Why, they fit perfectly!"

"Of course," said the Shining One proudly.

"And they have not even one spot nor tiny wrinkle," said Christian as he admired the quality of his garb.

"Nor will you find in them one thread of human devising," added the Angel.

"And look!" Christian said, as he prepared to don the last piece. "This wonderful coat has no seams!"

"This is your wedding garment," said the Shining One. "Wear it with pride! If you do, it will obtain for you a free and abundant welcome into the wedding supper of the Lamb. There you shall be seated with Abraham, Isaac, and Jacob and be served by His own hand."

Then Christian noticed the pile of dirty clothes lying at his feet and asked, "And what happens to my filthy rags, lying here all in a heap?"

"They stay here at the foot of the cross forever. Unless you choose to draw back."

"Oh, no! That can never be! I have put my hand to the plow!"

Upon hearing this, all three of the Shining Ones smiled broadly and said loudly, "Amen!"

Then the third Shining One addressed him saying, "Christian?"

"Yes?" answered Christian, turning to face the third speaker who held in his hand an iron, whose business-end glowed red-hot and trailed wisps of acrid, white smoke. The sight of such an instrument of torture in the hand of one of God's messengers gave Christian quite a start. He was even more startled when the third Shining One said, "This, also, is for you."

Then Christian shrank back a bit, saying, "Why 'tis a branding iron . . . an instrument of torture such as we use to mark evil convicts."

"Aye," said the angel gravely.

"And it glows red-hot," said Christian, eyeing the luminescent tip uneasily.

"Aye, because it comes fresh from off a live coal on the altar of sacrifice."

"Uh . . . what will you use it for?" asked Christian, glancing uneasily at the heat waves rising from its tip.

"To put a mark upon your forehead," said the angel, matter-of-factly.

"What?" exclaimed Christian, beads of sweat springing to his brow. "Must I truly be disfigured with such a scar?"

"'Tis the mark of ownership."

"Of whom?" asked Christian, hoping that there might yet be a loophole in this frightful affair.

"Of Him who upon the cross has bought your soul at the price of His own."

"My natural heart draws back from such an ugly scar," admitted Christian fearfully.

"Is not He upon the cross scarred because of you?" said the angel, casting an upwards glance toward the suffering victim.

"Well . . . uh . . . yes," admitted Christian, his eyes following the angel's.

"Is the servant better than his Lord?"

"Uh . . . no," answered Christian meekly. "I'm sorry. I be ashamed of my fear."

Then, standing brave and tall, with his eye fixed upon his suffering Lord, he faced the instrument of torture straight on and said, "You may proceed, sir. I shall be proud to bear about in my body the marks of my Lord."

"Stand still," commanded the marking angel, slowly but deliberately raising the glowing iron.

"Wait," said Christian, raising a hand in defense. "Uh . . . does it hurt very badly?"

"Does it matter?"

"Uh . . . no," said Christian, after a moment's reflection. "I guess not."

"Guess not!" exclaimed the angel. "Don't you comprehend 'that the sufferings of this present time are not worthy to be compared with the glory which you shall inherit hereafter?'"

"Aye," confessed Christian. "I am sorry. Have thine own way, Lord."

Then the angel raised the glowing iron higher, saying, "Stand still. Stand very, very still."

Christian shut fast his eyes and braced himself for the violent stab of pain that he knew was to come. In a flash he seemed to relive all the painful burns he had suffered as a little boy playing with fire. As he felt the iron press into his forehead he gasped involuntarily in anticipation of the monstrous wave of searing pain he knew would follow.

"Finished!" said the Shining One.

"F . . . finished?" stammered the pilgrim, blinking in amazement. "Why, it hardly hurt at all!"

"Because He has borne the pain for you," said the angel.

"My! Had I known it to be so easy, I would not have hesitated."

"Had you known, it would have been no test," said the Shining One.

"Ah," answered Christian. "Another test?"

"Yes," nodded the angel. "Another test."

"Why are there so many tests along this pilgrim way?"

"Because the devil continually accuses you of being unworthy to walk in white," said the first Shining One.

"And so your Lord gives him permission to test you," said the second.

"But when you pass the tests He allows," concluded the third, "you empower your Lord to stand proud and tall and rebuke him by virtue of your faithfulness."

"Ah," said he. "Like Job! Then thanks be to God that the test was not too difficult for me."

"The test will never be too difficult for you, dear Christian," explained the first Angel. "Everything that comes to you comes through Christ first. He weighs the strength of every temptation and absorbs in Himself all that you cannot bear. By standing close by your Lord, you avail yourself of His protection. You need never put Him to shame."

"Thanks be to God. Uh . . . ?"

"Yes?" asked the third Shining One.

"Forgive my curiosity, my lords, but may I look upon my wound?" he asked timidly.

"Certainly," answered the third Shining One, producing a mirror. "Here be a glass."

Christian peered intently into the mirror, and though he looked ever so closely, he was finally forced to admit, "Why, I see no mark at all!"

"'Tis a seal that cannot be seen by mortal man. 'Tis only for those who put it there."

"For what purpose?"

"It tells us, at a glance, who are His."

"Ah," he said. "I understand."

Then the third Angel handed Christian a scroll, saying, "Here, take this."

"Why 'tis a parchment roll tied with a green cord."

"'Tis for you to read as you run your course," said the Angel.

"Thank you. Thank you very much."

"Be sure that you open it often, for it grows stiff and hard to manage if you leave it closed for any long time."

"I shall."

"Guard it well," warned the second Shining One, "for you must present this roll at the far gate as your certificate of admittance."

"Oh, I shall. With my life! Thank you. Thank you very much!"

"And now, farewell, good Christian," said the first Angel.

"Yes, God be with you," said the second.

"Go in peace," added the third. "Your God shall be your guide."

Then Christian said, "Farewell, my friends. Might we perchance meet again?"

To this, the third Angel answered, "You may not see us with eyes fettered by mortality, but know for a surety that you shall have our company all along your journey. Godspeed, dear Christian."

Then the three Shining Ones faded from view, and Christian was left alone. Yet he felt neither alone nor lonely, for he knew that, though unseen, there were friends still close by his side. He also felt very close to Him who had suffered in his place. Moreover, his burden was rolled away, his rags lay at his feet, and in their place he wore a finer suit than that worn by any king upon a throne. Therefore did Christian give three leaps for joy and shouted, "Hurrah! Free! I am free! At last free! Free! Free! Free!"

I saw then in my dream that he resumed his journey. But oh, with what lightness of heart and swiftness of foot did he travel now! So he went on in his new-found freedom until he came to the bottom of the hill. There, just off to one side of the way, lay three men, fast asleep, with fetters of iron upon their heels. The name of one was Simple, of another Sloth, and of the third Presumption.

Christian, seeing them sleeping in captivity this way, straightaway went over to them to see if perhaps he might awaken them and encourage them to resume their journey. So he jostled the man named Simple, saying, "Sirs! What is this foolish sleeping all about? You behave like soldiers asleep on their watch!"

At this, Simple rolled over and, blinking at him with bleary eyes, muttered, "Huh? Wha . . . ?" before falling back in renewed submission to sleep.

Christian then shook Sloth by the shoulder, saying loudly, "Brother, wake up! Wake up, I say! 'Tis not safe to sleep on the road to Zion! There is danger!"

At the word "danger" Sloth made a feeble attempt at pawing the sleep from his eyes was only able to yawn and mutter, "Wha . . .? Is there danger do you say?" before falling half-asleep again.

Christian next turned his attentions to Presumption, saying, "Yes, danger! Grave danger. Wake up and come away with me. Here, I will help you off with your chains!"

"Bah!" snorted Presumption, rudely brushing Christian away from his irons. "We be doing just fine! Take your hands off me!"

"What!" exclaimed Christian, unable to believe his ears.

Then, to remove any doubt as to his meaning, Presumption said, even more rudely, "I said, go away!"

Christian, attributing the man's rudeness to his sleepiness, continued forward in his mission of mercy, saying earnestly, "No! If he that prowls about like a roaring lion comes by, you will surely become prey to his teeth!"

At the mention of lions, Simple started from his sleep, looked about him drowsily, and said, "Lions! Where? I don't hear no roaring lions."

"He will come upon you when you least expect him," urged Christian. "Awake out of sleep!"

Simple looked around a little more but, seeing no immediate danger, replied gruffly, while fluffing up the dirty rag he used for a pillow, "I tol'ja I don't see no danger! Now lemme alone so I can get some sleep."

"But . . . but . . ." Christian began to protest, only to be interrupted by Simple's insistent words, "No, no, no. Just go 'way!"

Undaunted, Christian turned his attention toward Sloth. "You there! Wake up!" he said, shaking him by the shoulders.

"Yeah, sure, just lemme get a little more sleep, and I shall join you."

"No!" insisted Christian, still trying to awaken him. "You must arise now. For now is it high time to awake out of sleep!"

"Would'ja stop shaking me!" groused the man, pushing Christian away.

"You must hurry for the day is far spent, the night is at hand!"

"I know, I know," he agreed. "You are right. (yawn) And I shall join you in just a little while. But first I must get my rest (yawn)."

"No!" exclaimed Christian, "you can rest in heaven. Come!"

But the man, unconvinced by Christian's urgent pleadings, only whined on, saying, "But the way is hard, and He who has called us is a hard taskmaster. Therefore I've got to store up strength for my journey."

"You are burying your talent in the earth!"

"I am not! I am simply playing it safe. When my Master returns He will be happy enough just to see that there is not one ounce missing."

"Oh," lamented Christian under his breath, "it is true what I have read: 'A little sleep, a little folding of the hands and sudden destruction cometh upon a man.'"

By this time Mr. Sloth had turned over and was well on his way back to dreamland. "Uh huh," he mumbled through his beard as he began to snore.

Christian then turned his attention toward Presumption, who seemed less sleepy than the other two. "And what about you?" he entreated. "Will you strive for your freedom and join me on my pilgrimage?"

"Join you on pilgrimage?" Presumption blurted out, as one offended. "We are on pilgrimage."

"But how can you call yourself a pilgrim when you are fastened in chains like this?" he protested. "To be a pilgrim is to break every fetter and let the oppressed go free! Come!" he said, kneeling down to examine the lock on the man's chains.

"Soon," he answered, firmly pushing Christian's hands away from his irons.

"No! Not soon!" cried Christian. "The example of the dreamer teaches us that soon will never come!"

"Not so! For I have seen it come and go many times."

"You must act now," insisted the pilgrim, "for the end of all things is near at hand and the time is far spent!"

At this, Presumption sat up a little taller and with no lack of pride in his voice said, "We have been in this pilgrim way much longer than you are ever like to be. If there were such a need to be running off all in a huff, the Lord of the way would have certainly told us before you."

"How?" asked Christian.

"Oh, uh . . . we shall surely feel a burning in our breast or at the least an article in the church paper," he said.

At this, sleepy Sloth managed to turn over and, from behind closed eyes agreed, saying, "Aye! At least an article (yawn, snore)."

"No! That is not enough! He has commanded us not to sleep as do others. He expects us to be diligent and press forward! We must stretch every nerve and muscle toward the mark of the high calling that is set before us!"

At this, Presumption sat up abruptly, planted his hands firmly on his hips and snorted loudly, "We are not athletes training for some worldly games! We are pilgrims who are meekly to wait, in simple faith, for the latter rain to fit us up!"

To this, Simple opened one eye long enough to concur, saying, "Aye. 'Twould be foolish to run before the time appointed."

"But . . ."

"And now, off with you!" ordered Presumption. "We are in the way of life and for now, that be enough."

"Nay! 'Faith without works is dead!' You must show that you have been called to the way by moving forward in the way."

"Bah!" barked Presumption. "You speak of legalism. Don't you know that 'twas all finished at the cross? Now be off with you!"

"But . . ."

"Away, I say!" ordered Presumption, pointing imperiously down the path. "'Let every man be fully persuaded in his own mind.'"

"But I speak the truth!" urged Christian.

"As you understand it," returned Presumption, trying to stifle a yawn. "Now let us resume our sleep. Perhaps God will give one of us a dream to confirm your warnings of danger."

"A dream . . . yes, a dream," Sloth managed to murmur between snores. Then Presumption adjusted his chains for comfort, pulled his coat over his head, and joined Simple and Sloth in their loud snores.

So Christian, with great reluctance, turned away to resume his journey. But he carried a heavy heart to think that men in such great danger could be so ungrateful. He had awakened them from a fatal sleep, warned them of mortal danger, and even offered to help them file off their leg irons, all to no avail.

Now, as he traveled on pondering what would become of those miserable men, he saw two men come tumbling over the wall on the left hand of the narrow way. The name of the one was Formalist, who said to his companion, "Make it down all right?"

The name of the other was Hypocrisy, who answered, as he jumped from atop the wall, "Aye, down I am."

"Good," said Formalist, dusting himself off. "Let's be on our way."

Then Hypocrisy, chancing to glance back along the path, saw Christian. "Say, chap," he exclaimed to his companion. "Look see! Another saint on pilgrimage. Hello there!"

"Gentlemen," answered Christian. "Whence from? And whither bound?"

"We were born in the land of Vainglory," answered Formalist proudly.

"And praise to God!" continued Hypocrisy, "we both be bound to Mount Zion."

At this, Christian's brow furrowed with concern for their safety and he asked, "To Mount Zion, do you say? Then why did you not begin your journey back at the gate?"

At this, they both looked upon one another with puzzled amusement. Then Formalist turned to Christian and said, "Gate?"

"What gate?" chimed in Hypocrisy.

"The wicket gate that stands at the beginning of the way," explained Christian. "The one manned by a great one named Goodwill."

"At the beginning!" exclaimed Formalist, haughtily. "The beginning begins wherever you happen to begin. Besides, that old gate you speak of is way too far out of our way!"

"What?" exclaimed Christian in amazement. "Have not you read where it is written, 'He that cometh not in by the door, but climbeth up some other way, the same is a thief and a robber?'"

"That does not apply to us!" sneered Hypocrisy.

"No. Not us!" agreed Formalist. "Everyone from the land of Vainglory is in total agreement that the way back to the wicket gate is much too far."

"Therefore," continued Hypocrisy, "we have followed the custom of our people in taking a short cut over the wall."

"But aren't you afraid the Lord of the Celestial City will count you as trespassers?" asked the pilgrim, more concerned than ever.

"Now why on earth would He do that?" demanded Formalist.

"Because you violated His direct command and came sneaking over the wall."

"Ha, ha, ha," chuckled Hypocrisy. "No need to trouble your head about that small detail."

"Why not?"

"Because what we do, we have custom for."

"Custom!"

"Yes, custom," confirmed Formalist.

"Custom long-standing," asserted Hypocrisy. "In fact, if you were to press the matter, we could produce testimony that our custom is nearly 2,000 years old."

"Indeed!"

"Indeed!" was Hypocrisy's confident reply.

"But will it stand a trial at law?"

"Oh, really now, good fellow," said Formalist with disdain. "Certainly there can be no doubt in any rational mind that a custom which has served us for soooo long . . ."

". . . And which has served to admit soooo many into the way . . ." continued Hypocrisy.

". . . Could certainly be counted as nothing but legal by any impartial judge," concluded Formalist smugly.

"And besides," said Hypocrisy, "if we get into the way, what does it matter *how* we get into the way?"

Formalist

"But . . ." began Christian, only to be interrupted by Hypocrisy, who said,

"No 'buts' to it, chap. To be in, is to be in!"

"Oh, I don't know," said Christian with a worried look.

"Listen to logic, friend," said Formalist, taking up the strain. "You are in the way, correct?"

"Most certainly so. Aye."

"Now you came in at the gate, correct?" said Hypocrisy.

"Aye."

"And we came tumbling over the wall," said Formalist. "Correct?"

"Aye."

Then Formalist jabbed a manicured finger into Christian's chest and said, "You are in the way." Then, pointing a thumb to himself he added, "I am in the way." Resting a hand on Hypocrisy's shoulder he continued, "He is in the way," to which Hypocrisy grinned in reply. Then, reaching his arm 'round Christian's shoulder he concluded, "We are *all* in the way! Now what, pray tell, is the difference? How are you better than us?"

Not in the least impressed by Formalist's logic or proud stance, Christian stepped back and answered boldly, "Chiefly in this: I walk by the rules laid down by my Master while you walk by the vain laws of your own imagination."

"'Tis custom!" bellowed Hypocrisy. "Tradition!"

"No matter," continued Christian, warming to his subject. "If our Lord counts you as thieves at the beginning of the way, I doubt that He will regard you as honest men at the end of the way."

"Did you hear?" sneered an indignant Hypocrisy. "Thieves he calls us!"

"What nerve!" scowled Formalist, squaring his shoulders and fixing Christian with an angry glare.

"'Tis true," affirmed Christian. "You came in by yourselves without His direction, and you shall go out by yourselves without His mercy."

"So sez you," snarled Formalist, with a curl to his lip.

"So says He!" answered Christian, unfazed.

Then Hypocrisy stepped up to Christian, chest to chest and nose to nose and growled through clenched teeth, "Best watch thee out where thou puttest thy nose, friend. 'Tis like to get bent."

"Aye," added Formalist, also stepping up in a threatening manner. "Best that you watch out for yourself . . ."

". . . And leave fellow travelers to their own peace and safety," concluded Hypocrisy, giving Christian a sharp shove as he spun on his heel.

Then I saw that they turned and began to travel on in a loose group, each lost in his own troubled thoughts. After a few miles Formalist finally broke the silence by saying, "And as to the laws and ordinances given to govern our behavior whilst in this way, we have no doubt but that we keep them just as well as you."

"Indeed," chimed in Hypocrisy. "In fact, I would venture to say that friend Formalist here keeps them better than you!"

"Indeed!" agreed Formalist.

To this, Christian replied, "You cannot expect to be saved by laws and ordinances, if you don't come in by the door."

"Bah!" snorted Hypocrisy. "We see no difference between you and us unless you count that, uh . . . fine suit you wear."

"These garments were given to me by the Lord of the way," Christian answered humbly.

"Probably to cover the shame of your nakedness. Heh, heh, heh," mocked Hypocrisy.

"'Tis true," answered Christian, meekly. "Before I met my Lord I had nothing but filthy rags. He Himself wove this fine suit in the loom of heaven and gave it to me as a token of His kindness."

"Well," said Formalist, proudly tucking his thumbs beneath his wide-spreading lapels, "take a gander at our garments."

"Aye!" put in Hypocrisy, with a bit of a swagger to his step. "I'll wager these are as fine as any you'll see in this way."

Christian looked at them briefly and answered, "But they have spots and wrinkles."

"Oh, come on!" protested Hypocrisy. "We be travelling men, good fellow! 'Tis impossible to travel this difficult way without picking up a spot or two here and there."

"Aye," added Formalist. "Surely the Lord at the gate has enough sense to realize that the way is hard, and that stumbles be many. Therefore, 'tis at the gate that He will give us a change of garments."

"Not at the head of the way!" said Hypocrisy emphatically. "For He knows good and well that if He did, they would surely become soiled and torn!"

"Not so!" protested Christian, strongly. "The great Weaver gives them to us at the beginning, and then gives us the power to keep them fully clean."

"And why should He do that?" demanded Formalist.

"Because," answered Christian, "the clothes are His, and by their beauty is He judged."

"Bosh!" snorted Formalist. "The kingdom of heaven is not food or drink . . ."

". . . Or shining white suits of clothes," sneered Hypocrisy. "Just so long as we are not filthy, or wretched, or poor, or blind, or naked, what does it matter?"

"Aye, what?" challenged Formalist.

"I only know that this lovely coat was given to me freely on the day that I surrendered all. And when I come to the gate, they will know that I am His because I wear His garments. And as I have worn His coat with pride, so will He confess me with pride before His Father."

"Bosh!" mocked Formalist. "Any coat will do!"

"Aye," agreed Hypocrisy. "Just so long as we are clothed."

"I also have a mark in my forehead," said Christian.

"Mark?" queried Formalist.

"Aye."

"Hmmm?" said Formalist, joining Hypocrisy in a careful scrutiny of Christian's forehead. Finally, after looking at each other with raised eyebrows and questioning eyes, Hypocrisy said, "We, uh . . . we see no mark."

"'Tis not for you to see," answered Christian, "'Tis for those who put it there."

"Hmmm," murmured Formalist. "And where did this 'mark' come from?"

Christian nearly came to tears as he recounted his wonderful experience at the cross, saying, "It came upon me as I stood beneath the cross over on yon, skull-shaped hill. I had just surrendered my all and watched my heavy burden tumble from off my shoulders."

"Well, then," said Formalist, failing to perceive Christian's tender emotions, "in that respect, we are better off than you."

"How so?" he asked, still a bit misty-eyed by reason of thinking upon the cross.

"In that we never had such a burden as you speak of," said Formalist arrogantly.

"Oh!" exclaimed Christian, coming back to the present. "So that's what let you come tumbling so nimbly over the wall! But let me tell you this, gentlemen. He who begins his journey by leaving his burden at the cross, ends it with none. They that behave as thieves and robbers and bypass the cross so they can travel lightly, shall be crushed beneath a stone at the end."

"Did you hear!" jeered Formalist. "The man waxes poetic."

"Is that what you call it?" snapped Hypocrisy impatiently. Then said he, turning to Christian with an arrogant air, "All right, sir! So you do wear those fine garments, and so maybe you do have some 'invisible mark,' and so you have left behind some imaginary burden on some skull-shaped hill! The fact remains, that we too are in the way!"

"I have also a sealed roll that I may read for my comfort as I travel on in the way," said Christian, showing them his scroll, bound about by its green satin ribbon.

"Bah!" poo-pooed Formalist. "Who needs a silly roll to read?"

"'Tis not only for reading."

"Oh? And what else?" inquired Hypocrisy, raising a curious eyebrow.

"I was also told that I must give it in at the celestial gate to certify that the price of my admission had been paid," said Christian solemnly.

"Paid?" queried Formalist, ears perking up at the mention of some new way to earn his admittance. "And what was the price?"

"The price is greater than all the universe could pay," said Christian, with gratitude swelling in his breast.

"That is an impossible price!"

"Yes," admitted Christian.

"But you said your admittance was paid. Who is it that can pay infinite prices?"

"'Tis He who hangs upon the cross. All of these things: the garments, the mark, and the scroll, are lacking because you came not in at the gate. Please, go back to the beginning and start your walk with the Lord aright," he pleaded.

To these things they had no answer to give, and, for a moment being under deep conviction, they could only look upon one another with blank stares. Then Hypocrisy broke the spell with a sly wink. Formalist responded with a knowing smile, and they both began to laugh mockingly. Then said Hypocrisy, between chuckles, "We have no garment . . . heh, heh, heh . . . because we were not naked."

"And no burden," bubbled Formalist . . ."tee-hee . . . because of our good lives!"

"And no mark," chortled Hypocrisy, "because . . . heh, heh . . . if it cannot be seen, it serves no purpose, and therefore cannot be needed."

"And no scroll for comfort," mocked Formalist, "because we be in no need of said comfort."

"Being quite comfortable already, you see," concluded Hypocrisy.

"Except when keeping company with obstinate, bullheaded bigots like you!" snarled Formalist.

"Therefore, alone shalt thou be! Farewell, foolish Pilgrim!" laughed Hypocrisy as he crossed his arms, turned his back on Christian, and paused to let him pass on. Then Formalist did the same as he snapped off a "Goodbye!" that really meant "good riddance." So they dropped back and let Christian go on ahead with no visible company but his own. Sometimes, as he looked at circumstances, he would sigh in discouragement. But then he would read a promise or two from his roll and pass on much encouraged.

As my dream continued, I saw Christian travel on until he came to the foot of a hill called Difficulty. Now, at the bottom of this hill, there was a spring bursting forth from beneath a great stone. At this place there was also a parting of the ways into three parts. One way meandered off to the left hand, and another wound off to the right. But that way which was straight and narrow, climbed right on up the hill (which I saw to be quite steep). When Christian came to the spring, he recalled Gideon's band of 300 and, without pausing on his way, deftly dipped his hand into the water to refresh himself. But not so Formalist and Hypocrisy. When they reached the spring, they fell to their knees, buried their faces in the refreshing coolness of the waters and slurped noisily. Thus it was that Christian got quite the lead on them as he began to ascend the steep Hill of Difficulty. Now, as he climbed he bethought himself of a poem, which, if I remember aright, he spoke thusly:

"This hill, though high, I covet to ascend;
The difficulty will not me offend,
For I perceive the way to life lies here.
Come, pluck up heart, let's neither faint nor fear.
Better, though difficult, the right way to go,
Than wrong, though easy, where the end is woe."

Now when the other two arose from their leisurely guzzlings, they smiled to behold each other with dripping chins and muddy knees. Then one of them belched loudly, and they both enjoyed a hearty belly laugh. Then, as they looked up at the tiny figure of Christian toiling up the Hill Difficulty, Formalist said, "Hmmm. Don't look like much fun to me."

"Steep," noted Hypocrisy.

"High," added Formalist.

"Dangerous!" said Hypocrisy.

"Difficult!" chorused both of them.

Ascending the steep Hill of Difficulty

"Especially with a belly full of water," chuckled Formalist, punctuating his comment with another belch.

"There must be another way," concluded Hypocrisy.

Then they noticed that there was not simply one other way, but two other ways: both of them flat, wide, and easy of travel. Now, since these two held fast to the doctrine that all paths lead to the same eternal destination, they reasoned that, by and by, on the back side of Difficulty, these two roads must certainly join the straight way again. No need for huffing and puffing all sweaty up some steep hill when a simple stroll round about would serve them just as well, they reasoned. So they began to debate about which way they should go. Now the sign pointing to one of those ways said "Danger," and the sign pointing off to the other said "Destruction." Since they disagreed on which way was safer, they temporarily (as they supposed) parted company. One of them took the way called "Danger," which meandered into a dense and overgrown forest where he was soon lost to my view. The other took the path called "Destruction," which led him into a wide field full of tar fields and gaping slime pits. There he was soon bogged down and ere long stumbled and fell. And, though I watched for quite some time, he never rose again.

I then turned my attention to Christian who, eager to please his Lord, had begun his climb at nearly a run. But because of the increasing steepness of the way, this soon slowed to a vigorous stride, then to a struggling walk, then to a crawl, and finally to climbing the steepest places upon his hands and knees.

About halfway up the hill was a pleasant arbor, placed there by the Lord of the hill, for the refreshment of weary travelers. Arriving there, Christian, all hot and breathless, said, "Ah, (pant pant) a resting place prepared for poor pilgrims. Phew! (pant pant) I shall sit here a few moments to gather strength for my journey. After I cool down a bit, I shall also read from my roll to refresh my soul."

So after he was finished with all of his huffing and puffing, he pulled his roll from his bosom and read therein, to his great delight and comfort. Then, recalling the muddy knees of his erstwhile companions, he took a new and appreciative look at the beautiful garments that had been given him at the cross. These served to remind him of his Lord's great love and mercy and set his mind at ease. Then, after a time, he stretched out on the bench, crossed his legs, put his hands behind his head, and said, with a yawn, "Ah, rest. Sweet rest for the weary pilgrim."

Soon, without intending so to do, Christian fell into a light sleep, which ere long turned into a deep slumber and detained him in that place until quite late in the day. As he slept, his relaxation grew deeper and still deeper, until his grip on his sacred document loosened. At last it fell out of his hand and rolled under the bench. Finally, as the westering sun began its late afternoon slide to the horizon, there came one of the Shining Ones to rouse him out of sleep, saying, "Awake, Awake!"

"Huh? Wha?" mumbled Christian.

"'Go to the ant, thou sluggard; consider her ways and be wise,'" said the Angel sternly.

Then Christian stretched himself and was soon wide awake. Said he, (yawn) "Oh, my! I . . . I must have fallen asleep for a moment. Hmmm. 'Tis getting on toward evening. Got to be on my way!"

And so, on his way he got. To make up lost time he set him out at a vigorous pace and was not long in coming to the top of the hill. Now, just as he was starting down the far side, there came two men shouting to him and racing headlong back up the hill! The name of the one was Timorous, who cried out, breathlessly, "Back! Back. Turn back!"

"And better soon than late!" panted out the other who was named Mistrust.

"Sirs," said Christian, "what be the matter? You run the wrong way."

"Easy enough for you to say," snorted Timorous.

"Aye," agreed Mistrust. "We were on our way to the City of Zion, the same as you."

"And we had already got-
ten past this difficult place,"
said Timorous.

"Puffing hard it was too,"
put in Mistrust.

"We thought that upon
reaching the top we would have
gained the victory," continued
Timorous, wringing his hands.
"But instead we found that the
farther we went, the greater the
danger!"

"Indeed?" asked Christian,
a bit unnerved.

"Aye," said Mistrust, miserably. "Oh, truly, it is a deadly,
dangerous way we have gotten
ourselves into."

Mistrust and Timorous

"More so than we ever imagined from Worldly-wiseman's description," put in Timorous. "That is why we have turned back the other way."

"Back! You are going back?"

"Of course back!" cried Timorous. "As will you if you have any wit."

"But this is the way laid out for us!" protested Christian. "You must walk in it!"

"Ho, ho," said Timorous, knowingly. "Sure, sure. Easy to say for you—from here! But we happen to know that just before us lie a pair of lionzzz in the way."

"Lions!" exclaimed Christian, eyes stretching wide.

"Aye," nodded Mistrust. "Great lions!"

"And," explained Timorous, still trembling from fright, "whether sleeping or crouched to spring we could not tell . . ."

"But we do know that if we had come within reach, they would have certainly torn us to bloody, bitty pieces," shuddered Mistrust, tearing an imaginary body to shreds with his hands while accompanying himself with graphic sound effects.

"Therefore," concluded Timorous, with a fearful glance down the hill, "we advise you to come along with us and turn back."

"Oh, my!" cried Christian, beginning to quake in his boots. "Now you have made me afraid."

"As well you should be!" declared Timorous. "Best you be wise and join with us."

"But where can I flee for safety?"

"Why, back home, of course!" said Mistrust. "Where else?"

"No! For if I return to Destruction, I shall perish in the fire and brimstone of its judgements."

"But who knows when it will be destroyed," whined Timorous. "'All things continue as from the beginning.' Why, you might live to be a ripe old age there."

"No!" said Christian with brave resolve. "If I turn back, my sins will come upon me again and crush me as wheat under the millstone. But . . . but! If I can somehow reach the Celestial City, I am sure to find safety. I must venture forward!"

"Better think twice," warned Mistrust. "You'll be walking right into the jaws of death."

"Right," whined Timorous, warming to his subject and beginning to stack imagination atop the facts. "Why, the longer we stopped to look at them, the greater they became. M'thinks they must be giant lions! Or perhaps some demonic apparitions!"

"Aye!" added Mistrust. "Compared to them we felt like grasshoppers! Truly, the danger is great!"

"And the land about them 'doth eat up the inhabitants thereof,'" whined Timorous. "Come back!"

"No!" exclaimed Christian. "Behind me lies certain death, while before me lies only potential death. And who knows but that love may cast out fear, and I shall conquer by faith. And if by faith I conquer, I shall find life everlasting beyond!"

"What?" cried Timorous in open-mouthed astonishment.

"Yea!" continued Christian, even more boldly. "Though the lions be ten feet tall, I will yet go forward."

"Are you sure?" pleaded Timorous.

"More than sure," affirmed Christian courageously.

"Well then, let me be off always before you go on," ordered Mistrust.

"Why so?"

"Why, to spare me the hearing of your tearing flesh and cracking bones of course," he whined. "Farewell."

"Best of luck to you, O foolish one," said Timorous, turning to flee back down the hill.

"Farewell," said Christian. "Though I can't see how you can."

So Mistrust and Timorous ran scampering down the backside of the Hill Difficulty in a cloud of cowardly dust while Christian continued on his way. But as he thought more upon the dangers so luridly described by the two traitors, he felt the need of courage from the Word. So he felt in his bosom for his roll . . . and . . . and . . . oh no! It was not there! Then cried Christian in utter despair, "Oh no! 'Tis gone! 'Tis gone! Oh, all undone am I! All undone!"

Then did Christian fall into great distress and confusion. His source of strength and comfort was gone just when he needed it most! Then, worse yet, he realized that he had lost his pass into the Celestial City!

"Oh no!" he cried out in desperation. "Where is it? Where could it be?"

At last he remembered that he had read from it before he had fallen asleep in the arbor.

"That's where it is!" he cried out in joy mixed with repentance. "'Tis in the arbor where I slept! In the arbor! Oh, dear, Lord, forgive."

Then, having fallen upon his knees and asked God's forgiveness for foolish neglect, he turned about and went in search of his precious roll, all the while saying, "Oh, foolish man. Foolish, foolish man! Oh, will it yet be there? Oh, foolish man."

And who is able to describe the sorrow of Christian's heart as he retraced his steps back down the Hill Difficulty? But I can tell you this much: sometimes he sighed, sometimes he wept, and oft times he scolded himself for indulging in sleep where he should only have paused for breath. Thus, therefore, he went back, looking carefully on this side and on that, hoping somehow to find the precious roll that had so often been his comfort.

At last he came within sight of the arbor, which only increased his sorrow by bringing to mind the evil of his sleeping.

"Oh, sinful sleep," he moaned. "Oh wretched man that I am that I should sleep during the hours of duty! How stupid of me to take my ease, as if I were already safe in the city! And how far along might I now have been if I had not slept! I must travel this road three times, when once would have sufficed. And now 'tis near to sunset and I shall have to travel in the dark! Oh! Oh, that I had not slept!"

By this time he had come to the arbor again, where, not finding his roll, he sat down and wept.

"Oh no!" he wailed through his tears. "'Tis gone! 'Tis gone! Oh, woe is me. All lost and undone am I! Ah, woe, woe, woe."

Here he sat for awhile, all sad and weeping and full of fears, supposing that he had forever lost his way to eternity. Then (as providence would have it), he chanced to cast a glance down between the slats of the bench. And there . . . there through the misty veil of his tears, he espied the green ribbon of his roll!

"Oh joy!" he cried, quickly kneeling down and clasping it tightly to his breast with hands all atremble. "Oh, thank thee, dear God! Thank thee, thank thee, thank thee!"

Then did Christian tenderly put his precious roll back into his bosom and resume his journey with joy and tears. Oh, but you can be sure that it was not with measured step and slow that he climbed the rest of the hill. Oh no, but rather with all the speed that heart and lungs would allow. Yet, as swift as he flew, the sun sped on swifter still. And so it was that, from atop the Hill Difficulty, Christian watched the golden orb slide behind the distant horizon which called again to mind the vanity of his foolish sleeping. Then said he, "Oh, sinful sleep! 'Tis because of you that I see shadows creeping over the path. 'Tis because of you that I begin to hear the noise of the doleful creatures of the night. All because of you, oh sinful, slothful sleep!"

Now, as he stumbled his way down the hill in the quickly fading light, there came again to mind the evil report of Mistrust and Timorous, which made Christian exclaim, "Oh no! These great beasts hunt for their prey in the night! And if they should meet me on this narrow path, how shall I escape being torn into pieces? Oh, but I must go on. Surely, God has some plan for my escape . . . I hope."

So he went forward into the gathering dusk of twilight, all the while fearing that any moment might be his last. But, as he was thus bewailing his unhappy circumstances, he lifted up his eyes, and behold, there were the lights of a very stately palace straight before him! The palace stood just alongside the pathway and its name was Beautiful.

"Oh, joy!" cried Christian with delight. "This must be one of the places of rest provided by the King of the hill!" So I saw in my dream that he made haste and went forward, that, if possible, he might get lodging there. Now before he had gone far, he entered into a very narrow passage which had, at its far end, two great lions. One of them stood on this side of the way, and the other stood on that side of the way. At sight of them, Christian came to a sudden halt, exclaiming, "Oh no! 'Tis true! Mistrust and Timorous did indeed see two great lions. Oh, now what shall I do?"

Now the lions were chained. But because of the gathering gloom of evening, this he could not know. Therefore was Christian greatly afraid and sorely tempted to follow in the steps of Mistrust and Timorous. Then said he, "Oh! What to do? Before me, almost certainly, lies instant death! And yet behind me, more than certain, lies another death, albeit maybe not quite so violent, and perhaps not quite so soon."

The House Beautiful

Now Watchful, the Porter of the lodge, having been told by his Lord to expect a traveler, was standing at an upper window with his spyglass stretched full length. Earlier he had watched with bated breath as Christian was accosted by Mistrust and Timorous. He had been puzzled to see him search frantically in his bosom and then, mysteriously, turn to hurry back over the Hill Difficulty. At the sight, thinking that Christian had abandoned his pilgrimage, his heart was nigh on to breaking. Also, he was not a little surprised, by reason of having heard better things of Christian. Later, just as the westering sun was sliding into darkness, he climbed the east tower for one last look and lo . . . Christian had reappeared at the top of the hill! With joy unspeakable he followed the weary traveler as he scrambled reck-lessly down the rocky descent. When Christian came to his halt to decide which death was the worse, Watchful called out in a loud voice, saying, "Is thy faith so small as that? Fear not the lions, for they are chained!"

Lions were chained

"What?" answered Christian, a silver edge beginning to line the dark clouds of doom. "Chained, do you say?"

"Yes, chained. Keep in the midst of the path, and no harm shall come unto thee!"

"But why are they here?"

"To show forth the faith of those that have it, and to send a-packing back those that have it not. Come straight on and all shall be well."

"Can it be?" asked Christian hopefully. "Can it truly be?"

"Aye!" said Watchful assuringly. "Only be careful not to venture too far left or too far right."

Then I saw that he gathered up courage from those brave words of the Porter and got himself into the very middle of the way; not too far left, not too far right. But still, it was with much fear and trembling that he came on. Now as he approached the lions, they began to stir . . .

"Oh dear," cried Christian.

. . . and to stretch . . .

"Oh! Perhaps they are ten feet tall!"

. . . and to roar as they jerked and lunged toward the middle of the road.

Now this extreme test of faith would have been trying enough in broad daylight, when a pilgrim could see the chains securely anchored in stone. But now, with sun well down and moon not up, Christian could scarcely see the path between, let alone any chains. Therefore, did he stop to speak with himself thusly, "Do I dare go on? Are his words really true? Do the lions wear chains?"

Then, with an invitingly smooth path behind him and a virtual bloody death before him, Christian paused to reason with himself again: "If his words be not true, then this entire pilgrimage business is but a pack of lies—a delusion. And if I am entered upon a delusion, then there be no hope for me. And if there be no hope for me, then just as well that I die at the paw of the lion as to die of despair. So it seems clear that I have nothing to lose and all to gain. Therefore I choose to believe His promise. The lions do wear chains!"

Then Christian, having chosen to believe the good words of the Porter, went forward in faith. Now, to make himself as small as possible, he let out his breath and turned himself sideways. Then he began to inch his way, oh, ever so carefully, between the two great beasts. As he came directly between the two ferocious felines, he could sense the moisture of their breath-roars fogging his face. He could feel the breeze stirred by the powerful slashings of their massive paws. The loudness of their roaring he not only painfully perceived in his ringing ears but also felt with the sympathetic vibration of his entire body. But, as he inched his way precisely through the midst of them, he found that their razor-edged claws always missed him by at least the breadth of a hair. And so, inch by fearful inch, roar by chest-crushing roar, and swing by air-splitting swing, he squeezed safely between them. Only then did he feel it safe to take in a breath of air and clap his hands for joy, shouting, "Oh, hurrah! His words were true! Hurrah, hurrah, hurrah!"

Then, leaving the lions to lick their hungry chops in angry disappointment, he went on till he came to the gate where the Porter joyfully waited. There Christian bowed politely and with a tremulous voice said, "Sir, I do thank you for your good counsel."

"'Twas only my duty," responded Watchful kindly.

"Sir, might this be a house set apart for wayfaring strangers? And if so, may I lodge here tonight?"

"To your first question, aye. This house was indeed built by the Lord of the Hill for the relief and security of pilgrims."

"Verily? Then may I enter in?"

"Answer me first. Who art thou? Whence from, and whither bound?"

"My name is Christian, although before I turned about, I was known as Graceless. I have come from the City of Destruction and be bound for the City of Zion."

"And how is it that ye seek for lodging so late? The sun is long set and the time for travel is far spent."

"I would have been here hours ago," said the chagrined pilgrim, "but oh, wretched man that I am, I slept in the arbor that stands on the hillside."

"Ah, a common mistake," said Watchful knowingly. "But it seems that you must have slept longer than most."

"No, 'twas not that I slept so long. I think I still would have gotten here much sooner except that, in my sleep, I lost my roll."

Then Watchful the Porter got a look of alarm about him and asked, "And where is it now? Do you have it?"

"Oh, yes, thanks be to God. I went back for it and was finally able to find it."

"Good! Very good!" said he with obvious relief. "Now, as to your second question. We have certain rules in this place about who may or may not enter in. Therefore, let me call out one of the virtuous maidens who will ask you a few pertinent questions. If she be pleased with your answers, she shall bring you in to the rest of the family."

So Watchful the Porter rang a bell, and there soon appeared a very beautiful and serious-looking damsel named Discretion, who answered, "Did you call for me, Father?"

"Aye, Discretion, my daughter," said he with a proud smile as he beheld Christian's timid look of admiration.

At the door of the Palace Beautiful

"To what purpose?"

"I want you to examine this fellow, my dear. He claims to be bound for Mount Zion. See if he be worthy to lodge with us this night."

"Yes, Father," said Discretion, bowing politely to her sire. Then Watchful took his leave of them saying, "I hope to see thee soon, brave pilgrim."

"Thank you, sir," answered Christian, a bit nervously, for he could tell by her regal bearing that Discretion would accept of neither fraud nor impostor in her home. Therefore, he resolved to tell her nothing more or less than absolute truth, knowing that without God's blessing, he would find no pleasant lodgings that night.

Then said Discretion, "Did you say you were bound for Mount Zion?"

"Aye, Ma'am."

"And you be come from the City of Destruction, I assume."

"Aye, Ma'am."

Then she looked at him closely and asked, "How did you get into the way?"

"I came in at the wicket gate."

"Not tumbling over the wall?" she asked, as she looked into his face, hoping to find there proof of an honest pilgrim.

"Oh no, Ma'am. Some did, but not I. I came straight on, through the way appointed."

So she continued to ply him with questions about what he had seen and done and learned on the way, and he told her all. At last, she smiled and asked, "And pray tell, dear pilgrim, what be thy name?"

"My name is Christian," he answered.

"And what would you have us do for thee at this place?" she asked.

"If you have found me to be an honest pilgrim, I would like very much to be lodged here tonight."

"Why?"

"Because it is my understanding that this place was built by the Lord of the Hill for no other purpose than the relief and security of pilgrims, such as I."

Upon hearing this, she smiled a gentle smile and turned away lest he see a tear of joy in her eye. Then said she, "I will call forth two or three of my family."

So she ran to the door and called for Prudence, Piety, and Charity, who all, after a little more conversation, brought him to the door. There, Watchful said, "Come in, thou blessed of the Lord. This house was built by the Lord of the Hill for the express purpose of entertaining just such as yourself. Do come in!"

So the pilgrim gratefully bowed his head and followed them into the house. Now, when he had been welcomed by all and comfortably seated, they gave him something warm to drink. While waiting for a rather late supper, the three sisters began to engage him in uplifting conversation.

Piety began by saying, "Come, good Christian. Do you mind if we ask you some questions about what has befallen you on your journey?"

"Yes, may we?" added Prudence. "It would be a wonderful way to invest our time while we wait for dinner."

"Oh, yes, but of course," said Christian with solemn joy. "You cannot know how happy I am to meet with those whose hearts incline toward the kingdom."

So they began to quiz him regarding his pilgrimage. Piety began by asking, "Do tell, dear Christian, what was it that first moved you to take on the hard life of a pilgrim?"

"I beg your pardon, Miss Piety," he answered, "But I was not moved at all."

"What? Not moved?"

"No, Miss. I was rather driven out of my native country by the firm conviction that if I stayed there, I would be destroyed."

"Ah, I see. But tell me, there be many roads claiming to lead to Mount Zion. How did you come to be in the only right one?"

"I am here only by God's grace, for he sent a man unto me, whose name is Evangelist."

At this, all the sisters looked upon one another with knowing smiles and Piety said, "Ah, dear Evangelist. There has no better man trod shoe leather in all the world."

"Aye, so I believe," agreed Pilgrim. "It was he who directed me to the wicket gate. There I was set in the way that has led me straight on to this house."

"And did you come by the house of the Interpreter?" asked Piety.

"Oh yes. I saw things there that I will remember as long as I live."

"What sorts of things?" asked Prudence.

"Well, three things especially stand out in my mind. One is how Christ maintains His work of grace in our hearts in spite of Satan's best efforts to put it out."

"Ah. And did he show you how Christ's work is done secretly?" asked Charity.

"Oh yes. He showed me how Christ hides Himself just behind the walls of our lives. To mortal vision He is not there at all! But to the eye of faith He is only one brick away! I like that."

"What else stands out in thy mind?" asked Piety, leaning forward eagerly.

"I was also impressed with how the man in the iron cage had quite sinned himself out of the reach of God's mercy."

"Ah, a sad case that," said Piety, shaking her head slowly. "His condition came about by a persistent refusal to repent. And what about the sleeper? Did you hear him describe his nightmare?"

"In all its horrible detail?" added Charity.

"Oh yes. His plight is one of the things that most stand out in my mind. You seem to know of the man."

"Oh, indeed!" said Piety and Charity together. Then Charity added, "He has been intending to repent of his sin since my great grandfather was a small child."

"Indeed! Then the Interpreter was right."

"About what?" asked Piety.

"When he said that 'soon doth never come, but recedes on before us like a desert mirage.'"

"'Tis a woeful story, his," said Piety, gazing sadly into the embers of the evening fire.

"Aye," said he. "It seems to me that he suffered just as much as the man in the cage. And yet he endured all of that mental anguish on account of one small sin. A tiny one he called it."

"'Twas not tiny at all!" exclaimed Piety, looking up abruptly from the fire.

"But he said it was," responded Christian, a bit taken aback by the intensity of Piety's reply.

"If it were so tiny, then why would he not trade it for all the riches of eternity?"

"Hmmm," said Christian, thoughtfully. "I don't know. I guess I'd never thought of that."

"If you will peruse the facts just a little, dear pilgrim, you will soon see that his so called 'tiny' sin was greater to him than all the world."

"Yes. I think I am beginning to understand. But do go on. Tell me more."

"'Twas a 'tiny' sin for Adam to taste the apple, but in so doing he believed the words of the serpent over the commands of God. From that 'tiny' sin have sprung all the woes that rest so heavily upon the world."

"Ah," nodded Christian again, as his comprehension began to deepen.

Then Piety added, "So do you understand now that there is no such thing as a 'tiny' sin? Do you realize that no one who clings to even one 'tiny' sin shall be made glorious and immortal at the trump of God?"

"Yes. Now I can see why he suffered so deeply. He was choosing sin over Christ!"

"Indeed," agreed Piety. "Was that all you saw at the house of the Interpreter?"

With that, he recounted all that had befallen him from the start of his way till his meeting with the two great lions. He ended his story by saying, ". . . and truly, had it not been for your good father telling me about the chains on the lions, I don't know but that I might have gone back with the others."

"Many have," said Piety sadly.

"But do tell, dear Piety," asked Christian earnestly, "why are the lions placed where they can so terribly frighten earnest pilgrims?"

"At some point in every pilgrim's journey each must choose between his senses and the Word of God. These lions were that point for you."

"Truly," said Christian, shuddering as he recalled the terror of his recent walk between the claws, "it seems to be a great test."

"Yes, but failed only by those who call God a liar. Those who believe the Word of God come straight through, as you have done."

"But you have to agree, dear Piety," interposed Charity, "that most have it easier than Christian did."

At this, Piety smiled and nodded agreement saying, "Aye, much."

"In what way?" asked Christian.

"In that they pass through in the light of day," answered Piety.

"And when we call their attention to the chains, they can actually see them," concluded Charity.

"Ah. And so for me, the test was the more severe because I had slept in the way and lost my roll."

"Aye," said Piety. "To fail one test makes the next more difficult."

"More difficult it surely was!" agreed Christian. "Thanks be to God that I am here, and thank you for receiving me."

"Tomorrow morning you must go take a closer look at the lions," said Piety, with a knowing smile.

"Oh? To what purpose?"

"To see that they have neither teeth nor claws," she said merrily.

"What!" he exclaimed, to the amusement of all three maidens. "Neither teeth, nor claws?"

"'Tis verily true," chuckled Piety merrily.

Christian cast a questioning glance at Prudence and Charity who both smiled and nodded agreement. He sat back in his chair, and after a moment's reflection said, "Then these lions were just like the warriors at the drawbridge! They were never intended to leave one scratch."

"Aye," agreed Prudence. "When we learn to see through the eye of faith, we soon learn that trials and temptations be mere paper dragons—deceptions of the enemy placed in our path to frighten us back."

"A lesson I pray to remember," he said solemnly.

Then Prudence spoke up, asking, "Dear Christian?"

"Yes, Miss Prudence?"

"Do you sometimes think back upon the country from whence you have come?" she asked in a kindly voice, her beautiful face even more lovely in the soft light of the dying fire.

Christian thought for a moment and then said, "Yes, Miss Prudence, I do. But only with feelings of shame and disgust."

"Truly? Not with a desire to return?"

"Yes, truly, Miss Prudence. If I had yet any love for Destruction, returning would have been much easier for me than coming on. But I desire a better country, that is an heavenly one."

Still seeking to know the true state of his inner heart, Prudence pressed her questions nearer home, saying, "How about some of the inner desires that were once so dear to you? Do you still carry any of them with you?"

"Well, certainly I used to enjoy my carnal thoughts as much as the next man. But now, when such thoughts seek to cross my mind, they cause me grief and shame. So, to answer your question, yes, my old thoughts do sometimes rise up to haunt me, but greatly against my will."

"Why so?"

"Why, because in my little book it says, 'Let this mind be in you, which was also in Christ Jesus.'"

"You do understand that your temptations are not sin in themselves, do you not?" she asked.

"I think I do. But do say more."

Then Prudence explained herself, saying, "There are some, who, having left their burden at the cross, think that their evil nature was left there as well. They expect that they will never be tempted again. Then, when old temptations and patterns of evil-thinking seek to arise, they think they have sinned and so fall into discouragement and despair."

"Ah. And what should they do?"

"Simply this. They must realize that temptation itself is not sin. The Scripture says that even our Lord Himself was 'tempted in all points like as we are, yet without sin.' Therefore, when an evil thought comes, seeking entertainment, we must resist it by the power of the Word. When we do, we follow in the footsteps of our Lord who turned all His temptations into victory."

"Ah. Stumbling blocks into stepping stones."

"Aye."

"And when there arises a temptation to dwell on evil thoughts, what part of the Word might I employ to strike it down?"

Then answered Prudence, "Well, there is one that says, 'Let the words of my mouth and the meditation of my heart be acceptable in thy sight, Oh Lord, my strength and my redeemer.'"

"Ah! A good verse, that one. I shall use it."

"Tell me, dear Christian, do you ever find that at certain times you have victory over temptations which at other times completely vanquish you?"

"Yes," he admitted sadly. "I do wish my victories could be more constant."

"When you do get the victory, can you remember what you did to obtain that victory?"

"Hmmm," said Christian, pausing to think a moment. "Well, for one thing, it always happens when I think of what I saw on the cross. When I picture Him hanging there for me and realize that any new sin will add yet another stripe to His back, why at such times carnal desire totally loses its power over me."

"Ah, very good. And when else?"

"Well, it happens again when I behold my fine linen garment woven in the loom of heaven. 'Twas given to me by His own angels and at His command. This white garment is proof of my salvation, and when I think of how my sinning will put stains upon it, why I hold me back from the act and get the victory again."

"Very good!" exclaimed Prudence with a joyful clap of her hands. "And when else?" she asked, leaning forward to hear.

As Christian began to realize how many keys to victory he already possessed, his heart began to glow within him. Then he continued with growing excitement, "It also happens when I spend time looking into my precious roll! And also, when I meditate and warm my heart about the realities of my eternal home, why, that will do it too!"

"Then you have already found many of the keys to consistent victory, have you not?" asked Prudence with a smile.

"Why, verily," said a pleasantly surprised Christian, "it seems that I have! If I would but choose to think continually upon these things, then sin would have no more power over me! I could ever walk in the sunshine of victory!"

"Yes!" exclaimed Prudence, accompanied by approving smiles from Piety and Charity. "'Twas thus that your Lord and Master got His victory over the world, over the flesh, and over the devil."

"Then may I do the same?" he asked excitedly. "Can it be so?"

"You certainly may," said Prudence, "if you will do these things, and yet two more."

"Being what?"

"First, you must decide that at the very first approach of evil, you will turn instantly from beholding it and cry unto thy Lord for help."

"I can do that! What else?"

"Next, when the world, the flesh, or the devil rise to tempt you, you must fling the words of Scripture in their faces, as did our Lord Jesus."

"And what does that do?"

"Oh, you cannot imagine the power thus unleashed. That word is sharper than any two-edged sword, and it cuts and hacks its adversaries to shreds. There is no temptation that can stand longer than a moment before such a weapon, and so they quickly scamper away."

"Amazing! This is a marvelous secret! And it really works, doesn't it!"

"Oh yes," affirmed Prudence with a nod. "Every time."

"But how? From whence comes such great power?"

"'Tis because the Word of God is creative and alive," Prudence replied, with a triumphant ring to her voice. "When we believe that the Word of God can do what it says it can do, and when we depend upon that word alone to do what it says it will do, then is all the power of heaven at our command."

"So let me see if I understand. You're telling me that if I keep my thoughts upon heavenly things, and if I am instant in prayer, and if I quickly draw out the Word of God against temptation, I may be as a warrior who never loses a battle. Is that right?"

"You have begun to understand," she nodded. "Now, you need only apply what you have learned."

"And that I shall do henceforth and forevermore," he said, almost eager to engage the enemy with his newfound powers.

Then Charity, who had been nearly silent until now, leaned forward and said softly, "Dear Christian?"

"Yes, Charity?" answered he, turning to face the fairest and sweetest of all the sisters.

"Do tell," she asked with deep interest, "what makes thee so desirous to go to Mount Zion?"

"Well, as I understand it, I am bound for a glorious land where there is no death and where there are no tears—a place where I will be freed from all those fleshly desires that are such an annoyance to me. There my companions shall be the unfallen angels and the noble ones of earth from all the ages. But best and most of all, I hope to see Him alive that did hang on the cross in my place. Yea, to think of enjoying His company forever! Oh, dear Charity," he said with tears in his voice, "this, more than anything, is what fuels the flame of my desire!"

Then Charity, yea, and Prudence and Piety too, felt a catch in their throats, and there was more than one misty eye glistening in the golden firelight. Then said Charity softly, "Then you do love Him."

"Oh, yes!" he cried, spilling his heart before them. "I love Him greatly because He first loved me."

After a few moments of silence, Charity asked, "Have you a family? Are you a married man?"

"Aye. I have a wife and four small children."

"And why did you not bring them along with you?" she inquired earnestly.

"Oh, how desperate I was to do so," he answered, his heart nigh on to breaking, "but they were all totally opposed to my going on pilgrimage."

Then Charity said earnestly, "But you should have talked to them and tried to show them the danger of staying behind."

"I did!" exclaimed Christian with a pained voice. "Oh, you cannot know how earnestly I tried to show them the glories of the better

Prudence, Discretion, Piety and Charity teach Christian

land! But it seemed too good to be true, and they called me a wild-eyed dreamer. Then I told them about the coming destruction of our city, but that seemed too bad to be true. So they called me a wild-eyed member of the lunatic fringe and would hear no more."

"And did you pray to God that He would bless your counsel to them?" she pressed.

"Oh, yes," he answered with a grieving heart, "and that with much affection, for you must know that my wife and poor children are very dear unto me."

"But what did they say for themselves to explain why they would not come?"

"Well, my wife was afraid of losing the things of this world, and my children were given to the foolish delights of youth; so, each, for their own reasons refused to join me. Then, I remembered the words of Jesus who said that if I put father or mother or wife or children ahead of Him, I was unworthy to be with Him where He was. Therefore, I determined in my soul that the instant I knew which way to run, I would come on alone."

"But did you, perhaps, by your vain life or jesting manner or light conversation, counteract all of your words of persuasion?" she asked.

"Well," he answered thoughtfully, "I would not say that my life was completely without fault. But I was most careful to set them a good example. But then they said I was too particular about little things and that I denied myself of things in which they saw no harm."

"Indeed? Well, then you must remember that Cain hated his brother because his own works were evil and his brother's righteous; and, if your wife and children have been offended with you for this, they thereby show themselves to be implacable to good. You have delivered your soul from their blood."

"So I believe," he said sadly. Then he brightened a little and added, "But I have hope that they may yet see the error of their ways and follow after."

I saw next in my dream that they sat talking in this manner till supper was announced. So, when all had washed and made ready, they sat down to dine. The table was furnished with fine things to eat and drink, all freely provided by the Lord of the Hill for the refreshment of pilgrims.

Now their conversation at the table was chiefly about that Lord of the Hill and the great exploits He had done. As I listened to their talk about Him, I concluded that He had been nothing short of a great and mighty warrior. They spoke of how He had laid aside His glory and His royal robes and come down in the garb of a common man to do battle in our behalf; how He had engaged the Prince of Darkness in mortal combat all alone, at the risk of defeat and eternal loss; how, by faith in the Word, and by the shedding of His own blood, He had gained the victory over he who had the power of death.

Oh, how the telling of those brave and selfless exploits filled my heart with more admiration and love than I knew it could hold. And what makes the tale all the more glorious is that He did everything voluntarily—purely out of love to this country wherein we humans dwell! Then, as they came to an end of discussing their Hero, Christian's heart seemed ready to burst with admiration, and he exclaimed, "Ah, what mighty love is this! That the Prince of Peace would lay down His glory that He might bestow it upon poor burdened sinners such as we."

Then Charity added, "And, He has sworn that He will not rest satisfied to dwell in Mount Zion alone; but that He will take all mankind who were born as beggars upon a dunghill, and make us into princes and princesses fit to sit with Him upon His throne!"

Thus they discoursed together far into the evening. After they had committed themselves to their Lord for protection, they went to their rest. The Pilgrim they laid in a large upper room, whose window opened toward the sun rising. The name of this suite was Peace, and there he slept peacefully till the break of day when the warmth of dappled sunlight on his face and the soft cooing of doves gently awakened him. So he sat up and could not at first remember where he was. Then said he "Ah! Where am I? Have I come to heaven? Is all of this a dream? Ah, yes, now I remember. This place is to show forth the love and care of Jesus for those that are pilgrims. Here I can gather a small foretaste of the glories of heaven (although, for me, heaven first began when my burden fell free)."

So they had him down to breakfast, and after prayers and some more discourse told him that he should not depart thence till they had shown him some of the rare possessions of that place. First they took him into the study, where they showed him records of the greatest antiquity. Here they showed him the pedigree of the Lord of the Hill, which proved Him to be the Son of the Ancient of Days from the years of eternity. Here also were recorded more fully many of His brave deeds on our behalf. Then was Christian seized with deepest admiration for his Hero and said, "My! These acts of the Lord of the Hill . . ."

"Yes?" asked Charity.

"They are so very brave! He is such a great warrior!"

"Yes," said Charity, proudly. "And such a warrior will He make of thee!"

"Of me? Oh no. I am but a common man."

Then said Charity solemnly, "Do not say, 'I am but a common man.' Were not the disciples of our Lord the same?"

"Yes."

"And what did he make of them?"

"Great warriors."

"Dear Christian," she continued, "'in the common walks of life there is many a man patiently treading the round of daily toil, unconscious that he possesses powers that, if called into action, would raise him to an equality with the world's most honored men.'"

"Such as the fisherfolk of Galilee."

"Aye. And such a man as that, are you," she continued. "All that is needed is 'the touch of a skillful hand to arouse your dormant faculties.' And I'll warrant you, good sir, that if you continue on as you have begun, your name will one day ride upon the tongue of thousands."

At this, Christian was silent for lack of an answer. He dared not contradict the dear damsel, who seemed to speak as a prophetess, yet neither did he dare to imagine that her words could ever come to pass. Therefore it was that he answered not a word.

After this they showed him the names of many hundreds that his Lord had taken into His service, and how He had reserved for them mansions of glory that neither time nor trial could ever take away. Then said Christian, having been thoughtfully silent for some time, "As I look upon the records of these ancient men it brings me to a conclusion."

"Being?" questioned Charity.

"That if He can take ordinary fellows, as these men were, and make of them great ones for eternity, why, then you are correct. He can do the same for me!"

"'Tis His greatest pleasure," said Charity, smiling broadly. Then she took him by the hand and said, "Come into the library and look at the great deeds of some of them."

So they read to him an account of the worthy acts that some of His servants had done; such as how they had "subdued kingdoms, wrought righteousness, obtained promises, stopped the mouths of the lions, quenched the violence of fire, escaped the edge of the sword, out of weakness were made strong, waxed valiant in fight, and turned to flight the armies of the aliens." Then Christian began to be inspired to do as they had done and exclaimed, "Oh! Such heroes. Oh, that I knew the secret of their strength that I might be a warrior such as these."

To this Charity only smiled and said, "Their secret thou shalt know soon enough. But for now, come."

So they took him into the armory, where they showed him all the weapons which their Lord had provided for pilgrims. There was a sword, sharp and two-edged, shields, helmets, breastplates, 'all-prayer', and shoes that would not wear out.

"Say!" exclaimed Christian, "I have seen these weapons before! This sword and its armor are exactly like the ones used by yonder stout fellow to hack his way into the beautiful castle!"

"Aye. They are of the same quality and made by the same smith."

"My," he said, as he admired their beauty. "I think that if I could use such weapons as these, I too could hack my way through any danger."

Then Prudence answered, "If such is your true desire, you may."

"Oh, no, no," he answered meekly. "Not I. Such armor as this must cost a king's ransom. Why, look at the fine workmanship!"

"But of course," said Charity proudly. "It was beaten out on the anvil of heaven by He who wove your garment."

"What?" cried Christian in surprise. "Is the Weaver of the Hill also a Smith?"

"Aye," said Piety, "and a Shepherd."

"And a Mighty General," added Prudence.

"And a Poet," put in Charity.

"And a Composer of fine symphonies," concluded Piety.

Then Charity pointed to an exceptionally fine suit of armor and said, "Would you like to wear some of His armor?"

"Oh, I am but a common man," said he. "I could never afford the fine outfitting of dukes and princes."

"Neither could you ever afford your fine wedding garment," said Charity. "They both come in exchange for a willing heart, without money and without price."

"Really?" exclaimed Christian, in amazement. "Then, yes. Yes! I would like to wear it!"

"So you shall!" exclaimed Charity triumphantly. "But first we would show you something yet more. Come."

So they led him into the museum where they showed him some of the instruments by which some of His servants had done wonderful things. They came to a rod that had leaves and blossoms, buds, and almonds on it. Then Prudence announced, "Here be Moses' rod!"

"The one he used to part the sea and open a river in the desert!" exclaimed Christian.

"Yes," said Prudence.

"But it has a name carved into its side. 'Aa . . . Aar . . . Aaron, it says. Is this also Aaron's rod that budded?"

"Yes, the same," said Charity. "'Twas given him by his younger brother. And here are the mallet and nail with which Jael slew Sisera."

"Ah! a brave woman, she," said Christian as he looked upon those odd instruments of war.

Then Piety said, "Here are the trumpets and lamps and pieces of pitchers wherewith Gideon put to flight the armies of Midian."

"Oh, my!" said Christian in amazement. "And not a sword among the lot."

"Aye," said Prudence, rehearsing her lesson, "because they did depend on the Word of God to do what it had promised that it would do; namely, to fight for them on that night."

"And what is this?" asked Christian, picking up a stout stick with an iron point.

"'Tis the ox's goad wherewith Shamgar slew six hundred men," answered Charity.

Then Piety picked up a whitened jawbone and said, "And here is the jawbone of an ass . . ."

"I know," interrupted the pilgrim. "This is the weapon wherewith Samson slew a thousand Philistines!"

"Yes," she replied, smiling at his youthful eagerness. "And here . . ."

"'Tis a shepherd's sling!" he exclaimed. "No doubt the one with which David slew Goliath of Gath."

"Right again," said Charity. "And here . . ."

"A sword!" blurted out Christian while reaching out to test the sharpness of its point. "Mightier and . . . ouch! Oooo! Sharper than all the others. Is it Goliath's?"

"No," answered Piety, smiling as she handed him a small bandage for his pricked finger. "This is the sword with which our Lord will slay the man of sin in the day that Michael shall rise up."

"Oh," he said. "And may that day come soon."

They also showed him many other famous relics, both ancient and modern. Then they opened to him prophecies and predictions of things that must shortly come to pass. These forecasts bring dread and amazement to enemies that plot our destruction, but great solace and comfort to pilgrims. With all of these wondrous things Christian was greatly delighted and said, "These things you have shown me give me great courage and hope. But they also make me eager to be on my way. Is it time for me to press on yet?"

Then Charity answered, saying, "Almost. Let us show you but two things more."

"Being?"

"'Tis an especially clear day and you can see with your own eyes the Delectable Mountains."

"Verily? Where?"

"Look to the south. Do you see yonder pleasant mountains?"

Looking as directed, he saw at a great distance a most pleasant, mountainous country. It was beautified with woods, vineyards, fruits of all sorts, flowers, springs and fountains—all very wondrous to behold.

"Ah! How I yearn to be there," he said longingly. "What is the name of this lovely country?"

"'Tis called Emmanuel's land," responded Charity. "And just as surely as you have come to this hill, so shall you come to that."

"I long to be there now," he said wistfully. "How much longer?"

Then answered Charity, with a twinkle in her eye, "Longer than you wish, sooner than you think."

"Ah," sighed Christian. "As always."

"But take heart," encouraged Prudence, "for once you attain that place, you will be close enough to see the very gates of the City."

"Truly!" he exclaimed in amazement. "That close?"

"Verily," affirmed Charity. "There you will find shepherds who will show you where to look and aid your vision by lending you their spy glass."

"Oh, now I am even more eager to be off," he said impatiently. "Is it time to go?"

"It will be, after we do one thing more," said Prudence.

"What thing?"

"Why, 'tis time to put on thine armor," she answered with a smile, a curtsy, and a graceful sweep of her arm toward the armory.

"Oh! Something I am most eager to do. Lead the way!"

So they took him again into the armory and there they harnessed him from top to toe with armor—fine armor that was time-tested and well broken in by those who had gone before. This armor would save him both from combat and in combat. It would save him from combat by frightening off many of those amateur villains who lurk alongside the pilgrim's way, even to this day. But should he chance to close with some powerful foe, who knew no fear, it would protect his vitals and so save him in combat.

Then being fully harnessed, he walked out with his friends to the gate. On his walk thence, he was amazed to find that his armor fit him as closely as if the Smith had fashioned it just for him (which I secretly suspect He did). At the gate they committed him to their Lord in prayer, and all bade him a fond farewell with tears in many an eye.

"Farewell, good friends," said Christian. "God bless you one and all."

"Godspeed, good Christian," said Watchful. "Remember the things that have been shown thee."

"I shall. Farewell, dear Watchful. You and your house have treated me as if I were royalty."

"Because thou art."

"Royalty? I?"

"Oh, yes," he said firmly. "Thou art now part of our 'peculiar people, a holy nation, a royal priesthood. He hath made us to be kings and priests unto God and His Father forever.' Therefore, Godspeed thee, dear Christian, son of the King."

These words, and those that had gone before, awakened within Christian the realization that the path he had chosen was more than just a simple journey from a vile land to a better. He now began to realize that he was also enrolled in a school which would render him a fit citizen of eternity. Yea, more than that, he was in training to become a prince worthy to serve under the King of kings and Lord of lords! This sacred realization brought high resolve to his heart and a joyful tear to his eye. After a few moments of silence he was at last able to ask the porter, "Have you seen any other pilgrims pass by during your last watch?"

"Oh yes! One whose name was Faithful."

"Faithful! I know him, for he is my townsman. My near neighbor! How far ahead do you think he may be?"

"Oh, I suppose that by this time he must surely be down the hill and well into the Valley of Humility."

"Well, I must hurry after him. It may be that we can travel on together. The Lord be with thee, dear Watchful. May He greatly increase your blessings for all the kindness you have shown me!"

Then, eager to be on his way and also to catch up to Faithful, he pressed forward. But, knowing of the hidden dangers on the way to Humility, Prudence, Piety, and Charity offered to accompany him down to the foot of the hill. And so down the hill they went, all the while repeating their former lessons. As they went down, Christian found for himself that the path into Humility was not all so easy as he had expected (as you too will learn, should you ever decide to bravely follow in his footsteps).

Then said Christian, after a near slip or two, "My, 'tis a steepish hill that leads down the back side of Difficulty. This climb down into Humility seems to replace difficulty with danger."

"Yes," said Prudence, "so it is. 'Tis a very rare matter for a man to descend into the Valley of Humiliation without a nasty fall or two."

"I can see why," he said, choosing his steps as wisely as he was able. "'Tis so steep and slippery and . . . oops! Uh, oh! Help!"

"I've got you!" said Prudence, seizing his arm to steady his steps.

Then Charity took his other arm and cautioned, "Careful now, dear Christian. Choose well each step."

Then said Christian, gratefully, "My! I am certainly glad for your company, dear ladies. I don't know but that I might have been severely injured without you."

"That is why Piety, Charity, and I have come with thee," said Prudence as she helped him over another slippery spot.

"Aye," added Piety. "For without us you would surely suffer many a slip on the way down."

And so down he went, but that very warily. Yet even so he grew a bit careless and did slip a time or two. "Uh, oh!" he cried out several times as he felt his feet sliding on the shale or slipping on slimy, green moss.

Many a time Charity would say, "Careful now." And Prudence would add, "I've got you! Here, hold fast to my arm."

Then I saw in my dream that these fair maidens finally got Christian safely to the bottom of the hill. There they gave him a loaf of bread, a bottle of wine squeezed that very morning, and a cluster of fine raisins. Christian bowed in gratitude and resolutely turned to pursue his journey. But behold, standing in his path was Charity who reverently held up before Christian a small, shiny key hung upon a golden chain. Upon seeing it, Christian was puzzled and asked, "Why, what key is this, dear Charity?"

"This is the secret of their strength."

"Of whose strength?" he inquired, his focus fixed firmly on the gently swinging key.

"Why, the strength of those who 'subdued kingdoms, wrought righteousness, obtained promises, and stopped the mouths of lions.' This is the key of promise, and by its power common men have 'quenched the violence of fire,' wrought 'escape from the edge of the sword, out of weakness were made strong,' and 'turned to flight the armies of the aliens.'"

"This little key has done all of that?" he asked in respectful awe.

"Aye," said she. "And when you come to your darkest hour, you may use this key to work any miracle that God has authorized in His Word."

"Indeed? Any miracle? Any miracle at all?"

"Yea verily. And much more besides. Indeed, any promise to be found in the Word may be applied to your life, as others have done before you. Simply depend upon that Word to do what it has promised it will do and there is no power on earth or in hell that can stop you from carrying out God's will."

"Then would you please place it round my neck, dear Charity," said Christian, removing his helmet and setting it on his knee as as he bowed reverently before the fair damsel. "I would wear it in my bosom, next to my heart."

So she ceremoniously placed the golden key round his neck, saying, "Go forth conquering and to conquer, dear Christian, for all power in heaven and on earth is at thy command. Only believe in the promises of God, and thou shalt triumph gloriously."

"Thank you, dear Charity," said Christian, brushing a tear from his eye as he rose to his feet. "Thank you very, very much. I shall count this key among my greatest treasures. Farewell."

After the noble damsels had once again wished him God's blessings, Christian addressed himself to his journey. But they, reluctant to part company with such a noble warrior, stood still in that place and watched until long after he had disappeared from view down the peaceful paths of Humility.

"God speed thee, dear Christian," whispered Charity softly.

"And forget not thy key," added Prudence. "Forget not thy key."

Farewell in the Valley of Humility

CHAPTER FOUR

NOW CHRISTIAN had not gone far into the Valley of Humiliation before he heard the ominous flappings of some monstrous bat's wings. Casting about him fearfully, he espied, swooping down from the North, a foul fiend.

"Oh no!" he cried out in terror.

As the evil apparition drew near, it circled round behind Christian and growled with a gutteral voice, "Halt where you stand, vile traitor!"

"This is surely the worst evil I have met with yet! What shall I do?"

"I'll tell you what to do, foolish fugitive," snarled the fiend, as he deliberately folded huge leathery wings after having settled to the earth amid a roiling cloud of dust. "Flee from my wrath to come, lest I devour you!"

Now the monster, whose name in the Greek is Apollyon, was most hideous to behold, being clothed with scales like a fish, having wings like a dragon, and the feet of a bear. Out of his belly fire and smoke belched up through his nostrils, and his mouth was as the mouth of a lion.

So Christian began to consider with himself what to do, saying, "What to do? Shall I run back or stand my ground?"

"You have no choice!" roared the beast, belching forth a cloud of sulphurous smoke. "Run, weak and feeble pilgrim! Run whilst you may!"

Well, you can be sure that this command Christian was very much inclined to obey—until he remembered that pilgrims are not provided with armor for their backs. And, recalling the treacherous difficulties coming into Humility, he quickly recognized the deadly perils of attempting a retreat back out. Therefore, to turn back must certainly prove to be the death of him. Therefore he planted his feet firmly and said boldly, "No! I must stand my ground. Oh, Lord of the Hill, be with me!"

Now Apollyon was quite taken aback by the boldness of this pilgrim whom he had taken to be no more than a common traveler who could easily be frightened back. He was also startled and pained in his ears to hear Christian cry out to his King so early in the encounter. Therefore, seeing that this pilgrim was impregnable to his fiery darts (having just put on the whole armor of God, you see), he was loath to run the risk of a direct attack. He therefore determined to use flattery and threats mixed with a good dose of diabolical deceit. With these subtle weapons of hell he hoped to disarm the man before resorting to more violent measures. He began his attack by softening his harsh demeanor and addressing Christian with the voice of Eden's gentle serpent saying, "Whence from and whither bound, O gentle traveler?"

"I flee from the city of Destruction, and I am bound for the land of Zion," Christian replied suspiciously, trying to look and sound more bold on the outside than he felt on the inside.

"The city of Destruction, do you say?" snapped Apollyon. "Well then," he hissed, squinting his eyes to narrow slits while pointing a sharp eagle's claw at Christian's breast, "since I am prince and god of that land, that makes you one of my subjects!"

"Nay, I am not!"

"Ah! But you are!" he countered with mounting anger. "You are mine by birth and by life! And, for your attempted escape, you deserve that I should smite you to the ground! I only hesitate," said he, calming himself a bit, "because I hope to gain yet further and better service from you."

"I shall never serve you again!" shot back Christian, instinctively fingering the haft of his sword.

"And why not?" demanded the fiend, casting furtive glances at Christian's sword hand.

"Because your services were hard and your wages were such as a man could not live on."

"What! Do you dare complain of my wages?"

"Yes," he cried, pointing an accusing finger. "Because the wages of sin is death. Therefore I have chosen to serve another Master whose yoke is easy and whose burden is light; a Master whose wages are eternal life!"

Now as Christian pointed the accusing finger and spake boldly for his new Master, Apollyon quailed and shrank back a few inches before shouting, "There is no prince that will lose his subjects without a battle, and I be no exception, Graceless!"

"My name be Christian," announced the pilgrim proudly. But this the giant ignored and, once more adopting a friendly manner, said, "But, heh, heh, dear Graceless, being by nature a kind and reasonable prince, I will give you an opportunity to go back in peace. If you do, I promise you easier work and better wages, as our country can afford."

"And why do you offer me such good wages?" asked Christian warily. "I be but a common man."

"Nay! Nay, nay," he said, assuming his sweetest serpent's voice. "Now that you have been a pilgrim, you can render me tenfold service by your fine example in turning back. That is how I can afford your raise."

"'Tis too late!" shot back Christian.

"'Tis never too late, dear Graceless," crooned the fiend. "Come back with me and be wise."

"Nay," said Christian nobly, "for I have betrothed myself to the King of kings. I should be dishonest thus to betray Him."

"Bah! Sheer nonsense!" snorted Apollyon, spewing a tongue of orange flame through a ring of acrid yellow smoke for effect. "'Tis a common thing for His professed followers to serve Him for a time and then come fawning back to me. Do you the same now, and all shall be well with you."

At this base suggestion, Christian said indignantly, "I have given Him my faith, and sworn Him my allegiance; how, then, can I turn back and not be hanged as a traitor?"

"Pah!" flamed the monster with a roar. "You have done the same to me! And hanging is better than you deserve! But," crooned the fiend, regaining control and slithering the sweet voice of the serpent between the clenched teeth of a grinning lion, "because I be so kind and fair, I am willing to let bygones be bygones and forgive your grievous injuries. You need only turn you about and strike out for home."

"So you can pierce my back with fiery darts?"

"Oh no! Not that! I, uh . . . I was only thinking of your comfort. Uh . . . surely you would not want to back your way out of Humility."

"Thank you, but no thank you."

Then Apollyon, losing all pretended patience with kindness (which he was much averse to use anyway, since it tended to make him nauseous), put aside his serpent's voice and roared as a lion, saying, "But you were born into my service! You have made me promises!"

"Promises gotten by deceiving a child before he knew a better way!"

"You have sinned much, though."

"Aye, so I confess," admitted Christian with no little shame. But then, remembering the cross and how his burden had tumbled into the sepulchre, he stood tall and refused to shoulder it again. Instead he said proudly, "But my new Master has power to absolve and to pardon what I did whilst deceived into your service. More than that, He has the power to keep me from falling. I need never serve you again, Apollyon. Ever!"

At this powerful onslaught, Apollyon cringed behind a leathery wing momentarily before roaring back, "No! Lies! All lies!"

"No! 'Tis very truth," countered Christian, growing more bold yet.

"Noooo!" bellowed the fuming beast with an involuntary shudder.

"And," continued the pilgrim fearlessly, "to tell the truth more plainly, I find His service easier, His wages higher, His servants kinder, His government fairer, His company sweeter, and His country lovelier than yours!"

"Nooo!" hissed the fiend. "No, no! Noooo!"

"Therefore, stop trying to deceive me! I am His and He is mine. I am of that number that will 'follow the Lamb whithersoever He goeth.'"

Meeting with such ill-success using mere guilt and guile, Apollyon thought it better to appeal to the man's natural fear of pain, saying, "Better think about what lies ahead and reconsider whilst you may, Graceless. Think of the many who have gone before you only to meet with shameful and painful deaths!"

"Aye," said Christian, resting his hand on his sword, "but 'blessed are those who are persecuted for righteousness' sake, for theirs is the kingdom of heaven.'"

This sharp thrust springing from the heart of the Word, made the fiend wince and blink serpentish eyes a few quick times. Fearing lest this unusual pilgrim might continue his deadly thrusts, he cast a quick glance behind him to spy out a path of easy escape. Then said he with feigned contempt, "This Prince of whom you speak so glibly is but a paper prince."

"Nay! Not so!"

"Yea! 'Tis so," accenting his words with a puff of smoke. "All the world knows how I have rescued my subjects from Him (either by fraud or by force), and so will I do to you!"

"He shall preserve me!"

"Pah! Name one time when He has come in person to deliver His own."

"How about when He stood in the flames with the three Hebrews?"

"Pah! Thousands of years ago!" roared Apollyon, visibly disconcerted. Then, belching forth a sheet of flame enveloped in a yellow-gray cloud of sulphurous smoke, he wrung his beclawed paws and said with fiendish delight, "But now we slow-roast them at the stake, and He does not so much as lift a finger whilst they writhe in the flames."

"While they sing in the flames you mean," countered Christian proudly. "And this they can do because He bears their pain in His own flesh. And more than that, they lay down their lives willingly, knowing that they shall inherit all the more glory when He comes with His angels."

"And do you hope to partake of said glory?" asked Apollyon, seeing a possible avenue of new attack.

"Aye. 'Tis already mine if I will be but faithful unto death."

"And why do you expect such goodly wages, seeing you have already been so unfaithful?" hissed the demon slyly.

"When?"

Then the fiend proceeded to list every sin, every stumble, and every doubting that he had ever seen Christian fall into, saying, "When you took your eyes off the light and fell into the Slough of Despond; when you went up to Sinai to be rid of your burden rather than waiting for your Lord to remove it in the proper manner; when you sinfully slept and lost your precious roll; and when you were almost persuaded to go back at the mere mewings of toothless lions!"

Then Christian's mouth went dry as he realized that the fiend possessed an exact account of every sin he had ever committed. This made him grateful indeed to remember that he had already sincerely repented. Yea, he had turned from his sins and sent them on ahead to the heavenly sanctuary where Christ did minister in his behalf.

"Aye," he confessed, "all is true, besides many fears and thoughts that you know nothing of. But I have repented of those foolish mistakes and have learned from them. My Prince has forgiven me and given me power to do better."

"Grrr-aaugh!" snarled Lion Mouth with a sheet of flame. "I am an enemy to this Prince! I hate His person, His laws, and His people! And I have come out of my den for the express purpose of stopping you! Turn or burn, Graceless!"

Christian, seeing that words had come to an end, drew his sword, lowered his visor, and gave Apollyon fair warning, saying, "Apollyon! In the name of the Lord, I declare that I am in the King's highway, the Way of Holiness. Here nothing can befall me except by my Lord's permission. Therefore, be careful what you do, for in opposing me, you oppose my Prince!"

Now, flattery, deceit and threats having failed him, Apollyon fell back upon those familiar weapons that he better knows how to wield: namely fear, torture, and death. Therefore he straddled the path that there could be no passage unless Christian should go out of the way. And this was the challenge that he flung out to Christian: "I despise thy Prince, and I am void of fear in this matter! Prepare yourself to die, Graceless; for I swear by my infernal den that you shall go no farther. Here will I spill thy soul!"

And with that, he slung a flaming dart at Christian's breast, but Christian had long since put his shield at the ready and so saved himself.

"So!" challenged Christian. "First words of flattery, then evil threatenings, and now it has come to combat, has it? Then in the name of the Lord of the Hill and in His power, I stand against you, O Destroyer and accuser of the brethren!"

Then did Apollyon attack with all his infernal skill, throwing darts as thick as hail. By these Christian was wounded in his head, his hand, and foot.

"Run for your life, wee coward!" snarled the fiend as he searched for a chink in Christian's armor.

"Nay," he cried out, skillfully parrying another flaming dart and countering with a swift thrust of his glittering sword. "Though I die on the spot, I will stand my ground! Ha!"

"You are thrice wounded, feeble warrior! Your blood spills on the ground, and you are falling back! Your Lord is ashamed of you!"

"Nay," declared Christian, "but proud, for I do the best I can! Let me pass, for you are a defeated foe!"

"So say you!" growled the beast, his bold facade beginning to wilt before the sharp arrows of painful truth.

"No!" he shouted, punctuating his words with a slash of his sword. "Not I, but my Book. Therefore, I will depend upon the Word to do what it says!"

"And what does it say?" Apollyon challenged thoughtlessly, to his instant regret.

Then declared Christian boldly, "It tells me that if I turn to God and resist the devil, he shall flee from me. Therefore, back off, foul fiend!"

Christian, taking new courage from the Word, resolved to play the man and began to gain new ground. Now the fierceness of this combat no man can imagine. Apollyon belched smoke like a dragon, fiercely roaring and hideously screaming the whole time of the conflict. And oh, what sighs and groans did burst from poor Christian's heart. Now this violent combat lasted for over half a day, and Christian, because of his wounds, found himself growing weaker and still weaker. Apollyon, seeing opportunity for a kill, began to circle tighter, round and round so as to make Christian dizzy. Then, seizing upon a weak moment, he rushed in like a flood, caught hold of Christian and, with a skill born of centuries of wrestling with flesh and blood, gave him a brutal throw to the ground. This knocked the breath from Christian's breast and sent his sword skittering just out of reach.

"Aha!" gloated Apollyon, savouring the moment. "No sword! Now shall I show you what I do to traitors!"

Then Apollyon, seeking to prolong and deepen the sufferings of death, pressed himself upon Christian to crush out his life and to smother him with his sulphurous breath.

"Dead man, Graceless," he fumed hot into his face. "You are a dead man."

And so it seemed, for Christian could scarcely find air to breathe. And what little air he could suck in was so befouled and sulphurous that it seared his lungs and turned his vision a blurry gray. Seeing that his situation was beyond hope (as did Jacob in his trouble), Christian yielded up his earthly life and committed the keeping of his soul to God. But it was not in God's plan to lose such a brave pilgrim so early on in his journey. Therefore, as Apollyon arrogantly reached for his last fiery dart, God filled Christian with a new supply of hope and strength. Instantly Christian's mind and vision cleared, and in good hope he reached out his hand, praying that God would guide it to his sword. Apollyon, already enjoying sure victory, only smirked a lion-lipped grin for the joy of seeing Christian's hand desperately stretching, scratching, searching, and clawing for his weapon.

"Dead man, sword-seeker," he hissed hatefully, "nothing but a dead man." Then Christian touched the haft of his sword with the tip of his finger and felt a new thrill of hope surge through his breast. But, stretch and struggle as he might, his reach still exceeded his grasp. Apollyon, gloating over Christian's futile efforts, sneered triumphantly and then pressed his entire bone-crushing weight onto Christian's chest. Hissing and fuming sulphurous breath into his face he taunted Christian, saying, "Your Master has left you to die, Graceless. Your sword lies but half an inch away, and your heavenly Lover leaves it lie. You are a fool!"

Thus did Apollyon seek to send Christian to a hopeless grave. But still, with heaven-born faith, Christian continued to flail about for that precious weapon, so near, and yet, so far. At last God, having shown the onlooking universe that Christian would never surrender his faith, no matter how bad appearances might be, gave the nod to one of the eagerly waiting Shining Ones. Instantly there was a flash of light, and a sword slapped firmly into that desperate, clutching hand.

"Aha!" cried Christian, feeling his body surge with new strength from on high and grasping the instrument of deliverance with viselike grip. "Rejoice not against me, O mine enemy!" he shouted triumphantly. "When I fall, I shall arise!" And with that, Christian gave him a deadly thrust which tore the scab off of that old, mortal wound inflicted so long ago on Mount Calvary. Screaming in pain and rage, the brute reared and fell back shrieking out his disbelief, "Auughh! Noooo! This cannot be! You were a dead man!"

Christian, perceiving that his blow had gone home, sprang to his feet and laid into him again, crying triumphantly, "Nay, but alive, for 'in all these things we are more than conquerors through Him that loved us.' Take that, foul fiend! Hah!"

So with latter-rain power, Christian slashed and hacked at the beast so fiercely as to force him into a scampering retreat. "Ah! What happened? You come at me as a new man!"

"And so I am!" shouted Christian, pursuing Apollyon's head with a swish/slash of his razor-sharp sword. "For I have waited upon the Lord and He hath renewed my strength. 'I shall mount up on wings like an eagle' and quite put an end to you, defeated foe!"

Apollyon, in spite of all his serpentine twisting and turning, saw fur and bloody scales flying fast as snow and soon judged it wiser to part with pride rather than life. Therefore he shamelessly turned tail, crying out, "Auughh! Away with me!" But unwilling to settle for partial victory, Christian flew at his backside with holy indignation and chipped out a few bloody divits from his scaly back, calling out, "What! Will you flee from a mere man?"

"Nay, but more than a mere man," whimpered the giant whose flame had gone cold by reason of his fearful wounds, "for you have compassed me with all the armies of heaven!"

"A thing you will do well to remember," shouted Christian, with a zinging slash of his sword, "'for nothing is apparently more helpless, and yet really more invincible, than a soul that feels its nothingness and relies wholly upon God.'"

"So say you now in the flush of victory!" cried Apollyon, finally limping up enough speed to get him airborne. "But it will be a different song you sing when I come to you in the Valley of the Shadow of Death. Adieu, vile follower of the dark force."

With that sinister threat, Apollyon spread his tattered dragon's wings and flapped an erratic flight down to the Valley of the Shadow of Death where he might nurse his wounds. Therefore, for a season, Christian saw him no more. Then, nearly exhausted, Christian fell to his knees and cried, "Oh! Thanks be to God, who has delivered me out of the mouth of the lion."

Then there came to him a mysterious hand holding some of the leaves from the tree of life. These Christian applied to his battle wounds and was healed in an instant. Then he sat down at the side of the path to partake of the bread and fresh-squeezed wine that had

I shall . . . quite put an end to you, defeated foe!

been given to him in happier times. As he thus ate and refreshed him-self, he looked about him and was amazed to see how powerful had been their battle. All about him the earth was gashed and torn by their violent struggles and everywhere lay the shivered shafts of Apollyon's fiery darts. Also there were scars upon some of the rocks from the by-blows of Christian's mighty sword. Then was he all the more thankful for the promises of God that had delivered him from the hand of the enemy. So after another prayer of gratitude, he struggled to his feet and addressed himself to his journey, saying, "Hmmm. Perhaps best that I go forward with my sword already drawn, for there is no telling what Apollyon might have in store for me in the Valley of the Shadow of Death."

Near the end of the Valley of Humility the green grass turned to brown stubble, and the perfume of fir and flower gave way to the stench of sulphur pits and rotting flesh. The singing of birds yielded to the muffled wing-flaps of vampirous bats and mysterious moanings. The westering sun glowed blood red as it reluctantly settled into the musty mist of the valley. As Christian watched it slide from view, he found himself standing at the mouth of the Valley of the Shadow of Death.

Now, if there had been any heights to climb, or seas to swim that would have taken him around this evil place, Christian would have done it in a flash. But the path laid down for him by his Lord led this way, and therefore, this way must he go.

Now this valley is a very fearful and solitary place—a place where all the woeful and miserable pieces of ground in all the world come together in one long, dreary valley. There is a section of lonely wilderness, a long stretch of swamps and pits, and a length of drought-parched earth. There is also a place where one side of the narrow way drops off into a slimy swamp while the other slides into viscous, sucking quicksand. It is a country void of people—one that none but a Christian with visions of a better land would ever pass through. It was here that Apollyon came to Christian again—this time in an even worse form than before.

As I beheld in my dream, I saw Christian look down toward the misty, bubbling swamp at the near end of the valley and stop to consider how most safely to pass through. Then I saw two men, children of the spies who had brought up an evil report of Caanan land (Numbers 13), making haste to go back. Christian, thinking them sent to guide and accompany him on his journey, was greatly encouraged and said, "Ho! Men! Where off to in such a haste?"

The first, named Shaphat, cried out with a fearful voice, "Back! Back!"

The other, whose name was Palti, added with breathless and quivering speech, "Back we say! If life or peace be prized by you at all, turn back with us!"

Christian, quite taken aback at such a show of cowardice from fellow pilgrims asked, naively, "Why? What be the matter?"

"Matter? What be the matter he asks!" whined Shaphat.

"Well, what?"

To this Palti sneered, as if Christian were asking the most obvious question in all the world, "What lies ahead be the matter, that's what!"

"And what be that?"

"'Tis the Valley of the Shadow of Death!" said trembling Palti.

"Aye," groaned Shaphat. "We were right on the edge of it and were just about to climb down the lip and begin our passage through. And we would have gone right on in too . . ."

"Except for the grace of God," interrupted Palti.

"Aye," continued Shaphat. "We were that close," he said, pinching thumb and forefinger tightly together, "to going down in except that (Oh, praise God!), we were lucky enough to see ahead!"

By now you can be sure that Christian's interest was thoroughly aroused, and he asked eagerly, "And what did you see?"

"Oh, truly God was merciful," answered Shaphat, "for if we had gone just a teeny bit farther, we would not be here to tell the tale!"

"Aye," added Palti.

"But what did you see?"

"What did we see?" said the trembling Shaphat in exasperation. "What did we see, he asks!"

"Well, what?"

"I'll tell you what we saw, blind one," blurted out Shaphat at last. "What we saw were the dark bowels of the valley itself!"

"'Tis dark as torch soot on dungeon wall," said Palti.

"We saw hobgoblins, and satyrs and dragons of the pit!" added Shaphat.

"Indeed?"

"Yea, and more," whined Palti again. "We could hear also the continual howling and moaning of dying pilgrims who had lost their way. And . . ."

" . . . And over the valley hung the depressing clouds of confusion," interrupted Shaphat.

By now Palti had begun to warm to his subject and to paint over grim reality with even worse imaginings. Said he, with grimaced face and erratic gestures, "There are dark and smoky clouds that hover over that place. They all take the forms of ghoul's faces and demon's claws and bat's wings!"

Shaphat, not to be outdone by his trembling companion, added, "The whole place is absolutely and totally dreadful! It has trees that reach down to claw you with their thorns. The tiny, narrow trail is all utterly tangled and confused and without any rhyme or reason."

From where Christian stood, the valley did indeed look like a terrible place. But these words were an evil report that made it seem ten times worse than it actually was. Then Christian asked nervously, "Was the path through straight and narrow?"

"Straight and narrow?" asked Shaphat, a bit bewildered. "Uh . . . aye, yes! Yes, it was straight and narrow. Especially narrow!"

Then Christian plucked up his courage and said, "Then from Goodwill's description of the path and your picture of the valley, this must surely be the way."

Christian advanced but Shaphat stood in the path saying, "What are you doing? You're not going on, are you?"

"I must! This is the straight path that leads to the Promised Land."

"Haven't you heard a word we've said?" shouted Palti. "This path will lead to your death! 'It is an evil land that doth eat up the inhabitants thereof!'"

"Aye," added Shaphat. "On the right side of the narrow road there lies a very deep ditch."

"More like a swamp!" put in Palti.

"Yeah, more like a swamp it was," continued Shaphat, "and in it we saw bodies floating! Bodies from all ages of blind followers who had followed blind leaders into death!"

"Ah," said Christian. "'Tis the very ditch that my book warns me of. Thank God we need not be taken by surprise."

"That's not all!" cried Shaphat. "On the other side of that teeny, tiny, skinny trail there is a very dangerous quag . . ."

"Quicksand, Shaphat!" injected Palti. "Tell'm it's quicksand. The viscous, vicious, sucking kind!"

"'Tis indeed quicksand," agreed Shaphat, bobbing his head for emphasis. "And, if even a good man sticks but his toe into this stuff, he'll not find the bottom."

"Not in a hundred years!" piped Palti.

"Aha!" said Christian. "That must be the quag of adult pleasure into which King David's eyes pulled him and whence he barely escaped alive."

"Probably so," said Shaphat, hands on hips in a cocky manner. "So do you think you can resist gorgeous demons better than he?"

"No," answered Christian with tight-set jaw. "But if I firmly choose to keep my eyes on the light, I believe that I shall be able to keep my feet on the path."

Then said Shaphat in utter disbelief, "What! You sound as if you still plan to go forward!"

"Yes, I must! This is the way!"

Said Palti, "But it be so pitchly dark."

"Better to go with God through the darkest night than to walk alone in the brightest day."

"Pah! You are a fool!" snapped Shaphat.

"I can do no other," answered Christian meekly. "God help me, for 'tis this way I must go."

"Well then, on to your death with you," said Shaphat smugly as he stepped aside with grave ceremony. "I'll bet my life that we shall hear no more of you."

"Except for your mud-muffled screams!" said Palti. "Be gone with you, O foolish one!"

"But wait," said Christian. "Can you not at least wish me God's blessing?"

"Blessing! Certainly not!" snapped Palti angrily as he turned to run.

"Why not?"

"Because God has no blessings for fools!" Palti shouted back as he joined his fellow coward in their futile flight from one death to another.

And so, alone and in dense darkness, Christian cautiously descended into the Valley of the Shadow of Death. The path seemed narrower and the air more vile than had been described to him. Therefore he went on cautiously, shuffling his feet to feel out his way—all the while walking by faith and not by sight. In this deadly place he found it all he could do to hold his balance for, as he sought to avoid the swamp on one side, he would be in danger of sliding into the quag on the other. But at such times it was as if he heard a small voice behind him saying, "This is the way, walk ye in it." Also, as he went slowly on, he soon realized that his sword was of no use against such things as were to be found in this valley. Therefore, he returned it to its scabbard and betook himself to the use of another fearful weapon of spiritual warfare called "All Prayer."

Now to add to his confusion, Christian heard the doleful voices of damned demons crying out from the pit. He also heard muffled wings rushing to and fro past his head. Moreover he heard the sounds of steel-rimmed chariot wheels pulled by great, whinnying stallions driven to a frothing frenzy by screaming demons. These came rushing toward him as if to run him over if he would not step sideways off the path. At this Christian cried out in desperation, "Oh, Lord, I beseech Thee, deliver my soul!" Then, just as it seemed that he would take a hoof in the face, the fearsome sounds would veer and rattle just over his head, or roar by scant inches to one side. But in spite of all these terrible noises, Christian remembered that he was on the path. Therefore he set his face like a flint and determined that he would not be diverted by mere noises, however fearful or loud.

Now he came on for many miles in this wise until, from somewhere off in the darkness, he heard a company of fiends flapping furiously forward to meet him. As they drew near, he heard a lead demon cry out, "Say now! Look what me sees."

Then a ghoul answered greedily, "Why, 'tis Christian, me doth believe."

"Aye," agreed the demon. "The one we almost stabbed with flaming arrows at the wicket gate."

"Christian!" slavered a starving fiend, eagerly licking his chops. "Mmmm, how delicious!"

"Me seen him first!" declared the demon.

"No," screeched the ghoul. "I recognized him first. He's mine!"

"We will share," ordered the fiend. "I gets 'is brains."

"And I his liver," hissed the demon. "Me loves liver. Loves it, loves it, loves it! Hee, hee, hee."

Then said the ghoul eagerly, "Let's take him back to the pit and have us a party."

In the Valley of the Shadow of Death

"Nay," whined the demon. "If we do, the big guys'll take him away from us."

"We eats'im here," commanded the fiend. "I'll cook him."

"But all of my infernally fiery seasonings are down below," protested the ghoul.

"I said we'll eat him here," snarled the fiend savagely.

"Then I gets to roast him," growled the ghoul.

"Nay," howled the demon, "but I do. You roasted the last one!"

"Nay!" complained the fiend. "You cook 'em too fast!"

"Do not!"

"Do too!" groused the ghoul. "They die before they're half baked!"

"I do not!" protested the hissing, spitting demon.

"I said I'll cook him!" rasped the fiend commandingly.

"Grrr!" growled the defeated demon.

"Are your demons ready for the capture?" asked the fiend eagerly.

"Me have two legions!" gloated the demon.

"And I four," boasted the ghoul with a sneer.

"Good," gurgled the fiend in a guttural voice. "I warrant you he'll be an easy one. Forward, ghouls and goblins, werewolves and fiends!"

"He who first strikes, first bites, hee, hee, hee," cackled the demon.

"I can hardly wait!" grunted the ghoul.

Now at this, Christian stopped and began to muse about what he should do. "Shall I run? Nay! I must not, for I have no armor for my back. And who knows but that I may be over halfway through. And, for all I know, the danger of going back may be greater than that of going forward. I shall go on!"

At this show of courage, the host of darkness was amazed and determined all the more to strike fear into his heart. Said the demon, "We be at him!"

Added the fiend, "Out with his eyes!"

"Pull out his tongue!" grunted the ghoul. "Legion!" commanded the demon. "Surround him all sides!"

Then Christian lifted up his voice in prayer and cried, "'Yea, though I walk through the Valley of the Shadow of Death, I will fear no evil.'" At this vicious attack from the key of promise, the fiend was stopped dead in his tracks and sputtered in shocked astonishment, "Wha'? Oh no! He's using the power of the Word of God!"

"Deliver me, O my God," continued Christian, "for in Thee do I trust."

Then the demon covered his ears wailing, "He's got 'All Prayer' to his use! Get me away!" With this, the demon and his dark legions streaked into the darkness and were silent. The fiend shook his fist at the fleeing backsides of the cowardly host and screamed, "Come back! He is weak!"

"And we are strong!" boasted the ghoul. "Back to the conquest with you, despicable demons," demanded the foul fiend.

"Aye," growled the ghoul, "We are the kind that only be cast out with fasting and prayer!"

"Oh, Lord!" cried Christian earnestly, "'be thou my strength and help . . . a shelter in a time of storm.'"

At this, the ghoul began to experience severe brain pain and bellowed out in abject terror, "Aaauugh! Off with me! He's praying again!"

Christian, seeing whence came his strength, cried out unto the Lord saying, "Help me, Lord, for I depend upon thy Word alone to deliver me."

Then the fiend began to shudder and tremble violently and screamed out, "Auugghh! All right! Enough is enough!"

"Auugghh!" groaned a ghoul. "And for me!"

And so, like a retreating wave of the sea, the dark spirits were utterly swept back by the power of the Word. So great was their terror, and so hasty their dismal retreat, that they tumbled and stumbled and scrambled over and around and through each other, all the while biting and scratching with screams and howls of total disarray.

My gaze turned to follow them and there, on the distant, murky horizon, I discerned the malevolent form of the giant Apollyon himself. In one of his mighty arms he held a blazing lightning bolt which he cast bitterly after the fleeing forms of his vaporous imps. In his thunderous voice he called down curses and imprecations upon them, saying, "What manner of spirits are you, that you flee in terror from the idle words of a mere pilgrim?" Then, when he was sure none would see, he whimpered and licked some of the festering wounds gotten in his fray with Christian.

Now after this victory, Christian had some good hopes that he might perhaps have an easier time finding his way. Ah! But not so, for all about him were noises and voices and diversions that distracted and confused. Yea, so badly mixed up was he that he could scarce recognize his own voice. Then, seeing his opportunity, there came sneaking up behind Christian a certain wicked spirit who spoke into Christian's ear in Christian's own voice. And the things he uttered were terrible blasphemies, loathsome lustings, and vile imaginings—yea, sins that Christian had long ago put away and forsaken. Therefore was Christian's heart full of sorrow to think that he could now blaspheme and curse Him who had died in his place and whom he loved. Not realizing that these thoughts were coming from without and not from within, he suffered great guilt and had not the wisdom to stop up his ears from hearing. Then he cried out, saying, "Oh, vile man that I am! To think such things! To say such things! I want to stop, and yet, though I clasp my hands over my mouth, the evil words go on without me. Oh, me!"

Then, as God would have it, from somewhere far ahead in the murky darkness he heard a voice—a voice of someone on pilgrimage—someone on pilgrimage and quoting words of hope! Now the solitary voice of prayer belonged to the long-sought Faithful, and these were the words Christian could faintly hear him say:

"'The Lord is my shepherd . . .'"

"What? Do I hear a voice?"

"' . . . I shall not want. He leadeth me beside the still waters.'"

"Can it be?" cried Christian, in hopeful amazement. "Is it a voice quoting Scriptures?"

"'Thy rod and thy staff they comfort me,'" he heard, trailing back to him from somewhere far off in the shrouding mists. Then shouted Christian triumphantly, "It is a voice! Praying to God! I am not alone! And if God be with him, then why not with me? And may I not soon o'ertake him and so have good company? Hello!" he shouted hopefully. "Good sir! Can you hear me?"

But Faithful, fearing some demonic decoy—another ploy of the goblins to lure him back into the valley, dared not answer. Christian called again and again, but there was no answer. Therefore he resolved to at least stay within earshot of that musical voice that so freely quoted the beautiful words of God. And oh, you cannot know what an encouragement it was to him to hear the wondrous words of Scripture come echoing through the babble of whimpering, whispering demons! Now, by and by, the morning broke behind him and brought new hope to Christian's heart. Said he, "Ah! Praise God! He has turned the shadow of death into the brightness of morning!"

Then Christian looked back and beheld by sight that which he had passed through by faith. He saw that the ditch on the one hand was much deeper and more slippery than he ever imagined. Yea, here and there, vultures feasted on many a floating body. Moreover, the bank was so steep, that, had he stepped aside to avoid the sounds of rushing chariots, he could never have clambered back onto the path. On the other side, coming right up to the pathway, was the sucking quicksand of the quag in which he saw an occasional hat or glove floating. He also saw how very narrow was the way which led betwixt them both, and how one misstep should have proved his ruin. Then did he tremble as he realized that the reality was much worse than the anticipation.

But also, to his joy, he saw the hobgoblins and satyrs and dragons of the pit, not as the great and powerful monsters they had personated in the night, but as they really were in the light of day; that is to say, nothing but shadowy vapors and hissy whisperings that began to evaporate in the sunbeams of truth. Then Christian glorified God saying, "Praises be to God, for 'He discovereth deep things out of darkness, and bringeth out to light the shadow of death.'"

As Christian looked back on everything from which God had delivered him, his heart was deeply moved. In fact, so touched was he that the springs of his head were loosed, and tears began to stream

The Valley of the Shadow of Death

down his cheeks. Then said he again, "Ah, greatly to be praised is the Lord my Rock! Greatly to be praised!"

Then Christian turned westward to look before him and saw that the path that lay ahead was even more dangerous than that which lay behind. Yea, a thousandfold more dangerous! As he looked, he saw here and there, left and right, before and behind, a path that was set full of snares, traps, gins, and nets. Moreover the light of the sun also showed the path to be so full of pits, dead-falls, and treacherous steps that, had it been dark, he must surely have perished away. Then Christian could not help but once again lift up his voice, saying, "Praise Him again, for 'His candle shineth on my head, and by His light I go through darkness!' Blessings be to God."

In the light, therefore, he most carefully picked his way among the wires, triggers, and pitfalls that were laid for him.

Now I saw in my dream that at the end of the Valley of Death lay much blood and ashes, and many bones and mangled bodies of men. These were the remains of pilgrims that had gone this way formerly, and 'tis likely from these remains that the valley takes its name. At first, I could see no reason for so much slaughter here, and I was puzzled as to what had been its cause. Then I espied, a little farther off, a cave where two giants, Pope and Pagan, had dwelt in times of old. "Aha!" said I to myself. "'Twas by their power and tyranny that the men whose blood, bones, bodies, and ashes I have seen were put to death."

Then I began to fear for Christian's life but soon saw that there was no need. For, at the time of Christian's passage, the giant Pagan had been sick nigh unto death for many a season and so was totally harmless. Furthermore, the giant Pope had also lost most of his former power and could only sit in his cave's mouth gnashing upon pilgrims with toothless gums and shouting threats after them, saying, "You heretics will never mend your ways till more of you be burned. And although you think me to be weak now, the day is coming when my deadly wound shall be healed and all the world shall wonder after me again. Then shall I show you pilgrims what I can do!"

But Christian remained silent and keeping his eye fast upon the light, passed by without hurt.

Passes Pope without much danger

CHAPTER FIVE

NOW CHRISTIAN had not gone much farther **on his way** when he saw Faithful before him upon his journey. So he called out to him saying, "Ho! Brother Faithful! Wait up and I will be your companion!"

"Nay!" Faithful shouted over his shoulder slackening his pace not one whit. "I cannot stop! The avenger of blood is behind me, and I am fleeing for my life!"

Then Christian foolishly allowed "old self" to rise up and be offended. So he redoubled his pace and was not long in catching up with Faithful, who smiled and saluted him. But Christian would not so much as look upon him but rather huffed and puffed right on past him. At this outstanding feat of athletic endurance Christian felt more than a little proud. So he turned him about with that leering grin that so often attends victory. He would let Faithful know that this was no ordinary pilgrim that he had spurned in the darkness. But as you may have learned, it is hard to guard your future while gloating over your past. And this truth Christian also discovered as his toe caught under the root of a pride bush and sent him rattling backwards to the ground. Now his fall landed him with such force between a rock and a hard place that his armor was jammed hard betwixt them. Indeed, he was stuck so fast that all his reaching and pushing, grunting and groaning did little more than make him look like a red-faced turtle stuck on his back. Finally he realized that, try as he might, there would be neither rising nor turning until some kindly hand should come offer him help. Soon Faithful came up to him and gazed gently down upon his helpless companion. As Christian willingly confessed his foolish pride, Faithful forgivingly and gently pried him loose from his stony prison. Then I saw in my dream, that they went on lovingly together and gave God glory by offering praise for all His great deeds on their behalf.

"Ah, dear Faithful," began Christian. "You cannot know how glad I am to have such agreeable company."

"As am I. I had wanted to accompany you from the beginning, but you got too much the head start on me."

"Oh? How long did you stay after I left?"

"Ah, till I could stay no longer," he sighed. "For it became the talk of the town that our city would soon be burned to the ground."

"What? The talk of the town?"

"Oh yes. For a time it was on everyone's tongue."

"And are you the only one to have escaped?" asked Christian incredulously.

"Aye, for although they all talked of the coming destruction, they did not truly believe it. They lived their lives just as they had done before and caused their children to look upon them as hypocrites. After the first fears had worn off I even heard some of them call your pilgrimage the 'desperate journey of a brain-sick lunatic.' But I believed in verity, and therefore have I come on pilgrimage."

"Did you see anything of Pliable?" asked Christian intently.

"Oh yes! We heard that he had followed you as far as the Slough of Despond, and all the mud caked upon his face certainly agreed with the talk. But he would not confess to having so much as left the village."

"Hmmm," said Christian sadly. "And how goes it with him now?"

"Poorly," said Faithful solemnly. "He is greatly despised and looked upon with disgust. Yea, he can scarce find enough work to feed himself."

"But why is everyone against him, seeing that they are in agreement with him?"

"Probably because he only agrees with them because he is too weak to do otherwise."

"Tsk, tsk, tsk," said Christian, shaking his head. "Then he has behaved according to the proverb."

"Proverb?"

"Yes. The one that says: 'The dog is turned again to his vomit and the sow that was washed to her wallowing in the mire.'"

"Ah," nodded Faithful, "'tis a true saying, as are the words of Jesus."

"Which ones?"

"Those telling us that when a man turns back from his pilgrimage, his lot is seven times worse than if he had not begun."

Christian meets Faithful who helps him up.

"Ah, indeed."

"And," added Faithful, "this is certainly true of poor Pliable."

"Well, let us talk of things more pleasant. How about you? How has your journey gone thus far?"

"Well," he began, "I profited from your mishap at the Slough of Despond and by keeping my eyes on the light, was able to cross over nearly dry shod. But shortly thereafter I met with a most lovely young lady."

"Oh?" puzzled Christian, having no recollection of any such person along his way. "A fellow pilgrim?"

"Nay, but rather a denizen dwelling offside one of the many byways," he said with disdain. "Her name, as I remember, was Wanton, and she was like to have been the death of me."

"Ah, indeed!" nodded Christian grimly. "I'll wager that 'twas she who nearly seduced Joseph and who put him into prison when he gave her the back. Oh, dear Faithful! 'Tis only by God's grace that you escaped the snare of that fowler!"

"Aye, indeed," he agreed, nodding solemnly. "I tell you, Christian! You cannot dream what a flattering tongue she had. She ran up to me and caught me and between kisses told me that she had been seeking me for a long time."

"Pah!" snorted Christian wryly. "Looking for anything that wore trousers, she meant. But do go on. How did God deliver you?"

"Well," Faithful went on, "then she purred and snuggled in close and looked up at me with painted eyes and told me that her bed was decked with coverings of tapestry and made up with fine linen brought with her from Egypt."

"Aha! From Egypt was she! Then it was that slithery serpent that sought to encoil Joseph!"

"Aye, it must have been," agreed Faithful. "Next she told me that her bed was perfumed with myrrh and aloes and cinnamon."

"Just like the whore of Proverbs 7!" exclaimed Christian.

"Aye," he nodded, growing a bit queasy at the memory, "just like. Then she invited me to stay and take my fill of love until the morning. Indeed, with all her flattery and fair speech, she almost caused me to yield."

"How was it then that God delivered you?" asked Christian earnestly.

"Well," said Faithful, mopping a bit of cold sweat from his brow, "just when I needed it most, God flashed into my mind the Scripture that says: 'Her house inclineth unto death, and her paths unto the dead. None that go unto her return again, neither take they hold of the paths of life.'"

"'Tis a true saying!"

"Aye!" he answered, shuddering slightly at the thought of his near escape. "And as soon as I heard it in my mind, I knew that I must instantly act or forever lose my life. So I said unto her, 'Get thee behind me, Satan! Thou shalt worship the Lord thy God, and Him only shalt thou serve!'"

"Ah! Bravo! Bravo!" cried Christian proudly. "What a brave use of the Sword of the Spirit! Then what did she do?"

"Why, you cannot believe the change! You would have thought I had uncovered a face full of leprosy the way she pushed away with an evil oath. Her lovely face twisted and became like the tortured face of a demon! And the siren strains of the seductress turned to the rasping curses of an angry harlot."

"Ah," smiled Christian knowingly, "so you got a look at her true colors, did you?"

"Aye," he agreed grimly. "All her beauty and talks of love were only bait upon a hook. And had I swallowed, she would have torn my flesh and pierced my soul."

"Aye, or worse! So did you see any more of her?"

"No. But as I was ascending the hill toward the wicket gate, I chanced to look back. As I did, I saw her enter a red-hued cottage that nestled tight against Beelzebub's castle. Then I saw something that set my blood to running cold."

"What was it?" asked Christian eagerly.

"By her back door I saw an iron gate set into the side of a hill. Even from a distance I could see smoke and vaporous fumes creeping out from around its edges, and who knows where it might lead to."

"Down to hell!" exclaimed Christian emphatically. "That's where! She is the one that destroyed the children of Israel at Kadesh Barnea, just as they were about to pass into the Promised Land."

"Aye. So do I believe."

"And she is also the one that brought Samson into his blindness," continued Christian.

"Aye. She has been the death of many a pilgrim."

"Truly it was only by God's grace that you escaped her," said Christian. "'Twas good that you had lodged said Scripture verse in your mind, for certainly if it had not been there, God could not have called it to your remembrance."

"Aye," agreed Faithful. "Glad I am to have learned it as a child."

"But tell me," asked Christian, "was that the worst of your encounters, or did you meet with other assaults as you came on your way?"

"Oh, indeed I did. When I was coming up to the foot of the hill called Difficulty, I met with a very aged gentleman who spoke with me thus:

"Greetings, gentle pilgrim," said the old fellow warmly. "Whence from and whither bound?"

"I be traveling from the city of Destruction to the Celestial City," I answered.

"Ah," smiled the old fellow congenially. "You look to be a right, honest fellow. Come dwell with me and I shall pay you good wages. Very good wages."

Then the old gentlemen took me by the arm as if to lead me down toward his home. But I gently, and yet firmly, resisted him saying, "Nay, not quite so quickly, sir. First I need to learn more of you. What be your name?"

"Does it really matter?"

"It might. How are you called?"

"Mmm," muttered the old fellow. "Uh . . . er . . . uh . . . Adam. Adam the First."

"Hmmm," said I, a bit suspiciously. "And where do you dwell?"

Then old Adam smiled me a toothless grin and, pointing back over my shoulder, said, "Over there. Down in yonder lovely town called Deceit."

"Oh?" said I, even more suspiciously. "And what is your work?"

At this, the old gentlemen cackled and nearly bent over double with mirth. Then, finally regaining partial composure, he said, "Ah, 'tis hardly work at all, lad! Heh, heh. Hardly work at all. For you see, my job is simply to indulge myself in many worldly delights. Then I writes me a little worldly paper once or twice a year to advise my worldly readers about which delights are most delightful."

"Indeed! It sounds like a rather pleasant occupation."

"Oh, it is!" he said with a merry bob of his head and a wink of his eye. "It is indeed! And you can rest assured that my house is well stocked with some of the finest dainties this world has to offer."

"Really? And what wages do you pay?"

"Ah," said the old gent, raising his hand in a solemn oath, "if you serve me well, you may become my heir and inherit everything!"

"Hmmm. And do you have any other servants?"

At this, the old bird broke into a wide, toothless grin and bobbed his head proudly as he pointed to the front porch of a very prosperous-looking house. Seated there I saw three very elegant ladies fanning themselves and idly chatting away the day. "Oh, aye!" he answered triumphantly. "Aye indeed! See there on my front porch? Three lovelies of my own begetting."

"Hmmm. Might I perchance know any of them?" I asked, straining to see who they might be.

"Mmmm, likely so," he nodded with a mischievous grin. "Yes, yes, likely so. Mmm, let me introduce you. Girls! Girls! Roll call!"

At this, the three of them rose and gracefully approached the white rail of the porch. There they all curtsied and waved their kerchiefs gaily. Then, one by one, he called out their names.

First he called for Lust-of-the-Flesh, who blew me a kiss and with one of her lascivious gestures gave me cause to quickly avert my eyes. Seeing my reddened cheeks the old fellow winked with a lewd leer and said, "Mmm. Not quite your cup of tea, eh? Then let me introduce you to to Miss Lust-of-the-Eyes."

This daughter was much more modest. She curtsied gaily and, with a smiling sweep of the hand, made a scene to appear before my eyes that nearly took my breath away. I seemed to see the kingdoms of this world, in all their glory, pass before my eyes. The sunlight lay on templed cities, marble palaces, fertile fields, and fruit-laden vineyards. Not the slightest trace of evil was to be seen, and I saw vibrant youth celebrating harvest time with music and dance. As the enchanting scene faded, Miss Lust-of-the-Eyes smiled invitingly and, with a final curtsy, stepped back.

Next he called for Miss Pride-of-Life who was dressed as a ballerina. She too waved her hand, and I suddenly seemed to see myself as the lead actor on the world's great stages. Again, I saw myself as a great orator driving crowds of thousands to their feet in thunderous applause. Next, I saw myself as a religious leader with multitudes bowing before me and kissing my toe. Then the scene faded and the old man asked with a sly grin, "Are you impressed with my progeny, young man?"

"Yes," I had to admit. "They are quite impressive."

"Good!" he exclaimed with great gusto. "Good, good, good! You may marry her who pleases you most, or all three of them for that matter, heh, heh—and live with me forever!"

"Well, dear sir," said I with much interest, "I must admit that these three charmings certainly have an attraction for me. My natural desires seem well inclined to join themselves to you."

At this, the old man grinned broadly, bowed low, and with an expansive sweep of his fine feathered cap toward Deceit said, "Well, good then! Good! Good! Good! Come along with me."

But as the old fellow grinned up at me from the depth of his bow, his hair fell away from his forehead, and I chanced to see what appeared to be words tatooed into his forehead. Then I grew deadly serious and asked, "But wait! What do I see marked on your forehead?"

"Why, nothing I trust," said old Adam, rising quickly from his bow with one arm held over his forehead.

"Why do you cover your head with your arm?"

"No reason. N . . . no . . . no reason at all," he stammered, searching desperately for some plausible excuse. "Uh . . . 'tis just that, uh . . . the shine from yonder bright light annoys me."

"Indeed?" I inquired, now more suspicious than ever.

"Yes," continued old Adam. "Light gives me headaches—terrible, headaches—pounding, throbbing vicious headaches."

"So," said I, beginning to lay out a trap, "you're only shielding your eyes then."

"Uh . . . yes," agreed the old man nodding head and arm and looking rather foolish.

"And you're not trying to hide anything from me, are you?" I continued, beginning to draw in my net.

"Oh, no," he said emphatically, shaking head and arm side to side and looking increasingly ridiculous.

"Hmmm," said I, "then certainly you wouldn't mind lowering your arm down over your eyes that I may see your forehead."

"There be no need!" protested old Adam. "No need at all!"

"I beheld something written there," I insisted, "and I want to know what it says. So please, sir, down with your arm!"

"Oh, very well! If I must!" he snapped petulantly as he threw down his arm. "There!"

"Why, it does say something!" I exclaimed as I peered intently at the old fellow's forehead. "It says: 'Put off the' . . . please, sir, stop shaking your head! It says: 'Put off the old' . . . Sir, turn back around, please! 'Put off the old man with his deeds.'"

"Take no heed to it!" whined old Adam. "An enemy hath put it there."

"Perhaps an enemy to you," I rejoined firmly, suddenly sensing the slaughter to which I was being led, "but a friend to me. I will not follow you!"

"What!" exclaimed the old bird, feigning shocked sadness. "And why not?"

"Because God has sent a new thought burning hot into my mind."

"Thought!" snorted the old trickster. "What thought?"

"That once you get me down into your town of Deceit and firmly married to one of your delicious daughters, you will bind me about with the chains of my lusts and sell me off as a slave!"

"Wha? No! No! 'Tis a wicked thought. Put it away! Please, my son, put it away."

"Nay, but I put you away!" I commanded. "Speak no more to me for I will not even look upon your house full of dainty deceits."

"Good sir," begged the old man who by now was groveling before me, "treat me not so harshly. I am a friend!"

"Nay!" I shouted, holding firm, "but I put you behind me! And now, Adieu."

"Come back. Come back!" he begged.

"No. Never!" I said, turning to go.

Leaping to his feet, the old devil cast aside all pretense of kindness and threatened me with an evil sneer, saying, "All right then, foolish refugee! I shall send someone after you who will make the way bitter to your soul!"

"With that, dear Christian, I gave him the back. But the vile fellow reached after me and gave me such a dreadful pinch that I thought

I had left a patch of flesh between his nails. I cried out in pain, "'O wretched man!'"

"Indeed!" exclaimed Christian. "Then what?"

"Why, I turned and limped onward up the Hill Difficulty. Now, I was about halfway up and had gotten to the place where pilgrims rest . . ."

"At the small arbor?"

"Yes. I had just arrived when, glancing behind me, I saw a man rushing after me as swift as the wind."

"Go on!"

"Well, he looked strangely familiar to me so, naturally, I smiled and raised my hand to greet him, but before I could utter a word, he struck me with his fist and laid me out nearly dead."

"What! Without cause?"

"So far as I knew," said Faithful. "When I had come a little to my senses, I staggered to my feet, nursing my swollen jaw and asked, 'Good sir, why have you attacked me, a perfect stranger, so roughly?'"

"'Tis as you deserve for your secret desires to follow after Adam the First! Hah!"

"And with that, dear Christian, he pummels my chest with many deadly blows and lays me nearly dead at his feet again!"

"Had he no mercy?" asked Christian indignantly.

"Nay," answered Faithful with a shake of his head, "for when I came to my senses again I saw him standing over me with an evil and angry look. His hand was raised to strike me again, and I cried out for mercy. But he only said,

"Mercy? Hah! Mercy I know not how to show."

"And with that," said Faithful, cringing a bit at the memory, "he knocked me again!"

"How did you ever escape him?"

"I did not! And I could not!" admitted Faithful, shaking his head ruefully. "No doubt he would have beaten me to death if Someone had not come to my rescue."

"Who?" asked Christian, leaning forward eagerly.

"I could not tell at first," admitted Faithful with a shake of his head. "The attacker had his hand about my throat and was pulling back his fist to smite me again when he got a look of terror on his face and fell back. Then through the slits of my swollen eyes I beheld a large man built powerful as a carpenter. He strode up, bold as David, and drove the bully back by His mere presence. Then He planted himself squarely betwixt us."

"God sent a hero to your defense then!"

"Aye, and what a hero He was! Yea, no matter what fierce threats came from the bully, my Deliverer never so much as flinched."

"Bravo!" cried Christian. "But who was it?"

"Well, I could not tell at first," said Faithful reverently. "But as He was leaving, driving the bully before, I saw bright beams shining from His hands, His head, and His side."

"'Twas our Lord Jesus!" cheered Christian. "It must be! For His scars are His glory!"

"Aye. Verily so," nodded Faithful, his eyes nearly spilling over. "'Twas the very One whom we saw on yonder skull-shaped hill. 'Twas He who freed us from our burdens."

"Then from that," said Christian knowingly, "I can tell who it was that attacked you. It was the man named Law. He spares no one and cannot show mercy to any that transgress him."

"Aye," agreed Faithful. "Now I remember when I first met him. 'Twas a day when I was supping at my table. He pounded on my door, and when I answered, he grabbed me round the throat and told me he would burn my house down about my ears if I stayed there."

"Then for sure it was the Law! He did the same to me! And 'twas he who leapt from the pages of my little book and lashed that heavy burden to my back!"

"Aye! Had it not been for him, we would both, no doubt, still be living peacefully in the city of Destruction."

"Peacefully awaiting our death, you mean," interjected Christian. "So in reality, he did us a favor, didn't he?"

"Aye," nodded Faithful, with a grim smile, "although he certainly did it none too gently."

"Well, gentle or no, at least he did his duty as a schoolmaster. It was his showing us our need that drove us to the cross."

"Aye. Rude as he is, he does have his work."

"Well, what other adventures did you have?"

"Around noontime," recounted Faithful, "I passed the chained lions. But since the sun was high, they were both snoring loudly with flies buzzing about their twitching ears. But even if they had been awake, they would have been quite harmless since they had neither teeth nor claws."

"Aye. Paper dragons," nodded Christian with a knowing smile. "Then what?"

"Well, I came to the House of the Porter, but having no need of lodging, I descended cautiously down into the Valley of Humility."

"Did you find it slippery going?" queried Christian.

"Oh, indeed I did! And would, no doubt, have taken many a nasty fall had not a lovely lady named Discretion guided me down. When I had gotten well into the valley itself, I met with a rather gloomy-looking fellow named Discontent. He hailed me thus. . ."

"Ho there! Whither bound?"

"Off to the Celestial City," said I proudly.

"Bosh! Go back," he sneered.

"And why should I do that?" I asked in surprise.

"Because, there is neither honor nor praise to be gained by slogging through this humble and obscure valley. You have nothing to gain and all your friends to lose."

"Which friends?"

"Why, the most important ones!" he announced, surprised at my ignorance. "Namely Pride, Arrogancy, Self-Conceit, and Worldly-Glory."

"But the path to eternity leads through Humility. If I must lose their friendship to walk it, then so be it."

"But they are your closest relatives!"

"They were," I admitted, "but since I have gone on pilgrimage, they have disowned me, and I them. Therefore, we are no longer related."

At this, he was somewhat taken aback and said, "'Tis a rather stiff price to pay for the drudgery of trudging through such a lowly valley, don't you think?"

"You are all wrong. Before the mount of Honor comes the valley of Humility. From all ages the great ones of gentleness and wisdom have traveled this valley and I merely follow in their footsteps."

"Like whom?" challenged he.

"Like Moses for one," answered I, "who spent 40 years tending sheep near here. And like Jesus for another, who for many a year kept a carpenter's shop just 'round yonder bend."

Pride, Arrogancy, Self-Conceit, and Worldly-Glory—Four Kinsmen

"Bah!" he snorted. "Exceptions to the rule!"

"Nay!" I shot back, "but makers of the rule. And as for you, I must warn you that you go the wrong way—a way which will surely end in a slippery slide down to your own destruction."

"Nay. I am simply going back to my relatives."

"Aye. To such relatives as shall consume you with their endless greed for greatness. As for me, I am bound for Zion, and so, adieu."

"You'll be sorry," he called after me.

"And so did you give him the back?" asked Christian.

"Aye. What else could I do?"

"Well done," nodded Christian approvingly. "Truly there is no end to their pride of life. And was this the last person to oppose you?"

"Oh, I wish it had been," said Faithful, shaking his head ruefully. "But sad to say, I met one other whose name was Shame. He was a very tall and lanky person who clung to me so leech-like that he was like to have been the death of me. He hailed me from one of the many byways saying . . ."

"Greetings, dear Faithful."

"Same to you, sir," I answered, happy to meet a fellow pilgrim.

"And what is a fine-looking chap like you doing down here in this lowly scrub of a valley?" he asked contemptuously.

"Wha' . . . what? Why, 'tis the way to honor!"

"Ah. So I take it that you consider yourself bound to Zion."

"Aye."

Then he got an arrogant air to his carriage and said haughtily, "Don't you know that this is not the way?"

"What!" I cried. "This cannot be!"

"Ah, 'tis even so," he said with unyielding confidence.

"What proof have you?" I demanded.

"The greatest of proofs," he said, motioning first up, then down the path. "Look about you. How many others do you see trudging along this miserable way?"

"Well," I had to admit, "at this moment, none."

"Uh, huh," he continued, following up his advantage. "And how many great men have you met with since you began your pilgrimage?"

"None."

"And rich?"

"None."

"And mighty?"

"None."

"And wise?"

"None."

"There be good reason for that."

"What?" I asked, growing weary of his grating manner.

"Chiefly this," he said with a twisted smile. "'Tis because there is no such place in all the universe as this Mount Zion. You chase a green rainbow pursued only by the ignorant and foolish."

"Nay!"

"But yea!" he shot back as he stepped closer. "The only people you are like to meet on this journey are the poor, the weak, the lowly, and the ignorant."

"They are humble."

"Because they have no choice," he snapped acidly. "They have no speed of mind nor might of muscle wherein to glory. So what is left to them but to affect great humility? Then they turn about and take great pride in not being proud."

"Why, I . . . uh . . ."

"I see you to be at a loss for words," he gloated. "And well you should be," he continued, crossing his arms and stepping yet closer, "for there is no defense for your feeble position. 'Tis unscientific and foolish to think that this world was created in six literal days. And that, by nothing more than the command of some imaginary God!"

"But you did not take into account that . . ."

"Hear me out!" he interrupted, poking a bony finger into my chest. "Do hear me out!" he demanded, pushing me back a step and emphasizing his words with painful jabs. "Just ask among any who have been educated by the establishment. I assure you that you will find it slim pickings indeed to meet even one who dares entertain such foolish notions."

"Now wait just a minute!" I tried to interject.

"Aha!" he spat out victoriously as he came nose to nose and glared down at me with piercing, bloodshot eyes. "Do I perceive thee to be glowing a little reddish in the cheeks? Shame on you, whimpy pilgrim! Your anger shows my words to be true."

"Nay! Not so!"

"Aye! Verily so!" he shouted, his pyorrheic breath directed straight into my upturned face, "for if there were such a God as you believe in, He would at least have power enough to keep your spirit from boiling over!"

"He does," I answered quietly (by God's grace), "or else I would have crowned you by now!"

"Awww. Tsk, tsk, tsk," he mocked. "What a shame that you are under the control of another and can no longer do what you would."

"Nay," I continued, "but rather lucky for you that the 'Spirit warreth against the flesh.' For I tell you true, sir, that before becoming a pilgrim I was a man of strong passions and would have bent your nose long ere this!"

"Awww," sneered he. "What a shame that mere words from the lips of some foolish preacher can make you repent of imaginary wrongs! And what a shame that you must go around to all of your neighbors to make right those imaginary wrongs!"

"'Tis a joyful duty for a pilgrim to make right all known wrongs," I countered.

"Nay!" he answered contemptuously, pushing me back with another painful jab of his long forefinger. "'Tis only a false humility in which the weak-minded take great pride."

"Nay!" I returned, standing my ground (to my great pain and to his greater surprise).

"Yea!" he snarled, right into my face. (If I recollect correctly, dear Christian, he had swollen reddish gums, crooked yellow teeth, and a couple of decayed molars). "Your strict standards have separated you from many a fine and great man," he continued. "And why? Why just because you happen to see them indulge a few little faults such as spending a bit of time at the ale house, or swearing by the Christ, or doing some other petty nothing."

"They are not petty nothings in God's eyes!" I answered firmly, still standing my ground.

"Bah!" he snorted, glowering down at me with both hands on his hips. "God has no eyes."

At this, I felt a holy boldness and after taking a deep breath, I stepped right up to him and said softly, nose to nose and eye to eye, "It is becoming clear to me that you have forced me to a point of decision."

"Between what?" he sneered, trying to maintain his advantage.

"Between the mockings of science falsely so-called and the Word of God," I said, advancing a step and unbalancing him.

"Between wisdom and foolish imaginations, you mean," he snapped contemptuously, giving back a step.

"Nay!" said I boldly as I commandeered another step, "but between life and death. And it is my decision that the worst foolishness of God is wiser than the best wisdom of men. Therefore I will believe God's way to be best even though all the so-called great men of the world be against it."

"Foolishness!" he sputtered, now on the defensive.

"'Spiritual things are spiritually discerned,'" quoted I, "and I perceive that you are spiritually blind!"

"What! Do you begin to revile me?"

"Nay! But I speak the Word of God concerning you."

At this he winced and made as if to cover his ears.

"Therefore, since God prefers that we believe His Word rather than the idle speculations of so-called scientific men, I will believe Him."

"Unscientific!"

"And since God prefers a tender conscience," I continued, "I will not violate mine."

"Bah! Womanish," he sneered.

"And since God calls them wise who become as fools for the Kingdom of Heaven, I will gladly be called a fool by thee and wise by He."

"'Tis foolishness! All foolishness!" he managed to stammer.

"So say you," said I, firmly walking forward into his continued retreat. "But, seeing that you are spiritually 'blind, and wretched, poor and naked,' your words have no weight with me! The fact is that they serve to confirm the truth of the Word of God, which says that . . . 'in the last days men shall be lovers of their own selves, covetous, boasters, proud, blasphemers, disobedient to parents, unthankful, unholy, false accusers, fierce, despisers of those that are good,' and many other things which you and your so-called great men do fulfill!"

"Such insult! Shame on you!"

"Such truth!" I shot back undaunted. "Therefore, since the poorest disciple of Christ is richer than the wealthiest king, and since the most foolish of His children are wiser than your greatest philosophers, I say unto you, Shame, depart!"

At this, Shame stopped his retreat, grasped my collar with both hands, and with his homely face bent down over mine, growled threateningly, "I must inform you, dear Faithful, that Shame is a most difficult one to leave behind."

"Away!" I commanded, trying to break his grip and get up-wind of his noxious breath.

"Nay!" he sneered, clinging tenaciously against my struggles.

"Must I call out against you the Word of God?" I challenged, "or will you go peaceably?"

"All right! All right!" he screeched, as bony fingers unclenched and thrust me back. "Have it your way, foolish pilgrim," he continued more quietly, but with bitter scorn dripping acidly from every word. "I shall depart for a time and a season. But I shall never be far from your ear. The voice of Shame thou shalt ever hear. Fare thee poor!"

"And so did he actually leave you?" asked Christian, who had hung entranced upon every word.

"Aye, finally," nodded Faithful, visibly wearied by the mere recitation of his encounter. "But only after I had greatly exercised my faith and brought out the Word of God against him. When he finally departed, God did give me a verse, which I spoke thus:

The trials that those men do meet withal,
That are obedient to the heavenly call,
Are manifold, and suited to the flesh,
And come, and come, and come again afresh,
That now, or some time else, we by them may
Be taken, overcome, and cast away.
O, let the pilgrims, let the pilgrims then,
Be vigilant and quit themselves like men!"

"Ah, my brother," said Christian thankfully. "I am glad that you showed such courage against that villain. He will, no doubt, dog our steps all the way to the Kingdom and try to make us ashamed of that which is good."

"Aye," nodded Faithful, "I fear we have not seen the last of him."

"But at least we can take comfort in the words of Solomon."

"Which ones?"

"Those that say, 'The wise shall inherit glory, but shame shall be the promotion of fools.'"

"Ah, 'tis a worthy saying. And should he be bold enough to show his face again, we shall more quickly cast against him the Word of God!"

"Aye. But do tell, did you meet any others along the way?"

"Nay, but I had sunshine all the way. And even through the darkness of the Valley of Death I felt the presence of God's Holy Spirit. But do tell, what adventures have you had along the way?"

Then did Christian recount all that had befallen him on his journey.

After this, I saw in my dream that Faithful chanced to cast a glance behind them where, at some distance, he saw a man walking. He was a tall man who was much better looking at a distance than when seen close at hand. Upon seeing him, Faithful called out, saying, "Ho, friend! Where off to? Perchance to the Heavenly Country?"

"Why, verily I am," answered the man merrily.

"Why then, come catch up that we may have your good company."

Then Christian said softly, "Caution, dear Faithful. I think that . . ."

"With a very good will shall I be your companion," interrupted the man, trotting up eagerly. "A very good will indeed. Indeed, with a very good will."

"Come, friend," said Faithful with a smile, "let us talk about our Saviour or something else worthy of our time."

Talkative

"Oh!" exclaimed the man, clapping his hands joyfully. "So happy I am to hear you speak thus. So very happy!"

"Good."

"There be so few along this way that choose to discourse upon serious spiritual matters and this is such a vexation to my spirit. Oh, such a vexation!"

"I can see it would be," agreed Faithful. "For what could be more worthy of our conversation than the things of God?"

"Oh! I like you wonderfully well, for your speech is so full of conviction, and the beauty of it is that there are so many things upon which we may profitably discourse!"

"Ah, that is true. And to be profited by such topics should be our goal."

"That's what I just said!" quipped the man.

"Yes and . . ."

"Furthermore, ahem, ahem," he interrupted with a strained smile, "furthermore, by good conversation we may learn the great promises and consolations of the Gospel. In addition, we may see how to refute false opinions, how to vindicate the truth, and how to instruct the ignorant."

"Ah," agreed Faithful. "I am very glad to hear these things from you."

"Why, thank you!" he said doffing his wide-brimmed hat and smiling cordially. Then his countenance fell as he solemnly replaced his hat and said, "Alas! 'Tis because of the rarity of such talk that so few understand the need of faith and the role of a work of grace in their soul in order to inherit eternal life."

"But if I may say so," put in Faithful, "such heavenly knowledge is the gift of God. No man can come to it by mere talk."

"Aye," agreed the man with a nod, "that I do know right well. And I could give you a hundred Scriptures for the proof!"

"Well then, seeing that we agree so well, what shall we talk about?"

"Oh, of whatever you will," grinned the man with an expansive gesture. "I will discourse of things heavenly or things earthly; things moral or things evangelical; things sacred or things profane; things past or things prophetic; things foreign or things near at hand; things more essential or things circumstantial. Provided . . . provided, of course, that all is done to our profit! So! What shall we talk about?"

Now Faithful, a bit overwhelmed by the vast array of choices, decided to seek counsel of Christian.

"Uh, just one moment while I ask counsel of my companion here."

"Very wise of you," nodded the man, grinning broadly and folding his hands piously together. "'In a multitude of counselors,' you know . . ."

"Brother Christian!" exclaimed Faithful, "do you see what a brave companion we have discovered here? Surely this man will make a very excellent pilgrim." When Christian responded with a wry smile, Faithful was puzzled and asked quietly, "What's wrong? Why do you smile so strangely?"

Then Christian motioned for Faithful to come close before saying softly, "This man with whom you are so impressed will do nothing but beguile you."

"What? Do you know him?"

"Yea," he nodded. "Better than he knows himself."

"Pray tell then, who is he?"

"His name is Talkative. He is the son of a man named Say-well with whom he lives on Prating Row."

"What!" exclaimed Faithful loudly.

"Shhh," whispered Christian, finger to his lips.

"What!" asked Faithful more quietly. "This man is Talkative from Prating Row?"

"Aye. This man is happy for any company and content with any conversation. As he cheerfully discusses religion today, he will as eagerly compare the girls at the dance hall tomorrow."

"Indeed?" said Faithful, still in shock.

"Yea. In fact, the more rum he pours into his crown, the more nonsense he rolls off his tongue. Religion has no real place in his heart, or house, or conversation."

"Well," said Faithful in amazement, stealing a furtive glance at their fellow traveler, "I would never have guessed it. I have been quite deceived by him."

"As have many," nodded Christian, casting a quick look at the man who, catching his eye, waved gaily. Christian nodded courteously but continued softly, "He is one of them that 'Say and do not.' He talks freely of prayer, of repentance, of faith, and of the new birth; but talking of them is all he knows."

"Tell me more," whispered Faithful.

"His heart knows nothing of prayer or repentance for sin, and his house is totally void of religion."

"Verily? Are you sure?"

"Aye. To all that know him he is a stain on, a reproach to, and the shame of true religion."

"My!" exclaimed Faithful under his breath. "Then he has surely caused the loss of many souls!"

"Aye. And unless God stops him, he shall stumble many more."

"Then he is a hypocrite!"

"Nay, but rather deceived. He knows not that in the judgment, God will look for fruit rather than mere talk of fruit."

"Then it is this man that Paul had in mind when he spoke of sounding brass and tinkling cymbals," deduced Faithful.

"Aye. By mere words he shall never earn a place in heaven, though he seem to speak with the tongue and voice of an angel."

"Is there any hope of converting him?"

Talkative at home

"Nay," answered Christian, casting another quick glance toward the object of their conversation. Again the man caught his eye and spread his hands as if to ask impatiently, "Well?" Christian held up a finger to indicate "just a moment" and continued, "Nay, he knows so much Scripture that he considers everyone else a fool and so cannot be taught."

"Then it would be a waste of time to hear all his empty words. How shall we free ourselves of him? I don't want to be rude."

"There is no need for that."

"How then?"

"Simply speak to him about the practical power of religion on his own heart. I'll guarantee that he'll lose interest right off."

"Well, that's easy enough," whispered Faithful. "I'll give it the try."

"I shall pray God to give you wisdom," said Christian softly as Faithful turned to Talkative, saying, "Well, sir. Back I am."

"Welcome," said Talkative with thinly veiled irritation. "But what took so long? We could have been deep into some lively conversation by now."

"Well, better late than never, I always say," said Faithful cheerily. "Let us go at it now, if you will."

"But of course," snipped Talkative. "Do you have a question for me?"

"Oh yes, many."

"Good!" exclaimed Talkative, crossing his arms and smiling confidently. "Ask me anything. Anything!"

"Answer me this, then. How may a man know when the saving grace of God is actually in his heart?"

"Well, uh . . . ahem . . ." stammered the man, a bit taken aback, "a, uh . . . heh, heh, a very good question, to be sure. To be sure, a very good question. And I, uh . . . answer you thusly: First, when the grace of God is in the heart, it causeth a great outcry against sin! Second . . ."

"Hold just a moment."

"Huh?" gawked the man, stunned at being interrupted so early on his voyage into eloquence.

"Wouldn't it be better to say that it shows itself by causing the soul to hate its sin?"

"Crying out against and hating! Hating and crying out against! What's the difference?"

"Oh, a great deal. I have heard many a man cry out against the evils of drink while stumbling home from the ale house."

"Hmmm," muttered the man under his breath, impatient to be getting on with his oration.

"Potiphar's wife," continued Faithful, "could cry out against Joseph with a loud voice as if pure as the driven snow; but just the same, she was quite willing to have him to her chamber."

"Bah!" grumbled the man. "You are picking at straws."

"Nay, just setting things straight. But do go on."

"Thank you," snipped the man tersely, relieved to once again have the reins in his hands. "The second evidence of grace in the heart is great knowledge of gospel mysteries!"

"Do hold up again," interjected Faithful once more, "for this is not needfully so."

"Eh? Wha . . .?" stuttered the man, stunned at Faithful's audacity.

"Yes. For a man may possess all knowledge and yet be as nothing if he hath not charity."

"Straws, my good man. You be catching at details again."

"I think not. I certainly agree that we have need of knowledge, but it is our acting upon our knowledge that shows us to be true Christians. To know without doing is the same as not knowing at all. As James has said: 'faith without works is dead.'"

"Hmmm."

"A man may know like an angel and live like a demon. Therefore, your sign is not true. As King David said, 'Give me understanding and I shall keep Thy law; yea, I shall observe it with my whole heart.'"

"Well!" snapped Talkative curtly. "'Tis obvious that I value knowledge much more highly than you!"

"Not so. I value it as greatly as you, if it be accompanied by action. But do go on. Give another sign to show that the work of grace is in the heart."

"Not I, thank you!" declined Talkative bluntly, "for no matter what I say, you catch at straws!"

"Then may I?"

"I care not."

Then answered Faithful, "The work of grace shows itself to a man thusly: first, there comes upon him great conviction of sin and the certainty of damnation unless he finds mercy by faith in Jesus Christ; then there comes a hungering and thirsting for righteousness—which appetites are fulfilled by Christ."

"Ummm-hmmm," intoned Talkative, staring blankly out across the field.

"And in proportion to the strength or weakness of his faith in his Saviour, so are his joy and peace; so is his love for holiness; so are his desires to know Him more; and so is his determination to serve Him well in this world."

Then Talkative stopped dead in his tracks, jabbed both hands onto his hips, and challenged, "And uh . . . how does grace in the heart show itself to others?"

"By confessing his faith in Christ."

"Aha!" brightened Talkative, feeling himself once again on vantage ground. "By talking, you mean!"

"Aye," agreed Faithful, making Talkative's face shine all the brighter. "And more," he continued (which once again drew a dark cloud over Talkative's countenance).

"More!" snorted Talkative. "What more?"

"Much more!" declared Faithful. "Such as by a life that agrees with the talk. That is, a life of holiness. Not by talk only, such as an hypocrite or talkative person might do, but by a practical submission of the life to the Word of God."

"Hmmm," murmured Talkative, once again staring over the field with a dour expression.

"Do you have any objections to what I have said?"

"Hmmm . . . no," murmured Talkative. "I suppose not. Carry on."

"Then, with your permission, I have a second question to pose to you."

"Ah, very good!" responded Talkative brightly, glad to change the topic. "I love to answer questions. Yes, yes, questions I love to answer. Go on. Do go on."

Then Faithful grew serious, and fixing his eyes on Talkative, said kindly, "Tell me, friend Talkative . . ."

"Hold, hold," interrupted Talkative. "I have not told you my name. How do you know it?"

"Oh, you are quite famous in these parts," announced Faithful. "My companion here told me all about you."

"Famous, you say?" crowed Talkative with an expansive grin. "Well, what do you know about that! Famous. Heh, heh. Oh, uh . . . excuse me. You had a question, didn't you. Well, do go on. I love to answer questions. Questions I love to answer." Then, under his breath, he said to himself, "Hmmph, famous he said. Fancy that. Even knew my name. My, my! Heh, heh, heh."

"As I was about to ask, friend Talkative," continued Faithful earnestly, "have you experienced the work of grace in your heart?"

Then was Talkative taken quite aback and stammered, "Wha . . . Why . . . uh . . . ahem."

"And does your life and conversation testify thereto?"

"Er, uh . . . ahem . . . ahem . . ." stammered Talkative, at a loss for words for the first time in his life.

"Or is your religion found more in your words than in your life? Answer me an honest answer I pray, for to call oneself righteous when life and neighbors testify otherwise is a great wickedness."

Then Talkative drew himself up to his full height and answered haughtily, "You have begun to meddle in things of private experience and conscience, which things I was not planning to discuss. I do not feel bound to answer you in these private matters of the heart, and so shall not!"

"As you choose," said Faithful pursuing the matter no farther for the moment.

After a few moments, Talkative broke the silence saying, "But tell me, why do you ask such personal, probing questions?"

"Well," answered Faithful with a matter-of-fact shrug of his shoulders, "you seemed so eager to talk about religion that I thought I might see if it was mere outer talk or true inner experience."

Then Talkative bristled, crossed his arms tightly, and with narrowed eyes asked tersely, "And . . . have . . . you . . . come . . . to . . . any . . . conclusions?"

"Not yet. But so far I have heard nothing to belie the things I have heard about you."

"Things!" snarled Talkative, bristling like a hedgehog. "What things?"

"That you are a man whose religion is long on talk and short on walk."

"What!" hissed Talkative angrily.

"People say you are a dark stain upon the Christian name and that some have already stumbled at your wicked ways, with many more in the same danger."

"Why the nerve!" exploded Talkative, his face livid with anger.

"They say also that you regard your religion with no more affection than you show for the alehouse—that your religion is on an equal footing with covetousness, uncleanness, swearing, lying, and vain company-keeping."

"Well! This is an insult!" exploded Talkative, the veins beginning to protrude in his neck. "A grave insult!"

Faithful, undaunted by his companion's explosive reaction, sent his shaft of truth deeper home yet, saying, "Not only that, but there is a proverb widely gone about regarding you."

Talkative in the alehouse

"Proverb!" screeched Talkative, beginning to tremble with rage. "What proverb?"

"'Tis the proverb spoken of the whore which says: 'As the whore is a shame to all true women; so is Talkative a shame to all true Christians.'"

"Well!" hissed Talkative, feigning great indignity at such cruel slanders. "Since you are so eager to believe any lie that floats into your ear, and so quick to make rash judgments, I must conclude that you are some kind of peevish or melancholy fellow, not fit to converse with a Christian gentleman, and so, I must bid you adieu!"

With that, he turned up his nose, spun on his heel and stalked off, turning the air blue with bitter words not fit to set before the eyes of gentle readers such as you.

"But wait!" Faithful called after the fast-retreating form. "There is much profitable conversation to be had."

"Not with the likes of you!" shot back Talkative over his shoulder. "Adieu!"

"Well, good Christian," said Faithful, a bit sadly, "there he goes."

"Aye. What did I tell you? Your words and his lusts could not see eye to eye, so he would rather part with your company than with his sins."

"Indeed. But do you think we should call him back?"

Christian shook his head sadly and answered, "Nay. Let him go. The apostle has said: 'From such withdraw thyself,' but he has saved us the trouble. Besides, 'tis his loss, more than ours."

"Yes, I suppose you are right," agreed Faithful ruefully, "but I am glad to have had this opportunity to witness to him, for it may come to his mind again someday. And at least I have dealt faithfully with him and so am free of his blood."

"Oh," chuckled Christian with a merry twinkle to his eye, "you did indeed speak straight on with him." Then, growing serious once again, he added, "Something which is seldom done in this age."

"Aye," agreed Faithful. "And I'll wager that this is the reason for so much sin in the church. And this is what makes religion to stink in the nostrils of those who pass by."

"Aye," nodded Christian. "Too many debauched and wicked talkers are allowed into the fellowship of the godly. And these hypocrites confuse the watching world, put a stain upon Christianity, and grieve the sincere. Oh, if only ministers were as true to deal with sinners as you have been. Then they would either change their ways or find the company of saints too hot for them."

"Say!" exclaimed Faithful. "I've just had a poem come popping into my head!"

"Oh, really? Let me hear it."

Then Faithful spoke in a verse, thusly:

"How talkative at first lifts up his plumes!
How bravely doth he speak! How he presumes
To drive down all before him! But so soon
As Faithful talks of heart work, like the moon
That's past the full, into the wane he goes;
And so will all but he who heart work knows."

Now Christian and Faithful were traveling through a long and weary wilderness. But because of their lively conversation and warm fellowship, the time passed easily for them until they found themselves nearly at its end. At this point, Faithful again chanced to cast his eye behind him and espied one coming after them.

CHAPTER SIX

CHRISTIAN! LOOK!" exclaimed Faithful excitedly. "Be that who I think it is?"

"Why, yes!" agreed Christian with joy. "'Tis my good friend Evangelist!"

"I thought so!" cried Faithful happily.

"Do you know him too?"

"Oh, aye! Very well. 'Twas he who rescued me from the law and set me in the way to the wicket gate."

By now Evangelist was approaching them wearing a broad smile and saying warmly, "Peace to you, dearly beloved."

"Welcome!" cried Christian, giving Evangelist a manly embrace. Then he stood back a bit, holding Evangelist by the shoulders and saying, with heartfelt emotion, "Welcome indeed, my good Evangelist! The sight of your face reminds me of all your acts of love and unwearied labors for my eternal good."

"Aye!" agreed Faithful as he too embraced the missionary firmly. "And a thousand times welcome again! Oh, how we poor pilgrims desire your good company, dear Evangelist!"

Then Evangelist looked lovingly upon them and said, "Do tell, my little children, how have things gone with you since our last farewell?"

Then Christian and Faithful rehearsed to him all the difficulties and trials that had beset them along the way, to which he answered, "Ah! Wonderful! Wonderful! Although I am not happy to have had you meet with such fierce trials, I do rejoice that you have gotten the victory by the faith of Jesus. And I am proud that in spite of your many weaknesses, you have continued along in the way to this very day."

"Oh, 'twas only by the grace of God," confessed Faithful.

"Aye," agreed Christian emphatically, "for truly the spirit is willing but the flesh is weak."

"But," warned Evangelist solemnly, "bear well in mind that the race is won only by them that endure unto the end. You are not yet

184 ◆ PILGRIM'S PROGRESS

out of gunshot of the devil. And though your trials have been fierce, you have not yet 'resisted unto blood, striving against sin.' Therefore, keep the Kingdom always before you and believe steadfastly concerning things that are invisible."

"We shall, dear Evangelist," pledged Christian firmly. "We shall!"

"And do not trust to your own hearts for 'they are deceitful above all things, and desperately wicked.' Set your faces like a flint toward the City, and you shall have all power in heaven and earth on your part. And now, farewell."

So Evangelist turned to go. But before he had gone even half a pace, Faithful ran 'round before him and, kneeling at his feet, pleaded, "Good Evangelist, wait!"

By now Christian had gotten to his side and taking hold of the pastor's arm, entreated him, saying, "Please, dear Evangelist, don't leave us yet."

"No, don't," entreated Faithful. "Stay awhile and tell us about things that lie ahead, for we know that you are a prophet."

"And what would you learn of me?" asked Evangelist, testing the depths of their desire.

"About trials and tribulations yet to come," said Christian.

"And how we may successfully resist them," added Faithful.

Then was Evangelist glad to have such sincere students and readily yielded to their earnest desires, saying, "You have learned the secret, haven't you?"

"Which secret?" queried Christian.

"That 'it is a part of God's plan to grant us in answer to the prayer of faith that which He would not otherwise bestow.'"

"Well, I've never heard it put into such eloquent words," said Faithful, "but Jesus did say that 'you have not because you ask not.'"

"Very well. Had you not asked, you would not have received. But since you have asked, it shall be given you. Hear me well," he commanded with upraised hand.

"Say on," said Christian reverently, "for we are eager to hear."

"My sons, you have heard that you must 'through many tribulations enter into the kingdom of heaven,' and that 'in every city bonds and afflictions await you.'"

"Aye," nodded Faithful, "some we have met with already."

"You will soon come to a town," continued the prophet, "where you will be fiercely beset with enemies more hateful and temptations more vicious than any you have met heretofore. And in that town one, or both of you, must seal your testimony with his blood."

At this saying, Christian looked upon Faithful with a lump in his throat before saying, "A fearful thought, dear Evangelist!"

"Aye," nodded Evangelist gravely. "But be thou faithful unto death, and the King of Glory will give thee a crown of life. And take comfort in the thought that, though his pain be great, he that shall die there will be better off than his brother."

"How so?" asked Christian sincerely.

"First, because it will seem as only a moment from his death to his resurrection; and second, because he shall escape many miseries that the other will surely meet on the rest of his journey."

"Then I could almost wish that I might be the martyr."

"As could I," agreed Faithful.

"God will choose for you. Only acquit yourselves like men and 'commit the keeping of your souls to God in well-doing as unto a faithful Creator.' And now, let us press on toward the place."

So I saw in my dream that when they came out of the wilderness, they saw a town before them. The name of that town is Vanity, and at the town there is a fair kept called Vanity Fair. That fair is kept open all the year long and is called by that name because the town where it is found is altogether lighter than vanity. It is also called Vanity Fair because everything sold or bought therein is vanity. This place is a living example of the words of the wise one that said: "All that cometh is vanity." Now, as they approached the place, they could hear the sounds of laughter, sharp bargaining, clinking coins, animals, children, machines, music, fighting, arguing, applause, and the many other sounds of the Fair.

Then asked Faithful, "What be all this hubbub I hear? Is there a riot?"

"Nay," replied Evangelist. "'Tis only the normal day-sound of Vanity Fair."

"Ah," he nodded. "I have heard me of this place."

"It seems to be quite a busy place," observed Christian.

"And so it is," agreed Evangelist. "Here are sold houses, lands, trades, places, honors, preferments, titles, countries, kingdoms, lusts, and pleasures."

"Oh, my!" exclaimed Faithful. "All of that?"

"More than that," said Evangelist grimly.

"More? Really?"

"Aye. Here also you will see merchandised delights of all sorts, such as whores, bawds, wives, husbands, children, masters, servants, lives, blood, bodies, souls, silver, gold, pearls, precious stones, and what not."

Amazed, Christian commented, "Quite an impressive list, dear Evangelist. But I trust that you have now come to the end of it."

"Nay, but 'twas just the beginning. Here, at any time of the day or night, you can see jugglings, cheats, games, plays, fools, apes, knaves, and rogues of every kind. Here too are to be seen, without price of admission, thefts, murders, adulteries, false swearers, and those all of a blood-red color."

"Well," said Faithful decisively, "since none of these things will help speed us toward the Golden City, I say that we avoid them altogether by going around this modern Sodom."

"And I second the thought," agreed Christian. "Tell us, dear Evangelist, which way to the path that leads around this moral pigsty?"

"There is no path around Vanity," said Evangelist gravely.

"What!" exclaimed Faithful. "No way 'round?"

"Nay, none. All who would reach the Celestial City must pass this way for this city lies squarely in the path to life."

"But why did the Master of the way lay the path through this place?" puzzled Christian.

"Ah, a common question. But 'twas not His doing."

"Whose then?" asked Faithful.

"'Twas nearly 6,000 years ago that Beelzebub, Apollyon, and Legion noticed that all pilgrims must needs travel through this narrow valley. Therefore did those demons establish this modern Babylon, square in the pathway, that they might thereby ensnare pilgrims."

"Hmmm," murmured Faithful as he scanned the cliffs on either side of them. "These mountains do seem impassable. And you are certain that there are no hidden goat trails or secret caverns?"

"Nay, none. He that would go round this town must find a way to sprout wings."

"Then have all pilgrims passed through this city?" asked Christian.

"Aye. The most famous of them being the Prince of princes Himself. Beelzebub did personally walk Him all the way through this town and invited him to buy of his vanities. When our Lord bravely declined to shell out even one penny, the fiend took Him from street to street and showed Him all the kingdoms of the world. Then, having shown our Prince his very best, he offered them all to Him if he would only bow the knee and do him reverence."

"Aye," said Christian proudly. "But He would not even feast His eyes on the beautiful sight of rich fields and vineyards, of grand palaces and gardens. He turned away from the sight of beautiful young men and maidens who would have served His every whim and instead struck the demon back with the sword of Scripture!"

"I perceive you know the story well," smiled Evangelist approvingly. "Yes, He knew that it was all a lying bribe, and He passed clear through this town spending neither cent nor second upon its vanities!"

"And so did set us a noble example!" affirmed Christian respectfully.

"Which I intend to follow with my whole heart," vowed Faithful.

"Well, now is our chance," noted Christian grimly, "for we are at the edge of the town. Will you go through with us, dear Evangelist?"

"Nay, for there is a price upon my head in this place. But I be off to seek more souls. God be with thee," said Evangelist as he turned to go.

"Farewell, dear Evangelist," said Faithful, sad to see him depart.

"The Lord prosper thee!" added Christian.

"So I believe He shall," smiled Evangelist. "And now, adieu."

With that, Evangelist turned him back toward the wilderness of this world to seek those honest souls (such as you and I) who might have a yearning to go on pilgrimage.

"Well," said Faithful, setting his jaw and looking straight before, "I move that we pass through as quickly as possible."

"And I second your motion," agreed Christian. "Forward!"

And so they strode straight into the town and looking neither to one side or the other, pushed their way straight on through, intending by so doing to shorten their time of temptation and also to remain as inconspicuous as possible. But they failed to take into account that, in this town, there are none who look straight before. None who move forward with determined purpose. And certainly none dressed in fine linen garments and armed with such brave armor. Therefore, although intending the opposite, they presented quite a singular spectacle and began to attract no little attention.

At first it was simply the cessation of idle chatter and the turning of admiring heads as they passed. Then, there was a small crowd of children and curiosity seekers who began to tag along behind them, laughing and giggling among themselves. "So far so good," they thought, and they were nearly halfway through before their troubles began.

It all started when a hard-faced real estate agent saw them pass by his colorful billboards without so much as a sideways glance. Now the ad man had assured him that no red-blooded man in his right body could pass them by without a second take. But here were two men in the prime of life striding by without a glance and he determined to know the weak link in his sensual advertising. Therefore he called out after them saying, "Ho now, men! Whither away with such haste?"

Then a shopper in the booth next door noticed their unusual garb and asked, "And why dressed in such white and shining linen?"

Upon hearing this, the portly proprietress of the fabric store across the lane bustled out to see, and, spotting their amazing garments, cried out, "Why, indeed! 'Tis unlike any fabric I've seen traded in this fair. How much will you sell it for, lads?"

"It's not for sale," murmured Faithful quietly, trying to ignore the interruptions and keep moving.

"Tee, hee," tittered the proprietress, her ample body jiggling in sympathy with her merriment. "'Not for sale,' he says! Nonsense," she snorted. "Everything is for sale in Vanity—at the right price! Just you name it, gents."

Then Christian's gleaming accoutrements caught the envious eye of a blacksmith who came up to admire the fine finish on his suit, saying, "Say, chap. Why dressed in such fine shining armor? Do you expect to meet with a dragon or two on the way? Ha! Ha! Ha!"

"We be bound for Zion's golden gates," said Faithful, impatient of delay, and eagerly seeking a path through the swelling tide of faces.

"Did you hear?" cried the realtor, misunderstanding their words. "They're miners for gold."

Then a jeweler, understanding them to be investors in precious metals, said greedily, "Gold! Tush! The price is the lowest ever. Wouldn't you rather have pearls? I sell some of the finest!"

Vanity Fair

"Nay," said Christian, hoping to steer the conversation aright, "but we seek the Pearl of great price."

"What! And what's wrong with my husband's pearls that you won't even turn in to look?" cried the jeweler's wife, offended that they should regard her husband's wares as cheap.

Then Faithful tried to set things straight by saying loudly, "Please let us pass, dear people. We are bound for a better land!"

"'Better Land,' you say?" cried the realtor gleefully. "Why, that's the name of my realty company, and better land is our specialty! Come, lads. 'Tis a buyer's market this time of year, and the interest rates are the lowest ever!"

"Nay," returned Faithful, "for I seek a better country whose maker and builder is God."

"Bah! What rubbish can you talk!" shouted the realtor. "All the world was made by God."

"Nay," said Faithful again. "We are not looking to buy anything here."

"What?" cried an indignant shop keeper. "Are not the wares of this fair good enough for you?"

"We are not looking for wares of any sort," injected Christian. "We seek to buy the truth."

At this, a minister of the social gospel perked up his ears, and, seeing potential for two more tithepayers, said piously, "Truth, do you say? Why, that's what I sell in my church."

"You do?" asked Faithful with some interest.

"Why, of course," he beamed broadly. "Services are just beginning, and you may come sample my wares—free and without obligation, of course. Without obligation and free."

"And of what persuasion are they?" inquired Christian.

"Why, any you wish," he said proudly. "We have Romish truth, Protestant truth, Eastern truth . . ."

"What about Jesus?" asked Faithful, a bit puzzled.

"Oh, heh, heh. Jesus truth. But of course!" said the minister, a bit chagrined. "How stupid of me to forget one of our greatest masters."

"But wait!" protested Christian. "There is only one Truth. All others be thieves and robbers."

"Well!" huffed the minister of the church universal. "Did you hear, everybody? He just called the better part of our people thieves and robbers!"

"Oh!" exclaimed the indignant realtor, "so my realty office is a den of thieves, is it?"

"And I suppose all my pearl salesmen must needs fall under the same condemnation," said the jeweler, sensing the swelling of a trend and hoping to catch a ride on the wave of popular sentiment.

"All I meant to say is that Jesus is the Way, the Truth, and the Life," said Faithful earnestly. "We must follow Him if we would be saved."

"Bah! There are many roads that lead home. How did you come to be a judge over us?" pontificated the minister.

"I say we box their ears!" shouted the realtor.

"Nay!" hooted the bejeweled shopper sarcastically. "'Tis too good for them! Hang them in the gibbet!"

"A den of thieves indeed!" the jeweler exclaimed. "You'll hear from my lawyer about this! Best you prepare for a lawsuit for slander!"

"Unless yonder mob does them in first," said the realtor with a wicked grin. Looking down the main street of the fair, Christian and

Faithful saw a rowdy mob of knaves and villains already deep into their cups and working themselves into an evil temper. Then said Christian, under his breath, "Things look not good for us here, dear Faithful. Best we be on our way."

"Aye," agreed Faithful. "Let us hurry on."

"What?" hissed the minister, blocking their way. "Away so soon?"

"Nay, but stay!" urged the realtor, grinning maliciously as he unfolded a plot plan of the local cemetery. "I have just the piece of real estate you deserve. 'Tis about six feet long, and I will give it to you free of charge!"

"Nay! We cannot stay, for we be bound for Mount Zion," urged Christian.

"Aha! Bound for Zion, are you?" scowled the angry minister. "So! By that I take you to infer that we who dwell here are not bound for Zion!"

"Nay! But rather for hell?" shouted the shopper.

"What!" snorted the portly proprietress, with a jiggle of her jowls. "They want to send us all packing off to hell?"

"Supreme insult!" screamed the jeweler, above the rumble of the gathering mob. "Stone them!"

"No!" squawked the jiggly lady. "To the inquisitors with them. For all we know, they be spies sent to sound out the land!"

"Spies?" asked one.

"Did you hear?" cried another. "Spies from an enemy land!" Now before one word of defense could be spoken, like a row of tumbling dominoes, the word spread quick as fire in the stubble. The city had been "invaded by spies, saboteurs, and molesters of children!"

Not realizing the futility of ever turning the tide, Faithful made a foolish attempt at the impossible, saying, "We be no spies, but faithful men bound on pilgrimage."

"Yes," cried Christian. "We are only passing through."

"What!" squawked the wealthy shopper. "Only passing through? Well! By that you infer that this town is not good enough for you!"

"And therefore, that the people in it are not good enough for you," added the proprietress with an offended quiver.

Then the realtor roared indignantly, "How dare you bring your fear-mongering insults into this peaceful town and stir up my poor wife. If you ask me, you deserve not to pass through alive!"

"Give them over to the mob!" screamed the jeweler.

"Here! Here!" bellowed the leader of the mob, pausing a moment from his self-appointed task of passing out clubs and staves.

"Nay, wait!" interceded the minister. "First take them to the basement of my cathedral. There we have instruments wherewith to draw out the truth."

"Please, good people," entreated Christian, "let us pass through. We mean no harm."

"Aha!" cried the minister. "He has just admitted that we are all good people!"

"Which proves all your former charges against us to be false," called out the jeweler. "Which means that we do indeed have a case against you in court."

"Aye, a case indeed!" declared the shopper. "And there'll be no passing through this town without paying for your crimes."

"Aye," glowered the realtor, nose to nosing it with Faithful. "I'll sell you a six-by-two yet."

"Hah! If there be any pieces left to bury," sneered the jeweler. "Here comes a right fierce mob of ruffians."

Then were Christian and Faithful beset before and behind by a mob of derelicts and drunkards. But first and foremost in the fray were the ladies and gentlemen of the town.

"So!" roared the realtor, picking up a handful of dust and throwing it into the air above them, "a den of thieves, are we? Hah!"

"Ministers of a false gospel, are we?" screamed the minister, neck veins bulging.

"So you have the only true way, have you?" bellowed the jeweler, wielding his finely-carved walking stick. "Take that!"

"Ow!" cried Christian, painfully.

"And that!" added the minister, taking a swing at Faithful with his pinecone-studded staff of office.

"Ooomph!" puffed Faithful, taking a vicious blow to his belly.

"And that again!" snarled the realtor, as another handful of dirt followed the first into their faces.

"Vile refuse!" screamed the shopper.

"Pull out his beard!" jiggled the proprietress viciously.

"Bring on the scourge!" called the jeweler.

"Nay!" argued the minister, wringing his hands gleefully. "Stretch them on my rack first."

"Send for the executioner!" raged the proprietress, her deep-set eyes glaring red with hatred.

"Set up the stake!" shouted the town woodcutter. "Four cords'll bring'm to ashes."

"Nay!" argued the shopper sadistically. "Burning be too gentle for such as these. Bring on the Clydesdales 'n ropes."

Then, just as it seemed that Faithful and Christian would be torn limb from limb, the magistrate of the town came striding round the corner. Upon seeing the melee, he immediately dispatched his men into the midst of the mob. So the officers pushed their way into the surging tide of humanity, all the while shouting threats and loudly banging clubs, maces, and swords against their shields as a warning to the mobsters. This diverted the attention of the mob long enough for the magistrate to climb onto the jeweler's display case where he shouted, commandingly, "Here! Here! Silence! All of you! There is a court of law in this fine town. If you have charges to bring against these men, there is due process to go through!"

Upon hearing this, the mob protested loudly, crying, "Nooo!" "Booo!" "Crush the wretches!" and other such like nonsense. This they did, not because they had any good reason (for not one in a hundred knew what he was shouting about), but rather because it was quite an adventurous way to trifle away another boring day in Vanity.

But at long last, the magistrate succeeded in quieting the mob long enough to ask, "Now, now! Quiet down! What is all this uproar about?"

"They be murderers!" shouted the realtor, shaking his dusty fist in the air.

"And thieves!" screamed the shopper.

"Liars!" bellowed the jeweler, raising his cane to the sky.

"Cheats!" spluttered the proprietress, quivering in red-eyed anger.

"Robbers of the poor!" threw in the realtor again.

"Deceivers!" hissed the jeweler, gnashing his teeth.

"False prophets!" snarled the minister with venomous hatred.

At this, the magistrate cried, "Stop! Stop! Stop! Surely these men cannot be all so bad as that. Why, I have not seen such a foul one as you describe since we crucified the Prince of thieves, down yonder trail."

"Nay," protested the jeweler, "but they are followers of that very One."

"Aye!" agreed the realtor. "Trained by His own Spirit and brought hither by that vile one named Evangelist!"

Upon hearing this, the magistrate's face took on a serious expression, and he looked upon the men with no friendly gaze. "Hmmm," said he most gravely. "This could be more serious than I thought at first. Dear sirs, I must frankly inform you that if you are truly followers of that vile deceiver and insurrectionist from Galilee, I doubt there is any way I can save you. But being a noble and just ruler of this principality, I shall appoint an impartial commission to study out your case and then bring you to fair trial. Uh . . . who will serve as unbiased commissioners for me?"

"I," volunteered the dusty realtor, with a malevolent grin.

"And I," growled the jeweler with curled lip and eyes narrowed to angry slits.

"I will serve," offered the minister, affecting his most pious and pastorly manner.

"Good, dear pastor," said the magistrate with an approving smile. "And seeing that this uproar seems to have a religious overtone to it, may I appoint you to be chairman of the commission?"

At this, the minister bowed low and said humbly, "You honor your humble servant, sire. Rest assured that we will, uh . . . pull out the truth . . . by one means or another."

"But surely we need the softening influence of the fairer sex, don't you think?" asked the magistrate.

"A good idea," blurted the realtor. "May I nominate my wife?"

"Will my lady accept the nomination?" asked the magistrate.

At this, the proprietress of the fabric store bowed graciously, tittered a teeny titter, and said sweetly, "Oh, but of course, good sire. And may I in turn nominate my noble neighbor?"

Upon being nominated, the shopper curtsied coyly and bubbled effusively, "Oh, thank you, dear storekeeper. Thank you, kind magistrate. I would just love to help. 'Tis so important that justice be served, you know."

"Certainly," said the magistrate, encouraged by such a good show of civic responsibility. "Well, since you are all responsible members of the craftman's guild and loyal citizens of the proud town of Vanity, I can safely leave this minor matter in your good hands. Do as you see best. Only remember to do what seems right and obey the laws of Vanity. Adieu."

As the magistrate and his officers turned to go, Faithful leaned over to Christian and said in ominous tones, "I think I see hard times ahead for us, brother Christian."

"Aye," Christian agreed. "I see not how we shall escape with our lives."

"Well," said Faithful, girding up the loins of his mind, "God knows best. Our only duty is to trust and obey."

And so the men were brought to examination; and they that sat upon the council asked them again whence they came, whither they were bound, and why they chose to dress in such unusual garb. The men answered them as they had done before and concluded with a plea that they had given no cause for such an uproar. But they that were appointed to examine them would not believe them to be anything but rabble-rousers or madmen, or perhaps saboteurs who had come to put the Fair into confusion. Therefore, they took them into the village square where they beat them, besmeared them with dirt, and then put them into an iron cage that they might be a spectacle for all the men of the Fair. There, during a lull in the crowd's mockery, Christian addressed Faithful thusly:

"Ah, friend Faithful," he said painfully, "how is your courage?"

"Well," he answered soberly, "to judge by appearances—not good."

"My thoughts as well," nodded Christian.

"But," continued Faithful hopefully, "to judge by the Word of Him that cannot lie, we have great cause for joy."

"How so?"

"In that we are counted worthy to share with Him in His sufferings."

"Aye, 'tis true," agreed Christian, regaining courage that had momentarily flagged. "I have heard it said that 'of all the gifts that

Christian and Hopeful in the cage of Vanity Fair

heaven can bestow upon men, fellowship with Christ in His sufferings is the most weighty trust and the highest honor.' Therefore, let us determine to keep our faces turned toward the cross that by beholding we may become changed."

"Amen!" said Faithful, encouraged to see Christian display such resolve. "And thus shall we be enabled to behave ourselves as befits His children."

Then the realtor, having a momentary lull in business, sauntered up to the front of the cage and in his most cordial manner said, "Top of the morning to you, lads. Do you find your accommodations to be comfortable?"

"Greetings, good Realtor," answered Faithful, as pleasantly as he could.

At this, the realtor took great offense, and pointing an accusing finger at Faithful, burst out saying, "Now, don't you go calling me 'good' when you don't believe a single word of it!"

"He was only returning a polite greeting," explained Christian meekly.

"Oh!" snarled the realtor, rearing back, hands on hips and eyes glaring. "And by that I understand you to say that it is I who should be blamed! Then here," he yelled, reaching down into the slime (slurp), "perhaps a handful of mud will mend your rude manners! (splat) And here (slurp), have some more!"(splat)

Now, as the realtor was reaching for his third glob of goo, a man named Hopeful drew alongside and said, "Good day."

"Huh? Oh, greetings, Hopeful," said the realtor, picking up some especially slimy mud. (slurp)

"I say, dear Realtor," said Hopeful, eyeing the mucky missile with concern, "why are you treating these helpless prisoners so roughly?"

"Because," the realtor grumbled, eyeing his targets expectantly, "they continually and purposely add insult to injury."

"From everything I have seen of them, they are nothing but men of peace who simply seek to pass through our town unmolested," protested Hopeful. "They have neither said nor done anything to warrant such foul treatment at our hands."

"What!" groused the realtor, fixing his angry glare upon Hopeful. "Are you also deceived? Can any good thing come out of the city of Destruction?"

"It seems to me the answer to that lies in their gentle manner and kind words," replied Hopeful, not noticing the approach of the minister behind him.

"Ahem," said the man of the cloth politely.

"Oh," said Hopeful respectfully. "Good day, Reverend."

"I could not but help overhear your conversation, gentlemen," he said with a thin smile.

"Good," snorted the realtor, his muddy hand weighing the heft of its oozing glob. "Then you can give us your professional opinion of the matter."

"Dear Hopeful," began the minister kindly, "don't you understand that in defending these base men you turn the finger of accusation upon us?"

"That certainly was not my intention, dear pastor," began Hopeful apologetically. "I was only . . ."

"Ah, ah, ah," interrupted the minister a bit curtly, both hands raised with head cocked forward and to one side, "intentional or no, the effect is precisely the same! An impartial panel of noble citizens have found these men to be insurrectionists and plotters of the worst sort!"

"I cannot believe this to be true!" responded Hopeful earnestly. "These men are quiet and sober and do not return evil for evil, but rather blessing. There are many that trade here in the Fair who are far more deserving of punishment than these men."

Then the realtor, with angry eyes glaring out from under bushy eyebrows, pushed his way forward, dripping glop of mud in hand, and snarled, "You do not yet understand the true issue here, friend! A man may be a foul and base opium fiend and yet, having found his place in Vanity, may cause no real harm. Those who abhor his ways avoid him while those who seek for escape seek him out and enter his smoky den."

"Those vile dealers in death are ravaging the very flower of our youth!" exclaimed Hopeful indignantly. "It is they who should be put in the cage rather than this sort."

"No, Hopeful," growled the realtor, unconsciously hefting the glob of slimy mud menacingly. "You still do not understand me! These men, by their very presence, threaten to upset the balance of nature. By their kind words and loving deeds they put even the best of us Vanitarians to shame! This causes guilt, and fear, anger, and insult. People begin to argue over their message, and therefore they are divisive!"

"Their message is full of hope!" cried Hopeful.

"There! There, you see!" groused the minister grimly. "They are divisive. Here, you and I, men who only yesterday were closest friends, are divided."

"Only because you are dealing with these men unjustly," protested Hopeful.

"So!" exploded the black-frocked minister, eyes glowering and a bead of perspiration springing to his brow. "Now you have joined them in their false charges! You, who should know better, are fast becoming more worthy of punishment than they!"

At this, Faithful, not willing that friends should be parted asunder on his account, said, "Good sir. Do not seek to defend us. Our God will stand by our side."

"Nay," answered Hopeful, now more indignant than ever, "but I intend that justice shall be done here!"

"As do I!" vowed a man named Honest who had come up in the midst of the latest exchange.

Ignoring Honest's interruption, the minister stepped up to Hopeful and hatefully hissed, "By your last statement, foolish Hopeful, you have called me unjust. Therefore do I strike you! Take that!" (slap)

"Unjust and unworthy minister of the gospel!" cried an infuriated Honest. "This calls for my staff upon your crown!" (thump)

"Ow!" cried the minister, now sporting a throbbing goose-egg on his bald pate. "Violent knave! Take that in return!" he said, taking a swing at Honest with his staff. This Honest easily avoided with a swift duck, only to catch a face full of the realtor's glop upon standing again.

"Ow!" he cried, eyes blinded.

Then the minister cried out for all the town to hear, "Hopeful and Honest have turned traitor! Down with the heretics!"

"What!" cried the Jeweler as he came trotting up. "Hopeful and Honest traitors? Why, the villains!"

"Knaves!" cried the stout lady, waddling up at full steam and puffing like a dragon. "Hang them all in the gibbet!"

"Irreligious wretches!" screamed the minister as he took another ill-aimed swing at Hopeful with his crosier.

"Into the mud with them!" cried the shopper.

"Put them in the pillory!" shouted the jeweler.

"'Tis too good for them!" snorted the realtor, searching about for some fresh mud. (slurp) "They are worse than those in the cage. Take that!" (splat)

"Ow!" cried Hopeful, as a glop of mud struck him full broadside on his face, nearly knocking him off his feet. At this moment the magistrate chanced to arrive with his men, and seeing another riot, cried out, "Ho! What be the cause of this new uproar?"

"Look and see!" cried the minister, pointing to Christian and Faithful, who sat meekly in their chains.

With hands on hips and face all in a scowl, the magistrate came strutting up to the bars of the cage where, with scarcely contained fury, he bellowed out, "Aha! So! 'Tis the men in the cage, eh? It appears that you have not yet learned your lesson, gentlemen. Even from within your cage you continue to cause riot and revolution. Well, perhaps a few bloody stripes from the scourge will take the edge off your rebellious spirit. Sergeant!"

"Sir!" shouted the sergeant, crisping to attention and snapping off a sharp salute.

"Beat these knaves without mercy and then hang irons upon what is left of them," commanded the magistrate.

"Yes, sir!" replied the sergeant, stepping forward with his heavy ring of keys. As he entered the cage and opened their leg irons, he muttered grimly under his breath, "This is gonna hurt you a lot more than it will me, boys. Should'a kept yer fool mouths shut!" Then, yanking each of them to their feet, he shoved them unceremoniously out of the cage and stood them before the magistrate, who said sternly, "If you will not respond to kindness and gentleness, then perhaps more rigorous measures will arrest your attention. You may proceed, sergeant!"

"Come on, knaves," ordered the sergeant, grabbing Faithful by the scruff of the neck. "To the post with you!"

"But these men are not worthy of stripes," protested Hopeful.

"Nay," agreed Honest, "but rather of honor!"

At this, the magistrate growled menacingly, "Best you cease these deceitful words, lads, lest we hang you beside them. The cat has nine tails, you know."

And so they beat them within an inch of their lives and hung irons upon them. Then they led them in chains up and down the Fair to strike terror into the heart of any who might dare to speak in their behalf or join themselves unto them. But Christian and Faithful behaved themselves with such wisdom and received their abuse with so much meekness and patience that it won to their side several more men of the Fair. This threw the princes and rulers of Vanity into such a storming rage as to make them conclude that neither cage, nor irons, nor torture could silence the witness of these two men. Some began to wish that they had merely allowed these two strangers to pass quietly through as they had wished to do in the beginning. But what was, was what was. Therefore, they were forced to conclude that only death could atone for the damage done in deluding the men of Vanity Fair. So the men were returned to the cage with their feet fast in stocks until the town could make ready to have a trial by jury.

There Christian and Faithful sat all alone in the dark. In the dark woods behind them they could hear the doleful sounds of the night

Then they led them in chains up and down the Fair. . .

creatures hooting and howling, whimpering and whining. For some time they sat in silence, hungry, thirsty, cold, and beaten raw. At last, Christian said painfully, "Ah, dear Faithful. How goes it with you?"

"Ugghh," he moaned. "I feel the full strength of David's words in the Psalms."

"Which?" queried Christian.

"The ones that describe Jesus saying: 'Truly I can tell all my bones, I have given my back to the smiters and they have plucked out the beard.'"

"Ah . . ." answered Christian with a nod that stretched the wounds on his neck, making him wince and cry out, "Ooohh. Ouch! It is the same with me. Every time I move, it causes more pain . . . Ah! . . . and yet, if I try to hold still, there is even greater pain."

"But surely we have great cause to rejoice in that the Lord Jesus has given us grace to behave ourselves as He would have done," encouraged Faithful.

"Aye! Indeed," agreed Christian. "I never felt His presence so near as when the scourge . . . aauugh! . . . was tearing my back."

"And we have good reason to rejoice because Hopeful and Honest and many more besides are studying the Words of Life because of our example," rejoiced Faithful.

"Aye," rejoiced Christian as the warm glow in his soul eclipsed the pain of his stripes. "I have great hopes that they may soon join us on pilgrimage."

"You know," said Faithful, smiling in the darkness, "the words of the ancient martyr really are true."

"Which ones?" puzzled Christian.

"When he said, 'The blood of martyrs is seed. The more of us you mow down, the more of us that spring up.'"

"Ahh! Aye, true indeed," responded Christian, careful to avoid the pain of nodding. "And we are more privileged than they in that we can already see a harvest of souls springing forth from the ashes of our afflictions."

"'Which are light and but for a moment,'" Faithful reminded Christian, who agreed and then began to quote a verse of Scripture, saying, "'My brethren, count it all joy when ye fall into divers temptations; knowing this: that the trying of your faith worketh patience.

But let patience have her perfect work, that ye may be perfect and entire, wanting nothing.'"

"Ah, blessed words from our brother James," said Faithful, his heart warmed by the power of the Word.

"Aye," agreed Christian. After a period of awkward silence, he asked the question that hung heavy on both hearts. "Do tell, my brother Faithful, which of us do you suppose will spill his lifeblood on this field of battle?"

"I could certainly hope for such an honor," said Faithful sincerely, "but I suppose that it shall be you, for you are more able to bear it than I."

"Truly," said Christian hopefully, "I would covet such a glorious fate as that. But sometimes 'tis easier to die than to fight on. Only God knows which path will bring most honor to His name."

"Aye," nodded Faithful stiffly.

"Only let us commit the keeping of our souls into the hands of Him who knows best and does well," Christian concluded.

Now I saw in my dream, that a convenient time having finally come, the people of Vanity hauled them into the courtroom to be arraigned. The judge's name was Lord Hate-good. His place was occupied by a high-backed, padded throne of a chair, ornately carved with all manner of occult symbols and decorations. The seat, lower back, and arm rests were all covered in fine scarlet velvet. The armrests curved forward and terminated in sculpted, claw-like hands that held polished marble globes. Behind him, high and exalted, rose the crest of Vanity wreathed with a carved wooden banner bearing the words that were the guiding force for the laws of Vanity. It said "Eat, drink, and be merry, for tomorrow we die." The judge himself wore a black, silken robe fringed with gold. The generous collar and cuffs were lined with white ermine. His head was covered with a black leather skullcap that gave him the appearance of being bald. His jaw was set, his mouth tight, and his eyes were deep-set pools of simmering anger. As he entered in regal majesty, all the court stood until he should be seated behind his large oak desk. He nodded arrogantly to the lawyers, witnesses, jurors, and observers and then, after seating himself, began the trial by asking for the indictment.

Lord Hate-good

"Bailiff!" he barked in a stern, high-pitched voice. "What be the charges against these men?"

Answered the bailiff, "The charges against these notable ruffians are these:

"First: that they are enemies to and disturbers of our peaceful trades.

"Second: that they have made commotions and divisions in this, our peaceful town.

"Third: that they have caused a goodly number of our citizens to align themselves with their own most divisive and dangerous opinions, and. . .

"Fourth: all of this has been done in open contempt of the laws of our prince Beelzebub."

"Hmmm," murmured the judge, his brow deeply furrowed in an angry scowl. Then, turning to the prisoners at the bar he asked, "Have either of you an answer to make?"

Then Faithful stood to his feet, albeit a bit stiffly due to his many wounds, and said, "I shall give my answer, your honor."

"Speak on," he commanded gruffly.

"My companion and I have not made any disturbance of the peace, being men of peace ourselves. As for winning men to our side, this was done by their own free choice when they beheld our truth and innocence. And I must comment, that in my opinion, they have only turned from the worse to the better."

"And what about being enemies of our Lord Beelzebub?" snarled Hate-good through clenched, tobacco-stained teeth.

"As to this lord you serve," responded Faithful boldly, "since he is Beelzebub, the enemy of the one true God, I have no choice but to defy him and all his angels."

"Did you hear?" cried out a frail, stoop-shouldered man named Envy.

"Aye! Hear I did," said another named Superstition, who nervously fingered one of his good-luck-charms. "Speaks to his own condemnation if you ask me. "

"I don't see why we gotta go through all this formality," groused a beetle-browed, barrel-chested man named Prejudice. "Let's just kill 'em."

"Yeah. Nail 'em up!" growled an ape-faced, nail-chewing man named Mr. Malice, a member of the jury.

"Order!" shouted the bailiff, pounding his gavel resoundingly.

"Booo!" complained Envy, eager to bypass all this formality and be on with the execution.

"Order!" commanded the bailiff again, pounding his gavel even more vigorously than before. "Order in the court!"

At last, order being somewhat restored (which is a rather rare thing to achieve in Vanity), the judge, Lord Hate-good, ordered the prosecutors to bring forth the witnesses. Envy was the first to eagerly raise his hand, saying, "I would speak, my Lord Hate-good."

"You may come forward, Mr. Envy," ordered the judge, with a nod.

Then, rising stiffly to his feet and approaching the witness stand, Mr. Envy said, "My lord, I have known this man a long time and I swear before this honorable bench that he is . . ."

"Hold! Hold!" interrupted the judge gruffly. "We have neglected to swear the man. Bailiff, give this man his oath."

Then the bailiff held forth a large, black book having many mystic markings engraved upon its covers. Beneath this, Envy solemnly placed his left hand as the bailiff droned, "Do you swear to tell the truth, the whole truth and nothing but the truth, as interpreted by, and as pleasing to, the Prince of Vanity?"

"But of course," he answered self-righteously. "What else is there to tell?"

"You may speak on now, friend Envy," ordered Hate-good with a nod.

"Well, sir, as I was about to say, this man Faithful, in spite of his gentle name, is one of the vilest men in our country!"

"Hear! Hear!" shouted an angry-looking fellow named Ill-will.

"Well said!" mumbled Superstition, fingering his beads.

"I don't see why we gotta go through all this formality," groused Prejudice. "These dumb trials always end up the same way anyway. So let's just kill 'em."

"Yeah!" snarled Malice. "Jus' nail 'em up!"

"Order! Silence, gentlemen," commanded Hate-good with an icy glare that quick-froze their exuberance. "You may continue, Mr. Envy."

Then said Envy, "This man has no regard for prince nor people, law nor custom, but does all he can to infect all men with his own peculiar notions of faith and holiness. Why, I myself once heard him say that Christianity and the customs of our town of Vanity were diametrically opposed, and could never be reconciled."

"Aye!" cried out Superstition, amulets held tightly in his upraised fist. "I heard that one!"

"By saying this, my lord," continued Envy with an evil glare directed at Faithful, "he not only condemns all our worthy enterprises, but all of us in the doing of them!"

"Good, Mr. Envy," said the judge with a slow nod and a hint of an evil smile. "Very good. Have you more to add?"

"Oh, much more, your honor," he said, with a slight bow. "I could go on all day. But first, let others give their testimonies, and if they miss anything, I shall fill in the blanks."

"Thank you, good Mr. Envy," said the judge politely. "You may step down."

Then they called one named Mr. Superstition, and bade him look upon the prisoner. After they sware him he began thusly: "My lord, I have no great acquaintance with this knave, nor do I desire more. However, from a short discussion that I had with him the other day, I know him to be a very pestilential fellow. At that time I heard him say that our religion was useless and one that could in no wise bring a man to please God. Now these words, my lord, necessarily lead us to the following conclusions: first, that all of our worship is in vain; second, that we are yet in our sins, and; third, that we shall all finally be damned. And this is all I have to say."

Then was a man named Pickthank sworn and bid say what he knew in behalf of their lord the king, against the prisoner at the bar.

"My lord," he began, in the style of a public orator, "and you gentlemen of the jury. This fellow I have known a long time and have heard him speak such things as ought not be spoken in this our town! He has railed on our noble lord, the prince Beelzebub, and has spoken contemptuously of most of his honorable friends."

"Names, Mr. Pickthank," droned Hate-good. "Give us names, please."

"Oh, but of course, your honor," said Pickthank. "Of course. I was just coming to that. The principal names that he has slandered are the Lord Old-man, the Lord Carnal-delight, the Lord Luxurious, the Lord Desire-of-vainglory, my dear friend Mr. Lechery, and Sir Having-greedy, along with all the rest of our nobility."

"Booo," sneered Malice.

"Ssssss," hissed Ill-will. "Down with the wretch!"

"Well said!" snapped Superstition.

"I don't see why we gotta go through all this formality," pouted Prejudice. "Let's just kill 'em."

"Yeah," mumbled Malice under his breath. "Jus' nail 'em up!"

"Order! Order!" bawled the bailiff.

"Go on! Go on!" urged the judge.

Then Pickthank, basking in his brief moment of glory, continued eagerly, "He has also said that if all men were of his mind, these noblemen would no longer be able to survive in this town."

"It sounds like a threat of murder to me," fumed the judge.

Then Pickthank turned to his right side and addressed the judge, saying, "Neither has he been afraid to rail on you, my lord."

"What!" hissed Hate-good, turning an acid eye upon Faithful.

"Aye, my lord, for he has called you an ungodly villain, among other rather unflattering terms—terms with which he has also bespattered the good names of most of the gentry of our town!"

At this, Hate-good stiffened, trembled with anger, and for a moment was speechless.

In the background Malice was heard to mutter maliciously, "He's dead meat now, boys. Get them nails!"

Then Hate-good gripped the arms of his throne so tightly that his knuckles went white and, slowly pushing himself to his feet, exclaimed bitterly, "You runagate, heretic, and traitor! Have you heard what these honest gentlemen have witnessed against you?"

"Yes," responded Faithful calmly. "But if I may speak a few words in my defense . . ."

Faithful Testifies at trial

"If the truth be known, sir," sneered the judge lowering his bony frame gingerly back onto the chair, "you deserve to live no longer but rather to be slain immediately upon the spot!"

"That's what I been sayin' all along," put in Prejudice. "Let's just kill 'em!"

"Yet," continued Hate-good, "in order that men everywhere may behold our gentleness toward you, we will hear you out, vile runagate!"

Then Faithful addressed himself to the court, beginning thusly: "Let me first answer Mr. Envy. Sir, I have never said anything but this: that any rule, or law, or custom, or person that is flat against the Word of God, is diametrically opposite to Christianity. If I have spoken amiss in this, convince me of my error from that Word and I am ready to recant. To answer Mr. Superstition. Sir, I said only this: that in the worship of God there is required a divine faith. But there can be no divine faith without a divine revelation of the will of God. Therefore, whatever is thrust into the worship of God that is not agreeable to divine revelation, cannot be done but by a human faith, which faith will not profit to eternal life. And as to what Mr. Pickthank has said. Sir, I say still that the prince of this town, with all the named attendants, are more fit for the company of devils than to be rulers over people. In this, I may have spoken a bit too bluntly, but I believe it still! May the Lord have mercy upon me!"

Then the judge, Lord Hate-good, shuddered and, trembling with rage, gave the jury their final instructions.

"Gentlemen of the jury, you see this man about whom so great an uproar has been made in this fair town. You have also heard what these worthy gentlemen have witnessed against him. Also you have heard his reply and confession. It now lies in your hearts to either dispatch him or to save his life. But yet I think it will serve our cause well to bring afresh to your minds some precedents from the ways of our law.

"You will recall that there was once an act made in the days of Pharaoh, the great servant of our prince, that, lest those of a contrary religion should multiply and grow too strong for him, their male children should be thrown into the river!

"Also, there was an edict passed in the days of Nebuchadnezzar, another of his fine servants, that whosoever would not fall down and worship his golden image should be thrown into a burning, fiery furnace.

"Once again, in the days of Darius the Great, there was a law passed that whosoever, for thirty days, should call upon any god but himself, should be cast into the den of lions.

"Now the essence of all our laws this rebel has broken, not only in thought (which is clearly against the laws of Vanity), but also in word and deed, which is obviously all the more intolerable. Therefore, since he disputes against our religion, as he has confessed, he deserves to die the death! Mr. Blindman! You may take the jury out to your deliberations. Be sure that you return a verdict that will be pleasing to the noble township of Vanity."

Then went the jury out, whose names were Mr. Blindman, Mr. No-good, Mr. Malice, Mr. Love-lust, Mr. Live-loose, Mr. Heady, Mr. High-mind, Mr. Enmity, Mr. Liar, Mr. Cruelty, Mr. Hate-light, and Mr. Implacable. These each held the private opinion that Faithful was guilty as charged and as they were polled by the foreman, Mr. Blindman, they answered him as follows:

"I see clearly that this man is an heretic!" cried Mr. Blindman, a large man, with thin, gray hair hanging down from under a black cap and reaching to a soiled, whitish collar. "What say you, Mr. No-good?"

Then Mr. No-good, a sleepy, handsome-looking chap, stifled a yawn long enough to say, "I say away with such a fellow from the earth!"

"And you, Mr. Malice?" asked the foreman, glaring out through sightless eyes.

"Aye! Away!" hissed ape face, removing his chewed to the quick fingers momentarily from his mouth, "for I hate the very look of him!"

"And you, Love-lust?"

The Jury agrees

"Hmmm?" he asked absent-mindedly, straining to peel his lecherous eyes off one of the shapely court reporters. "Oh, away! Definitely away! I could never endure him near me!" he said, as his optical tentacles once again encoiled themselves about the object of their lust.

"Mr. Live-loose?"

"Oh, dear," effeminated a pointy-nosed, debauched-looking man. "I could never bear to have him lingering about me! Oh, dear no, for his very presence would always be condemning my ways."

"And your verdict?"

"Why, I think he would look simply charming, swinging in the breeze," he said with sarcastic sweetness.

"Thank you. And you, Mr. Heady?"

Mr. Heady, a stout, short-haired commoner with a moustache and pointed beard, clenched his fist and snarled, "Hang him! Hang him! Hang him high!"

"Mr. High-mind?"

High-mind, an aristocratic-looking gent with ruffled collar, coifed hair, rosed cheeks, and manicured nails, leaned forward on his expensive walking stick and, looking down his large Roman nose, said in his most elegant accent, "A sorry scrub he is. Away with him!"

"Mr. Enmity?"

Enmity peered out from deep-set eye sockets with hateful eyes and snarled viciously from behind his hand, "Me heart doth rise against him!"

"Mr. Liar?"

Interrupted in the midst of relating a juicy tidbit to Mr. Cruelty, Liar snapped to attention and managed to mutter, "Uh, oh, a rogue! That's what he is, a rogue!"

"And your verdict, Mr. Liar?"

"Oh, whatever you wish, Mr. Blind-man. Whatever it takes to stop his lies about us. Whatever it takes. Some form of death I should suppose. Whatever."

"Mr. Cruelty?"

Then Cruelty, a devil-faced man with cropped hair, snakish eyes, pointed beard, and waxed moustache, leaned forward on his cane and snarled, "'Angin be too good for the likes uv 'im! We should 'ave him down to the torture chamber in the basement."

"Mr. Hate-light?"

Mr. Hate-light, a piggish-looking man with a hand continually raised to shield his eyes from the slightest glare, said, without looking up, "Let us dispatch him forthwith!"

"Mr. Implacable?"

Implacable sat stolidly in his robes and said icily, "Might I have all the world given to me, I could never be reconciled to the likes of him. Therefore, let us forthwith bring him in guilty and worthy of death!"

And so they did. Therefore, by command of Judge Hate-good, he was presently condemned to be put to the most cruel death that could be invented. First they scourged him, then they buffeted him, then they lanced his flesh with knives. After that, they stoned him with stones, then they pricked him with their swords, and last of all, they burned him to ashes at the stake. Faithful however, notwithstanding their evil treatment, behaved himself with utmost patience and love, even entreating God for his enemies that this thing might not be laid to their charge.

And thus came Faithful to his end. Then was their rage contained for a time by He who overrules all things, who had ordained that Christian should not fall in this place but should escape them. And so was Christian allowed to go on his way. Now as he stood, gazing upon the smouldering post where Faithful had sung his last hymn and prayed his last prayer, he spoke in verse, saying:

"Ah, dear Faithful, thou hast faithfully professed,
Unto thy Lord, with whom thou shalt be blest,
Aye, while faithless ones, with all their vain delights,
Are crying out under their hellish plights,
Thou shalt sing, Faithful, sing, for thy name shall survive;
For, though they killed thee, thou shalt be alive."

CHAPTER SEVEN

OW I SAW in my dream that Christian did not depart Vanity Fair alone. For standing by his side as he gazed pensively into Faithful's smoldering ashes was a young man whose name was Hopeful—a name he had chosen for himself because of his admiration of Christian and Faithful's courage during their sufferings at the Fair. As these two stood in that sacred place, they entered into a brotherly covenant to stand by, pray for, and encourage one another as Christian companions. Thus it was proven true that, whenever one dies for love of the truth, another rises out of his ashes to march in his stead. As the ancient martyr said, "You cannot destroy us, for our blood is seed."

"Ah, dear Hopeful," said Christian, as they set out on their way, "how it fills my heart with joy to have you as my companion."

"And a great joy it is to me to be going on pilgrimage with you, sir," returned the young man. "And I trust that Honest and Good-will and many other men of the Fair will soon follow after."

Now these two men had not gotten far off from the Fair when they overtook a man who was casually meandering on before them. This man's name was Mr. By-ends and Christian addressed him thus:

"Hail, good fellow! Whence from and whither bound?"

"Greetings, good sirs," replied By-ends pleasantly. "I hail from the city of Fair Speech, and seeing this is such a warm, sunny day, I am taking a stroll in the direction of the Celestial City."

"From Fair Speech, you say!" exclaimed Christian. "Can any good thing come from Fair Speech?"

"That you must judge for yourself," returned By-ends, slightly annoyed. "Was not the same said of Nazareth?"

"Then do tell, sir, what shall I call you?"

"Good sirs," he returned curtly, "we are perfect strangers. It is not my custom to share privileged information with just anyone. However, if you are going my way, I shall be glad to have your company. If not, I will be content to go it alone."

Hopeful joins Christian

"I have heard of this town of Fair Speech," continued Christian, still curious to learn the identity of their new companion.

"Mmmm, many have," replied By-ends proudly.

"Rumor has it that it is a wealthy place."

"Aye, 'tis indeed," he answered, with a smile and a slight bow. "In fact, I have many a rich relative there."

"Oh," answered Christian, sensing that he was coming closer to his goal. "And may I be so bold as to ask their names?"

"Certainly," replied the man, with a noticeable swelling about his chest. "Actually, I am related to nearly the entire town. But the most notable among them are these: my Lord Time-server; my Lord Fair-speech, from whose ancestors that town first took its name; also Mr. Smooth-man; Mr. Facing-both-ways; Mr. Anything; and the parson of our parish, Mr. Two-tongues, who is my uncle."

"My!" exclaimed Christian, amazed that any pride whatever could be derived from being related to such a long list of villains, "'tis quite a list you have made."

"Aye!" smiled the man proudly, mistaking Christian's shocked expression to be one of amazed admiration. "Distinguished men, every one of them. And I myself have become a gentleman of some distinction as well."

"Are you a married man?" asked Christian, continuing his probe.

"Oh, aye, to be sure!" boasted the man. "To a very virtuous woman, the daughter of a virtuous mother. She was my Lady Feigning's daughter."

"Lady Feigning, you say!" exclaimed Christian, nose hot to the trail.

"I see you to be impressed at her honorable descent," smiled the man, assuming a dignified air. "And she has built upon her heritage as well. Yea, she has attained to such a fine pitch of breeding that she can mix well with all classes, from peasant to prince."

"And are you trained in matters of religion?" Christian inquired.

"Oh, but of course!" he replied a bit pompously. "And a very important part of our lives it is too!"

"I am glad to hear that," said Christian.

"Thank you," smiled the man, tipping the edge of his broad-brimmed hat. "However, I am pleased to say, that from the stricter sort, we do seem to differ on a small point or two."

"Oh?" invited Christian. "And what are they?"

"First," he asserted, "we are wise enough never to row upstream against wind and tide. Second, we are careful to be zealous for religion only when he goes about in His silver slippers."

"Is that so?"

"Ah, yes!" smiled the man proudly, looking for all the world like a peacock strutting his feathers. "We especially love walking the street with Religion on warm sunny days, like this one. And we enjoy Him even more should He be so popular as to draw the people's applause."

"Hmmm, I see," said Christian, his worst fears now being confirmed. "Uh, please pardon me a moment while I confer with my companion here."

"Oh, but of course," agreed the man graciously, with a low bow and a sweep of his satin cape.

Then Christian stepped a little aside with his friend, Hopeful, and said under his breath, "Oh, miserable day!"

"What's wrong?" asked Hopeful, who had been rather puzzled by all of Christian's probing questions.

"By all that I have heard thus far," he confided, "I am convinced that we have stumbled into the company of a man named By-ends. If I am right, then we are walking beside as foul a knave as any in all of these parts!"

"Indeed!" exclaimed Hopeful. "Well then, ask him. It seems that he ought not be ashamed of his name."

"All right," said Christian, turning to the man. "Ahem. Sir, you talk as if you know as much or more than anyone in the world."

At this By-ends smiled and quipped, "Well, I am not freshly fallen off the cabbage cart, if that's what you mean."

"Uh . . . excuse me?"

"In plain English sir: yes, I have been around the block a time or two."

"Oh, thank you. Then, if I do not miss my mark too far, your name is Mr. By-ends of Fair-speech."

"Nay!" protested the man disdainfully. "That is not my name!"

"No?"

"No!" affirmed the man.

"No?"

"No!" snapped the man angrily. But Christian locked him in his gaze so tightly that the man's eyes had to drop. Finally he confessed, with an injured sigh, "Albeit, it is an evil nickname given to me by some that cannot bear my good company. 'Tis a cross that I must bear, I suppose."

"But have you not given men good reason to call you by this name?" probed Christian.

"No! Never!" protested By-ends. "Never! Why, the worst thing I ever did was to have the good fortune to anticipate a couple of religious trends and to earn a little spare change thereby."

"Aha! So you are the man! And from what I have heard about how you earned your 'spare change,' it seems that you deserve this name more than you be willing to confess."

"Well, if that is where your prejudice leads you, what can I say? But if you will be open-minded enough to go on with me for a few miles, you will find that I am quite pleasant to travel with."

"If you travel with us, you must go against the wind and tide," warned Christian.

"Hmmm," murmured the man. "That rather goes against some of my favorite opinions."

"So I thought. You must also confess Religion whether He hobbles about in rags or strolls abroad in his silver slippers."

"No!"

"Ah, but yes! And you must also walk beside Him whether He be hung in the pillory or carried through the streets with applause."

"Stop trying to lord it over me!" complained By-ends obstinately. "Let every man be convinced in his own mind, and let me go along with you."

"Nay! Not one step farther, unless you are willing to brave the wind and tide and to confess Religion even in rags and chains."

"I will never desert my old principles," proclaimed By-ends staunchly, "since they are both harmless to others and profitable to myself. If you will not have my good company, then I shall wait for someone who will. Therefore, adieu."

Now, I saw in my dream that Christian and Hopeful proceeded on at their former good pace while Mr. By-ends dawdled along as best suited his fancy for he was a rather rich and lazy fellow. But one of them, chancing to look back, saw three other men join themselves to Mr. By-ends. The men's names were Mr. Hold-the-world, Mr. Money-love, and Mr. Save-all. All three had been schoolfellows with Mr. By-ends, having been taught by one Mr. Gripe-man, a schoolmaster in Love-gain, a market town in Coveting County in the north. This schoolmaster had taught them the art of wealth-getting, either by violence, deceit, flattery, lying, or by putting on a guise of religion. So well had these four fellows learned their lessons that any one of them could have opened his own school in the art. Then said Mr. Money-love to Mr. By-ends, "Who are those jolly fellows up ahead of us?"

"Oh, just couple of far countrymen, off on their own private pilgrimage," he grumbled.

"Well then," exclaimed Money-love, "why don't they wait up for us that we might have their good company? Are we not all pilgrims, on this fine day, and brothers bound for the same country?"

"Fellow pilgrims, perhaps," pouted By-ends, "but brothers? Absolutely not!"

"Dear Mr. By-ends!" exclaimed Money-love. "How can this be? Please explain your meaning."

"Oh," complained By-ends dourly, "those two are so legalistic and so much in love with their own opinions that they will not keep company with any but those who agree with them."

"Indeed!" exclaimed Money-love.

"Indeed," affirmed By-ends, looking grimly up the road.

"Well, no matter," said Save-all, with a resigned air, "wherever we may go, we are sure to find some who are religious overmuch. But pray tell, sir," he continued curiously, "what were your differences?"

"Well," he began, "for one thing, these fellows are so bullheaded that they consider it their duty to press on their journey no matter what the weather while I am all for waiting till wind and tide be favorable."

"But of course!" exclaimed Hold-the-world sagely. "'Tis only good sailing sense. Why, ask any sailor. 'Sail with the tide,' they'll tell you. 'With the tide!'"

"So I told them!" proclaimed By-ends.

Money-love and friends

"What else?" inquired Money-love as he adjusted his fine ostrich-plumed hat.

"Another major difference is that they are all for making their religion the most important thing in the world while I am for securing to myself the comforts of this life. After all, did not the Lord tell us to 'abide till He come?'"

"Yes, indeed," agreed the parsimonious Save-all. "And what else, pray tell?"

"Well," said he, "they are all for holding to their belief though all the world be turned against them. But I am for religion only to the extent that it is popular to be so."

"Very wise," agreed Money-love. "'Go with the flow'—that's my motto. Is that all?"

"Yes," answered By-ends a bit gruffly, "except that they are for standing by their religion whether popular or contemptible, whether in rags or riches. But I espouse Him only when, on sunny days, He walks smooth streets in His silver slippers, wind at His back, and with good applause."

"Here! Here!" proclaimed Mr. Hold-the-world loudly. "And hold you to that opinion, good Mr. By-ends. 'Make hay while the sun shines,' I always say. 'While the sun shines, make the hay.'"

"We must be wise as serpents," proclaimed Save-all. "Does not God send both rain and sun? And if they be fools enough to slog ahead through muck and mire, at least let us be wise enough to take shelter till the sun comes again."

"Aye!" nodded By-ends. "I am in full agreement."

"Did not Abraham and Solomon grow rich and still hold to their religion?" asked Money-love, pulling out his fine gold watch to examine the time. "And did not Job say that a man should lay up gold as dust? Yes! I think so! And if God be kind enough to bestow these blessings upon us, then 'tis a sure sign that He expects us to keep and enjoy them for Him, yea?"

To this, they all beamed broadly and chorused, "Yea!"

Then By-ends proposed an entertainment saying, "Gentlemen, since we are all on this somewhat boring pilgrimage and have need of some diversion to pass the time, let me put to you a question."

"Say on," said Save-all with interest.

"Suppose a man, say perhaps a minister or a tradesman, sees before him a good opportunity to gain great riches . . ." he began.

"Ah," said Money-love, rubbing his hands together with a greedy grin. "I just love this sort of question. Go on. Do go on."

"But he also sees that he will not gain possession of these riches unless he is willing to appear very zealous over some small point of religion that before meant nothing to him."

"Hmmm," said Money-love, with deep interest. "I see your set-up, but what is your question?"

"Namely this," said By-ends. "May not a man use religion to attain his goals and yet still be counted a right honest man?"

"Ah," smiled Money-love sagaciously. "Allow me to address myself to part of your question."

"Which part, friend Money-love?" queried By-ends.

"Uh . . . about the minister."

"Ah, yes, the minister. Proceed," he invited with great gusto.

"It seems obvious to me," pontificated Money-love, "that if a minister must adapt some of his principles to gain a greater income, he may do this and yet still be called a right honest man."

"And your reasons?" challenged By-ends.

"Well, first," he began pompously, "his desire for riches is certainly very lawful since all opportunities for wealth are set before us by Providence."

"Umm, hmmm," said By-ends with an approving nod.

"Umm, hmmm," echoed Save-all and Hold-the-world.

"And second," continued Money-love, speaking as if he were Solomon himself, "in order to alter his principles intelligently, he will have to study harder. This will, of course, give him a reputation for being studious. It will also make him an open-minded preacher, able to skillfully defend any side of any issue. And last, it will adapt him for any company in any land and thus make him a better man. And all of this, gentlemen, I propose to be in keeping with the mind of God."

At this, his three auditors broke out in spontaneous applause and By-ends said enthusiastically, "Ah, well said, Money-love. Well said indeed. Do go on."

"Third," he continued confidently, "if a man is so adaptable as to be willing to abandon some of his most heartfelt convictions in order to be better accepted among his parishioners, this certainly speaks well of his self-denial and genial personality."

"Here! Here!" said they all.

Then By-ends spouted merrily, "Ah! Me likes the way you reason, Money-love. Likes it right well! And now, your conclusion?"

At this point in their journey, they came upon the stump of a great tree, which appeared to Money-love as a stage beckoning him to deliver an eloquent oration. So he nimbly hopped onto it and, clutching his fine feathered hat to his breast, began to orate his final scene, saying, "Therefore, gentlemen! (Oh, wouldn't our Professor Gripeman love to see me now?) . . ."

"Here! Here!" cheered they all.

"Therefore, gentlemen! The conclusion of the whole matter is this! Ta-da! A minister who exchanges a small thing—such as standards or principles—for a great, such as money, wife or lands, should not be judged as covetous! Mmmm, no! No No! No! But rather as wise and industrious—one who faithfully improves his talents while his Lord be away!"

"Hear! Hear!" said they all, with another rousing burst of applause. Then said Hold-the-world, "Well said, Money-love. Said well. And now may I take the stage and answer as to the propriety of a tradesman doing the same?"

"By all means, Mr. Hold-the-world," said Money-love, giving the older gentleman a hand up before springing down. "Please proceed, for I am eager to hear!"

"Well," began Hold-the-world, looking for all the world like a seasoned actor from the Globe Theatre, "suppose the tradesman under consideration be just an ordinary fellow with not much prospect of advancement by mere honest labor? Then let us suppose that, by becoming religious, he may open opportunities for working at higher wages or getting a rich wife or bringing in more and better customers to his shop. May this be lawfully done? Of course, it may be lawfully done! And for what reason may it be done lawfully? Why, it may be lawfully done for the following reasons:

"One, to become religious is a virtue, and to be virtuous is to be religious, no matter what the motivation."

"Hmmm," said By-ends, a bit uncertainly. "Virtue means religious—religious means virtuous. I think I see the circle of your reasoning, sir. Yes, yes, I get it now. My thoughts exactly! Do go on."

"Two," continued Hold-the-world, strutting to the other side of the stage, "it is not unlawful to get higher wages, or a rich wife, or more business for my shop."

"Well that's certainly true enough," nodded Money-love approvingly. "Carry on."

"Three," cried Hold-the-world, waxing warm to his conclusion, "the man becomes good, to get that which is good, from those who are good, which is good!"

"Hear! Hear!" said they all as heartily as if their talk of gain had actually tinkled coins into their purses. Then Hold-the-world concluded by saying with great conviction, "Therefore, to become religious to gain a good end is a good means. Indeed, as the 'Society of Jesus' has so aptly put it, 'The end justifies the means.'"

"Say now, gentlemen," said By-ends, tickled pink by their irrefutable logic. "Your reasoning processes are clearly void of either fault or loophole. Why not put the same question to those strait-laced fanatics up ahead and see what stuttering fools they make of themselves in their answering?"

"Hear! Hear!" they all chorused, Money-love even risking the soiling of his ostrich feather by throwing his fine hat into the air. Then, having safely caught it again, he reshaped it and placed it ceremoniously upon his head, saying, "A good idea! Yea, a splendid idea! But who shall have the pleasure of laying our question before the knaves?" he inquired.

By-ends answered saying, "I suggest Mr. Hold-the-world, since they do not know him and will thus be more off their guard. Will you do us that kindness, good sir?"

"Absolutely!" he answered with a bow. "'Twill be with great pleasure."

"Oh good!" exclaimed By-ends, eagerly rubbing his hands together. "I shall love to see those finicky fanatics squirm. Hey!" he trumpeted ahead to Christian and Hopeful. "Hail, good fellows! Wait up there!"

And so the pilgrims halted, and these four men, all decked out in their finest, fair-weather traveling attire, came puffing up. Then Christian asked, "Gentlemen, what can I do for you?"

Then answered Money-love, feigning deep respect, "Uh, my good brother here has a profound question to put to you."

"Oh?" asked Christian, surprised that such well-to-do men of the world would deign to converse with commoners.

"Yes," said Hold-the-world, glancing at his fellows with a sly wink. "And a simple one it is too. Simple, very simple."

"Being?" asked Christian, motioning for Hopeful to pray that his answer might bear the approval of heaven.

"The simple question is simply this: May not a man use religion to attain his goals and yet be a right honest man?"

At this, Christian and Hopeful looked at each other in disbelief. Then Christian answered firmly, "Why, even a babe in Christ may answer ten thousand such questions as that."

"Uh, I er, uh . . . Indeed?" stammered Hold-the-world, a bit taken aback. "Don't you, uh . . . need to think about it a bit? You know, ask your minister, consult a few commentaries, perhaps see which way the political winds are blowing? Heh, heh."

"No need for any of that when I can answer you straight from God's Word."

Hold-the-world glanced helplessly at his fellows who, unable to help in the least, refused to meet his eyes. Then he asked sheepishly, "Uh . . . God's what?"

"God's Word!" affirmed Christian. "If it is unlawful to follow Christ for loaves and fishes, how much more abominable is it to make of Him and religion a Trojan horse to get and enjoy the world! Indeed, the only ones that hold this opinion are heathen, hypocrites, devils, and witches!"

"What!" protested Hold-the-world. "Give examples," he challenged.

"Certainly. Of heathen first. Hamor and Shechem had a desire for the daughter and cattle of Jacob, and they saw that there was no way to get at them except by religion. Read of it in Genesis 34."

"Hmmm," muttered Hold-the-world, beginning to scratch at the earth with the toe of his fine, fair-weather shoe.

"And, as you may recall, they ended up quite dead for their well-planned greed. Of hypocrites second. The hypocritical Pharisees were also of this religion. Long prayers were their bait; but to steal widow's houses was their hook! And greater damnation from God will be their reward!"

Then, Hold-the-world began to loosen his fine, fair-weather collar, murmuring, "Ahem! Say, is anybody else feeling a bit warm?"

"Of devils third. Judas, possessed of a devil, was of this religion as well! He was quite religious that he might bear the bag, but to steal what was put therein was his goal. And in the end he did hang himself and was lost, cast away, and despised forever!"

Now by this time, Hold-the-world was glancing this way and that for some way of escape and saying, "Er . . . uh . . . interesting. Fascinating, actually. But I, uh . . . think it be time for us to be on our way."

"Nay, but hear me out," commanded Christian with an authority that none dared resist. "Simon the witch was also of this religion, for he would have bought the Holy Ghost that he might get money therewith. Therefore, did Peter rebuke him as being in the gall of bitterness and in the bonds of iniquity. In conclusion then, it seems obvious that he that will take up religion to gain the world will give up religion to keep the world. For you men to answer this question as you have done shows that your motivations are heathenish, hypocritical, and devilish; and your reward will be according to your works!"

"Uh, I . . . er . . . uh . . ." stammered Hold-the-world, speechless for the first time in his life.

Then, they stood there staring blankly each upon the other but had not one thought wherewith to answer Christian. Therefore did Mr. By-ends and his company halt on the way in order to let Christian and Hopeful outgo them. Then, when they were alone again, Christian said to Hopeful, "If these men cannot stand before the reasoning of mere men, what will they do under the judgment of God? And if they are silent when dealing with vessels of clay, what will they do when rebuked by the flames of devouring fire?"

Then with ease did Christian and Hopeful leave those four men of the world quite behind them, not only because of their dawdling manner of travel but also because there appeared a small cloud in the eastern sky which put them into fear of a storm. Therefore did they put in at an inn along one of the many by-ways to eat and drink and trade money back and forth among themselves, as determined by the fall of the dice.

Now, the pilgrims went on until they came to a delicate plain called Ease. Here the traveling was most easy and pleasant, but as you must know by now, plains of Ease are always rather short, and so they soon came to its end.

Now at the far side of that plain was a little hill called Lucre. It was a rather filthy place, but it had in its midst a silver mine, which many former pilgrims had turned aside to see. But as they came near to the brink of the pit, the ground, being undercut and deceitful, would often break away beneath them. Therefore, many were either killed by the fall or else terribly maimed. Only a few were able to return from their detour to the filthy hill of Lucre, and those who were able to rejoin the right way were crippled men till their dying day.

Then, I saw in my dream that a little off the road, across from the silver mine, there stood a man named Demas. He had once been a companion of the apostle Paul on his journeys but had forsaken him in favor of this present occupation. This man stood, dressed as a fine gentleman, to invite everyone to turn aside and see the rare sight of the silver mine. Now as Christian and Hopeful drew near, he addressed them thusly. "Ho, there!" he called out pleasantly. "Good sirs! Turn aside here and I shall show you a wondrous sight!"

"And what sight is so wondrous as to turn us out of the way of life?" queried Christian suspiciously.

"Why, just over the brink of this little hill there is an immensely rich silver mine."

"Oh?" answered Hopeful, eyes brightening with interest.

"Yes indeed, young man," continued Demas, encouraged by Hopeful's obvious interest, "and with but a little digging and scratching on your part, you may richly provide for all your present pleasures and future fancies."

"Come then, good Christian," proposed Hopeful. "Let us look into this timely opportunity."

"Not I, thank you," answered Christian firmly. "I have heard rumors about this place."

"Rumors! What rumors?"

"Ugly tales. Tales of pilgrims who, in turning in after their greed, have found their graves rather than their fortune."

"Bah!" snorted Demas. "Only the careless! Only the careless! But I see you to be cautious men—such ones as may safely carry away great treasures, as have others."

"Aye, we have heard of these others," said Christian brusquely. "Men who carried away so much silver that they had no strength to run their course to the end. As for me and my house, better to be a peasant who attains the Kingdom than a king who falls by the way. So thank you, but no thank you."

At this, Christian and Hopeful turned to go on their way. Then Demas cried out, "Why will you go on this miserable pilgrimage as beggars and vagabonds when you could hire porters to carry you forth on beds of ease? You'll be sorry! Especially you, young man! Very sorry!"

Then Christian turned about and said with righteous indignation, "Not so sorry as you when you shall meet with your just reward!"

"Good sir! You judge me wrongly. I am a brother with you, a son of Abraham."

"A son of Abraham, do you say? I'll warrant you are, Demas, as was Gehazi your great-grandfather, and Judas your father. And I perceive that you are following faithfully in their slithery footsteps."

"Sirs! Please! Your opinion is too stern against me!"

"Nay, but true!" cried Christian, not yielding his position one inch. "Your father was hanged for a traitor, and to gain your end you are using even more devilish pranks than he did. Therefore shall your punishment be greater than his. And be assured that when we come before the King, we will tell Him of your deceitful and cruel behavior toward His tender children. Come, Hopeful. Off with us."

And so Christian and Hopeful escaped the snare and went on their way. Then said Hopeful gratefully, "My! Dear Christian! You cannot know how glad I am for your good company. For no doubt I had turned aside were it not for your wise counsel."

"'Tis for this reason that God sends us two by two," replied Christian, "that each might uphold and strengthen the other."

"Aye," agreed Hopeful as he lifted his heart to God in thanksgiving. "I hope one day to return the favor."

"No doubt you shall."

Now Christian and his companion had not gone more than a league or two when their godly conversation was interrupted by distant screams. Stopping to listen, they thought they heard the terror-filled voices of By-ends and his companions. And such was indeed the case. For these men of the world, at the first sniff of silver, had gone scrambling up to the edge of the pit to have a look-see. Now, perhaps the brink collapsed and plunged them all to their deaths. Or maybe they managed to slide down the ropes only to be smothered by the fumes that always settle in such damp places. Or perchance, they loaded themselves so heavily with riches that they could never clamber back out again. Of the details I am not entirely certain. But this much I do know: that not one of them was ever seen in the narrow way again.

Now I saw that just on the other side of the plain, the pilgrims came to a place where there was an old monument set beside the highway. At the sight of it, they were both plunged into deep thought because of the strange posture and exquisite workmanship of the statue. Yea, they almost felt as if in the presence of someone yet alive.

"Dear Christian!" exclaimed Hopeful in awe. "What is this amazing statue?"

"I cannot tell, my brother," answered Christian quietly.

"My!" he whispered softly. "Such detailed sculpting. Why, here and there you can see even the weave of the fabric in her robe."

"Aye," agreed Christian almost reverently. "I can see the tiniest wrinkles upon her face."

"Such a sad face, my brother. See the expression of longing and sorrow in her expression? Who could this be?"

"Well, her face be turned back behind her as if she were going this direction against her will."

"Look! There be some writing above her head."

"What does it say?"

"Uh . . . I cannot tell," confessed the young man sheepishly, "for I cannot read."

"Indeed!"

"Aye," he continued sadly, "for although the schools of Vanity taught us many things, reading was not considered to be of much importance."

"Hmmm. Probably to keep you from reading the Word of God for yourselves," commented Christian dryly. "But be not cast down about it, for I shall teach you. But for now, let me try to read about this amazing person. Hmmm, time has almost erased some of the letters, but there might be enough yet to read. Re . . . remem . . . remember, remember someone's wife, it says!"

"Then this must be Lot's wife!"

"Taste see. Is it made of salt?"

"Aye! It is! It really is!"

Lot's wife

"Then this is indeed Lot's wife! My, what a timely lesson lies here for us," said Christian soberly.

"What do you mean, my brother?"

"Were we not tempted by Demas to look back into the world? And were you not inclined to follow him?" asked Christian solemnly.

"Yes," confessed Hopeful, lowering his head. "Much to my shame."

"And if we had turned aside, who knows but that we would have been made into a monument for pilgrims, just like this sorry woman was."

"And I would have deserved it," observed Hopeful, "for really there is no difference between her sin and mine."

"Except that God can read the heart's desire and is able to have mercy where it will do good. Come! Let us keep in mind this timely lesson and be on our way."

"Aye," agreed Hopeful, casting one last glance back at Mrs. Lot. "And let us always remember Lot's wife."

I saw then that they went on their way till they came to a pleasant river which David the King called "the river of God," but John, "the river of the water of life." Now the narrow way lay just along the bank of this river, and Christian and his companion walked beside it with great delight. They drank freely of the water, which they found pleasant to the taste and uplifting to their weary spirits. Moreover, there were lovely green trees on both banks of the river that bore many varieties of the most exquisite fruit. They found that even the leaves of these trees were good for medicine, and as they partook of them the aches and pains of their travels gradually began to fade away. On either side of the river were also meadows, curiously beautified with lilies and green grass all the year long. In this verdant pasture, beside those still waters, they lay down and slept in perfect peace, for here they might lie down safely. When they awoke, they gathered again of the fruit of the trees, drank again from the water of the river, and then lay down again to sleep. This they did for several days and nights.

When they were finished with their resting and waiting upon the Lord, they knew that their strength had been renewed like the eagles. Yea, they could now "run and not be weary and walk and not faint."

The River of Life

Therefore they proved the value of those words of Jesus when He said, "Come ye yourselves apart and rest awhile." So they ate and drank one last time and then set out once more on their journey.

Then, I beheld in my dream that they had not journeyed far before the straight way and the river parted company. At this they were not a little sorry, but they dared not leave the narrow path for that was their guide and protector. Now it was not long before the way, although still straight, became rough and rocky. Many a time they nearly twisted an ankle on a rolling stone, and before long the soles of their feet began to be most tender from treading upon so many sharp pebbles. Also, there were all manner of briars and brambles, branches and bushes to catch on their clothes or screech against Christian's armor. Now the going became so rough and the progress so slow that their souls began to be much discouraged. Then said

Hopeful, as he nursed a new scratch on his cheek, "Ah, dear Christian. How I yearn to be back at the river of life."

"As do I, dear companion," sighed Christian wearily. "As do I."

"Or at least to have a path with fewer rocks and potholes," said Hopeful longingly.

"Well," remarked Christian wistfully, "perhaps the Lord of the far country will hear the sighings of our hearts and show us a better way."

Now a little before them, they saw on the left hand of the road, a lovely green meadow and a well-built sturdy stile to help them over the fence. The name of the meadow is By-path Meadow, and at sight of it they were more than a little encouraged. Then, Christian stepped off the path and leaned against the fence to view the inviting scene more closely.

"Look Hopeful!" he said joyfully. "A meadow, all smooth and green and lying right alongside the way. Surely God has heard our groanings."

"But it goes along the way, not in the way," replied Hopeful warily.

"Ah! 'Tis not very much off the way," retorted Christian as he began to climb the steps. "Here, let me just climb over this stile and have a wee peek."

Bypath Meadow

So, Christian got him over and stood amidst the blossoms and the honey bees who were gathering nectar from the lush clover of By-path Meadow. He looked back as far as the eye could see, and saw that the meadow lay right alongside the narrow path. He looked ahead, as far as the eye could see, and saw that the meadow lay still right along the path. Then he turned to his companion with a grin as wide as the sky.

"How does it look?" asked Hopeful, with an equal mix of curiosity and caution.

"Good," replied Christian confidently. "Very good! Why, the meadow lies right alongside our pathway for miles and miles. Come on over, good Hopeful. This be an answer to prayer!"

"But what if this soft, green, meadowy path should lead us off from the way?" queried Hopeful nervously.

"'Tis not likely," affirmed Christian. "From over here, this seems to be the right way. And 'tis surely much easier! Come along now, chap. If we hurry along, we can make up the time."

"Are you sure?" quizzed Hopeful uneasily one last, timid time.

"Sure I'm sure!" encouraged Christian. "And besides, if it turns out that I am wrong, we may easily hop back over the fence."

"Well . . . all right," said Hopeful reluctantly, sacrificing good judgment on the altar of ease.

And so Hopeful hesitantly joined his companion on the way that seemed right. On that side of the fence, he found the grass to be indeed greener and the path to be indeed smoother (albeit inclined ever so slightly downhill). Then Christian smiled and suggested that they remove their boots and stockings, the better to appreciate the softness of the way. And this they did, with much relish.

"Ahh! There! You see!" crowed Christian cheerfully. "Isn't this way lovely to our eyes and tickly to our toes?"

"Yes! I must admit that to my senses, this certainly seems to be the right way," admitted Hopeful, beginning to share his companion's exuberance.

"Now say, aren't you glad we came this merry way?" queried Christian as they strolled along in the way of comfort.

"Yes," admitted Hopeful almost cheerfully. "Yes, I think I am!"

"Then stop looking back, chap," chided Christian. "Don't you see how easily we travel just alongside the way?"

"Yes," replied Hopeful, trying to partake of his companion's confidence. "But doesn't it seem that we're just a tad bit farther off from it than when we first began?"

"Mmmm. No, not that I can tell," answered Christian, remembering the thorny way, and seeing only what he wished to see. Just then, up ahead, they saw a man treading the same path as they. At this, Christian brightened and said, "Say! Look up yonder! Do you suppose that man to be a fellow pilgrim?"

"I certainly hope so, but I cannot tell," Hopeful replied cheerfully. "Come, let us catch up with him!"

So Christian and Hopeful set off in hot pursuit. Now catching up was no small task, for the man was striding along with a briskness and determination worthy of a better cause.

"Sirrah! Sirrah!" called Christian, "Wait up!"

"Why, good day, gentlemen," answered the man, reluctantly pausing for a moment. "Come along now, catch up! Miles to go before we sleep. Miles to go. Best put your boots back on, boys. Holiday's about over for us."

"What does he mean by that?" asked Hopeful quietly as they sat down to pull on their socks and boots.

"I don't know," admitted Christian. Then Christian addressed himself to the man who was standing over them, tapping his foot impatiently, all the while keeping his eyes fixed on the fast westering sun. "Good, sir," questioned Christian, "can you tell us where this peaceful path will lead us?"

"Why, to the Celestial City, of course!" he replied brusquely. "Say, aren't you two about ready?"

"There, you see, Hopeful!" exclaimed Christian as he finished pulling on his boots. "Didn't I tell you so?"

"Ask him how he knows," whispered Hopeful, standing to his feet.

"Shhh," hushed Christian. "We can't do that."

"Why not?" asked Hopeful in innocent simplicity.

"We don't want to hurt the man's feelings by questioning his good judgment," answered Christian a bit curtly. "Besides, you can tell he knows the way by how boldly he strides along the path."

"Aye," admitted Hopeful ruefully. "Confident he certainly seems to be. I hope it be not in vain."

"Dear Hopeful!" teased Christian. "You worry too much."

And so they set off to follow the man in that softer way which seemed so very right. Now, before they had gone many miles, the sun had gone down upon them and dark clouds began to overspread the sky. Yea, it was not long until they found themselves walking in dense darkness, without light of the sun, moon, or stars. But the man who led the way continued pressing forward with all confidence (for Vain-confidence was his name, you see). Then, sensing them to be falling quite behind he shouted back, "Come, come, boys! Don't let a little darkness slow you up any. There be many miles to go before we sleep. Miles to go. Miles to go."

"Come along, good Hopeful," urged Christian. "We be falling behind!"

"To be honest, dear Christian," grumbled Hopeful, "I would just as soon be going back. All the other paths provided by the King have safe havens for rest and encouragement. But this one provides neither pause nor ending."

"Well," confessed Christian, "I must admit that I feel the same. But where we are, is where we are. Our only choice now is to either keep up or be seriously lost."

"But he's so far ahead," complained Hopeful. "Can you even see him?"

Then Vain-confidence, in a burst of petulant impatience, called back, "I say, men! Are you coming or no . . . . . t" (thump).

"Oh, oh!" gulped Christian, his pounding heart caught fast in his throat.

Then, over the sounds of a rising breeze, they heard the last dying word of Vain-confidence, saying, "Hhhheeellllp" (gurgle, gurgle, sssss).

"What do you suppose happened to him?" asked Hopeful, with tremulous voice.

"I don't know. But don't move one single step," commanded Christian, trying to project a confidence he did not feel.

"You d . . . d . . . don't need to w . . . w . . . worry about that," stammered Hopeful, frozen fast to the spot.

Now Vain-confidence, walking by presumption rather than by faith, had tumbled into a deep pit which had been dug there by the evil Prince of that place. In the bottom there were great ragged stones interspersed with sharp sticks. Those who missed being broken upon the one were impaled upon the other. And so perished Vain-confidence in his ways.

"What happened?" queried Hopeful, limbs shaking like a leaf.

"I don't know yet," answered Christian, staring wide-eyed into the inky darkness, "but his voice sounded to be coming from far down below us. Here, let me feel with my staff and see if . . . gasp! Oh, no!"

"What?" squeaked Hopeful.

"The ground before us is gone!" rasped Christian, reaching down as far as his staff would allow. "It drops away into . . . into . . ."

"Probably into some great pit of death," groaned Hopeful.

"Aye," agreed Christian, stepping back to relative safety. "Either that or we stand on the edge of some fearful abyss."

"Oh, no," moaned Hopeful.

Then Christian, hoping against hope, called into the pit, "Good friend! Are you well? Can you hear me?"

After a few moments, Hopeful whispered hoarsely, "No answer."

"Aye," admitted Christian. "Only dead silence."

"Then it seems that our companion has breathed his last," said Hopeful sadly.

"Here, I'll cast down this small stone," suggested Christian. (sssssssss-thump) "My! 'Tis a long way down!"

"And a long way up," groaned Hopeful. "And this brisk breeze is beginning to chill my bones. I say we go back before we all end up dead!"

"I agree with you. But pray tell, in this great darkness, which way is back?" asked Christian hopelessly.

"I don't know. Just be sure to feel ahead with your staff, lest there be another pit," warned Hopeful.

"I shall," said Christian as he turned into the quickly rising wind to tap-tap his way along like a man born blind. Then there was a roll of thunder that shook the ground and quivered the tree leaves. "Oh, no! Listen!" moaned Christian as the first leaden drops of rain tink-tinked against his armor.

"'Tis beginning to rain!" Hopeful shouted, only to have the shrieking winds peel the words from his quivering lips and shred them through the ghostly branches of the low-bending trees.

And so, as they stood there in the darkness, it commenced to thunder and rain upon them. And that with such a thundering and a raining as only Noah could appreciate. Oh, it was fearful! Most fearful! Fearfully fearful!

"Oh, my. Oh, my! Oh, my!" whined Christian helplessly. But he might as well have spared his words, for the swishing rain pouring through the tangled forest washed them to the earth. There was thunder and lightning and water coming down in torrents! Soon the path (if you could call it that), turned into a creek rushing about their feet. Then the rising waters began to tug at their knees and threatened to sweep them away unless they could somehow find higher ground. So they began to climb. But the climbing was not easy because of the slippery, slimy clay. And the climbing was not easy because the bushes and briars were tangled every which way against them. And the climbing was not easy because they knew not where they were climbing to. Yea, for all they knew, their next step might hurl them over a precipice or splash them into some raging torrent. Oh, no! The climbing was not easy. Not easy at all!

"Oh, that I had stayed in the right way!" groaned Hopeful.

"But who could have dreamed that such a peaceful path could ever lead us out of the right way?" whimpered Christian. "Or who could have thought that yonder confident, dead man did not know the way?"

"'There is a way that seemeth right unto a man, but the ends thereof are the ways of death,'" quoted Hopeful miserably.

"As we have certainly seen," agreed a soggy Christian, squeaking along in his rusting armor.

"I had bad feelings about this from the very first!" bemoaned Hopeful. "Remember how I spoke those gentle words of caution?"

"Aye. I remember," confessed Christian, miserable in his guilt.

"I would have spoken more plainly," continued Hopeful, "except that you are older and more experienced in this way than I."

"Good brother, please be not offended," cried Christian, more miserably yet. "I am sorry to have brought you out of the way and to have put you into this great danger of drowning. Pray, my brother, forgive me. I did not do it out of any evil intentions."

"Be of good comfort, my brother, for I do forgive you. Not only that, but I truly believe that, by faith, even this mistake may be turned about to our good."

"I am glad that you are so merciful," said Christian, relieved in his soul. "But come, we must strive to somehow get back."

"Yes. Here," volunteered Hopeful, "give me your staff and I shall lead the way."

"And fall into some great pit of death, as did yon confident, dead man? Nay. 'Tis because of me that we are lost in this muck. I shall lead the way."

"No!" protested Hopeful forcefully. "You must let me lead!"

"Why must I?" demanded Christian, eager to atone for his former foolishness.

"Because you are so troubled about your mistake that you may lead us into an even worse way."

"Oh, what to do?" Christian cried out almost as a prayer. "What to do?"

Then, for their encouragement, they heard the voice of one calling from heaven. Stronger than the swish of drenching torrents, greater than the roar of raging waters, yea, even louder than the booming thunders came a voice from heaven, saying, "Let thine heart be toward the highway, even the way that thou wentest; turn again!"

"Did you hear!" exclaimed Hopeful.

"Yes! Praise God!" shouted Christian jubilantly. "Heaven has not forsaken us. Come!"

Then, they made many brave attempts to get them back. But by this time, the waters were greatly risen about them and they had like to have gotten themselves drowned nine or ten times. Indeed, they learned by fearful experience that it is much easier to get out of the way when in it, than to get into the way when out of it.

"Ah, weary. So weary!" complained Hopeful, scarcely able to plant one foot ahead of the other.

"These are the f . . . feelings of m . . . my bones as well," Christian managed to exclaim through his chattering teeth. "'T . . . 'tis certain that we shall not get back into the w . . . way this night."

"Oh, if only there were someplace to rest," moaned Hopeful, hoping against hope.

"There is!" cried Christian joyfully, just as a bolt of flaming blue lightning split a great oak tree and dropped a monstrous limb thundering down just behind them.

"What?" Hopeful squeaked, leaning against the wash of air from the falling timber. "Is there hope, do you say?"

"Look!" exclaimed Christian, shouting above the roar of the elements and pointing Hopeful in the right direction.

"What do you see?" whimpered worn and weary Hopeful.

"Over there! Do you see it?" shouted Christian, as off to their right another bolt struck. "By the lightning's flash you will see a rude shelter wherein we may rest for a time. There! Do you see it?"

"Yes! Praise God!"

"Do you think we dare stop there?" asked Christian, fearing lest he should lead them both into yet another trap.

"Well, the spirit is willing to go on, but the flesh is too weak," confessed Hopeful. "Therefore let us rest. Perhaps by morning's light we may make up the time."

"All right," said Christian, leading the way a few steps closer with each burst of light.

At last they reached a small shelter situated on a little knoll, well above the raging waters. Entering, they found the roof sound and an abundance of dry straw whereon to lie. Therefore they dried themselves off as best they could, and, totally exhausted, lay them down to rest.

"Ah, sweet rest," sighed Christian. "Though we be soaked to the bone and damp in spirit, how good it is to rest."

"Aye," agreed Hopeful, his spirits rising as he wearily fashioned himself a warm nest in the straw. "My, 'tis a nice cozy shelter we have run upon, isn't it?"

"Aye," nodded Christian with an unseen nod. "Nice indeed. A sound roof, dry straw, and look! Feel here! Even a pillow for us to share."

"I wonder who this land belongs to?" queried Hopeful. "And who is so filled with kindness as to provide this quiet little resting place?"

"Who knows?" replied Christian, at the moment little concerned with minor details. "Perhaps morning's light will reveal the answer. As for now," he said with a long drawn-out yawn, "I shall have my prayers and then dream of higher ground."

"As shall I," concurred Hopeful with a yawn of his own. "God bless you."

And so they snuggled down into the friendly fragrance of the crinkly, dry straw, feeling as warm and secure from the angry storm as if they had just been tucked into their cribs with a mother's prayers. Now, no sooner had their heads touched the pillow but that they were both fast asleep.

But this was not a wise thing to do, as you shall soon agree. For, as comfy and dry as their little shelter might have been, it was still out of the right way. And, it just so happened that not far off from that place, there was a dark and dreary castle called Doubting Castle. The owner of that gloomy place was an evil giant named Despair, who had for his wife a giantess named Diffidence (so named because of her timidity, although, to be frank, she never seemed all that timid to me). Now, it was the giant's custom, after each storm, to search along his string of shelters to see if perchance any pilgrims had come over his stile and trespassed in the kingdom of Doubt. And so it was that well before morning's light, he was out and about with his torch and club to seek out offenders. As he sloshed along through the mud and mire of Doubt, he hummed out-of-tune snatches of some gloomy funeral dirge and mumbled through his scraggly beard, saying,

"Oh pilgrims! Has me delightful little storm washed any of ye up on me delightful shores? (snoring) Aha! What hears me sleepy-snorey in me first little shelter? Hmmm. Why, if it isn't a couple of pilgrims! And sleeping they are! In my kingdom of Doubt! In my shelter! Without my permission! Do they not know that to sleep in the kingdom of Doubt means to go to jail? No! Likely not. Not likely. Then, heh, heh, heh, it falls my lot to tell them so. And so tell them so I shall."

So the giant kneels him down and crawls partway into the shelter to cast an evil eye upon his senseless prey.

"Hmmm," he growled, looking triumphantly upon his catch with a leering, snaggle-toothed grin. "Two in one blow! And one of them a knight in shining armor at that! Hey! Wake up!" grunted the giant. But in their exhaustion the pilgrims neither heard nor saw but slumbered on (snoring).

"Wake up knaves!" he snarled. But in their weariness the pilgrims neither saw nor heard, but slumbered on (snoring). So the giant began to prod them with his club shouting, "Hey! Wakes thee up, I said!"

"Huh? Wha?" mumbled Christian, all bleary-eyed.

"Thee gots ears, ain't thee?" bellowed Despair. "Wakes thee up, me says!"

By this time Hopeful had begun to bestir himself and managed to open one bleary eye. But upon seeing the evil face of a giant not two feet from his own, he decided that he was having a nightmare and quickly clamped his eye shut, hoping thereby to switch to a better dream. At this, the giant was offended and cuffed him a good one alongside the head, snarling, "Hey! Wake up, I said!"

Then Hopeful opened both his eyes and saw the giant, now hulking less than a foot away. He smelled the foul odor of his greasy body.

Captured by Despair

He tasted the air hung thick with the miasma of decaying teeth and fresh garlic. He felt the heat emanating off that huge, muscular body and realized that this dream was worse than real. A quick glance over at Christian revealed him to be shaking noisily in his squeaky armor.

Then said Hopeful diplomatically, "Oh, uh, er, uh, ahem, good morning, kind sir."

"Kind sir!" snorted the giant, puffing a lungful of foul fumes directly into Hopeful's face. "Hah! Thou dost me insult! For I am neither kind nor a mere sir. I am a king. A tyrant if thee pleases."

"Uh, then, good morning, your highness," said Hopeful, trying hard to rectify his breach of etiquette.

"And what's so good about a morning," snarled the giant fiercely, "when a king finds his grounds trespassed upon, and trampled upon, and lain upon in so fearful a manner as ye have arrogantly done?"

"Oh, dear, good king," apologized Hopeful, "I am truly sorry. We meant no . . ."

"Silence!" roared Despair, the blast of his stinking breath stinging Hopeful's nostrils and sweeping back his hair. "I told thee I be not a good king! My name be Despair and I am a tyrant! An evil, vile, foul-tempered, tormenting tyrant who delights in deeds of mayhem and murder."

"Gulp. Uh, pleased to meet you, Mr. King Despair, sir," choked Hopeful, cringing back against the wall.

"I'm sure you are," hissed the giant sarcastically. "But that I'll change forthwith. Let me start by informing thee that there be few who trespass into the land of Doubt what ever escapes alive. Tell me. Have you ever had cause for deep despair?"

"Uh, yes, your highness."

"Well let me inform thee that it was mere child's play compared to what has come upon you today. Now, gets thee up and march thee on!"

"Where are we going?" asked Hopeful, stiffly struggling to obey.

"'Tis for me to know and thee to go," snapped Despair as he snagged Hopeful by an arm and sent him spinning out of the shelter and headlong into the muck. As the clumsy giant backed himself out of the shelter, Christian scrambled up and was quickly outside the shelter helping his companion to his feet.

"Comes thee now," ordered the giant, tapping his club menacingly and pointing deeper into the already dense gloom of the forest. "Step thee right along."

And so they began their dismal march to who knew where. But they did know, all too well, that their worst times no longer lay in the past.

Then Christian whispered to Hopeful, saying, "I have reason to suspect that we may be in great difficulty."

"Aye," whispered Hopeful. "He seems to delight in his tyranny. What shall we do?"

"I do not know," Christian confessed. "We are obviously in the wrong for having entered his kingdom."

"We might run for it," suggested Hopeful optimistically.

"Nay," objected Christian, looking grimly at reality. "We are so weakened from last night's ordeal that a run will gain us nothing but a beating from his club. Let us pray for mercy."

"From him!" exclaimed Hopeful with a jerk of his thumb back toward the giant.

"No," answered Christian. "From God."

At this, the giant's ears perked up, a scowl scrunched up his greasy face, and he blurted out, "Did me hear the name of God?"

"Yes, sir," said Hopeful respectfully. Then, realizing that he had just broken Doubt's laws of etiquette, he quickly corrected himself, saying, "I mean, yes, Your Highness."

"Too late! Take that!" snorted the giant, giving Hopeful a resounding thump on the head with his cudgel.

"Ow!" cried Hopeful, recovering his balance and reaching up to nurse a growing goose egg.

"That was for calling me 'sir,' before saying 'Your Highness,'" sneered the giant. "Now," he continued, "who was it what called out the name of God?"

"'Twas I," replied Christian forthrightly.

"Then take that!" snarled the giant, landing a clanging blow on Christian's helmet.

"Ow!" he cried, reeling from the blow.

"'Tis against the laws of this kingdom to speak out the name of God here," explained the giant.

"But you never told us!" protested Hopeful.

"Sooo!" roared the giant with an evil grimace. "Now ye be berating me methods of instruction, are ye? Then take that!" he snarled, snapping off another blow from his club.

"Ow!" howled Hopeful.

"Good King, please . . ." pleaded Christian.

"I told thee I be not good!" insisted Despair. "So take that!" he bellowed, clanging yet another dent into Christian's helmet.

"Best we be silent," declared Hopeful under his breath.

"Aye," agreed Christian softly.

"Be thee silent," Despair commanded gruffly, bopping them each a good one on the head.

"Ow!" moaned Hopeful.

"Ouch!" groaned Christian.

So, the giant poked and prodded them through the drippy, grey forests that flourish in the land of Doubt. At last they came to the wide moat that surrounded Doubting Castle. Above the great outer gate was a sign hung, and engraved with these words: "Abandon hope, all ye who enter here." Despair gave them a few moments to consider the import of those dark words of doom. Then, for his amusement and their instruction, he snatched open a large wooden box that swarmed with ugly, black flies. From within he pulled out an oozing hunk of rotting horse meat all alive with squirming maggots. This he threw into the moat where it exploded in a boiling rush of slashing piranha jaws. Also there came gliding forth several great alligators, summoned from their murky depths by the tremor of Despair's footfalls.

After this show of terror, the giant prodded his hapless victims across the bridge and closed behind them a massive wooden gate. Then, taking a large key that hung from a human skull, he locked the protesting rusty lock. Next he marched them across the courtyard, densely littered with the bones and skulls of doubting pilgrims from all ages past. Finally he pushed them through the prison gate, which he fastened behind him with another great key. From the glowing coals of a long barbecue pit, smouldering under some suspicious looking cuts of meat, he lit himself a smoky torch. Then, pushing them on before, he led them down, down, and yet more down, through a maze of stairs and corridors until they came to the lowest level of the inmost dungeon.

"Now, laddies," teased the giant in mock merriment. "Here be's me darkest dungeon." Wrenching open the iron door, which screeched in rusty protest, he said, "'Tis as dark and dreary a place as any you'll find, laddies. In thee goes, boys," he quipped, sending them sprawling into the darkness. Stabbing the foot of his torch into a crack between stones, he stepped in after them and clapped their legs fast in irons. Then the giant knelt down on one knee, grabbed them both by their collars and pulled them close to his greasy, torch-lit face. "'Tis Wednesday morning, lads," scowled the giant, his foul breath biting at their nostrils. "I'll be back to see thee in a few days . . . maybe! Heh, heh. Ta ta, me children."

Then, humming some eerie and occultic ditty, he wrestled the rusty door shut and secured it with a stout chain and lock. After casting one last glance upon his wilted victims, he took up his smoky torch and went shuffling away, up, and up, and yet more up, through the labyrinthine stairs and corridors that comprise the dungeon of Doubt.

As the footsteps of the giant faded away, Christian and Hopeful began to explore their new lodgings.

"Ah, what a dreary land is the land of Doubt," moaned Hopeful, staring bleakly into the darkness through the bars of his cell.

"Aye. And what a dreary castle is the castle of Doubt," added Christian dismally.

"These bars are solid," observed Hopeful, clanging one of them with a heavy manacle.

"Aye, and this lock is secure," grimaced Christian, tugging at the heavy, locked chain on the door.

"And these chains on our legs," despaired Hopeful, "they be no dream."

"Nay, but rather a nightmare," croaked Christian through his parched throat.

After exploring their cell, the luckless prisoners set themselves to sorting rubbish and filth from the rotted straw. This they scrapped into a small pile in one corner and then sat them down in abject despair. As they sank into silence they thought they could hear, echoing to and fro amid the corridors of Doubt, far-off voices crying out for help.

"Listen!" whispered Christian hoarsely.

"Help," cried one feeble voice from some upper level. "Is there anybody there?"

"Food. Won't somebody please give me just a crust of bread?" echoed another weakly from far down the corridor.

"Water!" rasped a tortured throat from the other direction. "Just one drop of water. Please!"

"Help us! " pleaded another. "Somebody! Anybody! Help us!"

"We are not alone!" marvelled Hopeful.

"Nay, but there be many," answered Christian. "And how many more might not there be who have not strength enough to call out?"

"Strange," puzzled Hopeful.

"What?"

"The path we came on didn't seem all that well traveled. How came there to be so many here?"

"There be another and shorter route to the land of Doubt," gloomed Christian.

"Oh? What route is that?"

"'Tis one that leads here more directly. It comes straight on, through the walls of a nearby university."

"Ah."

"But we were not sent here by the words of doubting schoolmen," lamented Christian. "We be here because of me. 'Twas all my fault. All my fault!"

"Don't blame yourself overmuch," sympathized Hopeful. "The way was extremely hard, and the path did seem to run parallel."

"But it was not straight and narrow," moaned Christian, dropping his head into his muddy hands. "I saw that the way turned a bit in the distance, and I knew the words of Goodwill about the straight and narrow way. But because my feet were sore and the meadow promised soft meanderings, I chose to ignore his counsel. Oh foolish, stupid, lazy pilgrim!"

"Let not Despair rule you, my brother."

"How can I help but be? By my own choice I have put us both into his dungeon and entirely at his mercy."

"But you did not choose this!" protested Hopeful, alarmed at the violence of his companion's despair.

"Whenever one chooses to leave the narrow way, he always ends up in despair," answered Christian hopelessly. "It always ends like this. Always!"

"Is there nothing I can say to cheer you?"

"No. Nothing."

Now it came to pass, that on the night of his great catch, giant Despair was having dinner with his dear, timid wife, Diffidence. And, between bites of "long pig" (for he was a cannibal, you see), he proudly boasted of his good fortune. He chuckled merrily as he described in gloating detail how they had sought to please him by addressing him so politely; how they had not once tried to escape or even attempted to deceive him.

"Hmmm," she frowned, furrowing her forehead and staring intently at him with beady, piggish eyes. "These two sound as if they might actually be sincere pilgrims."

"Wha!" grunted the giant, alarmed at the fearful thought.

"If they are, they will be tough nuts to crack."

"Hmmm. You could be right," agreed the giant, sucking loudly through a cracked tooth. "What shall I do to them?"

Then said she, with a snaggle-toothed grin, "I suggest that you give them three or four days with nothing to eat but darkness. Nothing to drink but what drippings they can lick off the walls. Then, when you do visit them, take your favorite crabapple cudgel and beat them without mercy."

"Hmmm, yes," he grinned, snatching up another piece of long-leg. "Yah. That ought to soften them up a bit. Ah, wifey. You're a genius. A stark raving genius!"

And so, Christian and Hopeful lay in this desperate situation from Wednesday morning till Saturday night. And this, without one bit of bread to bless their belly, one drop of drink to ease their drought, one ray of light to brighten their eyes, or one word of cheer to soothe their ears. And so did the deepening pain of their thirst and hunger keep pace with their growing discouragement. Also, the rats and bats, and mice and lice, that thrive in Doubting Castle, did scurry and flap and squeak and bite, and stopped their sleeping through the night. And so

In Despair's Prison

did their discouragement deepen yet all the more. Then, on Saturday night, Christian was startled from his lethargy by the sounds of a key in some distant lock.

"Listen!" he whispered hoarsely, nudging his dozing companion. "I hear a key in the outer door."

"'Tis probably only Despair," moaned Hopeful weakly.

"Does I hear me name echo through these hallowed halls?" the giant crooned merrily, as he parked his torch and fiddled with the rusty lock. "Good evening to thee, me boys," he said, punctuating his speech with a loud belch.

"Good evening, Your Highness," said Hopeful, a bit encouraged by the giant's merry mood.

"Not so good as thee thinks," he said with a sinister grin. "For I have talked to me wife about thee."

"And did she recommend mercy?" asked Hopeful eagerly.

"Mercy!" exclaimed he, raising bushy eyebrows and leaning back in shocked surprise. "Did you say mercy?"

"Yes, sir."

"Me can't believe it. What? You think this is some sort of reform school for wayward pilgrims?" Then, leaning forward menacingly, he thrust his favorite club just under Hopeful's nose and sneered with a cruel chuckle, "Heh, heh, heh. See this?"

"Aye," replied Hopeful, eyeing the knobby weapon with crossed eyes. "'Tis a cudgel."

"Aye. Of fine crab-apple tree stock, it is. My dear wife, ah, bless her gentle heart, advised me to use this club to beat thee thus! . . . Hah!"

Then the giant began to beat them furiously from head to toe.

"Ow . . . !" cried Hopeful.

"Ouch!" moaned Christian.

"Take that, knaves," puffed the giant, quickly working up an odious lather from the exertion of his labors.

"Please, stop!" begged Christian, vainly trying to shield himself from the rain of pelting blows.

"Nay! Never!" snarled Despair, growing more cruel with each passing moment. "Not till ye be tenderized chow for the alligators and piranhas in me moat!"

"Ow!'" cried one.

"Ouch!" wailed the other.

And so he beat them without one ounce of mercy, till they were so sore that they could scarcely have scratched a flea or turned themselves over. Then he, being quite exhausted by his labors, took his wheezing leave of them with an evil promise to return soon with more of the same. Then did they mourn and lament under their distress, but there was nothing more they could do.

Now when the giant's wife, Diffidence, learned that they had managed to survive his beating without cursing their God (or even

Despair himself), she began to grow alarmed. So she advised giant Despair that tomorrow he should supply them with instruments of self murder and counsel them to do away with themselves. Meanwhile, down in the dungeon . . .

"Ah, brother Hopeful," groaned Christian, "is it day or night?"

"I cannot tell," he moaned.

"How long have we lain here this way?" he croaked through parched lips.

"I cannot tell," whispered Hopeful painfully.

Then were these two pilgrims silent throughout the remainder of the miserable night.

Next morning, Despair, who was nursing a hangover from his previous night's indulgences, came shuffling unsteadily down into his dungeon.

"Listen," said Hopeful, startled by the creaking protest of a distant gate.

"Oh, no!" lamented Christian. "He comes again."

"Perhaps to set us free!" exclaimed Hopeful.

"Pah," replied Christian, astounded at Hopeful's boundless optimism. "Hopeful be thy name, and against all reason, hopeful be thy mind."

"But he might!" persisted Hopeful.

"No," groaned Christian, not even lifting his head from his hands at Despair's approach. "No. Despair will never set us free."

"What? Alive still!" bellowed Despair as he angrily wrenched open the door.

"Yes, by God's grace," said Hopeful boldly, no longer fearing Despair's cudgel.

"Ye must not speaks that name here!" roared Despair, bitterly. "Take that!" he snorted as he struck Hopeful a lusty blow on the back.

"Ugh!" grunted Hopeful involuntarily.

Then the giant glared upon him and said, "I trust that henceforth there will be no more such vile language heard here in me drippy dungeon. Now then, back to business. Business? What business? Oh, yes! Business. Ahem. I have counseled again with my dear wife, bless her gentle soul."

Now at the mere mention of his wife's gentle counsel, the prisoners began to tremble in their boots but still kept their silence.

Despair

"Well?" scowled the giant impatiently. "Don't ye wants to know her good counsel?"

"No," said Hopeful.

"What!" snarled the giant angrily. "Insult me wife, will ye! Then take that!" he spat as he landed a resounding blow upon Hopeful's shoulder.

"Ow!" moaned Hopeful softly.

"And you there, in the rusty armor. Don't ye wants to know her good counsels?"

"Uh . . . yes," said Christian, choosing what seemed to be a safer approach.

"So!" snapped the beast. "Being nosey, are ye? Take that!" he shouted as he landed a clanging blow upon Christian's well-dented helmet.

"Ow!" cried Christian miserably. "Oh, please have mercy, gentle king."

"I have tolds thee that I be not gentle!" Despair screamed, blood-shot eyes bulging in fury. "I am a tyrant! A tyrant of the worst sort! I have no mercy, know no mercy, show no mercy. Therefore, take that!"

"Ow!" cried Christian, wishing that the giant would have the decency to simply murder him and be done with it.

"Now then," leered the giant as he waved the cruel cudgel under their noses like a charmed snake, "do ye wishes to know her good counsel?"

"Uh, as you deem it best, your Highness," answered Hopeful discreetly.

"And you?" he asked, glowering threateningly at Christian.

"Uh . . . a . . . as you deem it best, your Highness," he replied.

"Hmmph!" snorted the giant, disappointed at the lack of further excuse for cruelty. "Then listen up good, lads," he said as he got down on one knee and spread a light-colored leather bag before them. "Since I be of such an evil temper, and since I know no mercy, nor show no mercy, and since none have escaped from my castle of Doubt (except by way of my kitchen, heh, heh, heh), and since it is impossible that ye shall either, her good counsel to thee is that you should use these." And with those words, he drew out three deadly objects.

"What are they?" queried Hopeful.

"I have brought for thee a vial with deadly poison," he said, setting forth a tiny blue vial, "a knife, sharp and long," he continued, laying down a ceremonial dagger with jeweled handle, "and a noose for the neck," he concluded, bringing out a long, stout cord tied in a hangman's knot.

"What are these for?" quizzed Hopeful.

"What for!" blustered Despair, screaming into Hopeful's face. "Why, for to do with thyselves away, of course!"

"Kill ourselves?" asked Hopeful incredulously.

"Of course!" answered the giant with a sarcastic sneer. "For why should you choose to live on, seeing your life is attended with such bitterness? Especially . . . heh, heh, heh . . . especially in the depths of Despair's dark dungeon of Doom."

"We would rather be set free," cried Hopeful undaunted.

"Free!" screamed the giant, starting back in shocked disbelief. "Do you dare to speak of freedom from Doubt! Grrr . . . I will slay thee for that!"

With that, the giant seized the dagger and with a look of ugly hatred moved to make an end of Hopeful himself. But in the good providence of God, the clouds of that country parted for a brief moment. Then, by way of angel-held mirrors, a ray of reflected sunshine zinged its way into the darkness of the dungeon. This caused the giant to fall into one of those fits that always attack him when the light breaks forth. Therefore, since he was now unable to continue on with his murderous intentions, he locked the door and withdrew, saying, "I shall return. But let me assure you, that it will be a much more pleasant death if you do away with yourselves. For if I have to do it for thee . . . Heh, heh, heh . . . it could take daaaayyyzzzz." And with these words, the giant took his leave of them, although he weaved a bit more unsteadily due to his exposure to the light.

"Brother, what shall we do?" whined Christian, beginning to waver. "The life we now live is miserable. My soul almost prefers to strangle by the rope rather than by choking down this foul air. To lie down in my grave seems kinder than to lie here in this dungeon. Would it not be better to escape this life by our own hand than allow ourselves to be ruled by the giant?"

"Indeed," agreed Hopeful, "death does seem better than to forever live on in this misery. But remember that our Lord has commanded us saying, 'Thou shalt not kill.' And to kill ourselves would be more than the killing of a body for we would destroy our souls as well. You seem to imagine that it will be easier in the grave where the 'dead know not anything,' and where 'their hatred, and their envy is now perished; neither have they any more a portion for ever in anything that is done under the sun' (Eccl. 9:5). But have you forgotten the second resurrection when the wicked shall rise to receive the punishment of eternal death (Rev 20)? Others have escaped this kingdom of Doubt. Therefore, so may we. As for me, I am resolved to play the man and try my utmost to escape him at first opportunity. With God's help we might well succeed or perhaps be killed in the attempt and thus obtain sweet release. But let us not be our own murderers."

With these good words did Hopeful encourage the mind of his brother. So they continued together in the dark that day in their sad and doleful condition.

Later, toward evening, the giant came again, curious to see if the prisoners had taken his counsel.

"Well, me chaps," he growled to himself as he unlocked and re-locked a series of doors and gates. "I am eager to see how ye have done thyselves in. Have thee stretched thy necks with the rope? Or have you writhed under the painful potion? Or did you perhaps fall upon the bloody point? Let me cast but a little light upon thy twisted bodies to see how thou didst destroy thy souls."

Then, coming in with his smoking torch he saw them lying all still and deadish. At this he grinned an evil grin—until Hopeful bestirred himself and said weakly, "Greetings, Your Highness."

"What?" snarled the giant furiously. "Alive still!"

"We would be free!" persisted Hopeful.

"Free! Nay! But thou hast disobeyed my command and the counsel of my gentle wife! My wife, dearest Diffidence, is a gentle soul. But she does not take kindly to having her kind counsel rejected."

Then the giant snatched up the instruments of death and thrust them into their faces. "Here be the poison, the dagger, and the noose," he said with sadistic hatred dripping like acid from every word. "Do not neglect to use them this time! I be on my way to ask her counsel once again. But this time 'tis on how to stretch out thy punishment and tortures to the utmost. You can be sure of only one thing, lads," he grunted as he rose to go, "and that be this—I shall be back tomorrow with instruments of torture. And if I finds thee alive still, it shall go worse for thee than thou canst possibly, in thy wildest nightmares, ever imagine. Ta ta, chapssssss."

"Ah, dear Hopeful," moaned Christian after the giant's shuffling steps had faded into silence. "I am nearly persuaded to obey."

"Nay! Nay, my brother, be brave," encouraged Hopeful. "Your only danger is that you shall forget how God has led you in the past. Remember that Apollyon could not crush you nor could the Valley of the Shadow of Death smother you. The threats and tortures of Vanity

Fair did not stop you. What hardship, terror, and suffering have you already endured? And shall this one, so near to journey's end, send you packing home?"

"Ah, good Hopeful, you are a brave soldier of the cross."

"Nay, but I am a far weaker man than you," he rejoined. "Yet I have taken the same strokes as you. I am no less thirsty or starved than you. I too mourn the absence of warm light and pure air. But let us hold fast the hope we possess. Let us trust ourselves to the hand that was nailed to the cross for us!"

"I shall try," resolved Christian. "Only take these instruments of death away from me lest I seize them in a weak moment."

"Here," said Hopeful, gathering up vessel, blade and cord. "I shall toss them through the bars. Hah! There! They are gone from us."

Now while Christian and his fellow thus encouraged each other in the gloom of the dungeon, the giant and his wife were in bed snacking on some deep fried delicacies and discoursing thusly:

"And do tell, my love," droned the witch as she drowned her goodies in tabasco sauce and chili powder, "have the prisoners taken our good counsel?"

"Bah! No!" he grumbled, downing a large flagon of some fiery fluid in two gurgling gulps. "They be sturdy rogues," he continued, wiping his filthy beard with the back of his hand, "who choose to bear all manner of hardship rather than do away with themselves. I suppose I shall have to kill them."

"Kill them!" squawked the wart-nosed biddy, spewing out a greasy mouthful of fiery food. "No! For then will they rise in the first resurrection to meet their Lord in the air! No! We must induce them to kill themselves that their souls may die as well."

"But what more can I do, my gentle?" he asked, wiping off his face and pouring himself another dose of fuming beverage. "I have starved them, thirsted them, beaten them, hidden them away from the light which they long for. The lice and mice bite and torment. Tell me, my love, what more can I do?"

"I'll tell you what will break their spirit," she declared, poking at his chest with her yellow-nailed, bony finger. "Take them into the castle yard tomorrow. Show them all the bones and skulls of those whom thou hast already dispatched. Show them thy well-equipped torture chamber and lead them to believe that ere a week comes to an end, thou wilt stretch them, brand them, roast them, skin them, salt their wounds, and then tear them into pieces for fish food, as thou hast done to their fellows before them."

"Hmmm," said Despair, nodding thoughtfully with an evil grin spread across his face. "Ah, wifey!" he gloated. "A good idea! Yes! A good idea! M'thinks the older one is beginning to long for death already."

And so, when the next day came, he took them out into his castle yard, all white with the scattered bones of multitudes—bones of all those, who, down through the ages had wandered into Doubt.

"You see these skulls of millions?" he growled, tossing a bucket of picked bones onto one of the piles. "These were once pilgrims, the same as ye be. In their search for an easier way they wandered into my kingdom the same as ye have done. And when, over there in yonder fine torture chamber, I had made sport of them long enough, I tore them into pieces, as I shall do to you before ten days have passed. Look with thine eyes and see thy fate. Listen with thine ears and hear their dying agonies which shall soon be thine own. Then remember the peaceful potion that will let thee slip away into pleasant and blissful sleep. And be grateful that even the giant of Despair hath a touch of mercy. And now, off to thy cage with thee. Take that!"

"Ow!" cried Christian.

"And that!"

"Ow!" howled Hopeful in pain.

And with that, he beat them all the way back to their foul and hateful dungeon where they spent the day in more misery and pain.

Now when night was come again, Despair and Diffidence continued their conversation regarding their prisoners.

"Ah!" he snorted furiously. "Ah! Me can't believe it!"

"Believe what?" she asked absent-mindedly as she ceremoniously dropped thirteen bats' wings and a pinch of powdered spider's web into a great, bubbling cauldron.

"That neither blows, nor starvation, nor thirsting, nor fleas, nor threats, nor kindly counsel can bring these ones to put an end to themselves!" he grumbled.

"Hmmm," she murmured, staring fixedly into the fuming mixture before her. "Hmmm. Hope, do you say? Ah yes, of course! Hope!

Thank you, Tisiphone," she said to a familiar spirit, unseen by Despair.

"What have thee heard, wifey?" he asked eagerly. "Have thy ghouly ghosts offered up any wisdom?"

"Hope!" she squawked.

"What?" said he, scrunching up his face, while his mind stumbled amid the back corridors of memory, trying to call up the meaning of such a rarely used word. "What be thee talking about, wife?"

"Hope! You old fool!" she cackled. "They must still have some hope left to them!"

"Hmmm. Hope, you say?" he said, scratching his balding pate.

"Yes!" she affirmed, stabbing her ornately carved stirring bone in his direction. "Either they yet have some trust in their Lord, or they expect some friends to come and deliver them. Or perhaps they have picklocks upon them and plan to escape! Have you searched them yet?"

"No. No," he confessed. "But I shall search them thoroughly in the morning."

But about this time, Christian remembered the good example of Paul and Silas in their prison and determined that he, too, would consult duty rather than inclination. Therefore, near midnight the prisoners began to sing hymns, and to praise God, and to pray without ceasing! And as they did so their courage began to rise and rise again—higher and higher still, until Christian declared, "What a fool!"

"What?" asked Hopeful, amazed at the strength of his partner's voice.

"What a fool I have been!" he exclaimed again, even more loudly. "To lie here in a stinking dungeon when I might just as easily have walked at liberty!"

"What are you saying?" asked Hopeful, fearing that Christian's mind had at long last snapped.

"Look! Look!" cried Christian, reverently pulling something from around his neck.

"'Tis too dark to see," Hopeful reminded his companion, still fearing for Christian's sanity and yet hoping against hope that something good was in the wind.

"Then, here, feel this," said Christian, handing over his precious treasure, hands trembling with excitement.

"Why, 'tis a key," marveled Hopeful. "A tiny, rusty-feeling key!"

"Aye. Rusty because in my stupidness I have not used it sooner!"

"What key is this?"

"'Tis called the key of promise! The key of promise!"

"What is it for?"

"This key is given to pilgrims to make them 'partakers of the divine nature,'" Christian answered confidently. "Also to give them power over all evil, and to release them from any lock made in the land of Doubt!"

"But will it work for we who have wandered out of the way?" queried Hopeful, afraid to let his hopes rise too high.

"Absolutely yes!" affirmed Christian boldly. "I am persuaded that the Word of promise will open any lock in a thousand castles of Doubt."

"Well, then go to it, my brother. My eyes long to see the smile of God's sun."

"No more than mine, I assure you," said Christian, fetching back his key. "Here, let me at these chains." Then Christian, hands trembling with excitement, tried to fumble the key into the locks of his leg irons.

"How goes it?" asked Hopeful in an agony of suspense.

"I don't know yet. My fingers are cold and my hands are shaking too much. Oh, Lord, help me to apply thy promise! Ah! There!"

"Is it in?"

"Not yet . . . but . . . wait! Ah! There! In it goes! And why, it seems to be just the right size!"

"The right size, you say?" cried Hopeful, himself now trembling with excitement. "Could it really be the right size?"

"Aye," grunted Christian, trying desperately to turn the key against the rust of the lock. "As our needs are, so shall the promise be. Ah! There!" cried Christian as the lock dropped open. "Free!"

"Did it really work?" asked Hopeful eagerly. "Oh, Christian, did it?"

"Feel for yourself!" declared Christian as he triumphantly directed Hopeful's hands to the opened irons.

"Oh!" exclaimed Hopeful joyfully. "It worked! It really did work!"

"Ah, to be able to move again," rejoiced Christian, cautiously stretching his stiffened legs freely for the first time in over a week. "Praise God! Here! Let me have at your chains."

"My," said Hopeful reverently as he felt Christian's quaking hands searching out the keyhole. "'Tis a wonderfully fine picklock you've got yourself."

"Aye. 'Twas forged on the anvil of heaven by Him that came to set the captives free," said Christian, working up a cold sweat as he once again struggled against the rust of Doubt.

"Where did you get it?"

"'Twas given to me by Charity down in the Valley of Humility. Ah! There!" cried Christian victoriously, as the heavy manacles clanked noisily to the floor. "You are free!"

"Free!" marveled Hopeful. "Am I really free?"

"Aye, lad. Free as a bird!"

"Oh, praise God!" exclaimed Hopeful, rubbing his swollen ankles. "Ahhh! It feels soooo good to move my poor legs again."

"Aye, praise God indeed!" concurred Christian. "I wonder why I did not think of this key sooner?"

"I can't imagine," replied Hopeful, "but for sure, late is better than never."

"And after all this time," puzzled Christian, "I wonder what made me think of it now?"

"Do you think it might have been because we began to sing praises?" inquired Hopeful.

"Yes," replied Christian, after a moment's reflection. "Yes! That's it! Then 'tis no wonder!"

"No wonder what?" asked Hopeful.

"That God's word commands us to 'rejoice always,' and 'in all things to give thanks.' If we had looked to the Word of God and obeyed, instead of looking at circumstances and feeling sorry for ourselves, we would have used the power of promise long ere this."

"Well, having discovered the wonderful power of praise and promise, let us keep on moving," urged Hopeful, eager to see the light. "Shall we next try the door?"

"Yes. Ohhh, my aching back," groaned Christian as he creaked to his feet. "Ugh. My bones feel as rusty as these doors."

"I do hope I can still stand me up after all this time," grunted Hopeful as he rose and painfully shuffled toward the door. Then, after a few moments of searching out the lock by feel, his heart sank within him and he groaned aloud. "Ohhh! Oh no!"

"What's wrong?" asked Christian. "Why such deep sighs?"

"Look at the lock, Christian!"

"What about it?"

"What about it? Why, here, put your hands where mine are—here on the lock. See how much bigger it is compared to the ones on our chains."

"Aye," replied Christian, faith undaunted. "But now you put your hands where mine are—here on the promise. Go on, feel!"

So, in the darkness, Hopeful fumble fingered his trembling way down Christian's arm to the little key.

"Why, the promise has grown to meet the problem! The key is larger!"

"Aye," said Christian reverently. And even in the dark, Hopeful could tell that Christian wore a smile.

"Then can we trust that God's promise will grow to meet our needs?"

"So do I believe. 'Twould certainly be in keeping with the ways of God. And look! 'Tis too dim to tell for sure, but I think the key is becoming shiny with increased use!"

"Yes!" agreed Hopeful, noting a faint glow in the darkness. "Perhaps it shines of its own power."

"I wouldn't doubt it. I do know that this lock is easier to find than the last. Here, let me at it."

With that, Christian thrust the larger key into the larger lock.

"Why, it goes in easy!"

"Aye! And see how it turns! (click) With ease!"

"Away with this chain!" grunted Hopeful, wrestling with the weighty links until they snaked into a rusty pile at his feet. "Now help me push this rusty door! (creak) It opens! Praise God!"

"Come," commanded Christian. "Off to the yard gate. Peter will not be the only one to leave an empty cell!"

"Aye," agreed Hopeful, his heart pounding as much with joy as from his strenuous exertions. "Off with us!"

But lo, as the pilgrims began to hobble stiffly down the hall they heard the voices of other prisoners in the dungeon of Despair. Voices of those, who, hearing of their escape cried out, "Help us!"

"Don't leave us!" croaked another.

"Stop! Take us with you," rasped a third weakly.

So Christian and Hopeful halted in their flight just before the cage of one dressed in the cap and gown of a distinguished scholar. On either side of him and across the hall were several other prisoners dressed in the garb of students. Upon seeing these freed men stopped outside his cell the professor cried out eagerly, "Sirs! Stop! Help us!"

There, in the dim light of Doubt, Christian addressed the man, saying, "Friend, would you be free?"

"Free? Yes! Yes! Of course I would be free!" he cried, stretching a skinny claw of a hand out through the bars.

"Look!" said Christian, triumphantly holding forth the glowing golden key.

"Eh?" replied the scholar, scrunching up his face and peering down through his spectacles with puzzlement. "What be that?"

"This be your redemption!" exclaimed Christian exuberantly.

"Indeed?" marveled the man.

"Yea, verily."

"But uh . . . What is it?"

"'Tis the key of promise," Hopeful bubbled excitedly.

"Promise, do you say?"

"Aye," concurred Christian. "With this key you may open any door in the land of Doubt."

"But 'tis so tiny and rusty."

"It matters not, friend!" exclaimed Christian, a bit puzzled, for to him, the key seemed neither small nor rusty.

"But how can this same little key break my chains and open my cell door?"

"Because this is God's promise! It has power to free us from any bonds and all afflictions!"

"And what about the yard gate and the moat gate?" challenged the scholar, beginning to scoff a bit. "Do you mean to say that your key will grow or shrink to meet different needs?"

"Yes!" crowed Hopeful proudly. "Any needs! All needs!"

"Hmmmph!" snorted the wise man, adjusting his foggy spectacles and glaring down his pointed nose. "Nay! Nay, nay nay!"

"'Tis verily so!" declared Christian defensively. "It has just finished working for us!"

"But how can this be?" squawked the man in his high-pitched, scholarly voice. "The locks of Doubt are quite large and . . . and very rusty."

"No matter!" urged Christian. "Only believe in the promise and you shall be free!"

"Nay, nay, nay!" protested the man, folding his arms and leaning back. "I will never believe that such a small, wiry key as that can work such mighty miracles as you say."

"You must!" demanded Christian. "For behind this key stands all the honor of God's kingdom."

"What?" scoffed the man, pausing to brush aside the tassel which hung down to tickle his nose. "God's honor?"

"Aye!" affirmed Hopeful. "And all His power too!"

"Nay. Nay!" snorted the scholar. "God is not fool enough to stake His honor upon such a feeble instrument as that! Have you come to mock me?" he asked, eyeing them suspiciously through his spectacles and planting his fists firmly upon his bony hips.

"Nay, good friend!" urged Christian. "We are here for your salvation! Only reach forth the hand of faith and freedom shall be yours!"

"Aha!" spat the man vehemently. "You *have* come to mock me! For 'tis plain to any eye," he snarled, holding forth a grossly deformed hand that had hitherto been buried beneath his robe, "that my hand be withered and cannot reach out for said key!"

"Then I shall use it for thee," offered Christian. "Twist the chain so I can get at it."

"Nay!" snorted the man contemptuously. "Get you gone, knaves. 'Tis plain to any educated mind that such a tiny, deformed key can be nothing other than weak and useless."

"Nay, but 'tis mighty!" claimed Hopeful, "even unto the pulling down of strongholds and kingdoms!"

"Bosh! Do you actually believe that?"

"Yea, verily," affirmed Christian proudly.

"Then you be fools! Such a fantastical belief goes against all logic and wisdom."

"But look upon us!" exclaimed Hopeful. "We be freed by it."

"Aye. No doubt because you be fools and court jesters, tricksters sent out by giant Despair on a mission of mockery."

"Nay, dear friend," pleaded Hopeful earnestly. "This same promise which has freed us, shall do the same for you! Only choose to believe in it."

"Away with you!" cried the scholar with a wave of his deformed hand. "Bad enough to be entombed here in the land of Doubt without having buffoons assault my reason with fairy tales and magic keys."

"But . . ." began Hopeful.

"Nay! Begone! Begone! I will not give Despair the satisfaction of chuckling over my gullibility! Do you think that all these caps and gowns and degrees are for nothing? Does the wisdom of the ages contained in my great library of philosophy and religion count for nothing at all?"

"But . . ." began Hopeful again.

"Nay! Go!" commanded the professor, crossing his arms and turning to his books.

"But . . ." cried Hopeful, loath to lose the man's soul.

"Away, I say!" he ordered, turning his back on the men and opening a great volume of poetry. When they just stood there in stunned amazement, he turned to them and pointing a bony finger down the corridor, commanded, "Go! Go, go, go!"

"Come along, good Hopeful," sighed Christian, reluctantly turning away. "This man's learning has left him more hopeless than the man in the cage."

"But Christian, wait," said Hopeful, taking him by the arm, "there are others."

So Christian stopped and called to all that lay entombed in the dungeons of Doubt, "Is there a man among you, who will choose to believe God's promise, and act upon it?"

But there was no answer. No, not so much as a peep, a mutter, or a squeak. Then, after a long silence, Hopeful said sadly, "No answer."

"Aye," nodded Christian grimly. "Faith be dead in these halls. Come! Let us flee from this dungeon of Doubt lest their doom become our own."

"Aye. Off with us."

And so, they turned and continued their flight from the foggy dungeon of Despair. Their steps carried them down the crooked corridor, up the winding stairs, over, around, and under various obstacles. At last they came into the courtyard all white with bones, and worked their way to the yard gate. Here their conversation was in low whispers because just above this gate was the bedroom window of the giants.

"Here be the gate to the yard," whispered Christian. "Let us deploy our key."

"Will it really work?"

"Hopeful be thy name. Let hopeful be thy words."

"I shall try," agreed Hopeful, chagrined at his unbelief. "Try the lock."

"It goes in. Ugh," grunted Christian, "albeit, not so easy as at the inner gate."

"But does it open the lock?"

"I don't know," whispered Christian hoarsely as he pushed and pulled, fumbled and fiddled—and failed. "Oh dear."

"Oh, it be all stiff and rusty. We are doomed!"

"Shhh! Hush these words of doubt!" commanded Christian sternly. "The key of promise works only for those who choose to believe!"

"Choose? Then . . . then may I simply choose to believe in God's promise? Even if I do not feel belief?"

"Aye. Faith is not feeling. Choose to believe based upon the evidence of what God has done for us in the past."

"Why! . . . then . . . why glory be!" cried Hopeful in a whispered shout.

"What is it?" queried Christian, amazed at the cheerful glow on his young companion's face.

"I have chosen to believe! And God has made it a fact! I do believe! Try again brother, for now your key will certainly open the gate."

"All right," agreed Christian, renewing his attack on the rusty lock of Doubt.

"Does it yield yet to the attack of faith?"

"No. Not . . . y . . . Wait! Yes! Yes! I think so! Hear it squeaking!"

"Yes! Go hard at it, brother!" encouraged Hopeful with a furtive glance up at the open window, whence bellowed forth the snores of two slumbering giants.

"It opens! Victorious promise opens the doors of doubt!" cried Christian in his loudest stage whisper. Then putting his shoulder to the gate he forced it open. But not without a loud squawk of rusty protest.

"I knew it would! I knew it would!" Hopeful shouted out loud. **"Three cheers for the promises of God! Hip hip hurrah! Hip . . ."**

"Shhh!" hissed Christian, clapping his hand over Hopeful's mouth and looking fearfully up at the apartment window. There the curtains puffed outwards and sucked inwards in rhyme with the rumble of snoring giants. "We are not out yet!"

Meanwhile, in their dusty apartment, Despair and Diffidence were enjoying ghoulish dreams—dreams wherein they tortured pilgrims in the worst ways imaginable. Then Diffidence's dream dissolved into a nightmare. In it there was an escape and she heard prisoners fiddling with the yard gate! Then she shuddered involuntarily as she heard the lock give way before the power of a magic golden key. And then, horror of horrors! She heard a cheer of triumph! At this, she awoke with a start and viciously jabbed her bony elbow into Despair's ribs. "Hey!" she grunted into her husband's ear.

"Ooomph!" puffed Despair, suddenly dreaming that one of his prisoners had captured his cudgel and whacked him a good one in the ribs. "Why you ugly little. . . ."

"Hey! Wake up!" screeched the witch into his ear.

"Huh, Wha'?" he mumbled fuzzily. "Who hit me?"

"Did you hear something, my dearest?" croaked Diffidence nervously.

"Wha'?" grumbled the semi-comatose monster. "Wuss' wrong?"

"Did you hear cheering?" she persisted, although fearing a violent reaction from Despair.

"What!" he roared, snapping alert as the despised word pricked a seldom used portion of his foggy brain. "Wha'dg you say?"

"I could have sworn I heard someone cheering," she insisted, straining her ears for any hint that perhaps her horrific nightmare had some basis in reality.

"Cheering!" scoffed Despair with a snort. "My dear! Cheering hath not been heard in the land of Doubt since . . . since . . . since . . . uh . . . Hmmm, actually, I don't think it has ever been heard here. No! Never! Nor ever shall it be! Get thee back to sleep, eh?"

"Yes, dear," yawned Diffidence reluctantly as she fluffed up her greasy pillow and yanked the sooty comforter over her hideous head.

264 ◆ PILGRIM'S PROGRESS

As she was settling back into her grimy nest, her large black cat leaped to the windowsill and, tail twitching angrily side to side, stared intently at two emaciated fugitives easing their way through the partially opened gate. Then, through the foggy gloom of Doubt, he watched as they made ready to break for the main castle gate.

"Now what?" queried Hopeful.

"Now we dash across the courtyard, attack the great iron gate, and escape across the moat," Christian declared confidently, straining to see across the foggy boneyard.

"Shall we have at it?"

"Aye. But do tell, is it day or night?"

"Well, the sun be all hidden by the clouds of Doubt, but it must be day for all the chickens are clucking and scratching about."

"Unless the moon be hotly bright. Is the way clear?"

"Yes," whispered Hopeful. "The curtains still be drawn on the giant's apartment."

"Good. Next time they both snore together we'll dash across the courtyard and be out in no time. You cover our backs with prayer."

"I shall," promised Hopeful fervently.

"Ready?"

"Ready," affirmed Hopeful, casting one last edgy glance at the window. "Watch out you don't take a tumble over all the rolly skulls."

"I'm off!" Christian whispered loudly, pushing off the mossy wall of the castle and dashing over, around, and between the scattered piles of bones.

"I'm right behind!"

And so they ran the bony gauntlet and soon reached the relative safety of the great yard gate.

"We made it!" rejoiced Hopeful, bent over with his hands on his knees and panting heavily. "Hurry . . . (pant pant) with the lock."

This Christian had already proceeded to do and marveled to see how large his key had grown during their quick dash across the bone yard.

"How goes it?" quizzed Hopeful, glancing nervously back at the window.

"Hmmm . . . hard," grunted Christian, struggling to insert the key into the huge rust-clogged lock. "'Tis rusty and old. I don't think the key of promise has been brought against it very often."

"But be of good courage. Our God shall prevail over Despair."

"By faith I know 'tis true," grimaced Christian as he finally penetrated the lock with his shiny key. "But we should have been at this gate last week, before it got so rusty."

"Yea, but better late than never. How goes it?"

"Hard," grunted Christian, cold sweat springing to his brow, "and yet it seems to budge, ugh, a bit."

"Hurry," hissed Hopeful frantically. "I see the giantess opening the drapes of her window."

"Lord, keep Thy promise strong, for I am about to hang all my weight upon it!"

"God be with thee," encouraged Hopeful, frozen as statuesque as one of Diffidence's pagan idols.

"He is," grunted Christian through clenched teeth.

"Does it open for you?" whispered Hopeful, watching tensely as Diffidence picked up her black cat.

"No," confessed Christian, fatigued from his strenuous exertions. "I have lost too much weight. Here, I'll put this leg bone through the loop and hang on it. There. Here goes. Ugh."

"Did it work?"

"No. Come add your pounds to mine."

"Might we not break the key?" objected Hopeful, fearful of destroying their only hope.

"If the promise be not strong enough to hold all our weight, then the entire pilgrimage be in vain. Quick!" he hissed. "Grab on!"

"All right," obeyed Hopeful, reaching up for a grip on the bone. "Here goes."

Meanwhile, unable to resume sleep after such a harrowing nightmare, the giantess had roused herself and plucked her black cat, Lucifer, off the windowsill to lend herself a bit of comfort. She had just drawn the curtains to feast her eyes on the grimy, grey fog of Doubt, when she detected motion at the far yard-gate. Her eyes narrowed to angry slits as she watched one emaciated prisoner join another in hanging all his weight on a large shiny key. Then she saw the key turn and heard the lock squeak. Dropping the cat in alarm, she snatched the covers off Despair, kicked him soundly on his goose-bumped bottom, and shrieked wildly, "Despair! Despair!"

"Hmmm?" he mumbled through clenched eyes as he sent a hairy paw in search of his lost comforter.

"Wake up!" she screeched into his hairy ear. "Do you hear me? Wake up this instant!"

"What do you want, wench?" he growled, cracking one bleary eye and scowling angrily from the depths of his hangover.

"How many times must I tell you not to let the prisoners out to exercise in the open air?" she shouted furiously. "If I've told you once, I've told you a hundred times! Sunshine and exercise are tools of the enemy and only serve to increase the prisoner's health and lift their spirits!"

"What are you talking about, wife!" protested Despair, indignant to be the target of such a base accusation. "Me never lets me prisoners out into the open air. Sunshine be the death of me and my power over them!"

"Well then," squawked she, "why are those two scrawny pilgrims out? And why does one of them have a great big, shiny key that fits into your outer gate?"

"What!" He snorted in utter disbelief.

"Look for yourself," she screeched, drawing aside the curtains.

"You be crazy!" he bellowed as he finally sat up in bed and rubbed bleary eyes with hands still greasy from his last feast. "Stark raving crazy!"

"Just listen," she challenged as the sounds of a huge rusty hinge sent its complaining squawk echoing across the castle yard.

"What?" he yelled, heart pounding in a raging panic. "That be me gate opening!"

"And those be thy prisoners escaping!" she screamed, pointing to the large castle gate, hanging open on its hinges.

"Me club! Me club!" he commanded, exploding out of bed and landing on the cat's tail. The cat, feeling unjustly abused, returned the favor with a spitting hiss and a nasty scratch on a bare leg. "Ow!" roared Despair, sweeping the snarling, spitting ball of fur rolling down the stairs, while he jerked on his leather britches. "Get me me club!" he screamed. "None shall escape the kingdom of Doubt or the rule of Despair!"

"Run fast, dear," she urged, handing him his huge, spiked club. "They be crossing the moat!"

"I'm going! I'm going! I'm going!" he bellowed, his huge voice trailing off as he clattered down the stairs in his iron war shoes while still fastening his belt.

Now, by this time the prisoners were across the moat and hob-bling along as quickly as stiff bones would allow. But no matter how fast they tried to go, Despair went all the faster and it was not long before they heard his great clomping steps gaining on them, moment by moment. Then said Christian desperately, "Come quickly, friend Hopeful. I hear the steps of the giant!"

"Aye," panted Hopeful weakly. "But we are weak and ill-fed, and he is fat with the blood of martyrs. 'Twill yet take a miracle. Will your key open the clouds?"

"And why not? Oh, God of promise," he prayed earnestly as he limped along, "open unto us the sun of righteousness and blind the eyes of Despair."

Escape from Despair

At that moment Despair came bounding heavily across the moat, waving his blood-stained war club and uttering evil imprecations. "Don't think you can escape Despair so easy as that, knaves! Me have never opened me prison gates before this. Nor shall me now! Grrraugh!"

"He's coming across the moat!" cried Christian, casting a furtive glance back at the fearsome spectacle.

"Oh, where is the sun?" pleaded Hopeful, trying hard to control his rising terror.

"It will come," encouraged Christian, his faith growing to meet their need.

"When?" pleaded Hopeful fearfully.

"Just when we need it most."

"That 'tis now!"

"Quick! Turn in here," suggested Christian, turning down a little used by-lane.

"All right," obeyed Hopeful trustingly.

"A dead end!" cried Christian, screeching to a halt before a dense wall of briars and thorns.

"Oh, no! 'Tis a trap!" groaned Hopeful, turning to flee only to find the only escape blocked by the hulking form of giant Despair. He stood grinning sadistically and swinging his war club menacingly from side to side.

"Yes," concurred Despair with an evil chuckle. "Heh, heh, heh. A trap. And now me's got you. You're too weak to get away from me! Grrrr," he snarled viciously as he began closing for the kill.

Then the Spirit of the Holy One came mightily upon Christian who, casting off all fear, pointed his key at the giant's head and said, "Stand back or I'll use this key of promise to cut off your head!"

"Ptah!" spat Despair, advancing step by measured step. "Me curse thee by the gods of discouragement and depression, of dungeons and dragons. Me shall tear thee limb from limb and feed thee to the fish of the moat!"

"You come to me with a club and in the name of the god of force," cried Christian, advancing fearlessly to the conflict. "But I come to you in the name of the God of courage, whom you have defied!"

At this, Hopeful was amazed beyond measure. My! To see a starved and tottering prisoner, armed with nothing but a simple golden key advancing to give combat to a fearful giant. It was marvelous beyond words! Even the giant was taken aback for a moment and stopped to consider this exceeding rare spectacle. Then Christian stepped forward, bolder yet, saying, "Stand aside, feeble giant. For I swear that if you give not back, this promise of power shall pierce you to the marrow and lay your bones for the sun to bleach!"

"Promise! Bah! Me fears not a mere promise," grizzled Despair with a guttural growl.

"One last warning, Despair. Stand back and no more defy the God of creation, for if you persist in your folly you shall learn to your regret that the Lord saves not with sword or spear but by the power of His promise. Now back with you lest you show all the earth that there is still a prayer-hearing God in Israel!"

"Pah!" sneered the giant raising the visor on his war helmet in disdainful abandon. Then he rushed forward with great clomping stomps, club a'swinging and gnashing his teeth in furious anger. "Now me's got thee," he snarled, closing Christian into a corner and raising his bloody club, "and I'll tear thy head from thy . . ."

But! Just at this extreme moment when death was but a club stroke away, God split the clouds of Doubt and unveiled the sun shining in its noonday glory.

"The sun!" cried Hopeful joyously.

"Eh? Oh, no! Oh, no!" shrieked the giant, shuddering convulsively from head to heel. "Oh, me! The sun shines through! Got to get me into the shade before me fits start to act up! Got to get me into the shade! Aaugh! Out, cursed light!"

"Quick!" cried Hopeful. "Use your key to reflect the sun into his eyes!"

"Yes!" said Christian, catching a drop of golden sun and splashing its scorching ray, full force into Despair's unshielded eyes.

"Aauugghh!" screamed the helpless tyrant, dropping his club and clawing at screaming eyes as he staggered about like a drunkard. "No! Put up thy sword! Get thee gone! Aaauuuggghh!"

"Come!" shouted Hopeful as Despair staggered into a thorny briar bush and drew greenish-blue blood from a score of cuts and scratches. "Time now to flee!"

"Nay," called Christian, harrying the giant with his reflected lightning bolt. "I'll hold him off with the light while you get a good start."

"Aaauuuggghhh! Take it away!" snuffled Despair, now fallen to his knees and groveling in the dust.

"I'll not leave you," cried out Hopeful courageously.

"'Twas my fault we came here!" commanded Christian as he jock-eyed his way into a sunnier patch of light. "Therefore I shall bring up the rear. Go!"

"All right. But hurry," called Hopeful as he reluctantly turned to flee. Meanwhile, Despair had gone deep into his worst paroxysm of convulsions ever and was reduced to a babbling, gurgling blob of writhing pain.

"Come!" called Hopeful from far up the trail.

"I'm right behind you," answered Christian as he stabbed Despair in the eye with one last blazing flash from his key. "Go on!"

"Away! Please, take it away!" the cowardly giant continued to sob long after Christian and Hopeful had gotten far out of range of his doubtful threats.

And so, by the promise alone, did they escape from the hand of Despair. From thence, by light of full sun, they traveled on through the low-lying swamps of Doubt, through the dark, mossy forests of Doubt, through the windswept moorlands of Doubt, across the fair meadows of Doubt, and finally, back to the stile of Doubt that had first enticed them out of the way. There they noticed, for the first time, that the stile was stoutly built, well maintained, and easy to climb coming off the right way. But going back it was slippery and rickety and scarcely traveled at all. So they cautiously got them back onto the King's highway, where they were totally safe from Despair.

Now, when they were got over the stile, they decided to erect there a pillar of warning to save others from falling into the evil grasp of Despair. And this is what it said:

This pathway is rough, 'tis certainly true,
But not near so hard as what waiteth for you.
For over this stile, Doubting Castle doth lie,
So stay in the way, unless you would die!
Despise the Great King, the giant doth do,
And if you be a pilgrim, he despiseth you too.
So stay on the path and go not o'er there,
For the castle is kept by the giant Despair.

Many, therefore, that followed after read these words and so escaped the danger. So was it proven true what the apostle James spoke when he said, "He which converteth the sinner from the error of his way shall save a soul from death, and shall hide a multitude of sins."

As they traveled from that place, oh, you cannot imagine with what joy they hailed the rolly stones, the sharp pebbles in their shoes, and every single ankle-wrenching pothole, be it large or small.

CHAPTER EIGHT

THEY WENT ON then, from the land of Doubt, with no further event or mishap till they came at last to the Delectable Mountains. These are the mountains that belong to the Lord of that hill of which we have spoken before. So they went up to behold the gardens and orchards, the vineyards and fountains of water. There they drank and washed themselves and freely ate of the fruit of that land. Now there were on the tops of those mountains shepherds feeding their flocks, who stood by the highwayside. The pilgrims therefore went over to them and leaning upon their staffs, began to converse with them.

"Pardon me, gentlemen," said Christian politely, "but is this the way to the Celestial City?"

"Aye," answered the lead shepherd named Knowledge. "It is indeed."

"How far from here to there?"

"Too far for any, except those who actually get there," Knowledge replied, speaking in that cryptic style of speech that is characteristic of the man.

"And is the way safe, or dangerous?"

"Safe for all who trust and obey. But transgressors shall fall therein."

"As we have seen. Are there any provisions made in this place for pilgrims who have become weary and faint in the way?"

"Oh, indeed!" replied Knowledge with a broad smile. "The Lord of these mountains has charged us not to be forgetful to entertain strangers. Therefore, all the good of this place is before you!"

"Thank you," said Christian gratefully. "Thank you very much. Say, but these mountains are restful to the eye."

I saw also in my dream that the shepherds asked Christian and Hopeful many questions. Then, being pleased with their answers, Knowledge looked lovingly upon them and said, "Welcome! Welcome to the Delectable Mountains. Come to our tents and partake of our meal. We would also invite you to stay here for a time. Our Lord has named us Knowledge, Experience, Watchful, and Sincere. To the degree that you come to know and love us, you will find your journey safe and easy. Come, partake freely of the good things of this land!"

And so it was that the pilgrims spent many a happy day dwelling among the shepherds. On one occasion, as they were walking up and down upon the mountains, they came to the top of a hill called Error.

"My!" exclaimed Christian, coming suddenly to a steep drop-off at the top. "This hill of Error has a gentle slope on the way up, but going down the back side it becomes a sheer cliff!"

"Indeed," agreed Experience. "Look down at the bottom. What do you see?"

"Oh, no!" cried Christian, appalled at the sight. "I see several men all smashed and bloodied at the bottom!"

"Aye," nodded Experience sadly.

"How were these men destroyed?" asked Hopeful.

"Have you not read of them that were led into error by listening to Hymenaeus and Philetus, who spread lying doubts regarding a literal bodily resurrection?" quizzed Knowledge.

"Yes," answered Hopeful. "I believe their story was recorded by Paul. But what about them?"

"They whom you see below are those deceived ones."

"Indeed? But why are they left unburied?" quizzed Christian.

"They are left there as a warning to others to be cautious about dwelling too long upon things that are not revealed. Those that are careless in these matters often climb too high for safety or come too near the brink of this mountain."

"Hmmm," mused Christian. "We have enough challenge simply trying to understand what God has revealed. Therefore you may rest assured, sir, that our sole desire is to know and to do the bidding of Him who has called us and saved us by His blood."

"Mmm, good," nodded Knowledge. "Wisely spoken."

"What mountain is that?" asked Hopeful, pointing to a high hill that lay in the direction from which they had come.

"'Tis called the Mount of Caution," replied Knowledge. "Come and you shall see why."

Then, I saw that they led them to the top and bid them look down into the valley. This they did, and immediately noticed several men walking in endless circles, over, around and into the many tombs that were in that place. As they watched they saw that the men were blind because they kept stumbling endlessly into the same tombs.

"What does this mean?" asked Christian with puzzled concern.

"Do you remember, some way back, how the road became rough and full of potholes?" replied Knowledge.

"Yes," answered Christian ruefully, remembering all too well.

"And did you chance to notice a sturdy stile that led over the fence and into a meadow on the left-hand side of the way?" At mention of the nearly fatal attraction, Hopeful shifted nervously on his feet and stammered, "Uh . . . er . . . uh, yes."

"Why?" asked Christian, seeking to conceal the depth of his interest.

"From that stile there is a path that leads directly into the stormy land of Doubt," explained Knowledge. "There you will find Doubting Castle, which is kept by an evil giant named Despair. These blind ones were on the same pilgrimage as you, until they came to that stile."

"Oh?" said Christian nervously. "Uh . . . please . . . go on."

"Well, because the right way was temporarily rough, these lazy ones foolishly chose to walk alongside of it in a soft clover patch named By-path Meadow. There they became lost in a storm and were soon captured by Giant Despair."

"Ahem, uh . . . interesting," commented Hopeful, hoping that the shepherds would not pick up the quavering in his voice. "Uh . . . go on. What then?"

"Then," continued Knowledge gravely, "he cast them into the dungeon of Doubting Castle (which I hear to be as dark and dreary a place as any to be found on earth). After he had amused himself with them for a time, he put out their eyes and set them out to pasture among those tombs. There, they will grope blindly about until he comes for them or until they die."

At this Christian and Hopeful caught each other's eye for a split second, and then looked down to hide their shame. Knowledge, pretending not to notice, continued saying, "Herein is fulfilled the saying of the Wise Man who said, 'He that wandereth out of the Way of understanding shall remain in the congregation of the dead.'"

"Ahem," coughed Christian, clearing his throat and fighting back a tear.

"Is there any hope for them?" Hopeful inquired with an intensity of feeling perceived only by Christian.

"Nay," replied Knowledge, shaking his head sadly. "Virtually none who fall into the land of Doubt are ever set free again."

Then I saw that Christian and Hopeful looked at one another with tears streaming down their faces as they realized the greatness of their miraculous escape. But being ashamed to have gone out of the Way, they kept their thoughts to themselves and said nothing to the shepherds.

Then, I saw in my dream that the shepherds led them to another place in a valley where there was a steaming, fuming iron door set into the side of a hill. One of the shepherds donned heavy gloves and cautiously opened the heavy door. This done, Experience bade them look in, saying, "What do you see?"

"'Tis very dark," answered Christian, peering nervously into the cavernous blackness within.

"And frightfully smoky," added Hopeful, straining to see beyond the billowing, yellow-gray clouds.

"I hear the rumblings of some great fire," added Christian.

"And my nose stings from the odor of brimstone," said Hopeful, pressing his kerchief to his nose.

"What is this evil place?" choked Christian, as a wisp of the sulphurous smoke wafted over him.

"This door is a byway to hell," said Watchful.

"Oh?"

"Aye," added Sincere. "This is the way whereby hypocrites enter that place."

"Indeed? Can you give examples?"

"Certainly," said Knowledge. "Namely, such as sell their birthright, with Esau; such as sell their master, with Judas; such as blaspheme the Gospel, with Alexander; and such as lie and dissemble, with Ananias and Sapphira."

"But did not each of them appear to be a pilgrim, even as we do today?" asked Hopeful.

"Indeed they did," agreed Knowledge. "And they remained in the way quite a long time too!"

"My! How far along can a hypocrite go in this way?" Hopeful asked nervously.

"Most give out long ere this," answered Watchful.

"But some manage to get even farther than these mountains," added Sincere.

"Indeed!" exclaimed Christian, amazed to think such a thing possible.

"Oh, yes," Sincere continued. "Some ignorantly come right to the gates of the kingdom ere they realize their loss."

"And are there any other ways that lead into this dreadful place?" inquired Christian.

"Oh, yes many," said Knowledge. "Hundreds and thousands."

"Verily?" asked Christian, fearful at the thought.

"Yes," continued Knowledge. "In fact, all roads lead to this place, save one."

"Then all the more reason to cry out to the Strong for strength," said Christian, convicted of his need to stay near the cross.

"Aye," put in Knowledge in his riddle-like manner. "And when you get it you will find that you will need it too."

Then, with great echoing reverberations that seemed to resound forever, they slammed the heavy door that led down into the hypocrite's byway. Then the shepherds led the pilgrims back down to their tents among the sheep.

"Well," said Christian, beginning to get itchy feet, "our days among you have been pleasant and instructive, but we feel that we had best be on our way."

"Aye, and we agree," said Knowledge with a smile. "You only needed to become acquainted with us and to refresh yourself for your journey. But before you go, would you like to look through our glass at the Celestial City?"

"Can we truly see it from here?" responded Christian eagerly.

"Aye. Here," said Knowledge handing Christian his spy glass. "Can you see it?"

"Well," said Christian, peering intently into the glass, "my hands are shaking a bit from looking into the lake of fire, but what I can see seems all shining and glorious! Oh, how I long to be there and sitting at the feet of my Lord!"

Then, as Hopeful took his turn looking at the wonders yet to come, Watchful responded, saying, "If faithful, you shall enter there soon."

"How soon?" asked Hopeful eagerly as he returned the glass.

The Shepherds and the Delectable Mountains

"Much sooner than you think," answered Watchful with a play-ful wink at Christian, "and much longer than you wish."

"And now, Godspeed," said Knowledge, a bit sad to see them go.

And so they parted from the shepherds, who, each of them, gave them some important counsel. Watchful gave them a map of the way and told them to follow it closely. Sincere urged them to beware of the Flatterer. Experience warned them to take heed that they sleep not upon the Enchanted ground, and Knowledge bade them Godspeed and urged them to use their time wisely. Then they each gave them a fond embrace and several precious gifts.

CHAPTER NINE

OW A LITTLE below these mountains, on the left hand, there lies the contented little country of Conceit. Contented because all they that dwell therein account themselves to be in possession of all knowledge worth the having. Therefore, it is that they feel themselves to be in need of nothing besides. From that country I perceived there comes into the straight way a little crooked lane. As Christian and Hopeful passed this well-worn intersection they were joined by a very pert and forward young man whose name was Ignorance. As he joined himself to them, Christian said, good-naturedly, "Greetings, lad."

"Oh, hello, good sirs," he said briskly, looking up briefly from a storybook.

"Whither from?" asked Christian.

"Hmmm? Oh, I am from yonder, fine country of Conceit," said the lad with a noticeable rise of chest and chin.

"Oh?" continued Christian. "And whither bound?"

"I am off to the Celestial City," he said, exuding waves of boundless confidence.

"You are?" asked Hopeful, somewhat taken aback by such supreme assurance.

"Of course!" crowed Ignorance, as if repeating a journey travelled many times.

"But how do you expect to get in at the gate?" asked Christian, concerned for the lad's salvation.

"Why the same as everybody else does, of course," he answered coolly.

"But what do you have to show at the gate that will cause them to open it for you?" Christian inquired.

"Excuse me?" answered Ignorance blankly.

"What makes you think they will let you in?" Hopeful rephrased.

"Why, because I know my Lord's will and have lived a good life," offered Ignorance. "I pray every day in the streets, fast twice a week, pay tithes (even of my garden herbs, mind you), and give alms.

Besides, and greater than all that, I have left my country and all that I possess in order to go on pilgrimage."

"But you didn't come in at the wicket gate!" insisted Christian. "You are likely to be called a thief and a robber!"

"Dear gentlemen! Please!" protested Ignorance, his fur rubbed quite the wrong way. "You be complete strangers to me. How do you dare speak to me so bluntly, seeing that I scarcely know you?"

"Because we are concerned for your welfare," answered Hopeful earnestly.

"There be no need for that," blurted Ignorance with a confident wave of his hand. "No need at all. You be content to follow the religion of your country, and I'll be pleased to follow the religion of mine. I have good reason to hope that in the by and by all shall be well with both of us."

"But the wicket gate is the appointed way to begin this journey, no matter what our nationality," insisted Christian.

"Nay!" scoffed Ignorance. "All the world knows that said gate is a great way off from the country of Conceit. Why, I can't think of even one person in our parts who even knows how to get there."

"That should be a warning to you!" urged Hopeful.

"Nah! It matters not a bit!" responded Ignorance arrogantly. "Why, anyone can see," he continued, waving a hand back toward the intersection, "that we have a fine, pleasant, green lane that rolls down from our country right into the Way. Actually, we have quite the jump on most folks."

Then, realizing what manner of man they were dealing with, Christian took Hopeful aside and said softly, "There be more hope for a fool than for this man."

"Aye. He is certainly wise in his own conceit."

"What do you think, Hopeful? Shall we reason with him further or outgo him and hope that time will grant him wisdom?"

"He certainly feels no need of counsel at this time," said Hopeful, glancing at the young man, who, oblivious neither to their presence nor its lack, was licking at a sucker and buried once again in his storybook. "I say we try to help him later when he may appreciate it."

So they continued on their way at their former good pace, leaving Ignorance to meander along on his own, reading his story, savouring his candy, and completely unconscious of their disappearance.

Now, they had not gone much farther when they came into a very dark lane, where they heard a man named Turn-away screaming as if for his life (which, as you shall soon see, was indeed the case).

"Let me go! Unhand me, you vile beasts!" he screamed, and that for good reason. For the man was bound about the neck by many strong cords and dragged along by seven devils of the worst sort.

"Stop! Where are we going?" demanded Turn-away, seeking desperately to stall for time.

"To a little iron door in the side of yonder hill," leered Legalicus, a demon attired in the habits of a judge.

"Oh, no!" cried Turn-away. "Not the one called The Bypath to Hell!"

"Ah, so you know the place, do you?" gloated Baelzebub, a chief demon. "Yes. That's exactly where we're going. Heh, heh, heh."

"Noooo!" cried Turn-away, resisting with all his might.

"Yessssss," a spirit named Tisiphone hissed into his face with a demonic curl to his lip.

"Wait, wait, wait!" cried Turn-away, still trying to stall. "Where does it lead?"

"Now where would you guess a door called The Bypath to Hell might take you?" leered Legion sarcastically.

"I have no idea," lied Turn-away.

"Then let me be the first to inform you," volunteered Legion, glad to be the bearer of grim tidings. "It leads to the lake of fire where you must perish forever!"

"Noooo! Not to the lake of fire!" screamed Turn-away, trembling violently.

"Ah, but yes," chortled another dark one named Lucifer. "And to the hottest part of it too!"

"But I am a pilgrim!" he insisted desperately.

"As are many who have perished there," grinned Legalicus.

"Now just you wait a minute," screeched Turn-away. "I need to send a message to my Lord reminding Him that I have eaten with Him as a loving companion."

"Oh, have you now," crooned Tisiphone. "Well, so have we. Heh, heh, heh."

282 ◆ PILGRIM'S PROGRESS

"But I am a believer!" screamed the man. "I have said the sinner's prayer. I believe!"

"We do better than that," gushed Legion. "We believe and tremble! Ha, ha, ha."

"But I have worked miracles in His name!" pleaded Turn-away.

"We still do," Baelzebub howled. "And by the same power as you did."

"B . . . b . . . but I . . . I . . . have spoken in tongues!" Turn-away yelled, beginning to grasp at straws.

"As have the oracles of Delphi and pagan priests of all ages," countered Linguisticus. "Want to hear me?"

"Noooo!" he groaned, running out of hope. "Lord Jesus, help me!"

"Your Lord has said that He does not know you," sneered Legion. "Here we are."

"Open the iron door," commanded Lucifer. And so was it done. From great cavernous depths there belched forth billows of yellow-gray smoke. At the sight thereof Christian and Hopeful shook and trembled but were unable to tear themselves from beholding the fearsome spectacle. Then, Turn-away dug in his heels, and holding up his hands piously said, in as dignified a manner as he could muster (which was not all that dignified, given that he was shaking like a leaf), "Wait! Hold, hold, hold, jus' . . . just for one moment. I know you gentlemen have a job to do b . . . b . . . b . . . but I think there must be s . . . s . . . s . . . some misunderstanding here. Heh, heh."

"A misunderstanding, do you say?" asked Legion.

"Uh, Yes! Yes, a rather serious one at that," Turn-away continued, relieved to be halted, even if just for the moment.

"Well, we certainly don't want to make any mistakes in matters so serious as this," said Legion politely. "Let me introduce you to Legalicus. He deals with all these legal issues."

"Bad day," intoned Legalicus acidly as he produced a large black book. "Name please."

"Name? Oh, you mean my name. Uh . . .T . . . Turn-away they call me, although I never could understand quite why."

"Turn-away, Turn-away . . ." muttered Legalicus as he methodically turned to section T. "Hmmm," said he, running a sooty claw down the long list of names. "You come from a rather large family, don't you, Mr. Turn-away. Ah, here you are! Alouiscious P. Turn-away, from the town of Apostasy, right?"

"Yes, sir."

"Tsk, tsk, tsk. Looks like an open and shut case to me, boys."

"Beg your pardon," said Turn-away.

"Oh, nothing. Nothing at all, Mr. Turn-away. We just have to take care of a few formalities here, that's all. Let me ask you first, sir, did you come in at the wicket gate?"

"Well, uh . . . no. Not exactly," Turn-away admitted chagrined.

"Hmmm," said Legalicus, thumbing through another of his large black volumes and pausing to read aloud, "'Not exactly'—hmmm. Listen to this, boys. The Dictionary of Common Human Usages defines the phrase 'not exactly' thusly, Mr. Turn-away. 'Not exactly'— a euphemistic figure of speech by which humans mean to say 'exactly not.' Is that what you really meant to say, sir?"

At this, Turn-away hemmed and hawed and at last answered, "Well, no, not exactly."

"But! Say it how you will, the fact is that you came not in at the wicket gate," snarled Legalicus grimly. "Isn't that so, Mr. Turn-away?"

"Well, yes."

"Why not?"

"Well, uh . . . it was a long way, you see," Turn-away explained lamely.

"Yes, I do see," said Legalicus, scribbling something official in his ledger. "Next question. Have you your certificate?"

"Gulp. Certificate?"

"Yes, certificate. Do you have it?"

"Well, uh . . . no. Not exactly. I mean er, that is no, sir. Not with me," confessed Turn-away, his fears once again rising rapidly. "You see I . . ."

"Did you ever have it?" interrupted Tisiphone.

"Uh, where do we get them?" Turn-away asked lamely while trying to control an involuntary twitch of his face.

"At the foot of the cross, of course!" howled Lucifer, hovering hungrily in front of Turn-away's face. "Did you ever go to the foot of the cross, Mr. Turn-away?"

"No one ever sent me there!"

"And I suppose you never tell a lie either," Linguisticus sneered sarcastically.

"I try not to," Turn-away evaded.

"Only try? I'm happy to inform you that 'only try' doesn't count in this court of law, Mr. Turn-away," mocked Legalicus, ceremoniously snapping shut his black book with a malicious wink at his companions. "Case closed!"

"Say, I don't think I like the looks of this," Turn-away whined, once again beginning to tremble like a leaf in the wind.

"And we don't like the looks of you," said Lucifer as the pack began to tighten their circle of darkness.

"Best you be careful!" threatened Turn-away desperately. "I have cast out devils in His name, you know!"

"Because we allowed you to," hissed Tisiphone. "Try it now, nominal Christian."

"Stand back! I warn you!" commanded Turn-away unconvincingly as he inched back away from the hairy horde toward the fuming iron gate. "This is your last chance!"

"And this is yours," grinned Baelzebub, motioning them all into position. "Ready ghouls and goblins?"

"All right then!" screeched Turn-away, his eyes wide with fear and voice all aquiver. "You have forced me to it! In the name of Jesus of Nazareth, whom Paul preached, I cast you out!"

"Jesus we know . . ." leered Baelzebub icily as he oozed closer with a menacing leer.

"And Paul we know . . ." sneered Legalicus sarcastically as he filed the points on his long black nails.

". . . BUT WHO ARE YOU?" roared all seven demons in practiced unison.

Then Turn-away screamed desperately, "I'll show you who I am! Out! I cast you out! All of you!"

"In, false Christian! We cast you in! All of you!" echoed the seven spirits in sadistic glee.

"Ready? 1 - 2 - 3!" directed Baelzebub.

"No. Aaauuuugh!" screamed Turn-away as hands and claws, pincers and paws violently tore him off his feet.

"In with him!" seven demonic voices screeched and howled, cackled and yowled as they sent Turn-away spiraling away, down, down, and yet more down into the cavernous blackness of the hole in the hill.

Then, as Turn-away's fading screams were cut short by the echoing clang of the slamming door, Legalicus turned and cast a soul-stabbing stare toward Christian and Hopeful. Pointing a black claw at them he said, in an evil, guttural voice, "We nearly had you two, back in the land of Doubt. But your journey is not yet o'er. We shall meet again!"

Then the spirits, being totally helpless to harm true Christians, slowly returned to their vaporous state and were soon lost from sight. Said Hopeful, turning from the fearful sight with trembling, "Who was that man?"

"I am not sure," answered Christian weakly.

"I wonder if this could be the man named Turn-away who lived in the town of Apostasy?" Hopeful ventured.

"Ah yes, it must have been," answered Christian. "For there was a paper on his back which said 'wanton professor and damnable apostate.'"

"Ah, then certainly it was Turn-away! Then how great are the dangers of being a pilgrim in name only," he said gravely.

"Aye. Better never to profess than to live a lie."

"May God deliver us from ever becoming a Turn-away," prayed Hopeful.

"Aye," agreed Christian. "But say! This reminds me of another man named Little-faith—a good man who lived in the town of Sincere. As I remember it was right near this dark lane that he came into some hard trials."

"Oh? Tell me his story," suggested Hopeful as they resumed their travels.

"Well," said Christian, pointing up the hill, "you see yonder twisting lane that comes down from Broad-way Gate and meets with this path?"

"Aye."

"'Tis called Dead Man's Lane."

"Indeed! Why? Are there many murders done there?"

The robbery of Little-faith

"Aye, many indeed. Now this man, Little-faith, was going on pilgrimage, as we do now, and when he came to that lane he sat down for a short rest."

"A dangerous thing it would seem to me," commented Hopeful.

"Aye, dangerous indeed! But not having consulted his map, which would have alerted him to his peril, he felt quite secure and his rest soon turned into a deep slumber. It was not long until his loud snorings reached the ears of three brothers named Faint-heart, Mistrust, and Guilt. These three vultures smelled a carcass for the plucking and so came skulking down the lane just as Little-faith was rising from his nap. Then, these three ruffians broke into a scrambling run down the lane and with dark threatenings commanded him to stand still on the spot. At this, he turned white as a ghost and could neither fight nor flee. Then Faint-heart came up to him and said, 'Hand over your purse, knave!' But Little-faith was sickened at the thought of losing his only means of travel and so was slow to obey. Angered at his delay, Mistrust stepped up to him, reached into his pocket, and snatched out his bag of silver. At this, Little-faith finally pulled his wits together and cried out, 'Thieves! Thieves!' At that, Guilt strutted up and knocked him a heavy clout on the head that stretched him senseless on the ground.

"Before they could search him the thieves heard someone coming along the road. They, fearing it to be Great-grace, one of the King's warriors from the city of Good-confidence, took to their heels and left Little-faith to shift for himself. After awhile Little-faith came to himself and made haste to hurry away from that deadly place. And that is the story as I heard it told."

"Hmmm, sad," sympathized Hopeful. "And so was he stranded with no treasure left at all?"

"Not totally," said Christian. "They had no time for a search, so he at least kept his heavenly jewels."

"Ah," said Hopeful thankfully. "Lucky for him!"

"Indeed! But he was still deeply grieved for he had scarcely enough change to get him through the day, let alone finish his journey. I hear he had to find odd jobs and sometimes even beg to feed himself. But even so, he had many an empty belly for the better part of the way."

"And did they get his certificate?"

"Nay. And lucky for him too! For without that, there is no entering the Celestial City."

"As Turn-away learned," said Hopeful, with a nervous glance back toward the distant smouldering gate. "God must have watched over him."

"So I believe, for certainly 'twas neither wit nor wisdom on his part that spared him that loss."

"Well, at least he could derive some comfort from having retained his certificate and jewels."

"He could have if he had not allowed his blessings to be swallowed up by his curses. He consumed much of his pilgrimage in bemoaning his loss."

"Ah, poor man," sympathized Hopeful. "This must have been a great grief to him."

"As it would be to any of us were we robbed, wounded and left to die in a strange place! 'Tis a wonder he did not die of grief, poor heart! I heard that no matter where he went, or who he met, he told and retold the story of his loss."

"'Tis a wonder that his loss and his need did not drive him to pawn off some of his jewels," Hopeful commented absent-mindedly.

"That was an ignorant and foolish thing to say!" snapped Christian bluntly. Yea, Christian spoke in such a forceful manner as to nearly set Hopeful back on his heel in surprise. Then Christian continued his sudden lecture saying, "The jewels pilgrims carry are of no value here! And even if someone did buy them, how could he live off the money knowing that he had sold the jewels entrusted to him to carry to the kingdom? Better to meet ten thousand thieves than to lose eternity!"

"Why do you answer me so curtly, my brother?" complained Hopeful. "Esau sold his birthright for a mess of pottage. So what's wrong in supposing that Little-faith might have done the same?"

"There is a great difference between Esau and Little-faith which you do not discern, dear Hopeful. Esau's birthright was symbolic, but Little-faith's jewels were reality. Esau's belly was his god, but Little-faith's was not. Esau lived for fleshly appetites, but Little-faith did not. Esau could see no further than the meal of the moment when he said, 'I am at the point of dying! And what good will this foolish birthright do me then?' But Little-faith was, even with his weak faith, able to see the value of his jewels in eternity and would not have sold them at any price."

"Hmmm," answered Hopeful quietly. "Go on."

"Nowhere will you read that Esau had kept even a little faith. And without at least a measure of faith, no man can see to value himself as heaven does. Yea, he will sell birthright, self, and soul to the devil himself and think he has driven a sharp bargain. They are like the ass who in her season cannot be turned away. Likewise, when men with no faith set their minds upon their lusts, they will have them whatever the cost."

"Hmmm," mumbled Hopeful, his hurt feelings beginning to mend. "Say on more."

"But Little-faith was completely different. His affections were set on things above, where Christ dwells at the right hand of God. Therefore, he would no more sell his jewels for momentary comfort than you would shell out a crown for a flake of straw at dinner. So, you see, your mistake was no small one."

"So I see now," admitted Hopeful. "But your answer came so forcefully that it nearly made me angry."

"My apologies," said Christian sincerely. "I probably jumped to my brother's defense with heavier boots than were called for. But come, let us be more careful of each other's hearts and yet continue to draw lessons from this sad story."

"I shall be happy to," replied Hopeful with a smile.

"You may lead the way now. Have you any questions or observations?"

"Well," replied Hopeful thoughtfully, "as I think about those three robbers, it seems to me that they were nothing but a pack of cowards."

"Oh?" answered Christian, arching a questioning eyebrow. "And why do you think so?"

"Why else would they have run away at the mere sound of someone coming down the road? It seems to me that against such faint-hearted ones as that, Little-faith could have at least put up a bit of a struggle and not have yielded his silver so meekly."

"Ah," Christian answered sagely. "From a distance many others have called these three rogues cowards. But in the heat of actual battle, they have found them to be quite the opposite."

"Indeed!"

"Aye. And from your words it seems that you are in favor of only a bit of a struggle before yielding."

"Is there something wrong with that?"

"Well, if that's all the resistance you intend from a safe distance, might you not have second thoughts when you felt a dagger at your heart?"

"Hmmm."

"You seem to think that these fellows are only amateur highwaymen, but such is not the case."

"No?"

"No indeed! These are journeymen thieves; professionals who serve under the king of the bottomless pit. He hates to have his servants meet with failure and, if need be, will come to their aid in person! And since he roars about like a lion seeking whom he may devour, there be few that can resist him."

"So!" exclaimed Hopeful. "This is a more serious business than at first meets the eye."

"Indeed," nodded Christian solemnly. "Much more serious. And I speak from personal experience too."

"You do!"

"Aye. Some time back, while I was in the Valley of The Shadow of Death, Faint-heart, Mistrust, and Guilt set upon me full strength. And when I gave them some good stout Christian resistance, do you think they would fall back? Nay, but rather two of them continued to harry me while the other sounded the alarm for help. And I tell you true, dear Hopeful, 'twas but a moment before the Prince of the pit came rising to their aid."

"My!" said Hopeful, fully caught up in the drama of the story. "How did you manage to escape them?"

"First," answered Christian, breaking into a cold sweat at the memory of the ordeal, "I was wearing my gospel armor. Second, I called to my aid all-prayer, and my Lord did send reinforcements. But even so, I had to strive valiantly against these three villains and their prince. I tell you true, dear Hopeful, no one knows what mortal combat is except those who have been there. Why, even the memory makes my heart race a bit."

"You say they are not cowards. Yet they ran at the mere thought that Great-grace was coming down the path."

"You are right, they did! As has their master many a time too! But don't be too amazed at that, for Great-grace is the King's champion. But certainly you can see that there is a great difference between Little-faith and one of the King's great ones."

"Yes, I can see your point clearly on that one."

"Good. Then let me say more. Not all of the King's subjects can become His champions. And when it comes to feats of war, no common pilgrim can handle his weapons as surely and swiftly as Great-grace can. A child cannot knock down a Goliath and though you can yoke a sparrow with an ox, you cannot expect him to pull half the load. Do you see my drift?"

"Yes."

"Then you can see that some are weak, some are strong; some have a great faith, some a weak; this man was one of the weak, and therefore was he backed against the wall."

"I see your point. Perhaps I expected more from Little-faith than he was capable of. But I still wish it had been Great-grace they heard. Surely he would have soon laid those three rogues in the dust."

"Soon? No, Hopeful, not soon. Even he would have had his hands full with those three."

"Great-grace! But you called him the King's champion!"

"Aye, of a certain he is. But good as he is at his weapons, those three and their master are desperate villains. As long as a man can stand them off at sword's point, he fares well enough. But let just one of them get within dagger range and down he goes! And when once a man is down, with four against one, what chance has he then?"

"So, apparently, Faint-heart, Guilt, and Mistrust are more of a challenge than meets the untrained eye," concluded Hopeful, beginning to feel more sympathy for Little-faith's predicament.

"Aye," agreed Christian, glad to see that Hopeful was beginning to realize the power of the enemy. "Should you ever meet Great-grace in person, study his face. There you are sure to see many a cut and scar. Why, he has even been heard to say from the heart of combat, 'We despaired even of life.'"

"Verily! Great-grace?"

"Aye, and not he alone," exclaimed Christian. "Look to Scripture to see how these sturdy rogues drove King David to the wall with sighs and deep groanings! Yea, Heman and Hezekiah, even though they were the champions of their time, had many a bruise to show from their encounters with these three."

"My! I had no idea!"

"Oh, yes. Faint-heart, Mistrust and Guilt are more deadly foes than most pilgrims realize. Even Peter, the prince of the apostles, was so badly beaten by these three that he was made to fear a mere scrub-maid. And remember, he was the one who boasted that he would die for his Master!"

"I am beginning to see your point," Hopeful answered gravely. "But what can we do to protect ourselves against such rogues, seeing that they have all the forces of hell at their beck and call? Do common pilgrims, such as I, even stand a chance?"

"Aye. All the chance in the world."

"How?"

"The first thing we must do is to follow the example of the man at the gate of the palace and harness ourselves with the gospel armor. Especially must we obey the words of the apostle when he said, 'Above all, take the shield of faith, wherewith ye shall be able to quench all the fiery darts of the wicked.'"

"I can do that," Hopeful stated, greatly encouraged. "And what else?"

"Second," continued Christian, "we must ask the King to let us travel with one of His convoys, or in the presence of a mighty Champion such as Great-grace or Great-heart. Or, better yet that He Himself shall be our leader! His presence is what enabled David to rejoice when in the Valley of the Shadow of Death. And Moses would rather have died on the spot than to have gone one step without his God. Oh, my brother, it is the same with us! If He is at our side we need not fear though ten thousand such rogues be against us. But not alone, dear Hopeful. Not alone! Though I have survived some hard times against such as these, it was only by a swift employment of my shield and by His hand guiding mine to the sword. I fear that we have not yet met with the last of dangers. But, since the lion and the bear have not devoured me, I trust that God will also deliver us from the next uncircumcised Philistine."

"Well," said Hopeful thankfully, "I am glad that you have opened my eyes to my danger. And I am also glad to be in company with such an experienced warrior as you."

"We are what God has made us by our permission," answered Christian modestly. "But say? I have just thought of a poem full of lessons from the experience of Little-faith."

"Share it with me."

"All right. It goes like this:

'Poor Little-faith! hast been among the thieves,
Wast robbed, Remember this: whoso believes
And gets more faith, shall then a victor be
Over ten thousand; else, scarce over three.'"

"Very nice," smiled Hopeful. "And very, very true."

And so they continued on in their journey, with Ignorance trailing along, nonchalantly, far down the trail. They went on until they came to a fork in the road. Here they came to a halt because each path seemed just as straight as the other. As they stood trying to decide which way was the right, a man of a very dark and swarthy complexion, but clothed in a robe of white, came to them and said cheerily, "Why are you two intelligent-looking gentlemen standing here at a halt? There are many miles left in this day."

"We know, good sir," answered Christian. "But we're at a pause because we don't know which of these paths to follow."

"Perhaps I can be of some help," offered the man with a gracious smile. "Where are you trying to go?"

"We be off to the Celestial City," announced Christian.

"Ah! Just as I thought!" exclaimed the man with a broad grin and a joyous clap of his hands. "From your fine appearance and shining garments, I just knew that you must be fellow pilgrims. Come, follow me," he said with a deep bow and a gesture toward one fork, "for I know the way quite well."

So, trusting that his white robe had been woven in the same loom as their own, they followed him down the path that forked off to the left. Now, this path did, ever so slowly, by degrees too small to detect, bend away from the City until, some hours later, they were actually walking away from it. Yet, the man in white spoke to them with such friendliness and bantering humor, that travel was most pleasant and the time seemed to fly by. He asked them many questions about their exploits and, after each account of their adventures, praised their wisdom and courage. Yea, he lavished so much praise upon them that, had his words been rum, they would have soon been laid out quite senseless by the road. Indeed, so pleased were they with his merry company that they failed to notice that the light was now behind them. Neither did they notice when at last they were led under the snare of the fowler. Suddenly, the man leapt to one side, pulled a hidden cord, and dropped a heavy net that encircled them firmly in its meshes. Yea, though they tried, and tried again to free themselves, escape was impossible. Then, Flatterer laughed loudly, and with a grand flourish, threw off the white robe, crying, "Aha! I've got you now! Ha, ha, ha!"

"This must be the Flatterer!" groaned Christian.

"Yes," Hopeful concurred dismally. "Did not the shepherds warn us about him?"

"Aye, 'tis I!" exulted the Flatterer proudly. "And I shall return with the prince of flatterers shortly forthwith. Until then, I bid you most lovely, and intelligent, and gullible gentlemen a brief adieu."

With that, the man ran swiftly on down the trail, where he soon vanished into a dark and musty wood.

"Oh, me," lamented Christian. "The wise man was right when he said that, 'A man that flattereth his neighbor, spreadeth a net for his feet.'"

"Aye," bemoaned Hopeful. "Right indeed. Oh, how did we ever end up here?"

"'Twas because we forgot to look at the map the shepherds gave us," Christian answered ruefully.

"You're right," confessed Hopeful. "Oh, foolish pilgrims! When will we ever learn to follow instructions?"

And so, there they lay for some time bewailing their foolishness and praying for help. Christian tried his best to reach his sword, but alas, when bound up in the net of flattery, such a sword as that is of no use. Neither could he reach within his bosom to use the key of promise. And so they sat for a time with no defense except to pray that the Lord of the Hill would forgive and send aid.

Freed from the Flatterer's Net

At last they espied a Shining One coming down the winding path toward them. In his hands he carried a whip of small cords and at the sight of him Christian blushed for shame—for this was the same angel whom he had met at the Slough of Despond.

"Gentlemen!" said he with mild surprise, "I see that ye be trapped in the snare of the evil prince."

"Yes," admitted Christian, head hung low. "Much to our shame."

"Are ye not pilgrims?"

"Aye," admitted Christian reluctantly.

"Your voice," said Help, straining to catch a glimpse

of Christian's face. "I know that voice! Have I not met you before?"

"Aye, sir. At the Slough of Despond."

"Aha! I thought so! Well, I must comment that while your appearance has certainly improved, your situation has not. Did you take your eyes off of the light again?"

"Uh, not exactly," hedged Christian.

"No? Then pray tell, how did you come to be ensnared in this deadly net so far off the right path?"

"Uh . . . we followed a man who claimed to know the way," Christian admitted with shamefacedness.

"What did he look like?" asked Help suspiciously.

"Well, he was dressed all in white which made us think that he must surely be one of us."

"He said he was a pilgrim," added Hopeful.

"Was his face dark?" asked Help.

"Well, yes," admitted Christian.

"Very dark," added Hopeful.

"I thought so!" snapped Help angrily. "It was the Flatterer. He is a prophet of darkness who has transformed himself into an angel of light. Here, let me cut this net." So he went at it. But sharp as was his sword, and sure as were his strokes, the net of flattery was not an easy thing to part asunder. Yea, the Shining One had worked up quite the sweat before deliverance was complete. At last, however, he was able to part the net, saying, "Ah! At last! There you go."

"Ah, thank you, good angel," said Christian, glad to be able to move again.

"Yes. Thank you!" exclaimed Hopeful as he crawled out the hole and scrambled to his feet.

"Now, follow me back to where you left the way," commanded Help sternly.

And so follow him they did, over and around many a dense thicket and gurgley bog. This time, as they travelled with eyes open to see, they marveled that they could ever have been so blind. Great indeed, they decided, must be the power of flattery to close one's eyes to truth. At last they found themselves back in the way.

"Here you are, gentlemen. Back on the way that be straight and narrow."

"Thank you, sir!" exclaimed Christian. "Thank you very much."

"Yes, thank you," added Hopeful gratefully.

"Tell me," queried Help, crossing his arms and looking down upon them sternly, "how did you come to follow in the tracks of the Flatterer?"

"Well," stated Christian glibly, "we came to this fork in the road and knew not which way to go."

"I see," answered the angel suspiciously. "And where did you rest last night?"

"Oh, with the shepherds upon the Delectable Mountains, of course."

"And did they not give you a map?"

"Oh . . . uh . . . (gulp) yes, sir," confessed Christian.

"And when you came to the parting of the way, did you consult it?"

"Uh . . . well . . . no, sir," admitted Christian, head hung low.

"Why not?" asked the Shining One earnestly. "Why not?"

Then Christian swallowed hard and said simply, "We uh . . . forgot, sir."

"I see," said Help with a disappointed sigh. "And did not the shepherds specifically remind you to be on guard against the Flatterer?"

"Uh . . . er uh . . ." Christian stammered.

"Did they?" demanded Help, pointing at Christian and looking upon him with a stern and severe countenance.

"Yes, sir," admitted Christian.

"But sir, this man spoke with such elegance and polish that we had no clue he could be the Flatterer," exclaimed Hopeful.

Then the Shining One re-crossed his mighty arms in ill-concealed displeasure and commanded, "Lie down!"

"Lie down, sir?" asked Christian weakly.

"Yes," he ordered, pointing to the earth, "faces to the ground."

"Yes, sir," answered Christian meekly, as he moved to obey.

"Yes, sir," said Hopeful, nervously eyeing the cat-o-nine tails twitching ominously in the clenched fist of the angel. Then Christian whispered to Hopeful, "I think he is going to punish our foolishness."

"And we deserve it," answered Hopeful, stretching himself out next to his companion. Then said Help sternly as he raised the scourge, "'As many as I love I rebuke and chasten!'" And with that, he smote Christian two sound stripes upon his back. These Christian bore in courageous silence. Then, as he struck Hopeful one light blow on his back, he said, "'Be zealous, therefore, and repent.'"

"Ow!" squeaked Hopeful involuntarily. "Yes, sir. We were foolish."

"You may rise," said Help as he stepped back and once again crossed his powerful arms.

"Ah," groaned Hopeful, rising to his feet. "Thank you for your help, sir. And for our well-deserved chastening."

"Yes," added Christian. "And thank you for making it lighter than we deserved."

"You are welcome," said Help kindly. "Be on your way now. And take good heed to the other directions of the shepherds. They spoke for your salvation, not for the pleasure of hearing their own voices."

"Yes, sir," said Christian, turning to resume his journey.

"Yes, thank you, sir," said Hopeful gratefully. "Farewell."

After thanking Help once again for all his kindness, they resumed their travel. And you can be very sure that they were more than a little grateful to be got back into the right way. After a few more miles they thought as if they heard someone whistling some distance ahead of them. They looked and behold, there was an old man with a flowing white beard hobbling down the highway to meet them. This man carried a silver-headed walking stick, was dressed in bright-colored clothing and carried himself with the jaunty air of one who knows all worth the knowing. His name was Atheist, and at the sight of him Christian was quick to be on his guard, saying, "Look!"

"What?" asked Hopeful.

"Yonder is a man with his back toward Zion and coming down to meet us."

"Ah, yes. I see him now," said Hopeful suspiciously. "Let us guard our ears lest he should prove to be an even more skillful flatterer than the first."

Upon meeting them, Atheist bowed deeply and tipped his hat in a most jolly manner, saying merrily, "Ho, hey! Whither away, boys?"

"We be bound for Mount Zion," said Christian.

"Zion!" snorted the man derisively as he broke into a great spasm of laughter. "Zion, do you say? Ha, ha, ha."

"What is the meaning of all this laughter?" demanded Christian.

"Oh, nothing really. Really nothing. I am just simply amused to see what ignorant persons you are."

"What do you mean?" demanded Christian.

"You know as well as I," said he, trying to contain his merriment, "that you have undertaken to go on a tedious and dangerous journey, do you not?"

"But of course," replied Christian. "We counted the cost at the start."

"But!" said the man, slicing the air with sweeps of his elegant cane, "what you *don't* know is that when you come to journey's end, you will have gained nothing more than tourist's memories for all your many troubles."

"What!" stammered Christian. "Why do you say that? Do you think us unworthy to enter in at the gate?"

"Gate! Ha, ha, ha," laughed the man again, holding his side with one hand and wiping tears of mirth with the other. "There be no such gate in all the world! Ha, ha, ha."

"But there is in the world to come," protested Christian.

"No, no! No, no, no no. No such place," he said with a cocky smile. "No such place at all!"

"Why do you think so?"

"Experience, my boys! Experience! You see," he continued, lowering his voice and drawing very close, "I was once a pilgrim, the same as you."

"You were?" chorused both.

"Aye," he affirmed, chest puffed up like a cock on the strut. "And I have traveled much farther on this way than you are ever like to go!"

"And what did you see?" asked Hopeful, eager to know what lay ahead.

"See? You want to know what did I see?"

"That's what I asked you, sir," said Hopeful tersely. "What did you see?"

"Why, nothing!"

"Nothing!" exclaimed Christian.

"Nothing!" howled the man, barely containing his mirth. "Nothing at all! Because there is nothing to see! Ha, ha, ha. It is all a sham!"

"No!" barked Christian.

"Yes!" snapped the man, tightening his jaw and locking his steely gray eyes onto Christian's. "I have traveled this way for over twenty years, and at my journey's end I was no closer to the 'gate' then when I had first begun!"

"This cannot be! Are you sure?" demanded Christian, scarcely able to believe his ears.

"More than sure! Yes!" quipped the man. "And now," he continued with greasy images of lust and debauchery virtually dripping from every word, "I am on my way back to whence I came. And you can be sure that all the pleasures and enjoyments I formerly denied myself on the way up are being enjoyed to their full on the way down."

"This is amazing!" exclaimed Christian in utter shock.

"Isn't it though! I only wish I had never put away that which is seen for that which is unseen."

Then Christian took Hopeful a few steps to the side and said, quietly, "What do you say, Hopeful? Is it true what this man says?"

"What!" exclaimed Hopeful in stunned amazement. "Did we not see the City through the glass? Can we not walk by faith for a time? Do you not remember, brother, the words of the wise man who said: 'Cease, my son, to hear the instruction that causeth thee to err from the words of knowledge?' Come, let us flee this man before your faith grows even weaker!"

"My faith is not weak, my brother," encouraged Christian. "I only wanted to hear what answer you might give. It is clear as day that this man is blinded by the god of this world. Let us go on, knowing that we believe the truth and that no lie is of the truth."

"Oh, dear Christian," exclaimed Hopeful, greatly relieved, "you don't know how glad I am to hear you talking this way. I was afraid the angel might have to chastise us again."

"Well? Well, well, well, well? What is all this whispering about?" demanded the old man impatiently. "Will you turn away from your legalistic foolishness and follow me down to Sodom town, or no?"

"Sir," answered Christian confidently, "we be following the promises of the King—those written by the God who cannot go back on His word, though all men be liars."

"What!" exclaimed Atheist, his bloodshot eyes nearly starting out of their sockets in disbelief. "You will risk all you have on mere words?"

"Not mere words," Christian confidently affirmed. "The Words of God."

"Oh! Of all the harebrained notions!" snorted the man, shaking his head and giving them the back. "Fools ye are, lads. Fools! Fools, fools, fools! Ha, ha, ha . . ."

And so the man tottered off down the trail, stumbling in at every house of ill-repute or smoky den that could be found along the way. Now, whether he died of one of the loathsome diseases so easily acquired in such places, or whether he was murdered in some dark alley, or whether he lived out his short life of debauchery to its miserable end, I do not know. I know only that he disappeared from view, never to be seen again.

I then saw in my dream that they went on without further mishap or encounter till they came into a place where was a new and even deadlier danger. For they now came to a certain country where the water was clear and the fruit abundant. There was neither man nor beast to oppose them, and the air was so fragrantly sweet that it tended to make a traveler very, very drowsy. To make the place even more seductive, there were pleasant arbors placed, here and there, all along the way. These were comfortably shaded with fruit-laden vines and furnished with soft, silken couches. Great was the temptation to rest here in these enchanted grounds and, indeed, many did. But those who succumbed to this deceitfully pleasant air laid themselves down never to rise again. It was here that Hopeful began to be very dull of mind and heavy of eye.

"I say, dear Christian," said Hopeful, yawning widely. "I am (yawn), beginning to get sooo sleepy that I can scarce keep my eyes open. Let us (yawn) lie down in one of these pleasant arbors and take a short nap."

"No, friend Hopeful!" exclaimed Christian in sleepy alarm. "If we lay down in this land we may never wake again."

"Why do you say that, my brother?" yawned Hopeful, eyeing the soft couch in a nearby arbor (yawn). "Sleep is sweet to the laboring man. Can we not take just a wee catnap and be refreshed for our journey?"

"Hopeful! Don't you remember that one of the shepherds told us to beware of the Enchanted Ground?"

"Yes," yawned Hopeful. "So?"

"Well, this be it!" he warned, straining to squelch an incipient yawn. "And I can assure you that if we disobey this command, it will go worse for us than we can imagine."

"I don't see how a few minutes' sleep could do us any harm," grumbled groggy Hopeful.

"No? Well look over there into the mist," Christian challenged.

"Well," said Hopeful, straining to see through the gently billowing mists of the place, "'tis rather foggy and I don't see what you mean."

"Then step over to that arbor and see what greets your eyes on the other side," directed Christian.

"All right," said Hopeful, stepping into the arbor and looking into the soft whiteness. "Ahh!" he screamed, suddenly fully awake. "Bones! Dead men's bones! Positioned as if they were . . ."

"Taking a short catnap?" asked Christian ruefully.

"Yes!" answered Hopeful.

"Aye," nodded Christian. "A short nap is what they thought, but eternal sleep is what they got. These are the bones of those, from all ages past, who settled down to Laodicean ease rather than pressing forward to subdue the kingdom."

"My!" exclaimed Hopeful, now fully alert and trembling at the sight. "This pilgrimage stuff is serious business."

"Aye," agreed Christian. "And if we disobey the shepherds this time, we are sure to add our bones to the pile. Therefore, let us not sleep as do others, but rather watch and be sober."

"Well, I certainly see the need," agreed Hopeful, "but how?"

"Let us stimulate our minds by engaging in profitable conversation," suggested Christian brightly as he set out at a brisk pace.

"All right," agreed Hopeful cheerfully, stretching his stride to catch up. "What about?"

"About uh . . . about how you came to be a pilgrim," urged Christian. "What was your life like before beginning on this wondrous way?"

"Oh," Hopeful confessed reluctantly, "I was buried in the enjoyment of my sins and pleasures, the same as everyone else at Vanity Fair."

"Can you give me some examples?" asked Christian.

"If you wish. Like everyone, I pursued after the treasures and pleasures of this world. I also found temporary comfort in rioting, revelling, drinking, swearing, lying, uncleanness, Sabbath-breaking, and what not. But then I met you and brother Faithful, who was martyred for his pure faith and clean living. I tell you true, dear Christian, when I heard him pray for his executioners and judges, I could not believe my ears! When he sang praises to God from the midst of the flames, I realized that he possessed a joy that all my time-consuming and mind-numbing sins could never supply. On the night of his execution, long after idle spectators had gone back to their cups, I stood and watched Faithful's ashes smouldering in the gathering darkness. I realized that he had looked beyond what is perceived by mortal eyes. He had seen far beyond the present moment and dwelt in the very atmosphere of heaven. But as for me, I was 'bewildered and deceived and moving on in a gloomy procession toward eternal ruin—to a death in which is no hope of life, toward night to which comes no morning.' I and all of Vanity had chosen a ruler who had chained us to his car as captives, and who was leading us on to the brink of a hopeless eternity. I could see nothing in the future but death. And I had no recourse for the present, except the fogging of my mind so that I would not think of what lay ahead. I was convicted that I was lost. Eternally lost!"

"And did you yield to the power of this conviction?" Christian inquired earnestly.

"Oh, no! Stubborn swine that I was, I was not willing to know the evil of sin, nor the damnation that follows. Instead, I tried to shut mine eyes against the light."

"But what caused you to finally realize that it was the Spirit of God calling you?"

"Well, first of all, I did not realize that it was God who was working upon my heart," Hopeful answered thoughtfully. "It never occurred to me that God would begin my conversion by showing me the evil of sin.

"Secondly, sin still seemed sweet to my flesh so I was very loath to separate from it.

"Thirdly, I saw no easy way to part with all my old companions, especially since their company and amusements were still so agreeable to me.

"Fourthly, those hours of conviction were so fearfully, heart-afrighting times that, even now, the memory of them makes me break into a sweat."

Hopeful's life of sin

"So were you ever able to escape from your convictions?" asked Christian with intense interest, seeing in Hopeful's testimony a mirror of his own.

"Oh, yes," nodded Hopeful, "for short times I would bury my thoughts with music, plays, and pleasures. But when the lights faded, and the rum was gone out of my head, they would return. Always they would return! And when they did I found myself as bad off, nay, worse off than I was before!"

"Why?" inquired Christian. "What brought your sins to mind again?"

"Ah, many things," said Hopeful, shaking his head ruefully. "In fact, nearly everything."

"Such as?"

"Well, if I were to meet a good man in the streets; or if I heard someone read from the Bible; or if my head began to hurt; or if I had a mysterious pain; or if I heard that some of my neighbors were sick; or if I heard that someone had suddenly been killed; or if I heard the bell toll for some dead man; or if I thought of dying myself, especially whenever I saw a fire burn, or saw smoke ascending into the sky. Then I would think of dear Faithful singing his way into eternity—an eternity that I myself was unprepared to face."

"Then were you ever able to be rid of the sense of your guilt?"

"No, no! Not at all!" answered Hopeful, saddened at the memory of his hopeless condition. "I finally resolved to ease my mind by trying to live as you and Faithful had done. I did my very best to live a clean and sober life too! Yea, I tried my hardest to obey the law. But I found that there seemed to be another law in my flesh that was stronger than the desires of my heart. I found myself doing what I didn't want to do and not doing the things I knew I should do. Oh, Christian," cried Hopeful, beginning to sob openly, "you cannot know the torment of wanting to do right and yet being led captive by the flesh into some deeper depth of sin! Oh, it was double torment to me! I thought as if I had somehow fallen into the tortures of the second death before my first!"

"So what did you do?" Christian asked earnestly, himself on the verge of sympathizing tears.

"Why, I thought I must try harder to mend my life," answered Hopeful through misty eyes, "'or else,' thought I, 'I am sure to be damned.'"

"And did you?"

"Oh yes! At least outwardly. I fled not only from my sins, but from sinful company too! I began to apply myself to religious duties such as praying, reading, weeping for sin, speaking truth to my neighbors, and so forth."

"And did all of this make you feel whole?" inquired Christian tenderly.

"Yes, for a time. But at last my troubled conscience came tumbling upon me again and that in spite of all my reformations!"

"Why so, since you were now reformed?"

"It happened to me the same as to you."

"From reading the little book?"

"Aye. There I read such words as: 'All our righteousnesses are as filthy rags,' and, 'By the works of the law shall no flesh be justified,' and 'When ye shall have done all those things which are commanded you, say, we are unprofitable servants.'"

"Ah, yes," nodded Christian, returning in memory to his own sorry state back in Destruction. "I remember reading those very words myself. Then what?"

"From these sayings I began to reason with myself thus," continued Hopeful. "If all my righteousnesses are as filthy rags, and if, by the deeds of the law, no man can be justified, and if, when we have done all, we are yet unprofitable servants, then it is totally impossible to think of gaining heaven by my own obedience to the law."

"Well thought out," nodded Christian. "Go on."

"Well, then I thought of this illustration: Suppose a man foolishly runs himself a hundred pounds into the shopkeeper's debt?"

"All right."

"And suppose that later on he shall repent of his folly and from then on pay cash for every purchase?"

"Um, hmm. Please continue."

"But also suppose that his wife and children need every penny he earns in the mines just to survive? Suppose that all his scrimping and scraping and working to exhaustion only serves to keep him even. What happens to that old debt? Why, it is still standing in the book of records uncancelled. And at any time the shopkeeper may sue him, and cast him into the debtor's prison till he shall pay him the last penny."

"This is an all too familiar story," Christian answered, smiling wryly out of one corner of his mouth. "And how did you apply this to yourself?"

"Like this," he answered. "I have, even by my smallest sin, run myself an infinite distance into God's debt. So, seeing my dilemma, I reform my life and by sheer force of will never commit another sin."

"'Tis, of course, impossible in your own strength," Christian reminded him.

"Oh, true, and that I know from experience," agreed Hopeful. "Yet, even if I could live a perfect life, I would only be keeping current with the present. I have no extra righteousness to pay off my past infinite debt. My past is always there, lurking in the shadows, gathering interest, and waiting for me to die so it can collect its due."

"A very good application," nodded Christian. "But do go on."

"Another thing that greatly troubled me was this: If I looked closely at even the best of my deeds, I found that I was still doing them for selfish reasons. I would sometimes hear people remark upon how good my life was now that I had become a Christian, and I would feel proud. At other times, I would consider committing a sin and refrain from it because it would harm my reputation or business. So, I found that even my noblest deeds were still mixed with enough sin to bury me in the judgment."

"Very perceptive. Then what did you do?"

"Do!" Hopeful fairly shouted. "Do! I could not tell what to do! I was about to give up in despair! But because Faithful and I had become such good friends, and since I could see that he had the peace for which I longed, I finally opened my heart to him in his prison cell."

"And did he share a word of comfort?" asked Christian.

"No! He told me that unless I could somehow obtain the righteousness of a Man that had never sinned, I could never be saved. Not even if I added to my best righteousness all the righteousness of the whole world."

"Ah," said Christian with a knowing nod. "The shopkeeper's unpayable debt?"

"Aye."

"And did you believe him?"

"Well, I certainly didn't want to! And at first, when I was still satisfied with my good deeds, I would have called him a fool! But since I had seen my true self reflected in the Word and understood the sin that attached itself even to my best performances, I was forced to admit that he was right. Oh, so very right!"

"But were you able to believe that such a Man could be found? A Man who had never committed one sin?"

"No. Not at the first, but later, yes," stated Hopeful.

"And did you ask him who this Man was and how His righteousness might become your own?"

"Yes," smiled Hopeful. "And he told me it was the Lord Jesus! He told me that I might trust in what He had done for me, first by His life, and second by His sufferings upon the cross."

"Did you ask him how that Man's righteousness could be of such a quality that it could justify you before God?"

"Oh, yes. To be sure."

"And?"

"He told me that He was the mighty God!" exclaimed Hopeful, his heart brimming with joy at the remembrance. "The Creator of heaven and earth! He said that He had done His noble deeds not for Himself, but for me! He told me that His relationship with me was as full and distinct as if there was not another man in the entire universe to share His love. Then he told me that all

Faithful instructs Hopeful

His life and deeds would become my own, if I would simply believe on Him."

"Wonderful! And what did you do then?"

"I foolishly set my opinion of myself (as I then was) over God's opinion of me (as He would make me)," answered Hopeful. "'Surely,' said I, 'He would not be willing to save one such as I.'"

"And how did Faithful answer you?" inquired Christian earnestly.

"He bade me go to Him just as I was and see for myself! 'Taste and see that the Lord is good,' said he. Then I answered that 'It was presumption.' But he said, 'No, for you are invited to come.' Then he gave me a book inspired by Jesus Himself that would encourage me to come freely. 'In this book,' said he, 'you will find steps to Christ that the most ignorant babe could follow.' He also said that, 'every jot and tittle thereof stand firmer than heaven and earth.' Then I asked him what I must do when I came, and he told me that 'I must get on my knees and with all my heart and soul entreat the Father to reveal Him to me.' Then I asked him further, 'How must I make my supplication to Him?' Then said Faithful, 'Go, and you shall find Him in the most Holy Place upon a mercy seat. There He can be found at any hour of any day for His ministry in that place is to give pardon and forgiveness to them that come.'"

"'But Faithful,' said I, 'I don't know what to say to a noble Prince and God such as He!'"

"'Friend, Hopeful,' said he, 'you may speak to Him like this: God be merciful to me a sinner. God, cause me to know and believe in Jesus Christ for I see that if I have no faith in His righteousness I am utterly cast away. Lord, I have heard that You are a merciful God and hast ordained that Your Son Jesus Christ should be the Saviour of the world. I have heard, too, that You are willing to bestow His righteousness upon such a poor sinner as I am. And I am a sinner indeed! Lord, please take this opportunity which I lay at your feet, and magnify Your honor by the salvation of my soul through your Son Jesus Christ. Amen.'"

"Ah," sighed Christian. "A beautiful prayer. And did you then do as you were told?"

"Oh, yes!" exclaimed Hopeful, joy radiating from his face at the memory. "Gladly! Over, and over, and over again!"

"And did the Father reveal His Son to you?"

"No," said Hopeful shaking his head. "Not at the first, nor second, nor third, nor fourth, nor fifth; no, nor even at the sixth time either."

"What did you do then?" inquired Christian, edging closer to hear.

"Why! I could not tell what to do!" exclaimed Hopeful.

"Were you ever tempted to give up praying?"

"Oh, yes!" Hopeful cried out. "Yes! A hundred times twice told!"

"But you did not. Why not?"

"Because I had no choice! I believed the Word telling me that without the righteousness of this Christ all the world could not save me."

"Ah."

"'Therefore,' said I to myself, 'if I surrender my prayers I shall die. And if I must die, better here at the throne of grace than at the flesh-pots of Egypt!' And then this thought came into my mind fresh from the throne of God: 'Though it tarry, wait for it; because it will surely come, it will not tarry.' So I continued praying until, at last, the Father showed me His Son!"

"Hurrah!" exclaimed Christian joyously. "And how was He revealed to you?"

"It happened like this," explained Hopeful, his face radiant with joy at the memory. "One day I was very sad, I think more sad than at any time in my entire life. And this sadness came upon me through a deeper insight into the greatness and vileness of my sins. It seemed hopeless, and I saw nothing ahead of me but death and the everlasting loss of my soul. Suddenly, it seemed as though I saw the heavens open wide, and the Lord Jesus looking down upon me. After a loving smile, He said: 'Believe on the Lord Jesus Christ, and thou shalt be saved!'"

"'But Lord,' said I, 'I am a great, a very great sinner.'"

"'My grace is sufficient for thee.'"

"'But Lord,' I asked, 'what is believing?'"

"'He that cometh to me shall never hunger, and he that believeth on me shall never thirst.'"

"'Then are believing and coming all the same thing?' I asked."

"Any who come reaching out the heart and affections after me are believers in verity."

"'Then, oh, dear Lord,' I cried out, 'am I truly a believer in Christ?'"

"Thou art."

"Then was I so relieved, that the tears flowed down my face, but still I asked for more. 'But, Lord?' I asked, 'may such a great sinner as I truly be accepted of, and saved by Thee?'"

"He that cometh to me I will in no wise cast out."

"'But, Lord,' I cried, 'I want my faith to be a true faith. What must I believe of Thee in my coming to Thee?'"

"Chiefly, this. That Christ Jesus came into the world to save sinners such as you. That He bestows righteousness to everyone who believes. That He died for your sins and rose again for your justification. He loved you, and washed you from your sins in His own blood. He is mediator between you and your God and He ever lives to make intercession for you."

"From all of this," explained Hopeful, "I understood that I must look for my righteousness in Him and for satisfaction for my sin by His blood. I saw that the life He lived in obedience to His Father's law, and the death he died in submitting to its penalty was not for Himself but for me. For me! And He would have done it even if I had been the only one! The only one, Christian!"

"Ah! Blessed revelation!" rejoiced Christian, tears of sympathy running unashamedly down his cheeks.

"Aye, blessed indeed!" agreed Hopeful, his own eyes swimming at the memory. "And now was my heart full of joy, my eyes full of tears, and my affections running over with love for the name, the people, and the ways of Jesus Christ."

"This was a revelation of Christ to your soul indeed! But what effect did this have upon your spirit? Do share some details."

"Well, it led me to see that in spite of its so-called righteousness, all the world is in a state of condemnation. I saw that through His Son, God the Father can justify the repenting sinner and still be just. I became even more ashamed of the vileness of my former life and awakened to the sense of my own ignorance. I saw more clearly than ever the beauty of Jesus Christ. I was filled with love for a holy life and a longing to do something for the honor and glory of the Lord Jesus. Yea, I thought that if I had in my veins a thousand gallons of blood, I could spill it all for the sake of the Lord Jesus!"

CHAPTER TEN

I SAW THEN, in my dream, that Hopeful chanced to look behind them and saw Ignorance, whom they had left behind. Then said he to Christian, "Christian, look there!"

"What?"

"Off yonder," answered Hopeful, pointing down the trail. "Isn't that Ignorance coming along behind us?"

"Aye, I believe it is. But I'll wager he still has no desire for our company."

"Perhaps not," replied Hopeful, "but I'm sure that he would have learned some good lessons if he had stayed with us."

"Ah, certainly true enough," agreed Christian. "But no doubt he thinks otherwise."

"Probably so. But who knows?" said Hopeful optimistically. "Time may have opened his eyes some. Let's wait up a bit and see. Helloooo back there!"

"Helloooo up there!"

"Come, lad," urged Christian. "Hustle up a bit. We're waiting to enjoy your company."

"All right. Thank you," called Ignorance, continuing to saunter along at his own good pace. When he had finally meandered up to them, he said merrily, "Greetings, sirs. Thank you for waiting."

"We were glad to do it," replied Christian with a welcoming smile. "How do you do?"

"Oh, very well, thank you."

"Tell me, lad. Why do you loiter so far behind?"

"Oh, I just simply really enjoy my own company I guess, that's all," he babbled mindlessly. "So, you see, good fellow, when I am alone, I am sort of not really alone at all, if you catch my drift. Thanks for asking though."

Christian pulled Hopeful to one side of the trail and whispered, "I told you he had no desire for our company. But since he is here, let's see if we can bring him to his senses."

"Aye. I'm game, if you are."

Then, Christian addressed Ignorance, saying, "Tell us, lad. How do things stand between your soul and God?"

"Oh, very well, I hope," he answered nonchalantly while unwrapping another sucker and popping it into his mouth. "Say, either of you chaps wanna' sucker?"

"No, thank you," said Christian.

"How 'bout a storybook?" he said, pulling a worn, dog-eared penny novel from one of his pockets.

"No, thank you," said Hopeful.

"You sure? This skinny 'ole trail gets pretty dreary at times."

"We're sure," answered Hopeful.

"Suit yerselves, chaps," answered Ignorance, shrugging his shoulders and stuffing candy and books into his pocket.

"Tell me," queried Christian, "upon what do you base this hope of yours?"

"Hmmm? Oh, well, for one thing I am always full of good thoughts that come into my mind to comfort me as I walk."

"Oh?" answered Christian with arched brows. "And what good thoughts are these? Pray tell us."

"Why, I think often about God and heaven!" babbled Ignorance with great assurance.

"Hmmm," murmured Christian. "But so do the devils and damned souls."

"Ah!" said Ignorance, head cocked down to one side and forefinger raised to heaven, "but I think of them and desire them! And therein lies all the difference. All the difference in the world."

"But there are millions who desire heaven," protested Christian, "and not one in a thousand shall ever get there. 'The soul of the sluggard desireth and hath nothing.'"

"Ah! But there is a big difference between me and them."

"Oh?"

"Yes! For, you see, I not only think of heaven, but have left all to attain it!"

"That I doubt."

"And why do you say that?" asked Ignorance, a bit perturbed.

"Because leaving all is a very hard thing to do. Much harder than most realize."

"'Tis true!" sputtered Ignorance. "I have!"

"What makes you think so?"

"Well, for one thing," said Ignorance confidently, "my heart tells me so."

"The Wise Man says, 'He that trusteth in his own heart is a fool.'"

"This is spoken of an evil heart. But mine is a good one! One that will go on."

"Easy enough to say. But what do you have to prove your heart is good?"

"Well, for one thing," replied Ignorance with great assurance, "it comforts me in the hopes of heaven."

"That may be because of its deceitfulness!"

"Deceitfulness!" squawked Ignorance indignantly.

"Yes. A man's heart may falsely bring him great comfort by hoping for things to which it has no claim."

"But my heart and my life are in harmony and therefore my hope is well grounded!"

"And who told you that?"

"My heart tells me that!" replied Ignorance with the assured finality of a lawyer who had just offered up the proof of proofs.

"Your heart tells you so! Dear friend, the Word of God needs to tell you so! If it does not, then any other testimony is worth nothing!"

"But are not good thoughts the fruit of a good heart? And is not a life that is lived in obedience to God's commandments a good life?"

"Oh, but of course," agreed Christian. "But it is one thing to have these fruits and quite another to only think you do."

"All right! All right then!" challenged Ignorance in exasperation, "since you are wise so overmuch about these things, you tell me what you consider to be good thoughts and a life lived according to God's commandments."

"Well, there are several kinds of thoughts," replied Christian thoughtfully. "Some about ourselves, some of God, some of Christ, and some others. Which one shall I discuss?"

"I am most interested in thoughts about myself. So tell me, what are good thoughts about myself?"

"Good thoughts about ourselves are ones that agree with the Word of God."

"And when do our thoughts agree with the Word of God?" queried Ignorance curtly.

"When we pass the same judgment upon ourselves that the Word does."

"Empty words floating in a sunbeam," snapped Ignorance with a careless wave of a half-consumed sucker. "I want to know what these words mean! Explain yourself, if you can."

"Certainly, with ease. The Word of God says of the natural man, 'There is none righteous, there is none that doeth good.' It also says that 'Every imagination of the heart of man is only evil, and that continually.' Now then, when we think these thoughts about ourselves, then are our thoughts good ones because they agree with the Word of God."

"'None righteous!' 'Every imagination evil!' Hmmph. I will never believe that my heart is so bad as all that!"

"Then you have never had one good thought about yourself."

"Nonsense," scoffed Ignorance. "Sheer and utter rubbish! But let us talk about my life. At least I know my life is honorable."

"Not unless it agrees with the Word," warned Christian.

"Oh, bother," groaned Ignorance, rolling his eyes. "And what does the Word say about my life?"

"The Word of God says that man's ways are crooked ways—not good, but rather perverse. Now when a man humbly agrees with this, then his thoughts about his life are good because they agree with the Word of God."

"Bah! You look too much on the musty side of life."

"Not so, friend. We simply look at reality. Through God's eyes we see ourselves as we really are: wicked, perverse, selfish, and disobedient. And, when we see ourselves as He does, then we are in a position to ask Christ to change us into His glorious image as He has promised to do."

"Then our life and thoughts are full of the joy of Christ," added Hopeful, "as He Himself promised when He said, '. . . that my joy might remain in you, and that your joy might be full.'"

"Enough of that! Enough of that!" Ignorance blurted out, defenseless against the sword of the Spirit. "Tell me this, what are good thoughts about God?"

"The same."

"Being?"

"Being thoughts that agree with the Word of God."

"Which ones?" he challenged.

"Why, when we think that He knows us better than we know ourselves and can see sin in us where we can see none; when we think He knows our inmost thoughts and that our heart, with all its depths, is always open to His eyes. Also, when we think that our own righteousness stinks in His nostrils even in our best performances."

"Well, of course!" exclaimed Ignorance. "Do you take me for such a fool as to think that God can see no further than I, or that I would dare come to God in the best of my performances?"

"I don't know. It's hard to tell what you think. Give us your thoughts in this matter."

"Why, I think that I must believe in Christ for justification."

"But how can you believe in Him when you have such a high opinion of yourself?" Christian asked sincerely. "It appears to me that you feel no need of His justification."

"I just believe, that's all!"

"But what do you believe?"

"I believe that Christ died for sinners!" snapped Ignorance. "Can we at least agree on that?"

"But of course."

"And I believe that Christ, by virtue of His merits, takes my religious duties and makes them acceptable to His Father, and so I am justified."

"What!" exclaimed Christian. "Do you truly believe that?"

"Yea! Absolutely," said Ignorance, raising a proud chest and crossing his arms with a smug smile.

"Then let me answer you in four parts," proposed Christian.

"Certainly. Go on."

"First, you believe with an imaginary faith; for faith of this kind is nowhere described in the Word."

"Second, you believe with a false faith, because it takes justification from the personal righteousness of Christ and applies it to your own.

"Third, in this faith Christ does not justify you but rather your actions. Then, through your actions He justifies you. This is false.

"Fourth, you therefore rest your hopes upon a deceitful faith that will leave you under the wrath of God in the day of judgment."

"What!"

"Yea! True justifying faith takes we whom the Word has awakened to our sinfulness and sends us fleeing for refuge into Christ's righteousness. There, having thrown off our filthy garments, we hide our nakedness under His robe as a child fresh from the bath hides under his mother's cloak when there comes a knock at the door. And when God looks upon us He sees neither our filthy rags, nor our nakedness, but rather the pure garments of Christ."

"What?" squawked Ignorance. "Do you expect us to trust only in what Christ has done? Do our own works account for nothing at all? No! Anyone who believed that nonsense could freely indulge in all kinds of lusts since his own acts have no effect on his salvation!"

"Ohhh," groaned Christian in exasperation. "Ignorance is your name, and as your name, so your mind, for you are totally ignorant of the true effects of saving faith."

"What!" he snorted indignantly.

"Yea," continued Christian earnestly. "For true faith will lead a man to love God's name, His Word, His way, and His people. One with such a love will do nothing but good acts."

"Pray tell, lad," interjected Hopeful, hoping yet to awaken Ignorance to his need, "have you ever had Christ revealed to you?"

"What?" scoffed Ignorance. "Are we depending on revelations now? You and all you believe are the fruits of distracted brains!"

"Not so, friend," urged Hopeful tenderly. "Christ is so far above our natural thoughts that we cannot know Him unless God the Father reveals Him to us."

"Bah! That is your faith, not mine," sneered Ignorance with another wave of his sucker. "And I'll wager two-to-one that my faith is just as good as yours. Perhaps, even better since I have fewer legalities and technicalities buzzing around my brain."

"Friend Ignorance," urged Christian, "not only must Christ be revealed to you as a gift, but your very faith must come to you as a gift. I see that you are ignorant of true faith, and I plead with you to awake to your own wretchedness and turn to Christ Jesus for salvation."

"Come along with us," invited Hopeful, "and we will share all that we have learned."

"Thanks, but no thanks," growled Ignorance, planting his feet as firmly as if he intended to send down roots. "You old birds jog along too fast for me. I shall come along at my own good pace and in the enjoyment of my own good faith. And I'll lay odds that I'll get to the kingdom not long after you!"

"Friend, please!" begged Christian, loath to lose the man's soul. "You must flee to Christ or you shall never come to said kingdom."

"Perhaps so, perhaps no," said Ignorance icily, his arms crossed, his eyes staring into the sky, and his feet budging not an inch.

"But . . . but . . ."

"No! No, no, no," interrupted Ignorance rudely. "We shall see who is right by and by. Fare thee well, gentlemen. I trust to see thee in the Kingdom."

"If you do," warned Hopeful, "it will only be because you have conformed your thinking to the Word of God."

"My heart tells me that there is no conforming needing to be done. And so now, adieu."

"But dear Ignorance . . ." Hopeful persisted.

"Adieu, adieu, adieu!" intoned Ignorance, not even deigning to lower his gaze to look upon them.

"Come along, my good Hopeful," sighed Christian sadly. "Even Jesus uses no more force than to knock at our door. Therefore, we must leave him be and travel on alone."

"Aye," agreed Hopeful as they reluctantly resumed their journey.

After a long period of gloomy silence, Christian said, "Tsk, tsk, tsk. Ah, how I pity that poor man. He has a fatal surprise awaiting him at journey's end."

"The iron gate in the side of the hill?"

"Aye, so I fear. Turn-away will not be the last to perish in that place."

"But alas, dear Christian," mourned Hopeful, "in our town there are whole families, churches, yea, multitudes, who believe just as he does. And some of them pilgrims too!"

"Tell me, Hopeful, what do you think about such men?"

"What do you mean?"

"I mean, do you think they ever have true convictions of sin and so fear that their state is dangerous?"

"Ah, best for you to answer your own question on that one," answered Hopeful, "since you are the elder of us."

"All right. Here is what I have observed. At times, this sort of person may indeed have deep convictions of sin. But since they are ignorant of what God has said, they don't realize that such convictions are sent to them for their own good. Therefore, since the feelings they have are so unpleasant, they try to forget them, or stifle them, or bury them under some foolish pleasure. When they have thus eased their minds, they presumptuously assume that everything is now well with their souls."

"But what makes them think so?"

"Their hearts, that is to say their feelings, tell them so."

"Ah. But are not fear and guilt sent for man's good? Do they not help put their hearts right at the very beginning of their pilgrimage, as it did for us?"

"Aye," nodded Christian. "Right fear does. 'The fear of the Lord is the beginning of wisdom.'"

"How do we know if we have this right fear?"

"By three things."

"Being?"

"First, by its origin," Christian began. "Godly fear is caused by saving convictions of sin and deep feelings of one's lost and undone condition."

"Ah, yes," recalled Hopeful. "I know about that one. And?"

"And second, by its results. Godly fear will drive the convicted sinner to lay fast hold of Christ for salvation."

"As it did for me," agreed Hopeful. "And third?"

"And third, by its fruits," Christian concluded. "Godly fear creates and maintains in the soul a great reverence for God, His Word, and His ways. It keeps the soul tender and makes it fearful of turning, to the right hand or to the left, toward anything that might dishonor God, grieve the Spirit, or give the enemy occasion to accuse it."

"Well said, brother! And therefore, godly fear is much to be desired even though for a time we are in distress."

"Aye. 'Twas a heavy burden that lay on my back as I began this journey. But, praise be to God, it was taken from me at the cross."

Then, as there was a temporary lull in the conversation, Hopeful looked about him and asked, "Say, are we almost past the enchanted forest?"

"Why do you ask?" quizzed Christian. "Are you growing weary of our conversation?"

"Oh no! No! Not at all," affirmed Hopeful. "I am just curious to know where we are."

"Well," said Christian looking about, "as near as I can tell, we have only a couple more miles to go."

"Ah! Good!" he answered in relief. "I grow weary of this drowsy land of sweet-smelling mists. But let us continue our discussion. For us, conviction of sin drove us to the cross where we found our freedom. But what about the ignorant? What happens to them when they meet with conviction of sin?"

"At the first it arouses fear in them the same as it did with us."

"And what do they with said fear?"

"Well, sad to say, they do not realize that such convictions are for their own good to drive them to Christ; therefore they seek to stifle them."

"How?"

"Oh, there are several ways," said Christian. "First, they think that these convictions from God are actually from the devil! Therefore they resist them as valiantly as we resist evil temptations."

"Ah."

"Second, they believe themselves to have great faith when in reality they have none. Therefore, when these convictions of sin come upon them, it causes them to question whether their faith is indeed a true faith. Then, they are forced to either examine the depth of their faith or deny the conviction. But to admit that their faith needs examining is to confess that it may be a false one. And if their faith has been a false one, then it follows that their eternal hopes may be built upon a mirage, and they may be lost. This thought very few can tolerate, and so they harden their hearts against conviction."

"A dangerous course," said Hopeful solemnly. "Are they not resisting the Spirit by so doing?"

"Of course they are! But they comfort themselves with the thought that they are actually resisting the devil."

"You said there were several ways," noted Hopeful. "Continue with your list."

"All right," agreed Christian. "Third, such persons imagine that to even entertain such fears is a denial of faith and therefore ignore them and behave with presumptuous confidence."

"Ah."

"And last," he continued, "I say again that such fears tend to take away from them their pitiful, old robe of self-righteousness and therefore, they resist them with all their might."

"Well, speaking from my own experience, I can certainly attest to the correctness of your thinking," agreed Hopeful, "for that was certainly my state before Christ revealed my true self to me."

"And so it is still with Ignorance and his kin," said Christian sadly, "and probably will be until they come to their eternal destruction. But come, let us turn our attention away from Ignorance for now and look into another profitable question."

"Certainly," Hopeful agreed readily. "You lead the way."

"Tell me," queried Christian, "did you happen to know, oh, say about ten years ago, a man named Temporary? As I recall he lived in your parts and was very religious."

"Oh, yes!" exclaimed Hopeful. "I knew him quite well. He lived in the town of Graceless right next door to a man named Turn-back. Their town was just a couple of miles away from the town of Honesty."

"Yes, that is just the man I had in mind."

"What about him?"

"Well, if I remember right, that man is an example of one who was once much awakened to the sight of his sins and to the wages due to them."

"Ah, right you are. I remember that during the time of his conviction he would often come to me with tears in his eyes. I truly had pity for him and for a time, I thought him surely a likely candidate for the kingdom. But alas, I suppose it is not everyone that cries

'Lord! Lord!' that will enter in. But what was your experience with him?"

"He came to be very close to me as well," began Christian, "and once mentioned that he was resolved with all of his heart to go on pilgrimage."

"Then what?"

"Well, he let himself grow careless about guarding the avenues of his soul."

"What do you mean by that?"

"I mean that he let a man named Save-self have free access to his ear. And you can be sure that it was not long before he had found salvation in some easier way than through Christ. Once, when I tried to persuade him that conviction of sin was actually a proof that he was coming nearer the kingdom, he looked at me with an angry countenance, and from that time forth made himself a stranger to me."

"And to me as well," recalled Hopeful. "Tell me, brother Christian, in your opinion, what are the reasons for such sudden backslidings as his?"

"I think you may already have the answer to this one," observed Christian. "You lead the way."

"Well," answered Hopeful, pausing a moment to gather his thoughts, "I think there are . . . uh . . . four reasons for it."

"Being?"

"First off is the fact that their hearts are not made new," Hopeful began. "Their consciences may be temporarily aroused to fear the judgment. And for a time, they try to put away their evil deeds. But in their hearts they still long for the fleshpots of Egypt, and when the restraint of fear wears off, seven devils return to replace the one cast out."

"Well said," observed Christian. "What be the second?"

"The second reason is that they retain their fear of men, and as the Word says, 'The fear of men bringeth a snare.' So, for a time, their fear of punishment will lead them hot for heaven in spite of the opinions and opposition of men. But as their fears of the future grow cool, they begin to worry more and more about what people may think of them."

"Aye," Christian agreed with a solemn nod. "I have seen it happen many times."

"Then they begin to believe worldly counsel."

"Such as?"

"Such as the proverb that says not to 'put all your eggs in one basket.' So they decide to play it safe and begin to pull back from Christ so as to live in two worlds. But they soon find the words of our Lord Jesus true when he said, 'a man cannot serve two masters.'"

"Aye," agreed Christian. "They soon grow to 'hate the one and love the other,' as He also said. And usually it is the Lord that they come to hate rather than the world."

"Aye. Sad, but true."

"And what be the third reason for backsliding?" Christian prodded.

"I think it is the pride of the human heart," Hopeful stated matter-of-factly. "Being by nature proud and haughty the natural heart looks down upon religion as being low and contemptible. Therefore, as they take their eyes off the example of the meek and lowly Jesus, they find humility to be a stumbling block rather than a stepping stone, and so return again to their former ways."

"Ah, right you are! I have seen it a thousand times. The pride of our natural heart is too wide a burden to squeeze into the straight and narrow way. And what be the fourth reason?"

"The thoughts of a judgment and the punishment to follow are grievous to them," concluded Hopeful. "So rather than thinking about those things which will surely come to pass, they choose to ignore them."

"'Tis like a little child who thinks he cannot be seen because he shuts tight his own eyes," commented Christian with a wry smile.

"Aye," agreed Hopeful, "just like. They secretly hope that ignoring these things will somehow prevent their occurrence. But to ignore these things hardens their hearts and leads them to a life of backsliding."

"I see that you have a good understanding of these things, brother Hopeful," said Christian. "Truly the bottom line is that they do not seek first the kingdom of God, and yield the heart to the control of the Holy Ghost. Therefore, their hearts and minds remain the same as before."

"Or worse," said Hopeful. "Remember Turn-away and the seven demons leading him to hell's back door?"

"Aye! Quite well," said Christian, "and quite against my will, my knees begin to shake at the mere memory of it. He is a perfect example of those whose hearts were never changed."

"So it seems to me," agreed Hopeful. "Too many come to Christ out of fear of punishment rather than for love of what He has done for them."

"Aye. They are like the prisoner who trembles in contrition while standing before the judge, and yet picks a pocket or two on his way out of the courtroom."

"Repentance by fear I would call it," said Hopeful ironically.

"Aye, indeed. It was the gallows rather than conviction that shook his knees. But, in spite of all of his rivers of tears, when he is released, we find that he is a thief still."

"Sad, but true. But come. Now that I have showed you the reasons for backsliding, you show me the steps men take in doing so."

"All right," agreed Christian readily. "First, they choose to think on everything and anything except God, His law, and the judgment."

"Because such things are not agreeable to the natural heart," deduced Hopeful.

"Aye. Secondly, they gradually fall away from spiritual duties such as secret prayer, controlling their lusts, guarding the avenues of the soul and so forth."

"Probably because such things are a burden to a man who has taken his thoughts off of Christ."

"Yes," Christian agreed. "Thirdly, they begin to avoid the company of living and vibrant Christians."

"No doubt because they remind them of their own lukewarmness," concluded Hopeful.

"So it seems. Fourthly, they begin to ignore public spiritual duties, such as church and prayer meetings, where God's Word is read and His praises sung."

"Because by now their thoughts and hearts are out of place there," Hopeful observed.

"Right again," nodded Christian. "Fifthly, they begin to perceive specks of dust in the eyes of the godly."

"Why is that, do you suppose?" asked Hopeful, having noted the same thing himself.

"The answer is simple. This seeking out of other people's specks blinds them to the beams in their own eyes. They see all the hypocrites in the church and this gives them an excuse to throw all religion to the wind."

"Ah, that makes sense. And sixth?"

"The next step, of course, is to begin spending time in the company of loose and wanton sinners."

"Ah. And I'll wager I can guess the seventh step."

"Go on," Christian urged.

"They begin to enjoy carnal conversation and the contemplation of sin," stated Hopeful knowingly.

"Exactly," agreed Christian. "And if they can find the slightest evil in someone who is reputed to be honest, they rejoice greatly."

"No doubt because they have found an excuse to do the same."

"Right you are. The eighth step is that they begin to play with little sins openly."

"As if there were such a thing," commented Hopeful wryly. "And at that point what can prevent their hearts from becoming hardened and casting off all pretense of goodness?"

"Nothing at all," said Christian. "And that is the ninth step. And unless there be some miracle of grace to prevent it, they shall utterly perish in their chosen deceptions."

CHAPTER ELEVEN

OW I SAW in my dream, that by this time the pilgrims had gotten well past the fatal allurements of the Enchanted Ground. From there it was but a short distance to the country of Beulah, where the air was very clear and pleasant. Since the narrow way passed directly through this lovely country, they slowed their pace a bit to better enjoy its beauties and be refreshed. Here they heard the endless singing of birds and the gentle cooing of the turtle dove. Everywhere they looked they saw lovely greenery and found flowers of every description growing in rich profusion. In this country the sun shines night and day and its light totally dispels any darkness coming from the Valley of the Shadow of Death.

Here they were far out of reach of Giant Despair; in fact, from here they could not even see Doubting Castle or the misty miasma that continually hovers over that land. Here, also, they were within sight of the City to which they journeyed, and sometimes, even met and talked with some of its citizens. This was because they were now within sight of the very borders of heaven. Therefore, the Shining Ones commonly crossed over to encourage those who had come so far in their journey. In this land also the contract between the bride and the Bridegroom was renewed; yea, here, "as the Bridegroom rejoiceth over his bride so did their God rejoice over them." Here they had no lack of corn and wine; for in this place they found abundant supplies of all those things they had been seeking all along their pilgrimage. Here they heard voices from out of the city; loud voices, saying: "Say ye to the daughter of Zion, Behold thy salvation cometh."

"His reward is with Him," proclaimed another.

Here all the inhabitants of the country looked upon them lovingly and called them, "The holy people, the redeemed of the Lord."

Now, as they walked about and beheld the glories of this land their hearts rejoiced! And that, because they could see the kingdom so much more clearly from here. As they drew even nearer to the City they began to discern details and wonders not perceived from afar. They saw that it had twelve foundations made of precious stones. They saw it to have gates of pearl and streets that were paved with gold. The Lamb of God was the light of it and its glory far outshone the glory of the sun. As they gazed in amazement at just a few of its wonders, they found their desires for it growing stronger and yet stronger still. So mighty was Christian's desire to be there that he grew quite ill from lovesickness. Hopeful also had his desires drawn out by the sight, and he too had a bout or two with the same happy illness. Therefore, they stayed in the land of Beulah for many days to recover their strength. And as they lay resting in that land, Christian would sometimes cry out, saying, "Oh, if you see my Beloved, tell Him that I am heartsick because of my desire for the better land."

But it was not long before they grew strong enough to endure the glories of the place. Yea, they were soon able to walk about and explore right up to the very borders of that country. As they did they saw, opening off the pathway, gates leading into the most exquisite orchards, vineyards, and gardens. Now the law of this land was, that any who had any hunger might venture into any garden, orchard, or vineyard and partake freely of all that they desired. Therefore, Christian and Hopeful enjoyed many a dinner hour eating living food fresh from vine, bush, and branch. Now, as they came up to one of these places, behold the gardener stood in the way; to whom Christian said, "Good Sir, pray tell. Whose goodly vineyards and gardens are these?"

"They belong to the King!" exclaimed the gardener with a proud smile. "And they are planted here, not only for His own delight, but also for the joy and solace of pilgrims. Therefore, come in and refresh yourselves with its dainties."

"Why, thank you," said Christian with a grateful bow. "Thank you very much."

"'Tis a very pleasant task you have, sir," observed Hopeful, between bites of the sweetest and juiciest peach he had ever eaten, "working for the refreshment of weary pilgrims."

"Ah, more than you can tell," replied the gardener meekly, "for here I meet the bravest and noblest of all the earth. 'Tis indeed a great blessing that the King hath graciously bestowed upon me. I do hope you can pause for a time and explore all the walkways and arbors, and rest in its pleasant pastures."

The Land of Beulah

"Oh, we shall!" exclaimed Christian. "It feels as if we are almost within the gates of the kingdom already."

"So it may seem to you now," said the gardener with a sage smile. "But let me assure you that 'eye hath not seen, neither ear heard what the Lord hath prepared for them that love him.' This country, compared to that, is like comparing the desert of Sahara to the valleys of the Nile."

"Indeed!" exclaimed Christian, scarcely able to conceive the reality.

"I don't know," said Hopeful as he wiped sugary juice from his chin. "It seems that if Heaven were any better than this, human nature could not bear it!"

Now, I beheld in my dream that whenever the pilgrims lay down to rest they would begin to talk in their sleep. And this was not just a word or two, here and there, but complete conversations with themselves wherein they smiled and laughed and bubbled over with joy. Now this was something never done in their journey heretofore, and as I was pondering to find the reason for this, the

328 ◆ PILGRIM'S PROGRESS

gardener addressed me thus: "I see thee to be puzzled, dear story-teller. You see, it is the nature of the fruit of these vineyards to go down so sweetly as to cause the lips of them that are asleep to speak out the praises of the King of Glory."

"Ahh," said I, beginning to understand. So, I saw when they awoke that they turned their steps toward the great City itself. But, as I said, the reflection of the sun upon the pure gold City was so extremely glorious that they could not yet look directly upon it unless they viewed it through a glass darkly. I saw then, that as they went on they met two men in raiment like burnished gold and whose faces shone as the light.

These men asked the pilgrims whence they came; and they told them. They also asked them where they had lodged, what difficulties and dangers, what comforts and pleasures they had met with in the way; and they told them. Then said the first of the two, "You have only to contend with two difficulties more, and then you are in the City!"

"Good Sir?" entreated Hopeful. "Would you be so kind as to accompany us and guide our feet in straight paths?"

"But of course," answered the second. "But you must obtain the City by your own faith, not by ours."

"Thus it has been all along our journey," said Christian. "Come, Hopeful, I am eager to come at the City. Let us be off!"

So I saw in my dream that the four of them went on together, till they came into direct sight of the gate. Now the gate was higher, and broader, and lovelier than they ever could have dreamed in their wildest imaginations. It was made of luminescent pearl and the glory of it is greater than my feeble words can begin to describe. Moreover, like Paul, I am forbidden to describe its full glories lest you think me mad.

Now, at first sight of the walls and gates, the pilgrims were filled with joy and wonder! Oh, to think that they would soon be able to enter that place and to kneel at the feet of the great King Himself! But as they drew nearer they felt the earth start to quiver lightly beneath their feet and began to hear the muffled roar of a distant river. When they came within sight of it, they saw that it was extremely wide, very deep, and swiftly flowing, as it rushed on its way down towards the sea.

At the sight of this mighty river the pilgrims were brought to a stunned standstill. Standing on its banks they paused for many long moments to stare dismally at the sight. Then they looked this way to the left, and saw no way across. They looked that way to the right, and again saw no way across. Yea, as far as the eye could see in either direction there was neither bridge, nor fording place nor ferryman to get them across. Then said Christian mournfully, "Oh, no! Such a mighty and fearful river!"

"Aye," agreed Hopeful gloomily. "So deep and so broad!"

"And yet we cannot reach the gate unless we can somehow get over it!" moaned Christian.

"You are correct," said the first Shining One. "You must go through, if you would reach the far side."

"I was hoping for something a bit easier than this," groaned Hopeful. "Is there no other way to the gate?"

"Nay."

"But were not some carried over in chariots of fire?"

"Ah, yes, to be sure," answered the second Shining One. "But since the foundation of the world only Enoch and Elijah have been privileged to travel that special path."

"And may not we walk it as well?" pleaded Christian.

"Nay, my friends," said the first Shining One sympathetically. "None other shall tread that path till the 144,000 shall 'meet their Lord in the air, and so ever be with the Lord.'"

"Then, must we truly pass through this river of death?" asked Christian, fearing to hear with his ears what he already knew in his heart.

"Aye," answered the first Shining One solemnly. "You must pass through."

Then the pilgrims began to become discouraged because of the difficulty that lay yet before them. Again, hoping against hope, Christian looked up the river this way, and down the river that way, but still could see no way whereby he might escape the crossing.

"Ah, woe is me," he cried. "Woe is me!"

"Be not faithless," encouraged the first Shining One, "but believing."

"Sir," asked Christian, "do tell? Is the river as deep as it seems?"

"We cannot say," answered one angel.

"Why not?" Christian pleaded. "Do you not know?"

"We do not know," answered the other.

"Why do you not know?" Christian persisted.

"Because," explained the first, "according to your faith, so shall it be unto you."

"I am sorry," confessed Christian with troubled brow, "but I am not grasping your meaning."

"What he means," explained the second angel, "is that the depth of the river is inversely proportional to the depth of your faith."

Then Christian and Hopeful gave each other a blank stare before saying together, "Huh?"

"Let me explain," the angel continued. "If your faith runs deep then the river will seem shallow, even if it should be rolling on at spring flood. If your faith runs shallow, the river will appear deep, even if it is only an autumn's trickle. It all depends on you."

"Well then, brother Hopeful," said Christian, girding up his loins, "since the Lord of the City has promised that 'according to our days so shall our strength be,' let us pray for strength to conquer this mighty river."

And so they knelt beside the river and prayed for courage. Then they arose, took one last longing look at the City, and began their descent into the flowing waters. Now, they had hardly gotten as deep as their chests when Christian stepped into a low spot and began to flounder!

"Ah, Hopeful!" he cried. "I sink in deep waters; the billows go over my head; all His waves go over me!"

"Nay, but be of good cheer, my brother," encouraged Hopeful as he tightly gripped Christian's arm to bear him up. "I feel the bottom and it is good!"

But Christian was nigh to be choked and as Hopeful helped him back to the surface he flailed at the water and spluttered despairingly, "Ah! My friend! The sorrows of death have compassed me about; I shall not see the land that flows with milk and honey!"

And with that, the horror of a great darkness fell upon Christian. So dark was it, that he could no longer see the glories that lay so close before him. Also, because he was under the water as much as above it,

Passing through the river

he could never quite fully catch his breath. This caused him to lose much of his memory. Therefore, he could neither recall, nor intelligently talk of any of those sweet refreshments that he had met with in the way of his pilgrimage.

Then, the enemy of souls saw one last opportunity to take Christian down and thus avenge his ignominious defeat in the valley of Humility. Therefore, came he and some of his most vile demons to further torment Christian's distracted mind. "You are a dead man, Graceless," grizzled a raspy voice in Christian's inner ear.

"Ah, woe is me!" cried Christian. "I fear that I shall sink in this river and never get me in at the gate!"

"Courage, brother," cried Hopeful as he strove to keep his companion's head above water. "He will not suffer you to be tempted above what you are able to bear!"

"Your sins, Graceless," gurgled the ghoul. "Remember the sins of your youth. Foolish jesting, lustful thoughts, wasted years!"

"But my sins rise up before me and sap me of courage," Christian cried out between gasps for air. "Oh, wicked man that I am!"

"Be not afraid, my brother," Hopeful encouraged, "for your sins have gone up beforehand to the sanctuary, where our High Priest ministers in our behalf. If your sins come up to mind, it is only because Satan is trying to bring you into Jacob's trouble!"

"No, Graceless," fumed the prince of darkness. "He is there to minister for they that be good. Not for you!"

"But Hopeful! I see ghosts, and goblins, and evil spirits! Back!" Christian cried, futilely swinging his arms at invisible specters. "Get you back! I am no more yours!"

"Oh, but you are!" sneered the dragon. "Now and forever! Down under with you!"

"Ahhh! Help!" sputtered Christian as he felt himself being pulled beneath the waves by myriads of clutching hands.

On his part, Hopeful had all he could do to keep his brother's head above water; yea, sometimes Christian would sink clear under for a time and then he would rise again half-drowned.

"Brother!" gasped Christian. "I be sinking down!"

"You are dying, Graceless," snarled the fiend relentlessly. "Dying without hope of life!"

"I feel the seaweeds wrapped about my head!" Christian gurgled. "The pangs of death devour me!"

"Here brother," Hopeful cried, pulling Christian out of the depths, "come over this way and plant your feet on this solid Rock!"

"Oh, woe is me!" lamented Christian. "Woe, woe is me!"

"Nay, my brother," urged Hopeful. "Only trust all your weight to this Rock! I feel it to be a chief Cornerstone. Do you feel it?"

"Yes! Yes, I think I do!" Christian stammered excitedly as his toe felt the firm corner of the Solid Rock.

"Now look up!" directed Hopeful, pulling Christian onto the Rock. "We are only yards away from the far shore!"

"Oh, can it be!" Christian exclaimed in drowning desperation.

"Yes!" shouted Hopeful above rolling waters and fuming fiends. "I can see the path to the gate! Yea, there are men standing up to their chest in the water waiting to pull us out of the river."

"I can't see them!" cried Christian, his eyes blurred by the splashing waters. "I can't see anything!"

"Then rest your faith on mine," urged Hopeful. "Become not faithless in your last moments but believe! They wait for you!"

"No!" screeched the demon. "Not for you!"

"No, they are not for me!" sobbed the dying Christian.

"Yes!" insisted Hopeful. "For you!"

"'Tis for you they wait," Christian moaned. "You have been hopeful since I first knew you."

"And so have you, my brother," Hopeful encouraged.

"Nay. But you are a sinner!" hissed the serpent.

"Hopeful," reasoned Christian blindly, "surely, if I were right with God He would now arise to help me. But He cannot. Because of my sins He must leave me fast in this snare!"

"Nay, my brother! Remember what it says in the Word!"

"What does it say?" Christian gasped, clutching at any straw of hope.

"It says of the wicked that 'there are no bands in their death, but their strength is firm; they are not troubled as other men, neither are they plagued like other men.'"

"And how does that help me?" begged Christian.

"Don't you see? These troubles and distresses are no sign that God has forsaken you. They are only permitted to try you and to increase your reward at the latter end. Remember that even Jesus could not see through the portals of the tomb, but went through this river clinging to nothing more than the naked promises of God. Now is your chance to do the same and thus bring glory to His name. Go forward, brother! With one hand cling to the memory of His past goodness. With the other hang for dear life onto the naked promise!"

"Could it be? Could it truly be?" Christian cried, a touch of hope beginning to sound in his quavering voice.

"No!" screeched the demon. "Not so!"

"It could be so," Christian said, encouraging his own soul in the Lord. "He has always helped me before, so why not now?"

"Your God is a liar!" exploded the monster. "Curse God and die!"

"Nay!" cried Christian, his faith growing from contact with the solid rock. "'Yea, let God be true, but every man a liar'!"

"Not so!" squawked the archfiend, feigning boldness and yet trembling before the power of the promise.

"It is so!" declared Christian. "And in the name of the Promise-maker, I bid you evil spirit, be gone!"

"Noooo!" snarled the simpering spirit, feeling his mask being peeled off his face by the Word of God.

"Go!" Christian commanded in trumpet-like tones of victory. "'Get thee behind me, Satan.' Now!"

"Aaauuuugh!" wailed the fallen angel as he felt himself being hurled into outer darkness by angels who had been more loyal than he. "Let me goooooo!"

"Oh! Oh, glory be!" cried Christian.

"What is it, my brother?" queried Hopeful, amazed to see the transformation that had come over his companion.

"Oh, I can see Him again!" Christian rejoiced. "He speaks to me of faith, hope, and courage. I can hear Him saying, 'When thou passest through the waters, I will be with thee; and through the rivers, they shall not overflow thee.'"

"Yes!" exclaimed Hopeful, his wet face beaming with new joy. "Those are His exact words! Then be strong! Quit you like a man and be of good courage!"

"Yes! Yes, I shall! Oh! Thank you, dear brother. Without your help my faith might have left me forever!"

Then they both took courage, and from that moment, until they were all the way over, the enemy was as still as a stone. Christian kept his feet firmly anchored upon the Solid Rock and from there on the river grew more and more shallow. Soon they came within reach of the rescuers who drew them out with shouts and cheers of joy. And thus, they got them over.

Now, I felt as if I were beholding beforehand the scenes of the first resurrection. Yea, I saw upon the glistening sands of the far bank of the river, these two men as they once again met the two Shining Ones who, although unseen, had accompanied them through the river. Said the first, "Greetings, faithful pilgrims!"

"Greetings, dear sir," replied Christian with a bow. "But say, don't I know you?"

"Aye. We are your ministering spirits. On the day you set your hearts to seek the Lord you became heirs of salvation. And on that self-same day we were sent forth to accompany you."

"You mean, you have been with me all along my journey?" asked Christian in amazement.

"Aye," replied the second angel with a smile.

"And did you really leave the glories of this bright place to walk the dark and gloomy paths of our fallen orb?"

"Ah, yes!" exclaimed the first joyfully. "And I had to wait a good long while before my Lord blessed me with my commission."

"Indeed? Then, did you truly come on your own accord?" Christian asked incredulously. "And did you really have to wait your turn to come serve me?"

To this the first Shining One gave no reply, but only smiled with deep, heartfelt emotions.

"Then, sirs," said Christian, overcome with supreme gratitude, "I thank you for your noble sacrifice."

"Sacrifice!" exclaimed the second Shining One. "Dear Christian! 'Twas no sacrifice at all! Why, when news came that you had yielded your heart to the King, don't you know that all of heaven echoed with shouts of gladness! Don't you understand that all the bells in the kingdom were set to ringing! And don't you realize that there was a great host of angels, all of them desiring to be your ministering spirit? But as God's good providence would have it, it was we who were chosen."

"B . . . but why?" asked Christian, his eyes bedazzled by the beauty of the place. "It is so beautiful here!"

"Because," replied the first Shining One, regaining his composure, "to become a partaker, even in a small way, of our Lord's sacrifice is so great an honor that we all covet to share in it. You will soon see, dear Christian and Hopeful, that the law of self-sacrificing love is the supreme law of heaven. And now, on to the City! Prepare your certificates!"

Thus, they went along toward the gate. Now, although the City stood upon a mighty hill, the pilgrims went up with the bounding ease of mountain goats springing upon the rocks. This was partly because their ministering spirits led them up the way by their arms. But it was more because they had left their mortal garments behind them in the river. Yea, they were clothed with the same glorified bodies that will clothe all who, like they and others such as Faithful, come up in the first resurrection. Thus they climbed the hill with great agility and speed, even though the foundation of the City was planted upon a hill that was higher than the clouds. And as they climbed, they carried on sweet conversations with their ministering spirits and listened to breathtaking accounts of how they had been delivered from many a danger unseen and many a temptation undiscerned. They also rejoiced to have gotten safely through the river and to be attended with such glorious companions.

"Dear ministering spirits, as we ascend the hill of the Lord would you describe some of the glories of the place?" requested Christian.

"Ah, the beauty is greater than words can tell. But I shall try. First, there is Mount Zion and the heavenly Jerusalem, then the innumerable company of angels, and finally, the multitudes of just men resurrected and made perfect."

"And to think! We be almost there!" exclaimed Hopeful, his heart about to burst for joy. "Ah!"

Then the second Shining One picked up the description, saying, "You are on your way to the Paradise of God. There you shall see the tree of life and eat of its endless store of twelve manner of fruits. There you shall come together 'from one Sabbath to the next and from one new moon to another.' Every month there will be a new harvest of fruit on the tree and the leaves are for the healing of the nations."

"Ah, what a glorious thought!" answered Christian gleefully. "Tell us more."

"When you come to the City," said the first angel, "you shall be given white robes and you shall walk and talk with the mighty King every day throughout all the ages of eternity!"

"Oh!" exclaimed Christian, clapping his hands for joy. "This is too glorious. Can it be? Can it truly be?!"

"Oh, yes," affirmed the second angel, beaming his broadest smile. "These things and many more besides that cannot be described in mere words. And, in this place, you shall never again see things such as you saw in the lower regions of earth. There you saw sorrow, sickness, affliction and death. But not here 'for the former things are passed away.'"

"Ah, glorious heritage!" cried out Hopeful. "Long dreamed of, long seen by faith, but now! Now! The faith has become sight!"

"Aye," answered the first angel in triumphant tone. "You are now on your way to meet Abraham, Isaac, Jacob, and the prophets. Here you will meet the most noble and brave of all who ever trod shoe leather. Men such as Faithful, who scorned the flaying knife and sang amidst the scorching flame; men who were sawn in two; maidens who laid themselves down in their living graves dressed as if going to their wedding day. There are those who toiled in the galleys and with every stroke of the oar sent up a prayer for those who beat them with demonic delights. Here too, are those 'who were once foremost in the cause of Satan, but who, rescued as brands from the burning, have served their Lord with deep and intense devotion.' Men and women of whom the world was not worthy. Such men, dear Christian and Hopeful, will be your companions and friends throughout the endless cycles of eternity."

"And what shall we do in this holy place?" queried Christian.

"Ah, what tongue can tell?" answered the second Shining One. "There you will receive the reward of all your toil, and exchange joy for all your sorrow; you shall reap the fruit of all the prayers, and tears, and suffering you have sown for the king along the way. In that place, you shall wear crowns of gold and enjoy the perpetual sight and visions of the Holy One; for there you shall see Him as He is!"

"Ah! You were right," confessed Hopeful. "Indeed, what tongue can tell?"

"There also you shall continue to serve in person with praise, and thanksgiving, Him whom you first began to serve by faith upon earth," added the first.

"And there," picked up the second, "your eyes shall be delighted with seeing and your ears with hearing the beauteous form and pleasant voice of the Mighty One."

"There, too," continued the first enthusiastically, "'immortal minds will contemplate with never-failing delight the wonders of creative power, the mysteries of redeeming love. There the grandest enterprises may be carried forward, the loftiest aspirations reached, the highest ambitions realized; and still there will arise new heights to surmount, new wonders to admire, new truths to comprehend, fresh objects to call forth the powers of mind and soul and body.'"

"Oh!" cried Christian. "Stop! These thoughts are so grand as to burst our brains! Surely there can be no more!"

"Ah, but there is!" smiled the second Shining One, delighting in his ability to inflict such exquisite torture. "There 'all the treasures of the universe will be open to the study of God's redeemed. Unfettered by mortality, you shall wing your tireless flight to worlds afar! With unutterable delight the children of earth shall enter into the joy and the wisdom of unfallen beings. You shall share the treasures of knowledge and understanding gained through ages upon ages in contemplation of God's handiwork. With undimmed vision you shall gaze upon the glory of creation—suns and stars and systems, all in their appointed order, circling the throne of Deity. Upon all things, from the least to the greatest, you shall see the Creator's name written, and in all you will see displayed the riches of His power.'"

"Oh, stop! Please stop," chuckled Christian, even as his soul longed to hear more. Then the first Shining One said, voice bubbling over with joy, "There you shall enjoy the company of Christian friends and know that there shall nevermore be a sad tear of farewell."

"There, also, you shall be clothed with glory and majesty . . ." added the second.

". . . In a white robe of purest linen which is the righteousness of the saints!" continued the first.

"And!" exclaimed the second, "when He shall travel with sound of trumpet in the clouds, as upon the wings of the wind, you shall be dressed in the King's finest equipage to go out with Him!"

". . . and," carried on the first, "when He shall sit upon the throne of judgment, you shall sit with him; yea, and when He shall pass sentence upon all the workers of iniquity, let them be angels or men, you also have a voice in that judgment because they were your enemies as well as His."

"And so shall you ever be with the Lord!" proclaimed the second Shining One in a loud voice.

"Stop! Stop!" cried Christian. "I can bear no more. My soul is ravished with the mere hearing of these things!"

Now, while they were thus drawing toward the gate, behold, a great company of the heavenly host came streaming out the gates to meet them; to whom it was shouted out by the first Shining One:

"Behold, ye inhabitants of eternity! These are the men we have boasted upon. These are the ones who have loved our Lord when in the world and have left all for His holy name! He has sent us to travel with them, and we bear witness that they have conducted themselves as befits true princes of the realm! Now they are here! They have come to the end of their journey and we, their guardian angels, move that they be allowed to go in and look upon the face of their Redeemer with joy!"

Then, the heavenly host gave a great shout, saying, "Blessed are they which are called to the marriage supper of the Lamb!" Then several of the King's trumpeters came out to meet them. They, with their music, made the vast vaults of Heaven to ring with wondrous music, both melodious and loud. These trumpeters, and the countless billions of heaven, saluted Christian and his fellow with ten thousand welcomes accompanied with shouting and the sound of ten thousand trumpets!

When this was done, they surrounded them about on every side; some went before and some behind; some went on the right, and some on the left; all of them continually singing as they went with melodious notes on high. It seemed to the pilgrims as if all of heaven had emptied itself to greet them. Thus, therefore, they walked on together; and, as they walked, the musicians kept on with their music; the singers kept on with their singing; the shouters shouted all the louder. All this wonderful sound mixed with their looks of love, their smiles of gladness, and their loving words, told Christian and his brother just how welcome they were in this wondrous place.

Now, these two men felt as if they were in heaven before they had even gotten there. Their bodies were swallowed up by millions of angels; their eyes were bathed in a golden light; their ears were washed over with the beauty of the melodious notes. Here also, they had the City itself in view and above the festivities about them, they could hear all the bells therein ringing out their welcome. But above all, their hearts were warmed beyond measure as they realized that they were going to live in this holy place, with these holy beings forever and ever! Oh! By what tongue or pen can their glorious joy be expressed!

Thus they came up to the gate. Now, when they came to that massive door all high and lifted up, they saw inscribed in its pearly arches, by God's own hand, letters of gold saying, "Blessed are they that do his commandments, that they may have right to the tree of life, and may enter in through the gates into the City."

Then I saw in my dream that the Shining Ones bade these two men to call out to those who kept the gate, which they did. Then some from above looked over the gate, namely Enoch, Moses, and Elijah, to whom it was shouted by the first angel, "Ahoy! Ye men atop the walls of Zion!"

To whom Moses answered with a joyous smile, "Greetings in the name of the King. What bring ye?"

Then answered the angel proudly, "Two pilgrims are come from distant dark planet. They have braved all manner of trials and hardship because of the love that they bear to the King of this place!"

"Did they enter in at the wicket gate?"

"Yea!" affirmed the first angel with a triumphant shout.

"Have they their certificates?"

"Yea!" answered the second angel boldly.

"Give them in through the door," commanded Moses.

And so the pilgrims passed in the certificates they had received at the start of their journey. These were swiftly carried into the King, who received them with grave solemnity. Then, as He read them, His face began to beam bright with a joy and delight impossible to conceal. Then said He, "Where are those men who have braved all of these things for my sake?"

"They are standing just without the gate," answered Moses.

Then, I saw the Commander of heaven rise to His feet and all His court with Him. Then He waved His glorious right arm and shouted, "Command that the gates be opened 'that the righteous nation which keepeth the truth may enter in!'"

Now, I saw in my dream that these two men went in at the gate; and lo, as they entered, they were transfigured; and they had raiment put on that shone like gold! There were also some that presented them with harps and crowns—the harps wherewith to praise God, and the crowns bestowed as a token of honor. Then, I heard in my dream that all the bells in the City rang again for joy as it was said unto them by their Lord, "Well done, thou good and faithful servants. Enter ye into the joy of your Lord!"

I also heard the men themselves singing at the top of their lungs, and saying, "'Blessing, and honor, and glory, and power, be unto Him that sitteth upon the throne, and unto the Lamb, forever and ever!'"

Gates are opened to them

Now as the gates of the City were opened to let in the men, I looked in after them and beheld things never seen by mortal eyes. Yea, it is verily true that "eye hath not seen, nor ear heard, neither hath entered into the heart of man the things that the Lord hath prepared for them that love Him," for, as I looked in, I saw that the City shone like the sun; the streets also were paved with gold; and in them walked many men with crowns on their heads, palms in their hands, and golden harps wherewith to sing praises.

There were also some that had wings and they constantly called one to another, saying, "Holy, holy, holy is the Lord!" And after that, they shut up the gates; which made my heart to ache, so great was my longing to be among them. Yea, when I was returned to this dreary earth, I was for a time sunken into a deep gloom, for it is so dark here. Nor can I ever be content with the vain pleasures of this rebel planet again, for I have seen a better land.

While I was gazing upon all these things, I chanced to turn my head, and saw Ignorance come up to the riverside. Now when he came to the edge, he was puzzled for a moment as to what to do. But looking down the river a ways, he espied a man in a small rickety boat. The man's name was Vain-hope, and he was a deceitful ferry-man who

342 ◆ PILGRIM'S PROGRESS

lurked on that side of the river. So Ignorance hails him with a shout or two, pays his fare with four or five chocolates, and gets himself rowed across the river without half the difficulty which the other two men met. Then he, unlike the two pilgrims, climbed heavily all huffing and puffing up the hill, all the while saying, "My! This hill is worse than that 'ole Hill Difficulty I heard about! Oh, well. My heart tells me that once I get in the place I shall forget even my greatest sacrifices. Hmmm," said he as he looked about and wondered at the emptiness of the place. "I wonder where the welcoming committee has got off to?"

Now, Ignorance came all the way up to the gates alone and without the least encouragement. There were no shining companions, no silver trumpets, no ringing of bells, and certainly no clouds of angels. When he finally arrived, all a-huffing and puffing up to the gate, he looked up to the writing that was above and then began to knock (tap tap ta tap tap . . . tap tap), assuming that surely, as soon as they saw who was standing without, they would promptly swing wide the gates. But instead, he saw one lone face, which seemed to be a bit perturbed, peer down over the wall. Then Moses shouted down to him, saying, "Hellooo."

"Hellooo yerself," answered Ignorant.

"Who are you?" said Moses. "Where are you from and what is your business here?"

"I would enter in," crowed Ignorance proudly, tucking his thumbs under his lapels and wearing a confident grin.

Then was Moses' brow furrowed with puzzlement as he quickly thumbed through his books of record, all the while saying softly to himself, "Enter in? There are no more pilgrims due here today." Then, after a quick search of his records, he leaned over the wall and called down to the wee speck of a man far below, "Uh, excuse me, sir. What be thy name?"

"Do you really have to ask?"

"I'm afraid I do. I'm sorry."

"Hmmph. Somehow I expected them to know," said Ignorance to himself.

"Beg your pardon?" said Moses.

"Oh, nothing. My name be Ignorance!" he shouted up, tapping his foot impatiently.

"Ignorance, you say?" answered Moses, still puzzled.

"You got it, pal."

"Ignorance? Ignorance?" muttered Moses softly while doing another quick scan of the page. Then shouted he, "I'm sorry, sir, but we have no notice that any by that name shall be coming here today."

"Well," said Ignorance, not one bit dismayed, "perhaps the date is wrong. Check for tomorrow!"

This Moses did and saw no such name listed for the morrow, nor for the next day nor the one following. He then checked all the way to the end of the register with the same result. More puzzled than ever, he leaned over the wall and shouted, "There is no notice given that you are due to come to this place today or tomorrow."

"Hmmph!" snorted Ignorance. "I somehow expected better organization in such a rich-looking place as this. Well, then, check the register from beginning to end!" he commanded.

"I have."

"Well, good for you," snapped Ignorance. "At least you have more initiative than the rest of this place."

Then was Moses silent.

"Well?" asked Ignorance, after a long pause.

"Well what?"

"Well what!" exclaimed Ignorance. "When am I due into this place? That's 'well what'!"

"Upon close examination," said Moses sadly, "I find that there has never been, nor shall there ever be anyone named Ignorance who shall pass through this gate."

"What!" exploded the man. "Now wait just a moment! My heart tells me very clearly that heaven is my home. There must be some mistake."

"There are no mistakes made here," answered Moses with just a trace of righteous indignation.

"But I have eaten and drunk in the presence of the King," proclaimed Ignorance. "He . . . He has taught in our streets!"

"Indeed?" said Moses, momentarily impressed, "And did you come in at the wicket gate?"

Then Ignorance came to a stall and said, "Uh . . . er uh . . . wicket gate?"

"Just as I feared," murmured Moses to himself before asking, "Did your path come along in the straight and narrow way?"

344 ◆ PILGRIM'S PROGRESS

"Well, as a matter of fact, it did seem boringly straight and uncomfortably skinny to me, yes. Yes indeed."

"Good," said Moses. "Then, do you have your certificate that we may show it to the King?"

"Uh, I . . . uh . . . one moment please," said Ignorance as he began to search frantically through his pockets. His face broke out in a cold sweat as he scattered candy wrappers like the leaves of autumn and muttered to himself, "Certificate? Certificate? What in the world is he talking about? Perhaps there is a coupon in one of my books."

After a very long and very uncomfortable silence, Moses said, finally, "Come, my good man. Have you no certificate?"

"Uh . . . I . . . No," he said weakly. "But I want you to send a personal message to my Lord. Remind Him that I have eaten with Him as a loving companion."

"Oh?" asked Moses.

"Yes," he continued, gathering courage as he shared his resumé. "I am a believer! Prayed the sinner's prayer, I did. In fact, I have worked miracles in His name!"

"Oh?" said Moses, beginning to drum his fingers on the parapet.

"Yes," said Ignorance emphatically as he pointed authoritatively toward the Holy City. "You go tell your King that I have prophesied in His name and even spoken in other tongues!"

"Uh . . . er . . . one moment please," said Moses, withdrawing from his place on the wall.

"There," said Ignorance to himself with as much assurance as old Vain-confidence himself. "That ought to impress the Old Boy. Ate and drank in His presence I did. Spoke with the tongues of men—and of angels a few times, too! Moved mountains of difficulties with my faith and willing to be burned I was! Hah! What a shoe-in! I just wish they would hurry things up. It's so cold and dark out here."

So Moses went into the presence of the King with a message from the gate, saying, "My Master, there is a man waiting outside the gate who claims to be one of your followers."

"Indeed!" exclaimed the King, His lovely face lighting up with eager anticipation. "Well, throw wide the gates! Call for the trumpeters! Let us give him our royal welcome!"

"But Master," said Moses with downcast eyes. "He came not through the wicket gate. Neither does he carry a certificate."

"Oh?" said the King, his eager smile fading before a new expression of utter sadness. "And what be his name?"

"His name be Ignorance, Master."

"Ignorance. Hmmm. Ignorance," murmured the King softly to Himself. Then He bowed His head in sad concentration while He vainly searched His memory, hoping against hope that He could somehow, somewhere find that name. Finally, he looked up from His search and with a tear trickling down his cheek said, "I have never known any man by that name. Nor he Me. Sadly, though it breaks My heart, I must pass sentence that he is an impostor and not a subject of this kingdom. Bind him and cast him into outer darkness."

And so it was that a few moments later the great, pearly gate opened on silent hinges. But that, only long enough to give exit to the two angels who had been companions to Christian and Hopeful. Then, as the brilliant light momentarily spilled its golden warmth upon him, Ignorance was encouraged in his spirit and cheerfully addressed the angels, saying, "Ah! Officers! You are finally here! I am glad to finally see someone with some authority."

"Greetings," said the first angel solemnly.

"Same to you," said Ignorance brusquely. "Say, you know, before you bestow the harp and crown I should like to register a complaint."

"Complaint?" asked the second.

"Yes. I am a little surprised at the rudeness of this place!"

"Rudeness?" responded the second angel, raising his brows in surprise.

"Yes, rude!" exclaimed Ignorance. "It's freezing out here! And you have kept me standing here in the dark, all alone, for lo, these many minutes!"

"Do you have cause to believe you shall pass through this gate?" asked the first angel gravely.

"Now what kind of ignorant question is that?" blustered Ignorance.

"Do you?"

"But of course I do!" snapped Ignorance, highly offended.

"On what grounds?"

"Wha . . . What?" stammered Ignorance.

"On what grounds?" repeated the angel firmly.

"Why, uh, . . . on the grounds that . . . uh . . . that I . . . uh . . ."

"Produce your certificate, please," said the second angel stepping forward with outstretched hand.

"Uh . . . well, officer, you see, I uh . . . I have none," he confessed with a gulp.

"Why not?" demanded the first angel, also taking a step closer.

"Why, uh . . . because no man offered one to me," Ignorance lied.

"That is impossible," said the first angel, edging closer yet. "Every man that comes through the Way, the Truth, and the Life, receives a certificate."

"Unless they come tumbling over the wall or enter the path by some other forbidden byway," added the second angel, by now standing only a few discomforting inches from Ignorance's face.

"Did you come in at the wicket gate?" asked the first great angel bluntly, leaning forward closer yet.

"Uh . . . gulp . . . I . . .," stammered Ignorance, speechless for the first time in his life.

Then the second angel took Ignorance firmly by one arm and said, "Don't you know that there is only one way appointed for men to be saved?"

Then the first angel grasped Ignorance's other arm in a grip of steel and added, "And did not some pilgrims tell you, in no uncertain terms, that those who enter in by any other way be thieves and robbers?"

Then Ignorance smiled a wan, sickly smile, wiped the beads of cold sweat from off his brow and said, "I uh . . . say, chaps. Does it seem to be getting rather warmish out here?"

"Not yet," answered the first angel.

"Yet? Oh. Heh, heh. Uh, say, would either of you like a sucker?" he asked blithely, as he quickly managed to produce several from one of his pockets.

"The King has commanded us to tell you that He does not know you," said the first angel, ignoring Ignorance's foolish comment.

"What!" screeched Ignorance. "I mean, what?" he said, vainly attempting to disguise the rising terror in his quaking voice.

"He has further commanded," added the second, "that you shall be bound hand and foot and cast into outer darkness. Bind this man!"

Ignorance cast, bound hand and foot through the door.

"Nay, but I am a subject of this kingdom!" protested Ignorance loudly, as he felt mighty hands lifting him off his feet. "Let me go!" he screamed as his hands were firmly bound behind his back. "No! Stop! You tell your foolish King that He is making a mistake!" he squealed while his feet were being lashed with ropes. "I feel in my heart of hearts that I am a subject of this kingdom. My feelings tell me so! Do you hear?"

"Carry him away! For he is a stranger to this place," commanded the first angel.

"No!" screamed Ignorance biting, spitting and thrashing about as best he could. "Heaven is my home! I be a true pilgrim for my heart tells me so! I feel in my inmost soul that I do belong in this place. This is my . . . Get your hands off me, you! Let me go . . . !"

Then they carried him through the air to that door in the side of the hill where they had put Turn-about before him. Through that door, therefore, was Ignorance cast, bound hand and foot. Then I saw again that there are many ways to hell; some coming down from the very edge of the City as well as others which lead more directly from the City of Destruction!

So I awoke, and behold, it was all a dream.

Bunyan's conclusion

Now, reader, I have told my dream to thee,
See if thou canst interpret it to me,
Or to thyself or neighbor, but take heed
Of misinterpreting; for that, instead
Of doing good, will but thyself abuse:
By misinterpreting, evil ensues.
Take heed also that thou be not extreme
In playing with the outside of my dream;
Nor let my figure nor similitude
Put thee into a laughter or a feud.
Leave this for boys and fools; but as for thee
Do thou the substance of my matter see.
Put by the curtain, look within my veil,
Turn up my metaphors, and do not fail,
There, if thou seekest them, such things to find
As will be helpful to an honest mind.
What of my dross thou findest there, be bold
To throw away; but yet preserve the gold.
What if my gold be wrapped up in ore?—
None throws away the apple for the core.
But if thou shalt cast all away as vain,
I know not but 'twill make me dream again.

THE END

IN THE RIGHT HANDS, THIS BOOK WILL CHANGE LIVES!

Most of the people who need this message will not be looking for this book. To change their lives, you need to put a copy of this book in their hands.

> *But others (seeds) fell into good ground, and brought forth fruit, some a hundred-fold, some sixty-fold, some thirty-fold* (Matthew 13:8).

Our ministry is constantly seeking methods to find the good ground, the people who need this anointed message to change their lives. Will you help us reach these people?

> *Remember this—a farmer who plants only a few seeds will get a small crop. But the one who plants generously will get a generous crop* (2 Corinthians 9:6).

EXTEND THIS MINISTRY BY SOWING
3 BOOKS, 5 BOOKS, 10 BOOKS, OR MORE TODAY,
AND BECOME A LIFE CHANGER!

Thank you,

Don Nori Sr., Founder
Destiny Image
Since 1982